# Into Darkness

## Part Four of

# Changels Genesis

## by Peter King

Peter King Publishing
Wellington, New Zealand

## SPECIAL NOTE TO READERS

Into Darkness is the fourth part of Changels Genesis. It is not a stand-alone story.

Change of location due to teleportation ("bending") is marked with a new line and a centered "[+]"

Communication that starts as telepathy is rendered in *italics*

When the story moves back and forth from the narrator's present (in present tense) to his history (in past or perfect tense) there will be a new line with an ellipses "..." in the centre.

Translations the narrator understands are parenthesised e.g kara-kia (prayer)

Facts have been indicated with a superscripted dagger symbol† There is a detailed fact and fiction section on page 454 at the end of this part of the story. There is also a detailed section on language at the end of this book.

Non-English words have been hyphenated on their first use to expose the syllabic structure and ease pronunciation. The exception is Karearea (falcon) which is always hyphentaed e.g.Ka-rea-rea. Maori words ending in the 'e' have been given a non-standard accent acute (e.g. Tané) for the same reason.

## THANKS AND ACKNOWLEDGEMENTS

I must thank William Elachi of the Monusco mission in Goma, DRC and Sylvian Leichti for permission to use Sylvian's house fire picture before it was on Flickr.

I would also like to acknowledge the blog of the Virunga Park Rangers at Virunga.org. This was a vital source of background information on the operation of the park during the CNDP era. The rangers do a remarkable job safeguarding the mountain gorillas even as humanity fails so dismally to safeguard its own.

# AFRICA - TO SCALE

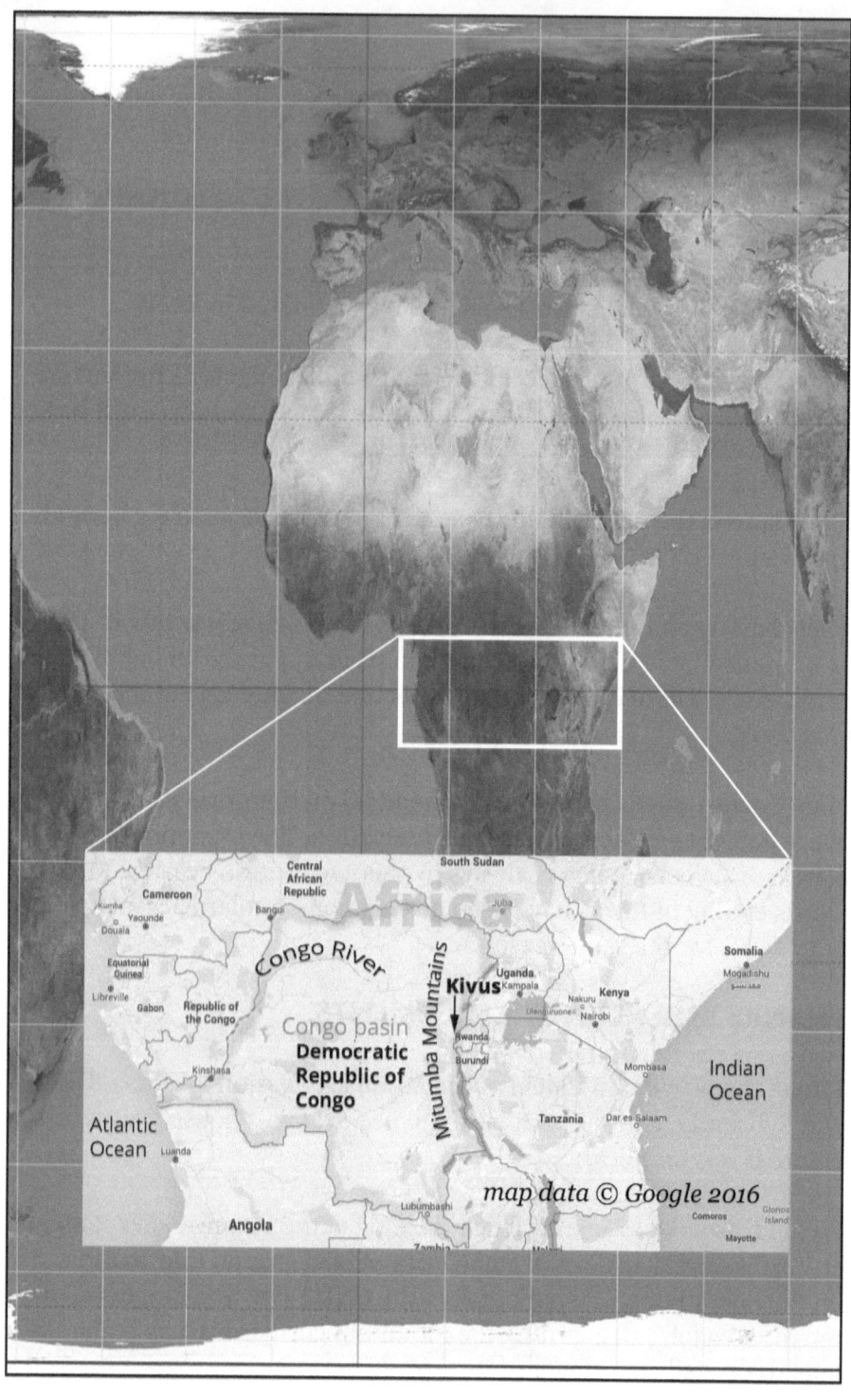

map data © Google 2016

*this thing of darkness I acknowledge mine*

**– The Tempest, Act 5, scene 1**

## CHAPTER FORTY TWO: NORTH KIVU

We knew something was different the minute we emerged into the briefing theatre. Dr Prosperov was waiting along with Bernard, Mrs Robinson and Mr Trân. Dr Prosperov and Grandpop were talking in low voices with serious faces.

We came into the theatre as usual but sat slightly further towards the back than we usually did. Dr Prosperov glanced at the faces of the parents in front of us. Mrs Robinson glanced back at Ashley. You could tell she was worried.

Dr Prosperov looked very serious.

"Temporal reconnaissance and UN announcement today indicates future African financier, Jeanne, in extreme danger. Yesterday soldiers of Bravo brigade of Laurent Nkunda's CNDP army abducted two hundred and eighty boys and girls from schools east of Masisi in North Kivu province of Democratic Republic of Congo†. Jeanne is among them."

Dr Prosperov looked around the parents.

"Everyone wanted more training. Situation demands training suspended. Tonight is first operational mission."

We all gasped and looked excitedly at one another. We were about to start making some serious money. Dr Prosperov indicated Grandpop should take over and stood back. Grandpop shuffled forward and then looked up us sharply.

"OK guys you heard it. We are now operational though I still think sending you kids into a war zone – even at four in the morning – is seriously risky so always remember this. Always remember you are volunteers. Unlike everyone else there you can get out. If you have any concerns come home. If anything scares you, come home. If you get a funny feeling, the way you guys do and you don't like it, come home. I don't want a repeat of the other day with the drug dealers. There is no law here. This is not a game. Kids your age and younger are killed there every day. Nobody wants any of you to be among them," Grandpop growled.

He was so serious I confess I started rethinking how much I really wanted to go to this place.

"Guys, the place you are headed is violence central. It's been at war since before you were born, it's got very active volcanoes, high mountains, gorillas of the animal kind, guerrillas of the human kind. It's King Kong country but with soldiers instead of dinosaurs and I know which I'm more scared of. Now Bernard will give you some background on why things are so bad."

With that, Grandpop sat down.

I admit my enthusiasm was giving way to a lot of nervousness. Bernard got up holding a sheaf of papers in front of him. He shuffled them a bit and licked his lips and then began in his rich, warm accent.

"The place where you are going is highly dangerous. Please make no mistake about that. Since you were born almost five and a half million people have died here in an ongoing war the Western world has ignored. It is the most deadly war since World War Two†. This place is very rich and business interests have exploited ethnic differences for their own advantage."

2

He nodded and the holograph came alive as he continued. "The Western Rift Valley of the African Continent. This is as it was last night our time. We are on the opposite side of the Earth so your work will be at night."

"The Virunga National Park of the Democratic Republic of Congo was founded in 1925 and was the first national park in Africa[†]. In theory it is still a park but war means the park operations are even worse than the park I worked in, in Zimbabwe. Rangers have to deal not only with soldiers fighting but also thousands of refugees in need of food and fuel. Despite this it seems that tourists have been able to visit the gorillas or the volcanoes. All sides regard tourism as an important business[†]."

The map zoomed in to show the area from a jumpable sixty thousand feet. There was a big lake named Kivu at the bottom, with a city named Goma at the lake's top right and some large volcanoes in clouds further north up the valley. On the left and on the right the huge valley sloped up into hilly country. Our view began to wander north and there was another lake further up the big valley.

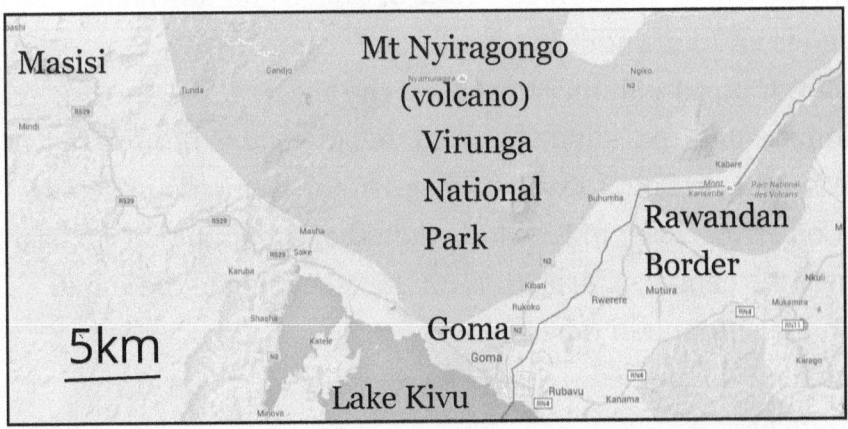

*Map data © Google 2016*

3

"The whole area is highlands, about four to five thousand feet above sea level. The volcanoes are even higher. The volcanic soil is very fertile and so the area can grow a lot of food and support many people. There is good rainfall in the wet season which is just beginning. Before the fighting people could grow a lot of crops such as coffee, tea, bananas and manioc and in the past tended many cattle."

"The land is mostly open agricultural hill country. It looks very much like this country. Even the Friesian cows are the same. Just like New Zealand, the population of North Kivu is 4.2 million although its area is much smaller. Just like the city of Auckland, here there are live volcanoes, extinct volcanoes and bush. The main difference is that it is on the equator so it is always warm and the bush is tropical jungle."

"The volcanic valley has old lava flows. But the last eruption of the live volcano, Nyiragongo, here, was in 2002 and destroyed a part of the main city of Goma and greatly shortened the city's airport†. But the natural hazards are nothing to the dangers posed by the fighting."

"The main political feature of this area is the border, here, between the Democratic Republic of Congo and Rawanda, Uganda and Burundi."

Yellow transparent lines traced out the borders.

"Goma is only one kilometer from the Rawandan border. In fact the North and South Kivu provinces of the Democratic Republic of Congo are closer to Rawanda than they are to the Congo basin where the capital, Kinshasa, is on the other side of the snowy Mitumba mountain range here."

Suddenly we zoomed right out so we could see the whole continent.

"You see most of the Democratic Republic of Congo's area is here on the left or east side of the big Mitumba mountains. It's a huge river basin for the huge Congo river and all the way down here is the capital Kinshasa. It takes about a month by barge to travel up the river from Kinshasa to Kitsangani here at the foot of the Mitumba mountains[†].

Roads between Kitsangani in the Congo river basin and the highland Kivu provinces are bad. So you can see that East side of the Mitumba mountains has little to do with the rest of the DRC while settlement along this border with Rawanda, Uganda and Burundi is continuous with relatives on both sides and frequent crossings."

Bernard gave a nod and we zoomed back down to the volcanic valley.

"What I am trying to show you is these borders do not really reflect the local people's history. This is because the borders were changed when the Belgians, who used to be in the Congo basin, invaded the Rawandan Kingdom, which was under German control, in 1916, during World War One. In 1922 the Treaty of Versailles changed the borders permanently without referring to any Africans[†]. The Belgians had ruled the Congo with extreme cruelty but preferred to rule Rawanda through traditional African Kings as the Germans had[†]."

"Before, and even after World War Two, the Belgians adopted a racial policy similar to the Nazis by defining everyone in terms of race on their identity cards[†]. They preferred the Tutsi Kings and cattle barons over the Hutu farmers and peasants[†]."

"Today the main ethnic conflict in the area is between Tutsi and Hutu. To outsiders they have more in common than either will admit because there has been intermarriage. They also both speak Kinyarwanda, but as with many peoples, from Ireland to Sri Lanka, the closer they have become to outsiders' eyes, the more keenly they assert their differences between each other." Bernard looked up from his notes and spoke to us earnestly. "You see Africa is no more naturally violent than Europe. Both can be violent. I know you will see some bad things in this place. They are everywhere and we cannot hide them from you so I think it is important that you understand why they came to happen. If you don't know the reason for the violence it seems to spring from nothing, which implies the people are primitive or mad. They are not."

The map shifted to the right and centred on Rawanda. Its borders were with Uganda to the north and east and Burundi to the south as well as the Democratic Republic of Congo. He returned to his notes.

"After World War Two many African peoples wanted independence from the European colonialists. The Hutu were tired of the Tutsi and the Belgians who ruled them. Seeing the Hutu had greater numbers and wanting to keep their influence in Rawanda after they were forced to grant independence, the Belgians switched from supporting the Tutsi to supporting Hutu leaders. The Tutsi were forced to give way although they fought back. This led to a mass killing of one hundred thousand Tutsi in 1959 in the so-called 'Wind of Destruction[†]'. That led many Tutsi to flee to Uganda and the Congo[†]. You see they had family all over this region because the Belgians had moved them around as labour on their plantations even before 1922."

"The Hutu and Tutsi continued to fight and kill each other through the 1960s in Rawanda and neighbouring Burundi. In general the Hutu had the advantage because of their numbers[†]."

"The Tutsi in Uganda in the 70s lived in refugee camps on the border with Rawanda. They were not allowed to become Ugandans nor would Rawanda, which was now mostly run by Hutu, allow them to live there either[†]. "

"Starving, and facing destruction, the Tutsi refugees formed the Rawandan Patriotic Front which ten years later played a decisive role in Uganda's civil war during the 1980s. The National Resistance Army fought against the Ugandan government of Milton Obote who had taken over from the lunatic Idi Amin. The tough Tutsi joined with the Ugandan resistance and fought well. The resistance defeated Obote and in 1986 occupied Kampala, the capital of Uganda. As in Zimbabwe the resistance then became the Ugandan Army and the Tutsi army hid inside it. In return Tutsi refugees were allowed to settle in Uganda[†]."

I have to admit there is nothing like knowing you are about to go into a war zone to make you pay attention to a history lesson. Mr Wakefield never got so much close attention from us, e-v-er.

"In 1990, a few years before you were born, the Tutsis in the Ugandan Army deserted and invaded Rawanda. They wanted to negotiate a Tutsi return with the Hutu-led Rawandan government from a position of strength. Unfortunately all they did was scare the Hutu leaders."

"The Hutu government became more extreme. They blamed all their problems on the Tutsi. In April 1994 Hutu extremists, led by Colonel Bagosora, assassinated the Rawandan Hutu president by shooting down his aircraft as he returned from peace talks[†]. Bagosora and others then mobilised soldiers and citizen militias to hunt down and kill all Tutsis and any Hutus who wanted peace. Some were shot, some were burned but most were hacked to death with machetes."

7

"By the time you were born, in June that year, half a million Rawandans, mostly Tutsi, were hacked or stoned or burned to death, and many fled across the border to their kinsmen around the city of Goma in the north, and Bukaru on the south of lake Kivu[†]."

Bernard stopped and looked up at us both sad and serious. "I must stress the Rawandan genocide was not a case of the Hutus being crazed African savages seized by a sudden murderous impulse. This murder went on for weeks."

He stopped to think, let a pause build, and then continued speaking clearly and slowly.

"This mass murder was exactly like a Nazi-style genocide. Identity cards specifying race had been given out[†], lists made and the stock of half a million extra machetes ordered in advance[†]. This killing was a coldly calculated mass-murder no different to the Serbian murders in Bosnia at the same time. It was planned and organised."

"In some ways it was even more psychologically clever than the European murders. The Hutus had to kill their victims themselves, one-by-one, face-to-face. There were no strange trains, or death squads in the night, that the Hutu might have pretended they hadn't seen, like some Germans did. This mass murder was designed to bond the whole surviving Hutu society in mass guilt."

I have to confess I gulped a bit at this. Coming from a minority myself, the idea that the majority race of a country could decide to murder the minority by cutting them down with machetes made me feel sick. Then I realised every one of us came from a minority. Ashley, Scotty, Tarik, and Tahira. Cam couldn't remember a time she wasn't a minority. It made we wonder at what people could do to each other. I felt cold. Bernard looked back down at his notes and began reading again.

"The Hutu victory was very short lived. Almost immediately the Tutsi army mobilised and it was not long before it had taken control of Rawanda. Many Hutu, fearing for their lives, now also fled into Zaire, as the Democratic Republic of Congo was then called, and formed the FDLR army in Zaire threatening the many Tutsi who lived there."

"The presence of these new Tutsi and Hutu refugees in Zaire led to the First Congo War in 1998[†] when you were all four. The Hutu killers and the Tutsi fought each other, but the Rawandans and the Ugandans supported the Tutsi and won easily. What happened then was that they joined forces with the people of Zaire, who were tired of the insane misrule of CIA-supported President Muboto. Adopting Zairian leader Laurent Kabila in a campaign that crossed the Mitumba mountains and then swept down the Congo river, they soon wiped out the few who supported the useless and hated Mubuto[†]. It was barely reported by Western media who focused on the white genocide in Bosnia."

"Unfortunately the end of Muboto did not bring peace. It did not take the new president Laurent Kabila long before he realised that his people were not happy to be ruled by Rawandan and Ugandan troops, who started looting, and he told them to leave the country. That started the Second Congo war[†]."

"At first Kabila had no chance. His disorganised army was no match for the battle hardened Rawandans and Ugandans but he started doing deals with other African leaders promising them access to the Congo's enormous mineral wealth in return for military assistance."

"The first to agree was Robert Mugabe who had Solomon Mujuru turn the Zimbabwean Army into his own private mercenary force. Other supporters were Namibia, Angola and Chad. Even Libya's Muhammar Ghaddafi helped out†. So there were five armies all fighting in the Congo. Of these Angola's tough soldiers, who had been fighting the Fretilin guerillas for decades, were the most important†."

"The pressure created a split over loot between the Rawandans and the Ugandans, and half way through they even started fighting each other, as well as everyone else. The UN sent a large force of French and Indian soldiers called MONUC† who have done very little except watch atrocities take place around them."

"Eventually Laurent Kabila was assassinated in Zimbabwe in 2001, and he was replaced as president of the Democratic Republic of Congo by his western educated son, Joseph†. The Ugandans and the Rawandan Armies pulled out of direct action in the Congo and all the other armies went home too."

"Unfortunately while the five national armies have gone, large numbers of armed groups remain."

"The UN force, MONUC, is all over North Kivu and has a large base in Goma. This is mostly made up of heavily armed Indian Army regulars who have a bad reputation with the locals†."

"The Democratic Republic of Congo army, the FARDC, have tried to pacify the Hutu FDLR army by incorporating them into their ranks, but the FARDC is so badly run in the East that what is happening is the other way around. The FARDC troops are really being brought into the rebel Hutu FDLR army because they pay more†."

"The main opposing army of both the FDLR Hutus and the FARDC in North Kivu is the Tutsi CNDP army† which is based around Masisi to the west and Rutshuru in the east, here and here."

The CNDP is almost certainly being supported by the Rawandan national army just over the border from Rutshuru. It is supplied through the Virunga National Park which is full of trails and runs along the border with Rawanda. The CNDP is led by Laurent Nkunda who claims the CNDP is there to protect the Tutsi population in the North Kivu from the Hutu FDLR[†].

"So as you can see there is a kind of curve from these volcanoes in the west here on the right by the Rawandan border, running around the top of the north of the Nyiragongo volcano in the middle, out to Masisi in the east and south, down to Sake at the top of Lake Kivu twenty-five kilometers east of Goma. This is the CNDP territory which is also where most of the Tutsi live."

"On the other side the FDLR is still run by some of the Hutu who carried out the 1994 genocide[†]. They are supported semi-secretly by the government of the Democratic Republic of Congo and their headquarters are in France and Germany. They operate like an illegal company running mines, extorting money which they call taxes, and trading with Uganda, Burundi and Tanzania."

"They are based around Kibua and Kalonga here, and have been attacking the Tutsi CNDP in Masisi and Rutshuru recently. That means they are simultaneously blunting the CNDP thrust south at Sake and cutting off its supply lines from Rawanda at Rutshuru."

"The Congolese Army, FARDC, is between them here in the west in Masisi. MONUC (which supports the FARDC) is based in the North Kivu capital, Goma, in the South East by Rawanda and lake Kivu. In amongst all of them are gangs of armed Congolese called mai-mai who are just out for themselves."

"What they are all fighting about is the mines. There is gold, which is getting very expensive now; diamonds, of course; and a mineral called Coltan, which is a key ingredient in the batteries of cellular phones and laptop computers[†]. They sell this through Uganda, Rawanda, Burundi and Tanzania, All of these armed groups fight over mines but also trade with one another. So it isn't so much a war as ruthless businessmen with guns pretending to be national armies, but really out to get rich."

"The result of their business is that eight hundred thousand people have been forced off their land and live in refugee camps[†]. You must remember that in this place you don't get food from supermarkets. Without land you can't grow food. This means that although their land is fertile and climate good there is much poverty and malnutrition. Most people go hungry." Bernard paused. Then he looked up at us and seemed a bit embarrassed.

"There is one final very important matter I must also alert you to which is most important for the safety of this girl, Jeanne. "

"I am sad to say that throughout this war rape has become a way of life for the armed men in the Congo. Tens of thousands, perhaps hundreds of thousands, of women, and girls – some much younger than you – have been raped by soldiers[†]. Some many times over. Jeanne will almost certainly face this threat if she hasn't already."

I snuck a sidelong glance at Tahira. I could see Ashley frowning too. They looked ... well ... really angry.

"Tens of thousands of girls have been injured and killed by both rape and pregnancy. Given many men in this area also carry the HIV virus Jeanne's chance of survival to achieve her task could be ... greatly reduced."

With that Bernard sat down and Grandpop stood up again. "Thanks Bernard, that was uh ... bloody depressing. So guys as you heard Jeanne is in serious danger – like everyone else in this place. And like it or not our chances of finding her are very small."

"But we have someone with us who worked as a courier in the Vietnam war when he was about your age. He knows how it feels to be a kid in the middle of a war. He knows how the children in this place will be feeling. We thought you might like to listen to his advice. Nguyen?"

Mr Trân stood up. He seemed nervous about making a long speech in English but determined at the same time. He looked especially at Cam.

"When I grow up was war all 'round. People scared and life very cheap. Many, many die. Americans in Saigon everywhere. My father and mother spy for Vietcong working in Colonel house. I must carry report to Vietcong."

"In war everything very confuse. Is sometime good, sometime bad. Is good for children when adult very busy. Don't notice child so much. But is very bad when notice. American soldier good and bad. Some very good. Give candy. Some very bad. Very, very dangerous. Shoot child for fun. I see that. Very bad."

"In war everyone scare at night. Even child scare American. Even goat. Soldier shoot anything at night. Vietcong not so scare. Very quiet. When I take message at night I am very quiet. Keep away from American. Also important not followed or leave footprint. Must keep eyes wide and listen. If trouble, then comes very fast. You run home any thing scare you."

Mr Trân seemed to have run out of things to say so he shrugged and sat down again. Grandpop got up.

"Thanks Nguyen."

He paused for the shortest time thinking about the children he had known in Vietnam and how Mr Trân could have been one of them. Then he shook off the memory and went on.

"So that gives you some idea of how the kids where you are going will feel."

Right. Now to specifics. The weather in the area is very wet right now. It's just started raining heavily and there is probably lightning too which is perfect. From the looks the rain could be around for some time. In war everyone sits out rain."

"It's about four in the morning local time. On the equator the sun comes up at six and goes down at six and there isn't much halflight. So you have two hours of darkness left."

"The territory we are putting you down into is not jungle. It's a combination of bush and crops. Close and open country. It's very steep – just like our island here in fact."

"So here's the plan. Tell us what you think of it."

"Jeanne and the other children are being marched through the hill country here to the CNDP base at Bizwe, north of the settlement, and refugee camp of Kitshanga. At Bizwe they will train them to fight and the girls, like Jeanne, get given husbands whether they want them or not."

I heard a gasp from Tahira and Ashley. They were pale with shock. Grandpop went on.

"The road the abductors have taken goes through these hills then it comes out into the plains north of Nyiragongo volcano. We aren't entirely sure where they all are. They could be on the road or they could be at Bizwe already.

So what we need to do is sweep the whole area. It would be nice

to bend and dive over but the rain is pouring down so nothing can fly. Unfortunately you're just going to have to leg it.
We've split you into three teams. Ashley and Scotty? You are the Bizwe team. Your job is to see if you can find anything near, but not inside, the camp working back to the two thirds point here. Sam and Tahira, you start at the one third point here. You will work up the road toward a rendezvous with Ashley and Scotty."
"The abducted kids will not be on the road so don't walk down the middle of it looking like lost lambs. If they are out in this weather they will be sheltering under trees so that is what you are looking for. Move parallel to the road but well off it looking for the column. You will need to keep moving reasonably quickly or you'll be walking all night."
"Remember these guys will have sentries posted and they will be armed. You have the advantage of comfort – which is very important – your own powers, thermal imaging and audio enhancement plus adaptive camouflage. They just have a lifetime of tough living and knowledge that their enemies will torture and kill them if they catch them napping. Don't underestimate that."
"Now that leaves Tarik and Cam. Hekator has sent through this... "
He held up a tube.
"It's a spray-on radio interception paint. All you do is spray it on an aerial and stick on this sand. It will intercept anything the aerial transmits or receives and send it to Control. We want to intercept communications at the CNDP camps, the FARDC units and Monuc."
"It's going to be intense. We will put you as close as we can. Your job is to spray the paint and get out. Alright, any questions?"

We all looked at each other. We were all a bit scared but nobody wanted to admit it. On the other hand we had been scared of gravity too, and people just weren't as unstoppable.

"OK, off to the jumpstation. Let's get this thing started."

"One moment," Dr Prosperov said as we leapt to our feet. He held the floor looking very serious.

"Please to remember. You go to make world better place. For yourself and all children. Is not game for amusement. Is possible you will see some bad things. Remember stopping them is why we go. This girl, Jeanne, will be important to Africa and whole world only if she lives. In many futures she will not. Nothing is certain. Please to be careful."

And for the first time ever we realised Dr Prosperov really was worried about us. We went to the jumpstation feeling a bit daunted by what lay before us.

Control was waiting and Grandpop followed us down and watched us.

"OK, Tarik and Cam wait. I have more for you. You others. Good luck," he called as we sealed our facescreens.

Control said, "bending in five, four, three, two, one."

## [+]

Time slowed down, the colour drained. Everything folded. I fell back, spinning, and then forward. There was brilliant light and presences. They faded. I opened my eyes. It was very dark and raining heavily. The ground was steep and muddy. Tahira was just to my left. I knelt quickly as we always did so we could get our bearings.

The hillside we were on was above the road which we could see opposite. It was very steep and seemed to climb up to our left forever. There was a distant flash in the sky and we could see palm trees shaking in the wind all along the hill. The rain was like a hose pouring down on us. The air wasn't as warm as you'd think but the smells of rain and trees were strong. Not being in the suit would have been horrible. It made me wonder if the kids we were seeking were out in this.

We extended our claws because we needed the grip.

"*Let's get going,*" I suggested.

I felt nervous and thought the sick feeling in my stomach might go away with exercise. Tahira agreed and we set off at a light lope following the slope of the hill.

Running in the suit was always easy. It made you stronger and adapted as you got hotter. But even our climbing claws didn't always grip in the wet ground and you had to watch where you put your feet to avoid sliding down the hill.

We came to a gully. It was only about 20 meters deep but it was obviously going to be far easier to jump it than to go down one side and back up the other. I cranked up the gravity deflection, started to glow and leaped. Tahira followed after me. On the other side we went back to normal weight and vanished again into the night.

We were running as normal where the hill flattened out a bit and we were coming up on a small village among the tall waving palm trees. Somehow we knew at once the village was deserted. But as we slowed down and walked towards it we also became aware we were not alone. It was suddenly cold inside our suits in a way we knew at once had nothing to do with the rain. In the shadows figures watched us. They were neither curious nor angry. They just watched us, dark like shadow people, without faces or eyes.

It was impossible to miss the first body. He was lying against the

**17**

side of his hut, his head twisted to the side, eyes closed almost as if he was asleep, shirt torn with dark stained holes. The water poured off the roof onto his legs. The sight of him made me curious and sad at the same time.

We knew there were more. Lot's more. The cold was in our bones. We felt sick. There were shadows moving among the houses watching us. We couldn't ignore them. We turned down a lane between the leafy huts. The shadows fell back before us. They seemed to be muttering to each other. Passing three, four, five, houses we came to a small church that had mostly burned down. The cold was intense. The charcoal remains were covered in puddles. Only the front remained. As we looked we realised that the church was filled with burned bodies. As we came to the side we could see half a dozen slumped against the inside door. The cold was on your soul.

"*They burned us,*" a male presence behind us muttered quietly. "*They told us we had to come to a meeting in the Church and then they locked us in and set the church on fire,*" he said.

"*I escaped,*" a girl whispered.

"*I got out with my sister and we ran over there. She got away.*" We went up the dark lane that led behind the church. The shades followed us muttering in a way that could not be truly heard. We came upon a body in the middle of the muddy lane. A little girl about Rewa's age in a pale dress with pink flowers in it. There were big holes in her little back but the blood had washed away in the pelting rain. I knelt down by her.

"*They shot me,*" the shade cried quietly, half-pitying her own body lying face down in the mud.

We just stayed there looking at that little body in the rain, Tahira thinking of Asal, me thinking of Rewa. It was as if our minds were stuck, unable to imagine how anyone could shoot a little girl in a white dress with pink flowers with a machine gun. It was a small thing compared to the horror of the whole church full of people burned to death behind us but that was too much for us to think about now. This little girl like a broken doll in the rain, gripped our minds and closed an icy hand on our hearts.

"*Who did this? Why did they kill you?*" I whispered to the presences who remained in the shadows.

"*They wanted to punish us for changing sides,*" the crowd explained in a soundless rush of emotion.

"*They said we had not been loyal,*" they added.

"Who did? I shouted out loud into the pouring rain and the empty street. "Who did these things?"

"*The soldiers. The FDLR,*" they whimpered.

They seemed both angry and fearful at the same time. More lost and confused than anything else.

"We should get back to the road," Tahira said.

"What about her?" I asked.

"We cannot 'elp 'er now," Tahira said softly.

I looked back at the little body. I wanted to bury her. Have a Maori funeral, a weeping, or Tangi. Do her justice. But looking at her in the rain, like a discarded rag, I couldn't help but think she wasn't mine to bury. She lay that way because she had been left that way and that in itself said more than any number of speeches that might be made at her funeral.

I stood up and we back past the Church. Now the horror of it made me feel sick and I had to fight to stop throwing up. With the cold sad shades behind us we splashed back out of the village and continued along the ridge looking down at the ridge opposite.

**19**

We had to make up for lost time so we started running through the pouring rain, leaping the streams and gullies that cascaded down steep hillside, now and then losing track of the road that glowed pale in the darkness below us because of the trees and brush.

The lightning still flickered in the sky with distant rumbles. The ridge we were following was sloping down toward the road. We were running along, focusing on not slipping when suddenly a goat bleated barely ten meters away. I was so surprised I threw myself into a deep muddy puddle.

Tahira burst out laughing. I lay there for a moment still unsure whether I was actually safe while Tahira giggled like an idiot in the safety of some trees behind me. I remembered Nguyen saying goats scared the American soldiers at night. Now I had experienced it myself I didn't think it was as stupid as Tahira obviously thought it looked.

I rolled over a few times and got up. The goat was bright orange in the dark to my left. Goats meant houses and houses meant people.

"*There's a village over there,*" I warned Tahira.

She slipped through the trees behind me to catch up.

"*Move by turns,*" I said.

Tahira scampered past me through the rain. Without the green outline my suit placed over her she would have been invisible in the darkness. Her squelching footsteps were soon lost in the continuous racket of the rain. Then it was my turn and I moved forward. The trees were quite high making it very dark. Through the gloom I could still see huts to my left. Suddenly there was a flash of lightning and I saw an orange head glowing in the dark of a window. I knew they hadn't seen me clearly – I was a chameleon in the dark – but they had seen something. I ran on until I found some cover.

"*I think someone saw me,*" I told Tahira.

"*Is it safe?*" she asked.

"*I dunno I'll check,*" I told her.

I snuck forward so that I was behind a rise of dirt with a good view of the huts. If it was some kid unlucky enough to be checking for monsters in the dark the instant I passed we were OK. If it were a soldier, we were in trouble.

The face in the darkness was glowing a bright orange. It definitely wasn't a kid. In fact another one had joined the first one. They were peering out into the dark unsure of what was outside. The first one seemed to be aiming something. I could feel they were soldiers. They were a small band worried about being caught before dawn.

"*Come up slowly and quietly. They can't see us but they are looking,*" I told Tahira.

She started moving. She was slow and steady. The soldiers made no sign they had seen her when suddenly Tahira tripped over something and grabbed a tree to steady herself. The soldiers noticed at once. Suddenly I realised they were preparing to shoot.

"Keep down!" I shouted.

A deafening bang bang bang spat lethal red lines out of the dark window. I focused on the two orange blobs and a blue light flickered twice, silently, and knocked them down.

"Well done Sam!" Grandpop called.

"*Tahira are you alright?*" I asked.

"*Yes.*"

I dashed back to find her pulling herself out of a deep muddy

**21**

pool. I had to stop myself smiling. Then the smell hit me. It wasn't mud. Tahira was swearing in Persian. My suit was translating and she wasn't as girly as she pretended to be. I couldn't help smiling.

*"We've gotta go. There are others."*

We crept on through the bush. For a while we said nothing.

*"I don't know if they saw me zap the two who were shooting. The rain effects the zapper quite badly. The charge goes everywhere. I don't think we have much range,"* I told her.

We came out of the bush surrounding the village. The road was closer now. No more than a few hundred meters. We picked up the pace and ran on until we came to the end of the ridge.

*"Sam? What's that?"* Tahira asked silently.

There was a strange orange glow in the sky. We were both thinking of our encounter in Greenland. The glow wasn't moving.

*"Grandpop? Control? What is that?"* I called in.

There was a brief pause.

"It's the glow from the Nyiragongo volcano Sam. Nothing unusual. Ashley and Scotty saw it an hour ago. You guys are a bit behind too. Pick it up. Dawn's coming in an hour."

We ran on. The slope which had been so steep was now just easy. We ran along popping up occasionally to check the road. We had gone for about 15 minutes when we spotted a group of orange blobs hiding in trees. They weren't doing anything much. We slipped up on them as quietly as possible.

It was a family. Mum, dad, grandma and three kids under some plastic sheeting with a handcart in some bushes hiding on the side of the road. We moved on thinking how glad we were to have suits.

As the land flattened out the number of groups we found on the side of the road were growing. There were already some people walking in the darkness north towards Bizwe. We just kept running. If anyone noticed us nobody said anything. While it was dark everyone seemed to be keeping their heads down under the pounding rain.

We were starting to get tired now. The nervous excitement that had kept us going when we started was giving way to nervous exhaustion. Tahira called a stop before we had to cross a bridge and we fell down in a grassy patch about a hundred meters back up the road.

We checked our situation. Ashley and Scotty were five kilometers further up the road. That meant we could expect to meet up with them in ten minutes if we all kept up a steady speed.

"*How are you guys?*" I called Scotty and Ashley.

"*Busy. The refugees are starting to move. It's hard to stop bumping into them,*" Scotty said.

"*Maybe we should stop trying to blend in and just run along the road,*" I suggested, tired and wanting to go home.

"*Well, it is raining,*" Ashley agreed. "*Kids in the dark running fast in the rain with hoods up and dark faces. It's out of place but so is Scotty's white face.*"

"*And it makes more sense than sneaking along a busy roadside,*" Scotty agreed.

"*What do you think Tahira?*" I asked her.

She had been lying on her back letting the rain fall on her. She sat up.

"*Whatever,*" she said.

We switched from blend to dark green but kept our facescreens

23

dark. Then we broke cover and began to run up the road.

We were only thirty meters from the bridge when we saw a soldier under a tree on the far side. Looking around we could see five more. That was all we needed. We slowed down. They were watching us although they didn't seem to be doing anything other than keeping out of the rain.

"*There's soldiers on this bridge,*" I warned Scotty and Ashley.

I walked on, very aware how small and unarmed I suddenly felt.

"*How many do you see?*" I asked Tahira.

"*Ten.*"

"*Me too.*"

"*You take the five on the left, I'll take the five on the right.*"

"*OK.*"

We kept walking quickly toward the bridge. I felt my mouth getting dry.

"Guys you can bend home you know," Grandpop said softly.

We kept walking our feet making no sound on the road over the pouring rain.

As we were about to cross the short bridge the men showed some sign of getting ready to stop us.

"*Tahira? I have an idea.*" I said as we walked on.

"*Let's walk right up to them and bend out. It'll freak them out.*"

"*Good idea,*" she agreed.

Just for good measure we gave them eighty decibels of spooky eighteen Hertz infrasound as well, to make them uneasy as we approached.

"*Ashley, there is a checkpoint on the bridge here. We will go home if we cannot get across,*" Tahira called.

We marched directly across the bridge. They were watching us in the dark shelter of the trees on both sides of road. Their guns looked very big. It was now obvious they always manned this bridge like a toll gate. I was just glad we could vanish.

"*Tahira, Sam? We could fix you a landing spot if you want to join us,*" Ashley said.

As we got closer nobody had moved to stop us. I wondered if we would get past anyway. Then as we drew alongside the checkpoint a voice spoke.

"Hey! You must pay the toll!" a man called out in a deep voice in French. He didn't seem particularly interested in us, he just wanted to hassle us to make sure everyone knew you couldn't past without paying.

I stopped.

"*Ashley they have stopped us. I think we have had enough. We will go home,*" Tahira reported.

"*OK, we're nearly done here too,*" Ashley told us.

The soldier who had stopped us was crouching under the cover of the tree. He looked cold, pissed off and red-eyed. He had a cigarette in his mouth, an AK under his arm and a blue plastic sheet over him. The other soldiers were busy trying to get a small stove started.

"*So do we go now?*" Tahira asked turning so we were back to back.

"*I dunno,*" I replied and shrugged.

The man noticed my shrug and took it to mean I didn't understand.

"You must pay us five thousand francs each," the man scowled cocking his gun.

He still couldn't be bothered getting up. I stood in the rain staring at him.

"*I can get all of them on my side. How about you?*" I asked.

*"Three of five. They're behind a tree. Perhaps I could talk to them."* she suggested.

*"Then they'll know you're a girl,"* I warned.

I took her silence to mean she wasn't keen to let these guys know that either.

*"We should just go,"* she said thinking of home.

*"I want to shake them up a bit."*

He couldn't see our faces in the dark. I used the suit to say in a deep, low voice. "No money," in French.

It was a statement not an excuse.

Now we were hooded little men with deep voices who stared at him. The voice caused a few of the men to look around at us. The man who had challenged me's eyes widened with surprise. The rain kept pouring down. Then the soldier stood and pointed his gun.

"All your money and I will decide whether it's enough not to kill you."

*"Ready?"* I asked Tahira.

*"Go!"* Tahira said.

I zapped him and in the blink of an eye the electric blue charge crackled through the rain knocking him down.

**[+]**

Time slowed, the colour drained. The world folded and I fell spinning into brilliant light. The presences came and went.

I opened my eyes. We were back under the oil in the light of jumpstation with the rain bubbling off our suits around us. We waded forward out of the tank the oil washing away water and dirt from our suits and emerged slowly dripping into the control room. Grandpop was sitting at the desk.

"Those guys on the bridge are still yelling at each other about you," he chuckled cheerfully.

We smiled but we were just tired out.

"Go and get changed," Grandpop said.

We went through the briefing room back to the changing machines. Somehow everything seemed a bit unreal. We looked at each other as we walked to the changers. We both knew we wanted to say something but we didn't quite know what so with a shrug we got into the changers.

There was something about that process. The hood removal, the disconnection from the suit, the unwrapping of the top, the journey through the tunnel and the removal of the bottom that felt different to previous times. When the drawer opened and I climbed naked back out into the changing room with my ordinary clothes hanging up I felt a strange feeling of being reborn.

I pulled my pants back on and felt strangely vulnerable. I put my shirt on and it made no difference. In my suit I was safe from everything. Soldiers, ghosts, even little dead girls. And now I wasn't.

I felt funny in my stomach as if my undressing had taken away the distance between me and the village full of people who had been burned in their church, the little girl shot, the soldiers I'd zapped. I felt nervous and weird as if the place I had been in was just around the corner and I might be back there at any moment.

I put my shoes on and went back to the briefing room.

I sat there by myself for a while feeling as if I was waiting for a movie of my life to start. Then Tahira came down. She looked the way I felt.

We exchanged "Hi's". We were still not sure what to talk about. We were waiting quietly when Ashley and Scotty came in, still

27

suited up. Somehow I found it easier to talk to Scotty and Tahira was the same with Ashley.

They hadn't seen any newly recruited child soldiers either. They had mostly come across refugees in pitiful conditions including little kids with nothing to eat and no-one to look after them. They were shocked to hear about the dead village we'd found and the fact we'd been shot at. We all laughed about Tahira taking cover in the cesspit. But she explained she was never in danger because of a bank between her and the soldiers. She said she was glad Grandpop had given us that gun training.

Scotty and Ashley were about to get changed when Cam and Tarik came in bickering over who left first. Cam was never shy about arguing with Tarik in her logical and persistent way and he was looking a bit got-at.

It turned out they had had the trickiest time of all. The antennas they were sent to bug were guarded and even using the adaptive camouflage and taking advantage of the heavy rain they had been spotted twice. Luckily no-one had shot at them, though. The spray had been a problem in the heavy rain. They had to dry the antennas to spray them which was almost impossible. The frustrations had led to squabbling.

Grandpop came in just as they started arguing again and sent them all off to the changers. Grandpop sat down with us while we waited.

"How you feeling?" he asked Tahira.

She shrugged, "OK."

Grandpop looked at her with eyes that told me he knew exactly what she was feeling but he just smiled and looked away. The others took their time so he looked to me next.

"Your Aunt's proud of you Sam. She said she was amazed how

well you did."

Tahira seemed to notice but said nothing.

"Your mum and grandmother are pretty stoked with you too, young lady," he added.

That seemed to wrap the cold feeling I had in my stomach in a warm blanket, but it didn't get rid of it. Tarik and Scotty came out and then, just as Grandpop was going to send Tahira in to get Ashley and Cam, they came out, chatting away. Grandpop stood up looking over his glasses.

"Guys, if anyone had asked me what a bunch of thirteen-year-olds would do on a mission in the most dangerous place in the world a year ago I would have said get lost, get confused, and probably get killed. But you showed us all that you've been listening and you did far better than any of us expected. We're all very proud of you."

He looked at his notepad.

"Now it was obvious the rain was going to have a big effect on this mission and it did. The lack of aerial observation was a real problem and I'm going to take that up with Hekator when I get a chance. The spray did not do well in the rain and poor Tarik struggled to get coverage. Cam you did a great job providing cover and distractions."

"The rain didn't stop Sam zapping two trigger happy soldiers endangering Tahira. Good work taking them out so fast Sam but it also showed how much the rain interferes with your stun ray because it gave away your position badly. If there were others you could have been in big trouble."

"You all suffered from poor grip on the ground and you may need better claws for wet weather."

"So that was my take on equipment. On the operational side

**29**

I think you need to formalise your comms a bit. It's a bit too vague at the moment. I'll take you through that later. Other than that I thought you were all bloody brilliant. I'm proud of you and I know your parents are too."

"But more important what do you guys think?"

He sat back with his arms crossed.

"I tink we need to bring some food wid us. Some of dose kids was starving. It wouldn't hoirt us none to have someting in our pockets to give 'em," Ashley said.

"Yeah, I hear you Ashley. Food is better than currency. People respond to it," Grandpop said writing in his notebook.

"Even pencils or solar calculators are valuable in places like this. They were where I come from," Scotty suggested.

"That's good thinking too Scotty," Grandpop agreed.

"Would be good to have better things for distracting," Cam said. "I had to throw stones," she added.

"That's another good idea, Cam. I'll see if Hekator can send anything through," Grandpop said writing it down.

"In France zey av a pill zat stops babies forming after…" Tahira flushed a bit. "Eez for girls like Jeanne."

Grandpop frowned. "Yeee … ah Tahira I can see what you're thinking about … but … I'll have to talk to your parents about that one. Pills like that are a bit more complicated to get hold of than pencils. Anyone else?"

"We seemed to do a lot of running. Couldn't Control have just scouted the whole road?" I asked.

Grandpop looked at me and chuckled.

"He already had. Your parents wouldn't have let you go without us checking it out first. It was a test for everyone. You and us. But we can't see everything. We thought the village where everyone had been murdered was just abandoned and we didn't see those guys who shot at Tahira. And we don't know what this Jeanne looks like. We don't know where she comes from. Only you guys can find her and we had to make sure she is with the others in Bizwe not hiding on the side of the road."

"Besides we have a problem. Bizwe is a big camp. The CNDP is not small. Putting you in there on your first mission was too dangerous. Finding this girl is an elephant-sized problem and the only way to eat an elephant is one bite at a time."

"Once we start getting intell from the signals we'll have a better idea of how the land lies. But for the moment the main thing is to do this slow and steady. This Jeanne is in big trouble but that's no reason to get you guys in trouble too. Our first priority is keeping you safe. Then we worry about the mission. That was the deal you and your parents signed up for."

I couldn't help thinking how incredibly lucky we were to be able to choose our level of danger. The people we had just visited just had to live with it all the time. We broke up the briefing and went up to dinner. Aunty Liz ruffled my hair and gave me a hug which made me feel better. I noticed both Tahira and me were much closer to our sisters than we normally were. And I noticed we all appreciated the food more than we normally did, thinking of those refugees on the side of the road.

That night Aunty Liz stayed with me when I went to bed. I told her about what I'd seen and how it just all seemed so hopeless. She told me sometimes she felt the same way going into other people's houses when she knew something bad was happening but nobody would report it.

"You've got to think about the good you do Sam. If you worry about the bad others do, or might do, you can't keep going."

"But what if the good you do is really small and the bad is everywhere," I asked, thinking just how bad it was.

"Then if you stop there will be no good at all," she said simply.

"We have to keep going and just hope that things will get better," she said standing at the door and flicking the switch. "What else can we do?" she said as she left me.

I thought about that for a while. I couldn't see anything wrong with her reasoning at all. I must have fallen asleep because I was running through the bush at home. Ax was looking for other children with a machine gun and I was helping them to run and hide. Every now and again there was a lot of shooting. The kids were all running, getting away into the jungle (which was what the bush had become). I went back making sure there were no stragglers. Then I came into a clearing and found Ax resting on a stump, smoking a cigarette. He was like a giant. At least four meters tall, he was all muscles, bullets and camouflage gear. He greeted me with a smile.

"It's hot work." he grinned, "but it's gotta be done."

He put out his ciggy on the stump and picked up his weapon.

"Rounded them all up? Good work boy!" he said and strode off in the direction of the kids I'd been helping. I was appalled. Then the thought struck me.

"How do you know you are helping?"

It was such a powerful thought I woke up. The rain was rattling on the window and the sea crunching loudly on the beach. I lay, curled up, warm and snug, thinking about kids curled up under a tree in a rainstorm. How did I know I was helping? So far I hadn't done anything. But how did I know I was even on the right side? How did I know Jeanne was going to be on the right side? I lay there thinking about it, but nothing came and I fell asleep again.

## CHAPTER FORTY THREE: FINDING JEANNE

It was weird to go back to school the next day knowing you had been to the scene of mass murder the night before. One of the smaller girls was wearing pink and white and I found myself staring at her at lunchtime thinking about the little murdered girl in Africa. Tahira noticed her too and looked over at me. A shared understanding passed between us and I turned away in time to catch something die in Emma who looked away. Man, that pissed me off!

I went to the library and found Scotty and Ashley there looking at a book on gorillas. All three of us went through the pages looking at these huge black-eyed creatures. Somehow we found it relaxing and fascinating to look at animals that lived in that place without murdering the young of their own species. We survived an afternoon of maths, and returned home listening to a Putamaya African collection Mariko played on the bus.

After work we went and got changed as usual and found ourselves with Bernard and Grandpop in the briefing room. We went forward again and took our seats as usual.

"Hi everyone. You might like to know we've spent the day poking around Bizwe and monitoring the radio traffic. The situation is getting interesting for Nkunda's Tutsi CNDP who have Jeanne. They are under attack both in Masisi in the south and Rutshuru

in the north. The UN, the DRC army (FARDC) and the Hutu
FDLR plus the mai-mai bandits are putting Nkunda under
pressure. Meanwhile the rain is getting intense in Uganda,
Rawanda and Tanzania with flooding likely if it doesn't ease[†].
Met forecasts show little sign of that."

"Control has been getting pictures of the eighty or so young
girls in the Bizwe camp during our night. Dr Prosperov is doing
what he can with them. Bernard and I have been trying to work
out what we can get you guys to do. And the only thing that
makes sense is to send you into Bizwe itself. The problem is that
five in the morning their time is too late. We need to get you
in much earlier in the morning. So we've decided to wait until
your holidays which must be pretty soon and get you to do some
other things in the meantime."

It was true. What with the visitors and all the training, six weeks
of term had zoomed past, and there were only two weeks of term
left.

"But what about Jeanne?" Ashley interrupted.

Grandpop looked a bit uncomfortable, but it was Bernard who
spoke.

"While she is in the middle of this armed camp there is not
much we can do for her, Ashley. She is surrounded by hundreds
of armed men. You could not get her out without killing her and
probably yourselves. Dr Prosperov thinks it won't be until she
has finished her training that she will be able to escape. Then we
can help her."

"But won't they...you know?" Ashley persisted.

Now Grandpop coughed and spoke softly.

"Yeah, Ashley. I know we wanted to help her escape from that
but it's too late. It's sad and horrible but in North Kivu it's the

reality and we can't stop it. Unfortunately we can't prevent bad things happening to good people, all we can do is make sure they survive to do something about them when they grow up. We know Jeanne is not going to have a good time. We have put some YouTube videos about DRC girl soldiers on your PCs for you to have a look at later which will give you some idea of these kids' lives. But while she does what she's told in the camp she will live. It's the village women the soldiers attack who often don't. So she is not as safe as she could be, but a lot safer than she might be."

"She will try and run away at some point once they send her somewhere to fight. They all do. So when she does, our job will be to make sure she gets to safety. Is that okay Ashley?"

I was surprised he asked her like that. It wasn't sarcastic, or talking down to her, he meant it.

"I jus' wish dere was somethin' we could do to stop 'em," Ashley said.

"So do I Ashley, I really do," agreed Grandpop. "But the problems in this place are way bigger than one girl. Their whole society is ...well..."

"It even makes the mess in Zimbabwe look good," Bernard said.

"Yeah," Grandpop agreed. "So we have to do what we can do and take our chances to help when we can. Tahira? Cam? What do you girls think?"

"I think we need know which girl is Jeanne very soon," Cam said.

"Exactly! 'ow else can we 'elp 'er escape?" Tahira added.

"Good! that's exactly what we thought too," Grandpop said. "But the camp in Bizwe is the wrong place to do it. It's 5:20 a.m. right now, the camp is waking up, and to send you there now would just put you all in unnecessary danger. Much better to put you in where no-one notices," Grandpop told us.

"So instead of searching Bizwe we are going to get you to look for Jeanne's family," Bernard said. "We know where she's gone but to help identify her we need to know where she came from. We need to know whether she will be able to go back or if she will have to go elsewhere."

"The main clues are the schools. Dr Prosperov says the vision of the school was very strong and he was able to identify it from Control's pictures today, as the Institute de Musami."

A view of the school appeared in front of us and we began moving around it. It was a pretty run down set of wooden buildings on a steep hill surrounded by green jungle plants and red earth. I couldn't help thinking it was only a little bigger than our own school on the island. A man in a red shirt was organising a group of quite small children to dig a garden. They all looked pretty spooked while the man was trying to keep them together. I couldn't help thinking what a total hero *that* teacher was. Here he was still trying to teach kids after all his oldest ones had been abducted by soldiers. I wondered whether our teacher, Mr Wakefield, would have the guts to do the same.

"We think the best solution is to find this man and ask him about Jeanne. Keep your eyes on him so you get to know his face."

We watched as he talked soundlessly to the children in a room with broken furniture and hardly any paper. The little kids had hard dark eyes. I wondered what they had seen.

"Like every teacher in the DRC this man probably speaks French. So our plan is that you will fan out, in your pairs looking for him." Bernard said. "When you find him Tahira will have to bend in to ask him about Jeanne and her family," he added.

"Yeah but, won't 'e find someone materialising out of thin air in a blaze o' light a bit odd?" Tarik asked.

Bernard's dazzling white teeth showed in his smile.

"We are counting on it Tarik," he said.

Grandpop took over.

"Guys we've been rethinking our policy a bit for this place. We're starting to think that given you will only be active at night, and given that this place is fairly ... well to be blunt ... fairly backward ... We can get away with being a bit *less* secretive," he said.

Bernard picked up, "You see here, magic is *alive*. That is how they will explain your appearance to themselves or others. They will probably see you as spirits, Abuzimu, who dwell in the volcanoes around them. Now, of course they are not stupid. They are practical people. But appearance and disappearance is either a trick or true magic. If they can learn it, it's a trick. They can see others can learn white tricks like flying helicopters so they are not magical. But the things which you do, *nobody* can do, so they will see you as magical."

"But none o' da others is black," Ashley pointed out.

"And I hope you will excuse me for saying that you obviously aren't an African either Miss Robinson. You just don't move like an African. Which is why it is best if you *all* keep your hoods sealed," Bernard replied.

"That will make you seem mysterious and powerful. As Scott knows in Africa magic is normal. So perhaps it's not so bad to be more obvious about your powers in front of these people," Bernard finished.

Grandpop added, "Not too flashy, though. We have to assume

the guys in the saucer you met in Greenland watch our news, there are some reporters here, and news of vanishing children might attract their attention. So try to keep your audiences small."

"Now tonight we are going to put you down in pairs around the school. You are to fan out and try to find this teacher. If you do, Tahira is to bend over to ask him about Jeanne."

"Now to make it simple we've put Control's pictures on your suits. You can display the pictures on your wrists or your fronts or your facescreens. That way you can ask who these girls are." Grandpop told us.

"Best not to put the pictures on your facescreens," Bernard interrupted hastily. "They may think the girl is dead which will distress the family," he explained.

"Good point," Grandpop grunted. Then to wake us up he yelled "OK, let's go!"

## [+]

We went to the jumpstation and a minute later Tahira and I were standing in the pouring rain again, in the dark with the school behind us, under the shivering palms and trees.

We were facing south along the line of the ridge. Tarik and Cam were on the north side while Scotty and Ashley were up-slope to the west. There were loads of houses and huts in front of us along a path that wound around the hillside.

"*What do we do now?*" I asked silently.

"*You have to let your feelings guide you,*" Scotty told us.

Tahira and I looked at each other. Then a dark presence ambled forward from the trees in front of us. He was a young man. He looked a bit annoyed. Other shadows had appeared and started coming from the school and houses. They were all ages. Boys, grandmothers, little girls and uncles.

"*You guys getting a lot of ghosts?*" Tarik asked.

We all said we were.

The presences were uncertain what to make of us. They seemed grumpy.

"*Why have you brought us here?*" An older man challenged us from the darkness.

"*We are looking for a girl of this school,*" I told them silently.

"*Jeanne,*" Tahira added.

There was a ripple of discussion among the shades, who remained in the dark shadows, beneath the trees and beside the sleeping huts. I noticed that out past the volcano with its orange red glow, the sky in the east was slightly lighter. But the Shades had a question.

"*Which Jeanne? There are many Jeannes among us,*" a woman called through the wind.

"*She is not among you, she has been taken by the soldiers,*" Tahira replied.

This sparked a flurry of anger. They obviously hated soldiers. Then a smaller presence stepped forward from the darkness. He was a boy a bit younger than us.

"*My sister is Jeanne. She was taken two days ago. I went to the soldiers for my mother and father. They thought they would pity a younger brother. I asked them to give her back to us. They shot me dead.*"

The presences raged silently. The shadows beneath the trees seemed alive with anger.

"*What is your name?*" Tahira asked.

"*I was called Phillipe,*" the small shade replied sadly.

"*What was your family name Phillipe?*" I asked.

"*Mazuri.*"

"*Mazuri?*" I asked to make sure I had it right.

"*Yes.*"

"*Where do your parents live Phillipe?*" I asked

He said nothing but looked at us doubtfully. They all were. I realised they trusted no-one.

"*We have been sent to rescue Jeanne,*" Tahira explained silently.

"*Why?*" An older spirit asked annoyed,. "*Why rescue that girl and not my niece Beatrice?*"

"*Or my cousin Marie?*"

"*Or my son Bertrand?*" complained another.

"*Who are you?*" An older woman demanded.

We looked at each other.

The problem with presences is they are don't really listen even if you do answer them. At best you can get them to calm down but explaining anything is a waste of time. They have no memory.

"*We have been sent by God, to save Jeanne,*" Tahira told them strongly.

The shades seemed kind of frozen. Tahira had confused them. They had no answer. They could not contradict her, but they weren't convinced. We did not impress them as godly but they could think of no better reason for us to be there. I took advantage of the stillness to question Phillipe.

"*How far is your parents house?*"

He answered in ideas that meant it was just over a kilometer down the path.

"*Only we can finish your mission,*" Tahira told him gently.

"*We have the magic you needed,*" I added.

Philippe was reluctant but he couldn't see any reason not to guide us so we set off down the path, Tahira in front.

*"Hey everyone we've found Jeanne's brother's ghost. He's guiding us to her parent's house. Her name is Mazuri,"* I told them.

"Good work Sam. But you others keep looking. There may be more than one Jeanne. It's a fairly common name and we need to make sure there isn't another one."

*"We think we have found the teacher's house but he's still asleep. How do we find out for sure?"* Tarik called in.

"Wake him up. Use sound and light," Grandpop said. "No point being shy."

*"What about everyone else?"* Cam asked.

"Look scary," Grandpop replied.

*"OK,"* they said doubtfully.

We followed the track with Philippe leading the way and some of the shades following behind. The rain was still pouring down and it was still dark but the light gray band in the east was getting bigger quickly. The glow of the volcano was still visible in the distance though it was smaller than the night before.

Tahira was keeping an ear out for Cam or Tarik who might call her over to talk to the teacher. I was leading the way. The path was muddy and slippery and we needed our claws to hold on to it.

Then as we rounded a bend in the hill we found ourselves facing a group of soldiers coming the other way. There were about a dozen of them, their faces smudges of black, under caps or just dark hair. They were wearing camouflage that didn't match together with a mixture of jackets and plastic sheets with holes cut for their heads. But their Ak47s looked well used and their jog had a purposeful tread to it.

Phillipe simply faded out in front of them. We had our hoods

**41**

up and our facescreens dark. It was still very dark and our suits looked like dark jackets, pants and shoes. Even with the mud spattered around our legs we still looked a bit new.

The leader of the soldiers was a tall, quite good looking man in his late 20s. The others were all younger. The youngest was only a few years older than us, though he looked like he had eaten nothing but lemons all his life.

It was all so fast, they were on us before we could decide what to do. We both fell back out of the way against the side of the path. Then the leader yelled for them to stop. All eyes turned to us with our backs to the bank in the slippery mud. The flash of white teeth suggested these guys expected to have some fun.

I'd been bullied by bigger kids before but not by men with guns. In some ways I almost wanted to zap them all. The leader came around to look at us.

"What have we here? Deserters or spies?" he said smiling in a way that was anything but friendly.

We said nothing.

"*Tahira, the teacher is awake. Though he's pretty annoyed. Could you calm him down?*" Tarik asked.

"*Moment, Tarik.*"

The leader walked over to us and bent down to look at us.

"So which is it? Spies or deserters?"

He would shoot us for either. We looked at him silently. He couldn't see our faces.

"*Two sites please Tarik,*" Tahira said.

"*Make it four. We're wasting our time here,*" Scotty said.

"*Got four,*" Cam said.

"Answer me. Spies or deserters?" the leader yelled in our faces then made to slap us.

If we'd planned it he wouldn't have got the charge he did. We both zapped him at the same time, blue lightning leaping at him from our chests instantaneously. Smoke rose. He sank to his knees. It was definitely time to bend out.

**[+]**

Time slowed, drained of colour and turned to a line and we reappeared in a flash of light in a ring around a man who had been threatening Tarik with a stick and was now looking at us surrounding him. He looked like he had been physically struck as he dropped the stick and turned to stare, his eyes bulging, at our faceless cowls in the pouring rain.

Suddenly he sprinted for his hut. There was a flash of light from Tarik which hit him in the middle of the back and his legs collapsed sending him sprawling in the mud. He looked over his shoulder at us, his face contorted in terror and tried to crawl desperately to his hut. A woman inside, apparently watching, started to scream.

Tahira ran forward to him and knelt down next to him.

"Professor, professor, listen! We are not devils. We are searching for your lost student Jeanne. We seek to protect the children the soldiers stole."

He stopped dragging himself and rolled over on his back looking up at her into the rain with an expression of extreme mistrust on his face.

"Go away! Leave me alone! In the name of Jesus Christ begone!" he shouted in French.

Tahira backed off to let him calm down.

The woman was still shouting for us to go away and for Claude. She seemed too scared to come out but she wasn't going to be quiet. The man went back to crawling away.

**43**

*"He thinks we're evil spirits,"* said Scotty said.

*"We* look *like evil spirits,"* Cam observed.

*"Let's light up and fly. Maybe he'll think we're angels,"* Ashley suggested.

It was getting a lighter. The sky was still gray and misty but it was definitely no longer night time. The rain had eased a little.

*"Would* you *believe it, if evil spirits turned into angels?"* Scott asked. *"He'll just think we're tricking him."*

*"Yeah, probably."* Ashley sighed.

*"OK, let's come back tomorrow as angels,"* Tarik said.

The teacher had got back to his house. The woman had calmed down when she realised we were not going to attack Claude any more.

## [+]

So we went home. Grandpop was upbeat at the debrief.

"Well, we have one name and one, maybe two, places to visit tomorrow. Control will keep the teacher under observation today to see what he does."

"What happened to that guy me and Tahira zapped?" I asked.

"Don't know yet. He was still unconscious when I came in. Control will watch him too. No criticism of Sam and Tahira, you probably found that guy a bit scary, but in reality you didn't need to zap him. Vanishing would have been spooky enough. And Tarik you didn't really need to zap that teacher in the back either. I know it's nice not to have to feel defenceless in a scary place but your weapons are meant to be as a last resort for the protection of others, not because you don't like someone's lip. So let's just have less zapping and more moving."

And we went off to dinner. I didn't really answer Rewa's questions. I just told her we had been talking to ghosts. She didn't like ghosts much so she didn't ask much more. Aunty Liz did though. I noticed she was paying a lot more attention to me at bedtime these days. I told her about Philippe. It made us both a bit sad that these crazy men with guns would think so little of killing a boy. She suggested I say a prayer for him, so I did, and that helped a bit.

I watched Mr Wakefield more closely the next day. I thought about Claude, the teacher we had attacked the previous night. I wondered how Mr Wakefield would cope with dark-faced little goblins surrounding his home at night and temporarily paralysing him. On the other hand how would he cope if soldiers came and dragged us away and shot our younger brothers and sisters who asked for us back. I had an unpleasant feeling that so long as *he* was safe he wouldn't really care very much.

The day passed dreading another scary visit to North Kivu. It was the combination of darkness, violence and rain that just made you wish we could go somewhere else instead.

I think we all did our cleaning a bit slower because we just didn't want to go there again. And yet by five we were back in the briefing room ready to go. Grandpop, looking over his glasses, was quicker than normal.

"The good news is. The rain has lifted for a while. The better news is, it's foggy. So the story tonight is to visit the teacher again. What we thought would be best would be to only put Tahira in as a mock angel. The rest will be in a circle out of sight protecting her."

"Tahira will be dropping in from above all wings and glow once the rest of you are in place. Your job is to watch out for neighbours who might find Tahira a tempting target."

"The rest will be up to Tahira to sweettalk this guy into

cooperating."

"Now we watched this guy all day."

The display came to life showing the hut in the morning in fast motion. Then it slowed. Claude seemed able to walk again but he was definitely spooked. He went to school as usual but he still looked worried. His wife (if that was what she was) had a small child, aged perhaps one or so. She went to the market but also to the church. Claude also went to the church. Then as evening fell they barricaded themselves into the house.

"We think he's feeling guilty about the children and that you guys are demons come to prick his conscience. So the idea is that perhaps you bad fairies wake this guy up and then Tahira, the good fairy or angel, drives you off. Any thoughts or questions? Yes Tahira?"

"Do zeez people 'av guns?"

Exactly what I wanted to know.

"We had a bit of a look around and the answer is no. The main weapon is machetes or metal bars which are dangerous enough at close quarters. Anything else?"

"If we find Jeanne's brother's ghost do we follow him?" I wanted to know.

"Well, *you* don't, you're Tahira's buddy. You never leave your buddy. But if she's safe one of the other pairs may."

There were no more questions so it was back to the jumpstation.

"We're putting you back at the school so the light flare doesn't confuse the story too much. You can walk to the house."

The world went and came as usual.

## [+]

In the fog the empty school buildings seemed even more spooky than they had before. Once again the crowds of shades began to trickle out from between the buildings and along the paths, shadows in shadow. This time we ignored them.

"*Hey guys, check this out,*" Tarik said.

He had made a skull pattern on his face screen.

"*It's good, but it's too bright,*" Scotty said. "*Try this.*"

Scotty's one was dark gray but it looked far spookier under the hood.

"*And fingers as well.*" Cam said.

She had made her fingers gray and skeletal looking.

"*This is a bit like trick or treating on Halloween,*" Ashley said as she copied the others.

So disguised as little ghouls with an audience of real ghosts, muttering in the dark we followed Tarik and Cam in the direction of the teacher's house.

The mist reduced visibility to about twenty five meters but there were a lot of huts and houses in this area. I wished we had whatever it was Tabika had used to keep everyone asleep. But we made no sound at all as we slipped around the teacher's house following the little worn paths between the tall tropical trees and bushes.

As we moved into position around the house the shades gathered around us – but remaining in the shadows. They seemed more curious about us now than irritated.

"*OK, we're ready,*" Tarik called in.

"*Better wake him up first,*" Grandpop suggested.

"*OK, 15 to 30 cycles, 80 db,*" Tarik called. "*All together on 'Go'. Five, four, three, two, one, go!*"

The rumble was deep, loud and even vibrated our stomachs. It was sort of like a big truck idling outside. We kept it up the whole time.

47

We knew we had woken him up because people were sticking their heads out of neighbouring houses and shouting at us until we gave them a look and a blast of spookiness. Their eyes went wide in the dark and they ducked back inside real fast. I got the impression that the news about the soldier we had zapped the night before had spread. Whatever it was nobody seemed keen to rescue Claude.

We heard hushed crying inside the hut. They were obviously terrified. I felt a bit bad about that.

"Tahira's on her way," Grandpop called.

We looked for her in the fog above us.

"*Let's start trying to break in. It will increase the relief when Tahira comes,*" Ashley said.

So we all started scratching at the hut with our claws. There was a glint of steel.

"*Look out for his machete!*" I warned everyone.

Scotty started growling like a hungry animal. It was a weird, unearthly noise. The child started screaming. I *really* didn't like doing this.

"Get away in the name of Jesus Christ!" Claude shouted, his voice high with terror.

At first we didn't notice the golden light above us but Tahira slowly lowered herself down glowing like the sun. Her wing beats were as low as one every two seconds so she must have been at maximum gravity deflection.

Ashley lifted her head made a brilliant noise, a high screeching wail as if in pain.

"*Back to the school,*" she thought.

And vanished. The others screeched like they were being driven away and vanished too but this put me in a difficult situation.

If I went back to the school Tahira was unprotected. There was only one thing for it.

"*Going up a grand,*" I told them, doing my screech as I vanished.

## [+]

Time slowed and the scene folded. I passed though light into cloud. I was falling so I unfurled my wings and cranked up the gravity deflection and my suit's brightness. I fell for six seconds very slowly. The cloud and the dark were impossible to see through but I knew where Tahira was and as my wings hardened I reduced deflection so I could get down to her quicker.

I was above Tahira as she started to call to Claude softly. I could just make her out through the fog, hovering over the house making a golden light all around the small hut. I could also see people looking from the neighbouring huts. They had their mouths open with astonishment.

I circled around lower and saw Claude come out of the house. Tahira must have looked magnificent. I noticed he saw me too, but Tahira now flew down from the roof and landed lightly by the door. I realised we were remembering how Tabika had seemed to us, when we were in poor Claude's place.

I hovered, flapping slowly because gravity was down to ten percent, over the house about ten meters up, keeping watch around us. Tahira waved Claude toward her. She was so bright she was hard to look at. Then she tried something we had never done before. She tried telepathy on him.

He seemed to get something, but it wasn't enough. So she spoke in French, her voice changed slightly to sound like a woman's. Claude was simply stunned. It took ages to get him to say there were only two Jeanne's taken by the soldiers. Mazuri and

**49**

Kamejeru. The wife and the child were watching from the door equally mesmerised. A crowd from the other houses had been drawn out, awestruck, by Claude's unearthly visitors. For the most part they were in awe except one little pest behind some others threw a rock at me. I picked him out and dazzled his eyes so that was the end of that little game.

Finally Tahira had had enough adoration, beat her wings and took off. We had to flap a bit to get going but as soon as we were out of sight in the fog we bent home.

**[+]**

The others were away quite a lot longer. It turned out that Tarik and Cam followed Philippe home and Scotty and Ashley found an old man named Kamejeru who led them to his son's house. They didn't do anything, just identified the places and left. Grandpop was very pleased.

"So now we have two names to give Dr Prosperov for further work. This is going much better than I expected," he told us.

We talked about it over dinner – which was Moroccan chicken and couscous. None of us had liked frightening Claude's family much. Tarik said it reminded him of the Turkish police and Scotty said it reminded him of when they were surrounded by war veterans. But we agreed that the bad fairy, good fairy trick was one way to get people on side.

When I talked it over with Aunty Liz that night she asked how I felt about going to North Kivu.

"Tired," I said. "It's dark, and the place is depressing. It just makes you feel like there's no hope in the world."

"I think you guys need more variety," she nodded.

## CHAPTER FORTY FOUR: THE BIG APPLE

G uess what guys? No war zones! Tonight you are going to Noo York!" Grandpop told us as we came into theatre the next night. The screen showed us a view of the famous city all lit up below us. It looked fantastic.

"This is as she is, right now. It's a cool twelve degrees – that's Celsius Ashley – with a slight breeze, but otherwise a normal fall evening in the big Apple."

"What about Jeanne?" Ashley asked.

"Dr Prosperov is the problem there," Grandpop admitted. "He's not sure which Jeanne it is. He's not getting anything from the names we found for him. He says it's probably him because the more information you have the harder it is to separate your thoughts from your guesses. He needs a little more time to get the insight he needs to be sure we're on the right path. That's what he told me anyway. So rather than hang around North Kivu, he wants you to do some spying for him in New York. Sound like fun?"

It sounded a lot better than dealing with the ghosts of war victims.

"OK, so what this, and the next few missions, are about is tapping communications. You will do that with Hekator's bug spray and transmitter grains that Tarik and Cam put on the antennas in North Kivu and a new device – this!"

He held up a half meter long silvery thing that looked like a fat earthworm. He had three of them.

"It's a worm," he said, then he glanced at it and changed his mind. "Well, it's a robot worm. Hekator knocked three up and sent them through. It digs into the ground and taps into large fibre-optic cables."

"I thought Hekator wasn't allowed to help us?" Scott asked. Grandpop smiled.

"Technically he isn't, but he likes making robots for us for fun. He slips them to us through the lighthouse. It's just the bigger things he's not allowed to work on."

Then Grandpop pulled out of his pocket three matchbox sized containers.

"We also have these. In here are a dozen tiny robot flies. They will fly around the target buildings recording and placing more bugs. If someone sprays them they pretend to die in hard to reach places, if they get smashed ... well nobody will be able to tell the difference. We were flying them around the house today and they work really well."

He put them back in his pocket.

"Now, I have been asked to remind you that what you are being asked to do is illegal in the United States – and just about everywhere else as well. Does that bother anyone?"

We all looked at each other.

"Not especially, Sir, but what are we buggin' and why?" Ashley asked.

"Exactly, Ashley! Good question. OK, so New York is the home of the United Nations and some of the world's most powerful banks. There are also some interesting corporate headquarters there. Dr Prosperov wants to find out more about what they are up to. His main reason is to get a better idea of what is going on in global finance. That is partly to understand the secret deals that motivate politicians but also to help him make money to pay us. So we are breaking every law in the book. Anyone bothered by that?"

Ashley wanted to be clear.

"So we'll be helpin' Dr Prosperov cheat Wall Street?" she asked seriously.

"Yeah, that's pretty much it," Grandpop confirmed.

"Woo hoo! Go Dr Prosperov!" Ashley whooped and high-fived Tarik and Scotty next to her.

We all laughed.

"OK, well, the technology makes this mission pretty simple. There are a few main sites of interest. These buildings here, because they host cell towers. The UN building joins the Manhattan fibre ring here, and the Verizon headquarters here on Manhattan next to what used to be the World Trade Center. Wall Street itself about here. The Empire State Building, because it hosts a number of microwave dishes, and the Verizon operations centre in Basking Ridge, New Jersey just over the Hudson river there. Verizon, for those who don't know, is a huge telecommunications firm that supplies most of the State of New York."

"Now this is just the first wiretap mission. We will be doing a whole bunch of these while Dr Prosperov sorts himself out. So you are going to be getting some practice in. We are starting with civilian sites because the security isn't as tight as military ones. That doesn't mean there isn't any. It just means it's not as vicious. Even so the security people may be armed so don't take any chances. Any problems and you vanish. Got that?"

We mumbled agreement. Actually we hated bending out. It felt like giving up.

"OK, now kids your age on the streets of Manhattan at one in the morning are out of place, so hide. Use blending, and be quick. It may be late but Manhattan rooftops aren't as empty as you might think either. The city is always busy and relatively noisy even now. There is also lots of light about."

"If a few people see you, it's no biggy so long as they don't have cameras. Don't forget cellphones are cameras too. Cameras will get you on Youtube or, worst case, breakfast TV. So we think bending directly onto rooftops is the best way in for most sites. It's certainly better than climbing up the sides. The exception is the Empire State Building where the roof is mostly a TV mast. That one will be a bit trickier and harder to get at."

The view of Manhattan vanished and was replaced with some large buildings surrounded by trees.

"OK, this is the Verizon operations centre. It's very new and shiny because it only opened a fortnight ago[†]. As you can see it's large and has a couple of thousand people working at it. It's pretty much the communication command centre for New York so it's very important."

"Tonight though you don't have to do much, you are just there to carry the worms and the flies and get them close enough to be useful. We'll put you inside the grounds pretty much on target."

"OK, so here are all the targets."

Nine little buildings all came up with the antennas in false colour like models on the stage.

"Come down and pick your targets and we'll give you more detail on what you are doing."

I have to admit this was way more fun than North Kivu. We were all really excited.

Tahira and I cruised the models. We agreed on the Empire State – beating out Tarik and Cam – and the Western side of the Verizon Center and for a third target got given a smaller cellular centre near Central Park.

Control cloned himself three times, one for each pair, and had some extra advice on wind dynamics around the Empire State, and the things we could hang on to. He also warned the observation deck was still open for another hour although there was no-one on it at the moment. The antenna was blacked out for September[+] so we would be obvious if we glowed too much on it, so we would have to be normal weight up there.

Then it was off to the jumpstation. We chose to start with the rooftop cell tower first and end with Verizon with the Empire State in the middle.

"Drop in five, four, three, two, one..."

**[+]**

Time slowed, space folded and span. The dead came and went and we found ourselves on a rooftop of a tall building in the dark next to a whole lot of fan units which were part the air conditioning. The noise of traffic and air conditioning was much louder than some of the places we'd been lately. The tower itself was not so large so we jumped on to it and climbed around spraying the antennas. The extra strength we got from the suits, our grip-whips, wings and gravity reduction (if needed), plus the fact that the height to the roof wasn't much more than our trees at home, made it all quite easy. We could see the city around and below us but it wasn't very distracting. Tahira even started whistling as she worked.

**55**

But the whole time we were looking up at the Empire State. It was huge and made the building we were on seem small even though it was twenty stories. We knew the bend up there would be a bit more of a problem. We released two flies and were all finished in ten minutes.

The plan for the Empire State was to bend above it and fly onto the TV mast. The reason was the observation deck, which was still open to tourists for another three quarters of an hour, was monitored by cameras, so we couldn't bend onto it. When we were ready we told Control and folded into the night.

## [+]

A moment later we burst into the sky like little fireworks. Immediately I was plummeting to the city below. It seemed so, *so* high when you had tall things near you. It made the falling sensation much worse. The Empire State was almost immediately below us. Our gravity deflection came up faster than our wings so we fell slowly in balls of light for about three seconds, dropping down above and being blown closer to the famous landmark.

I was so focused on the observation deck looking for tourists with cameras I completely forgot to check out the view. It seemed though that half past one in the morning on a windy Wednesday night was not the busiest time on top of the Empire State.

As my wings hardened I started them beating. I became aware the wind was actually quite strong and was pushing us toward the building. We flew quickly to the side of the TV mast which towered above beside us. The suit warmed us so we knew how much radiation there was. It was more than we expected.

The whole building was simply enormous and the city spread

out below us in all directions.

"Let's do this as dark as we can!" I called to Tahira.

"Yeah," she replied.

We both felt very obvious glowing against the blacked out antenna tower of one of the most famous landmarks in the world, in a city famous for not sleeping. Below, the lights on the building were yellow and red for some reason[†]. We buzzed over to the looming tower and found some glass surfaces and applied our palm and knee pads like a couple of fireflies.

We were worried we'd pull this glass off the building if we put too much weight on it. Still we felt very obvious glowing as we did. Slowly I reduced gravity deflection. It was bloody scary feeling my full weight come back on, and knowing how high I was. There was something about being stuck to the side of a very tall building that defied all sensible knowledge about our equipment. You just felt really, really high and really, really scared. It didn't help that the surface was worn and very rusty in places. I had to take a couple of breaths before I was ready to move. If I had forgotten to look at the view before, now I was deliberately trying to ignore it. All I could feel was this emptiness below that wanted to pull me into it. I tried to imagine I was anywhere else, but that was hard because the city was reflected in the glass all around us.

One of the nasty surprises was discovering the building was swaying very slightly in the wind[†]. The suits would not let us unstick more than one limb at a time. The suction was very good. The only question was whether the windows we were stuck *to* could hold our weight. We had to test every new hold. This slowed us down but made us feel a little more secure.

I slowly crawled down, and over, to the first antenna very,

**57**

very slowly and carefully. Tahira was doing the same on the other side. The whole place was buzzing with TV signals and I was probably ruining someone's late night TV reception. The first microwave was a big, old one which was quite high power. Unfortunately I had to lean around it to spray and I couldn't avoid looking down. My head reeled. The height was so much higher with things to see all the way down and I had to fight down an impulse to bend to safety. I got out the spray and concentrated on getting good coverage, with my knee pads sticking firmly to the building. The wind made the spray go everywhere. Then I placed the grains in the rapidly drying glue. The microwave was very hot – the suit's warning for intense radiation – because it was about the same strength as a microwave oven with the door off. I had to be quick. I tried to avoid getting near the beam.

Then I climbed around a bit further to a couple of long, radio antennas and sprayed them. It was all a lot slower than I would have liked, but the amount of rusty metal and dust meant we had to take extra care that our pads were sticking properly. All the time the yawning height below us felt like it wanted to suck us off the building and down into the streets and traffic unbelievably far below.

We crawled around to get to the last microwave. It was hanging off a ledge and hard to get at. I could hear Tahira taking deep breaths as we crawled over to it. The drop was straight down. The trick was to spread your weight over as much of the building's side as possible, almost hugging it. Working together we sprayed the round dish and placed the grains. We were finished.

"Ready to bend on." I called in.

"I need you to unstick before I can bend you," Control told us. Let go? I thought he had to be kidding. My whole body was clinging on.

"*Can we fly in to Verizon. Say from two grand?*" Tahira asked telepathically.

"Of course," Control replied.

"*Can you bend us while we are falling from here?*" she added.

"Easily."

Tahira glanced at me. I couldn't see her face but her thoughts were plain.

"*Let's jump!*"

"*We'll need our wings to get clear,*" I told her.

She shrugged.

The covers on her wings popped open like a bug's. I did the same. They began to beat – a loud buzzing sound above the city. The wings couldn't lift us, but they could pull us clear. We started them up, even while the suits held us fast to the building. Somehow the idea of letting go seemed a bit dumb.

"*Ready?*" she asked.

"*Yes,*" I said, lying on the side of the building that fell away below us like an enormous plain. It was so, so high. You had to have faith in Control otherwise you'd still be still clinging to the building, crying with fear, when the sun came up.

"*Go!*"

I unstuck and immediately began falling. The wings dragged me away from the building as it flashed past. I twisted around to face down. Tahira was further out and further down. The wings weren't lifting us, just pulling us clear of the bits that stuck out. My heart was beating like a mad thing. Falling in the empty sky did not give you this sense of speed, or danger. The other buildings were still far below but they seemed to be climbing up to me rapidly.

Then Control said, "bending in three, two, one," and we were gone.

[+]

The Verizon complex looked like a park below us as we tumbled into the night. We fell a bit, but with our wings out, and our suits already in diving mode, it was much easier than with a city around. It was a fabulous night to be flying. There was not much light here, and if we had felt exposed on the Empire State, this just felt calm and restful.

We flew in from over the country club shedding height at a ratio of ten meters forward to one down doing about 200km/h and checking out potential landing zones. For some reason we had total confidence we could land here without bending. We manoeuvred around, doing a right hand wheel about to shed speed, while balancing the lift from our wings and the energy from falling. We were doing about a hundred kilometers an hour as we swooped over the fence, over the grounds and climbing hard into a steep turn. We reduced gravity so that we swooped back again, doing about fifty kilometers an hour, with our wings buzzing furiously so we could land, glowing with reduced gravity, at a run. It just seemed so natural with no distractions to ruin everything.

We'd done it! Our first bend dive to the deck! We were totally stoked. We killed gravity deflection, unsealed our facescreens and high-fived, as our wings deflated, and folded away in the dark parklike grounds. We wanted to shout "Yeehah!" but we knew *that* was stupid.

It was almost two o'clock in the morning eastern standard time.

We were still about a hundred meters from the buildings and had ended up running among some trees. There were a lot of crunchy leaves about and the trees themselves were a bit bare. After all the noise from our wings the night air seemed very quiet even despite the motorway no more than half a kilometer away.

I was carrying the worm, so I kicked a hole in the ground with my claws, picked it out of my pocket by the tail, and lowered it down. As soon as its body touched the ground it began to shimmer and twist. We watched, fascinated, as the shiny body disappeared under the earth in less than a minute.

We heard the sound of footsteps in the distance following the paved path. There was a cough of static from the security guard's radio in our ears. The controller was checking in. The guard told him all was clear.

A torch flashed into the trees.

Glowing orange under thermal imaging was a big, round looking, white, security guard with a goatee. He carried a torch, radio, and a night stick. We lay down, almost transparent thanks to the adaptive camouflage, and listened to him whistle his way past us, the sweep of his torchlight over us showing him nothing. Tahira slipped the box out of her pocket and after a short pause the two remaining flies zoomed out into the night. We lost track of them in the darkness as the guard walked off exchanging crude jokes over the radio with the controller. Me and Tahira felt relieved at finishing, and a certain lightheadedness. It had been fun and now we could go home, so we did.

## [+]

When we got out of the pool I noticed the mood in the changing room and around the table that night was much happier. We

were telling stories and jokes. Tarik and Cam had been spotted
by a police car and climbed a wall in full blend camouflage
to escape. Scotty and Ashley had had to blind some security
cameras to do their work, and then freeze on a ledge standing
over a thirty storey drop while a guard searched around them
no more than ten meters away. I noticed Grandpop watching
us carefully. He even asked me how I thought the mission had
gone.

"It was awesome," I told him.

"Great," he said and ruffled my hair.

Dr Prosperov called us together and told us we would be doing
a psychic probe of a bunch of computer security geeks. These
guys had the passwords to the security systems of the biggest
computer companies of the world. It turned out their security
was more important than anyone else's because their designs
held the key to unlocking the security of all the other important
systems in the world, such as telecommunications firms, the
military and finance.

We were sent to our rooms where our screens had feeds from
Control showing each of the men we had to read. Our job
was to record the passwords for each of these guys. You had
to watch them for a while to start to build a connection with
them. It really helped if you knew their names, and it also really
helped if they were at work and busy on the security system.
You got their personal and document passwords very quickly
that way. Watching someone sleeping or driving got you a lot
of information but no passwords. You couldn't do it for long
periods at a time or your head hurt.

Once we had the passwords the next step was bugging.
Hekator's big, underground worms were great for the computer

firms which had buildings spread around parks. But they were no use when the fibre rings were behind concrete walls in cable conduits. They would have to wait.

But we were happy because instead of getting depressed in North Kivu we spent the next week or so bugging the world. We went everywhere! Well, everywhere it was dark. We bugged the transatlantic cables. We bugged buildings and complexes. In most cases all it meant was appearing on a rooftop, or a beach, dropping the bugs and vanishing again. It wasn't hard, but it gave us a great sense of being useful.

Once the bugs were placed Dr Morozov and Control would go to work, carefully and gently changing settings so they could get access to the networks without being noticed. It reminded me of chess and Tarik was fascinated by the whole business, often spending time with Control (Dr Morozov was much less patient) asking questions about the techniques they used to break in. Once the break-in was sorted Dr Prosperov would begin analysing the data with the help of Control. His plan was to use the information to trade on international markets and make money. He said he had to make more money now because the cost of paying us was a lot more than he had counted on. We were making almost twice as much as our parents and there were six of us. Dr P also used his prophesy engine as well to predict future changes in the market. It wasn't long before he had doubled and even tripled his already large income, averaging a million dollars a day.

With all this going on at home it was hard to go to school these days. Mr Wakefield's new enthusiasm was for plants so we had to draw leaves and stuff. Most of them were really dumb. Other times we'd grow cuttings or do surveys of patches of ground or identify plants from books. Marshall usually found an excuse to flick dirt at people. He and his gang were also into any plant with prickles on it. They'd trick kids by asking them what a plant near the prickle was, and then say "take a closer took" and push them into the prickles. They found that hilarious.

But when he wasn't being a dick at school Marshall was spending more time with his older brother Mitchell who had a new car and was out most nights speeding around the island like an idiot. Marshall bragged about driving it and doing doughnuts. I had my doubts that Mitchell ever let his annoying little brother drive his precious car, but Marshall's friends lapped it up.

Although the weather was getting warmer and we could go outside at lunch and break, we found the games the other kids played a bit lame. I suppose it wasn't surprising really. We tended to stay together and talk about stuff. Sometimes we talked tactics, and other times we wondered about the Fae or Dr Prosperov. The other kids left us alone. At the time it didn't bother us. It should have done.

In November all the others except the Khumalos, Dr Gursoy and Mrs Khadem, got letters from the Immigration Department asking them to clarify whether or not they were working in the country or not. Everyone had been so distracted by our contact with another world we had forgotten about the boring laws that tied up this one.

Mr Trân was very nervous because he knew he had been working in the country illegally for years. Mrs Robinson was nervous too because she was still meant to be a willing worker on an organic farm, and wasn't sure that this story was going to hold water for long.

And although Dr Gursoy had been hired reasonably legally, he was worried that the New Zealand authorities might give his position away to the Turkish government, which might then fall into the hands of Ergenekon.

Both Dr Gursoy and Mrs Robinson had another problem too. Their own parents were still vulnerable to the gangs that were chasing them. Mrs Robinson had called her mother to warn her she was in danger from some of her brother's old friends, and that her mother should avoid anyone from back in New Orleans. That wasn't so hard because Mrs Williams had settled into Houston with her sister and saw nobody from her former home. Dr Gursoy had not called his parents because he feared the calls could be traced, so he simply worried about the health of his father and old mother. Of course none of the old people in their old countries used computers so email was impossible and posting letters would have left evidence they were in New Zealand so that hadn't been safe either.

But now that we could effectively travel anywhere both Mrs Robinson and Dr Gursoy wanted to send letters home. Dr Prosperov said that it was up to us, but that he wanted to hear the security plan. At first we were hard-out planning these visits to the Post Office. But it turned out, of course, that random kids going to a Post Office to send a letter was so routine we stopped worrying. We never went back to the same Post Office, and they never questioned us. The result was that Ashley and Scotty ended up getting up early in the morning to bend into all sorts of little towns all over the United States to post letters to Patricia's mum. Tarik and Cam also regularly started travelling to Post Offices in Turkey to send letters to Adiyaman as well.

Replies were sent to Poste Restante services in Post Offices

in cities in other countries we chose for being as far away
as possible, and easy to deal with. By sending pictures of
us in these places we also gave them the impression their
grandchildren were constantly on the move.

Communication for the Khadem family was much easier. They
simply called relatives and friends either in Paris, the US or in
Iran. It was sometimes hard to remember nobody was chasing
them although they had to be careful of getting their Iranian
relations in trouble by talking about religion on the bugged lines.
The same was true for Zoe's contact with her mother and father
in Harare. Her dad reported that there had been questions
from the Government about the diamonds some agents had
seen Bernard selling, but Justice Appleby said he had no idea
what his son-in-law had been up to and suggested they ask
Bernard directly. Of course, he knew full well the cash-strapped
Zimbabwe Government had no way of tracking Bernard down or
making him return either.

The local law firm that Sir Michael had hired warned that the
Robinsons and the Trâns might have to leave the country for a
while to reapply for the jobs they already had. No-one was very
interested in that if there was a possibility that they might not be
allowed back in again.

Dr Prosperov asked Hekator if there was any way the adults
could be bent back into the country. He said that there certainly
was, but he needed to clear such things with Morganne and a
few others because it meant more technology and there were
political problems among the Fae Council.

The answer came back the next day. A hologram from Queen
Morganne told Dr Prosperov that the Fae would not be
supplying such technology and many had misgivings about

the technology they had supplied already. She had not been impressed by Dr Prosperov's use of their technology to monitor banks or crack software. She seemed to think that he was just using Fae technology to become rich. At the same time they were already worried about the risks of being detected by the Center. "We created your facility on the clear understanding that we may close it again. There are limits to our patience and you would be advised not to test them," she warned.

Morganne's message was a bit of a shock to us all. The way Dr P had told it, the Fae had fully supported Lucky. Once again we were discovering our leader wasn't above telling us porkies to keep us happy. The parents wanted to know what the truth was. Dr P arranged a talk with Hekator who was one of the strongest Fae supporters of a return to Earth.

Hekator told the adults Morganne wasn't being mean. She was just telling us where we stood. The Fae Council had met since Lucky had spoken to them and was beginning to have serious doubts about what they were getting involved in. They were still very nervous about Lucky, even if Raman and Ishtar were not. Queen Morganne herself did not like Lucky, but she did believe him.

But two important Fae Councillors – Horne, and Isis – who had led the Council when it had questioned Dr P/Lucky on Earth, were beginning to have doubts about him. They associated Lucky with their old enemies and weren't sure that Lucky was trustworthy. They also doubted there was any real need for the Fae to have an outpost on Earth at all. They were asking what the benefits were, and how much they outweighed the risks. The problem was, Hekator said, that the benefits he was getting from working with us, weren't considered very important, while the risks of losing strategic technical leadership were.

The other problem was the Fae did not like having a potential provocation to the Center out of their control. If we were found the Center could use it as an excuse to increase its own level of intervention on Earth. This could escalate into war just as it had before. The Fae were aware of Hekator's theories of a deep split inside the Center but as far as they were concerned that was an internal matter for the Center, not their problem. The presence of infiltrators on Earth was a matter for Center security, not the Fae. Horne and Isis argued that if Renwick was discovered to be a Fae base on Earth this would just increase the level of Center intervention here and it was for our own good that our base was closed.

The counter-accusation made by Raman was that Horne and Isis weren't concerned about Earthlings, just concerned for their own safety and wellbeing. He, and Ishtar were certain that the weaving they had found meant Earth would become pivotal in the future of the Galactic Center and, if things went the wrong way, not only would Earth be destroyed but so too would Fae. Unfortunately while they were respected, they were alone. Horne and Isis were merely expressing a popular opinion on Fae that confrontation with the Center in any way had resulted in too much grief and loss of life, and most did not want to return to the bad old days of war. They simply wanted peace and safety, without any risks.

## CHAPTER FORTY FIVE: STORM WARNING

Queen Morganne's warning made us wonder whether we would be closed down. I noticed a lot of conversations about it among the adults. Together with the new immigration worries, the idea that Dr P might be shut down by the Fae made the adults more worried than ever. After all our training, and hard work, the idea that they might take everything off us again really stang.

The bugging had given us a lift. We were using our training and we were getting it right. True, all we'd really done is walk around some beaches, streets and roofs after midnight but it was fun and exciting. We also knew that the real challenge was when we went to find the kids, and if our first experience with Jeanne had been anything to go by, that wouldn't be so much fun.

The last day of the term made us feel more nervous than excited. We knew the holidays would be intense. There would be long missions instead of the short ones we had done so far. Even Emma noticed we seemed to be less excited about two weeks off than the others.

"See ya round in the holidays," she said to me as she went towards her mum's car with her brother Andrew.

"Maybe not. We have to work again," I told her.

She could tell from the way I said it that I wasn't looking forward to it either. But she also looked disappointed. To be honest I still thought about the summer we'd had together and I knew she did too, but I didn't know how to tell her that.

Mariko picked us up for the last day of term and gave us good news. We would get the whole weekend off. No cleaning, no missions. *And* we were going to the big, hot water swimming complex north of Auckland. The idea we could just play made us feel great.

The next day we had to be up early to catch the early ferry and so breakfast would be on the ferry. Mariko and Gunter loaded Aunty Liz, me and Rewa; Scotty and his mum Zoe who was taking a break from Patience; Ashley and her mum, Patricia; and Tarik and Cam and their dads, into Betty the bus and off we roared.

We were all happy because we hadn't been off the island together for a while and it was nice just to get away from the place. The weather was also perfect for swimming in a hot pool. Windy, overcast and cold. Of course it made the ferry ride a bit bumpy, but Aunty Liz and Patricia avoided being sick by not having breakfast until we arrived.

It took about two and a half hours to get to Waiwera from the island. We sang in the bus. We played games and we jumped about. Mariko and Gunter sat up the front and talked, while the mothers just yakked and yakked and yakked. Dr Gursoy and Mr Trân mostly talked to us. They were a bit stiff at first, but you could tell they were relaxing as the island, which was both their home and work, got further away.

We reached the pool at ten. It was the best time.

We just ran, and squirted each other, and chased like idiots. We didn't have to be responsible or careful, or deal with heights or

ghosts or anything. At midday we ate heaps of greasy junk food
just because it was there and we were starving. Then, after a bit
of a break, we were back into it again.

It was about two when the fun stopped. I was chasing Ashley
down a slide and had just come up and got the water out of my
eyes when a voice beside me said, "long time no see Sam-the-
man."

I looked around, and there, standing next to me, was my cousin
Clive. He was taller now, but very thin. His eyes were harder too.
"Where you been Sam? Bit irregular taking off like that."

I wondered where he got a word like "irregular" from.

"We moved to Auckland. Aunty Liz got a job," I told him.

"How come you're here?" I asked cautiously.

"Been visiting in Auckland eh. Stopped in here on the way back.
Could have visited you *if* we knew where you lived," he added
accusingly.

I was looking around the adult tables beside the pool. I was
worried Ax would be there. Finally I spotted some families from
home. Rebecca was sitting with Sharon, her neighbour, both
wearing mean-as shades. Moana was busily texting while baby
Riki tottered about. Amy was tormenting Sharon's son Hema,
and Matthew was playing quietly by himself in the corner.
Tarik and Ashley came over.

"Hey Sam, are you playing or what?" Tarik asked.

Clive turned to look at them.

"Who are ya mates Sam?"

"Guys, this is my cousin Clive," I said half warning them.

"Hi," they said staring at him like he had an extra head.

Clive looked back, aware something was wrong. I started to
move towards the others.

"So who are you then," Clive asked.

"Abdul," said Tarik seriously.

"Charley," said Ashley.

I was amazed how they managed to keep straight faces. Then Scotty came up.

"What's going on?"

"Nothing Tom," Tarik answered. "Sam just met up with his cousin Clive. But Charley and me were just coming to tell him we were going."

"Oh yeah, right," Scotty replied. "Well, you'd better hurry up," he added.

"Gotta go," I explained to Clive.

"Yeah, right," Clive said, not believing a word.

I escaped with the others. We went out and back to avoid Clive seeing where everyone was based. But just as I looked back I saw Clive had cornered Rewa and Asal as Tahira went back to them. I went quickly up to Aunty Liz.

"Clive's here with Rebecca and Sharon," I told her.

"Where?" she asked quickly looking around.

I saw Clive looking at us, where Rewa was pointing.

"What is it Liz?" asked Patricia.

"My kid's aunt and her family. They're probably in contact with their father," Liz admitted.

There was a bit of alarm, but it still took a while for everyone to agree we had to leave. The more time we spent here the more information they would get. Rewa and Asal came back. Rewa was looking worried. She was scared of Clive and didn't like Amy anyway. I asked her if she had told Clive where we lived, but she said Clive hadn't asked that. He'd just asked everyone's names. It was a real bummer to have to get changed and dry again. I felt guilty and apologised to the others. Tarik and Scotty were good about it though, and told me not to sweat it.

But it wasn't over that easily. The table Rebecca was sitting at was by the exit and there was no way we could leave without walking past them. We formed a big group and started walking but Rebecca, who had been alerted by her son, called out to Aunty Liz and she was forced to stop.

Rebecca was as crafty and rude as she could be, saying there was no need to hide from her brother. According to her he was, "a real Christian now" and only wanted what was best for us kids. Liz tried to fob her off but she stuck fast. Mariko organised the others to keep going. That cut the length of the conversation short, but as we got into the bus I noticed Moana come out into the carpark too.

We loaded up and started going as she pretended to rummage in the car. But as we went past she straightened up, and held up her phone, to take a picture of Betty the bus. I realised then she'd been sent out to get Betty's plates.

I felt terrible all the way home. The others reassured me that my dad was no match for Dr Prosperov, and the Fae.

"Suited up, he's no match for you either," they said confidently. That was if the Fae didn't close Renwick. Without them we were a bunch of people on the run, and some of the others were already getting into trouble with Immigration. Having lost one home, back in the Hokianga almost a year ago, I wasn't in a hurry to lose another. I also just didn't feel lucky where my dad was concerned.

It was hard to explain. It wasn't what my dad could do or say that worried me. The others were right. He was just a man. But I worried that he might find a way to ruin what we had at Renwick

House, just as he had organised the destruction of Hua Kai. It was his singlemindedness that scared me. If he found out where we lived he wouldn't stop until he got what he wanted.

Our return to Renwick was not as great as I had thought it would be. We had had a great few hours but the feeling of being surrounded by enemies had overtaken us. I even found myself in the gallery looking out at the beach almost as if expecting to see them outside. I started to wonder if that was why the ghosts were usually in there.

The next day the weather was crap again. But to our surprise Dr Prosperov came down at breakfast and gathered us together at a table. He was smiling in his tricky way.

"My wife says thanks to your work, we have North Atlantic intelligence data sources to rival old KGB. This achievement in limited time very impressive. Mr Kahu says that intelligence gathering mission has given time to practice skills and recover from shock of North Kivu. Unfortunately very soon must ask to return to see to the safety of Jeanne Mazuri. Mr Kahu asked to 'give them a break' for few days and is my intention. However is possible is mission which is fun and potentially very profitable. Is real treasure hunt. If interested, please to meet me in suits at briefing theatre in thirty minutes."

And with that he turned and left. Outside the gray, windy day looked miserable and dull. We looked at each other. Then we all jumped up and raced down to the base and got changed. If we weren't going to have the suits much longer a bunch of treasure might help a lot.

Dr Prosperov was waiting, sitting in a chair, as if expecting us the whole time.

"In 1621 Spanish galleon 'San Andreas', sank somewhere in

Marianas archipelago. San Andreas one of Manila Galleons that is sailing around Pacific carrying precious cargoes from South America, Philippines, Japan or China and to Acapulco, Mexico. Galleons carried porcelain, silk precious metals but have reason to believe San Andreas also carrying smuggled treasure."

"There are many possible sites where San Andreas sank. Many too deep for you to dive. However is many possible places around Guam and Saipan where is coral reefs. Is good diving. Is also pleasant beaches. Have identified possible locations on map."

A big map appeared behind him.

"All guesses of equal value. Suggest you bring credit cards for lunch. Guam is American. Good luck," he shrugged and left us to it.

**[+]**

The weather was fantastic, the sand fine, the water clear as glass. We bent in and swam around Saipan for two hours. The coral was fantastic. Unfortunately for us it was ruined a bit because there were also a lot of old World War Two presences like the ones at Renwick. Underwater ghosts are especially spooky because they just form in the sea in front of you. So one minute you see beautiful coral, and the next minute, sea-rotten bodies like a trick of the light in the sunlight among the old war wrecks. We learned to keep moving pretty fast to avoid them. Luckily high speed and adaptive camouflage meant we also avoided the tourist dive parties too.

We took Dr Prosperov's advice and had lunch on a sandy beach at the south of Guam. Tahira gave Tarik a hard time because it was Ramadan[†] but Tarik said Alevi don't observe it with fasting anyway. We had nothing fancy, just some hotdogs and fries, and

75

the man in the shop was friendly. We played on the empty beach
for a bit letting our suits recharge our air supply. Then we went
into the water and bent to the Santa Rosa reefs south of Guam.
These reefs sit on top of an old volcano and are pretty shallow
considering how deep the ocean is around the mountain. A big
storm, an overloaded galleon, and it wasn't hard to imagine a
ship in trouble. We swam over the coral like dolphins in the
clear blue water. Sometimes you'd come to the edge of the
seamount and swim out over the edge above the blackness
below. It seemed to want to suck you down like a height – suck
you down into a darkness, full of blind and deformed fish.
We went back to the light and beauty of the reef and the pretty
fish that darted about. We zoomed around it for something like
an hour. Then Cam spotted something.

About twenty meters down she led us to the wreck of an old
galleon, lying on its side in the deep. It was flat, as if crushed by
a giant foot and buried in sand, half-overgrown by coral.
We swam around it, noting the broken mast, the rusted
cannons, the coral that intruded into and over it. It looked
totally beautiful resting there. Like some old movie star. Scotty
spotted the first gold coin. Soon we had gold fever and were
searching around. We found gold chain, coins and jewelry.
Tahira found a small box, which was rusted closed and took
some opening. Scotty helped her with it, and when they finally
got it open it was full of pretty gray pearls.

After two-and-a-half hours Control was in our ears telling us
we were out of time. He made us wait for five minutes while he
checked the contents of our pockets and then bent us home.

## [+]

Mariko and Gunter were waiting with Dr Prosperov and we all

inspected our finds. Dr Prosperov was pleased, but obviously regarded our finds as small change, because he said we should keep our trinkets. Mariko wanted to use some of the pearls for jewellery. Tahira was into that, as long as she got to have some of it. I just had four gold coins. I gave one to Rewa, and one each to Aunty Liz and Grandpop. Rewa was fascinated.

"I hope one day they let me be a mermaid," she said.

"If they don't stop us all," I warned her.

"Yeah, but you get all the fun stuff. I just want a turn," she complained.

"I also get the scary stuff too, remember," I reminded her.

"But is the scary stuff as scary as the fun stuff is fun?"

I thought back to the ocean depths we had swum over and the sense of endless darkness below us. It made me think of the rain and the darkness and the little girl in the pink flowers, machine gunned in the back as she ran from the screams of her family as they burned to death.

"I think ... I think the scary stuff is way worse," I told her.

The next day we discovered how true that was. Mr Trân made us a big breakfast of eggs Benedict with all the trimmings but then at eight-thirty Grandpop rounded us up with a serious look on his face and we trooped off to get changed.

Dr Prosperov and Bernard were also waiting when we emerged into the briefing theatre. Grandpop in his half-moon glasses was waiting.

"OK guys, playtime's over. It's back to the grindstone again today. Dr Prosperov is going to give you a rundown on what he's been doing. Bernard will tell you about North Kivu. Dr Prosperov?"

Dr Prosperov stood up and started in his usual style.

"Tracking Jeanne Mazuri difficult. Main problem is she changes identity several times to evade problems. Does not reveal full story until very old. Future projection is very faint given probability of survival is so low. However am now very confident we have the right Jeanne, and this is she."

A black girl's face appeared behind Dr Prosperov. She had short cropped hair and a cap on. She wasn't especially pretty but she did have nice skin. The picture moved. She seemed to be in a lineup of some kind, with others behind her. Sometimes she swallowed. Other times her mouth moved as she shouted the required response to whatever the leader had said. She had clever, almost cocky eyes, but she also seemed nervous and had a slightly beaten look I'd seen before at home among the kids who got regular hidings. It seemed to me she was doing her best to hide in the crowd and not stick out. She was just a bit older than Ashley.

"Jeanne says as adult that treatment in camp toughened her. Is very harsh. They train her to run ammunition to frontline fighters. If she is too slow they beat her, if there is not enough they beat her. She also has to act as a wife to them and if she doesn't they also rape anyway. If she tries to escape they will shoot her[+]," Dr Prosperov said.

The unfairness of it made me furious. Ashley and Tahira looked very angry too.

"Unfortunately we have dilemma. If she escapes she may be killed as deserter or may not make the mark in history needed to safeguard world. If she does not escape she may be killed by enemy or not gain the lessons needed for future. Is no simple solution."

"For moment Control has Jeanne under observation. This is

not good enough for future operations therefore Hekator has supplied operational tool."

He held up a clear tube. Inside was a large wasp-like insect. It was completely black.

"Robotic injection system plants nanotag on Jeanne allowing constant monitoring of mental and physical signs by Control. Tag will track infections, cardio-vascular system, digestive system and hormone levels. Is vital to assist Jeanne at low points in early career."

He looked quite pleased about this. There was a pause as he realised his enthusiasm was not shared by us. The way we saw it this way we could sit back and let them treat her like this for months. We wanted her out. The girls were seething, and us boys were pretty unhappy about the treatment this poor kid was getting too.

"Is problem?" Dr P asked.

"So we just gonna *watch* while dey abuse her?" demanded Ashley hotly. "What right have we got to stick any more in her dan dey have? What about *her* rights? Dis ain't about savin her, it's about makin it easy for us!"

Dr Prosperov smoothed his hair looking uncomfortable. He looked at Grandpop. Grandpop and Bernard were looking equally bothered.

"Uhh well, Ashley ..." Grandpop began but stopped because he couldn't think of a good reason either.

Bernard had a go.

"Ashley, compared to the other ways Jeanne's is being abused, monitoring her health without asking her is a very small thing."

"But that don't make it right, yeah?" Tarik shot out, surprising Tahira and Ashley. "uh ... does it?"

Bernard looked at Grandpop who looked in turn at Dr Prosperov. The adults were looking pretty uncomfortable now. "What is objection?" Dr P asked, obviously not understanding us.

"We was told we was goin' to rescue Jeanne! Dis is jus about seein how much more she kin take!" Ashley replied.

The adults looked at each other.

"But is too dangerous to rescue now," Dr P replied frowning.

"Dangerous for who? Us or her?" Tarik argued." She's the same age as us, right? And she 'as to face it everyday! We should decide if it's too dangerous for us!"

"Guys, if you tried to get her out now *she* would wind up dead because she can't bend and she isn't bulletproof. These guys kill kids your age without a second thought," Grandpop objected.

"Should not Jeanne 'av some say?" asked Tahira.

The adults stared at us.

"We must show them," Dr Prosperov said half to himself. The other two were not so sure.

There was a bit of a debate. Grandpop and Bernard kept saying we were too young. Dr Prosperov said we had a right to understand all the information before making a moral trade-off. Finally Dr Prosperov said:

"We need all parents to make decision. Full meeting and review of material. Is only way," he insisted.

This Bernard and Grandpop agreed to. We were told to go get changed again and summon the parents for a meeting at the theatre. Mariko and Gunter were to supervise us while the parents did whatever it was they were doing.

So we went back upstairs and the parents went down. We didn't even have to clean so we made some things that Mariko was working on for celebrating Eid. We ended up making our own lunch and having quite a bit of fun in the kitchen as well.

Then at about one Patricia, Aunty Liz, Mitra, Soraya and Mr Trân came up from the base. They were all pale and had tears in their eyes. They gave us big hugs and seemed to be shaking a bit. They were soon followed by Dr Gursoy, Grandpop, Bernard, and Zoe who looked shocked and slightly sick. They had no appetite. Finally Dr Prosperov and Mrs Jones came up talking quietly. They gathered us together.

"Your caregivers have agreed a package of information about Jeanne if you would care to see it. You don't need to get changed," Mrs Jones told us.

I have to admit I was now pretty nervous about it. In fact we all looked a bit scared as we went down to the briefing theatre with Dr Prosperov and Mrs Jones. It felt funny not getting changed. We felt a bit naked. In the theatre Mrs Jones stood in front of us. Dr Prosperov passed along some plastic bags indicating we should all take one. We had no idea what they were for. Mrs Jones spoke.

"Children in my ... extended ... life in this world I have seen many ... many horrors. Executions, mutilations, torture, disease, starvation, murders, massacres, wars. I have suffered some of these at times myself. Sometimes I have even wondered if I would die of the cruelty in my own memories. But I lived. I kept on."

"What your parents will *let you see* of Jeanne's world is not the worst of human behaviour. There is far worse in North Kivu they would not let you see. Acts of evil no child should see or even know about. There is also worse that I have seen that does not even happen here. But it is enough to give you some idea."

"The important thing I want stress is this is *not about you*. This is not a sick horror show for entertainment. Nor is it to scare you. This is about Jeanne's understanding of life. This is what she knows about *her* world. She lives with this every day."

The first image was a kid our age having his arms cut off with a machete[†]. It got worse from there. Beatings. Beatings with bars and bats and canes. Real people, just like us, just like kids at school, not actors. I'd laughed at horror movies but this wasn't funny. Women screaming being dragged away by laughing men with guns. Endless shootings of people all ages. Not movie shootings. This wasn't some story for fun, it was someone's life, someone's mother, someone's little boy screaming as his mother was killed in front of him, screaming with his little heart torn up in grief. The dead, hopeless, eyes of horror. It was the little kids that made it impossible to watch. Just to make it harder there were also everyday pictures of mums playing with laughing children as well. People working in the fields. People being normal or helping one another mixed in. It only lasted ten minutes. It felt like forever and by the end we had all used the plastic bags. It was a sad and smelly waste of a good lunch. We were all shaking with red eyes and the girls weren't the only ones weeping openly.

Dr Prosperov stood up in front of us. He looked very serious. "Everyone thinks he is normal. You ... you think you are normal but many say you have tough life. Lose home. Lose parent or parents. But normal for many children is horror like this. See horror every day and think ... this is life. This is normal."

He paused to think.

"Some try to master horror and violence by doing it. Seek to reach depths of violence and cruelness. Is no bottom! At bottom only monsters fighting to get lower. Is place which can only end in death. Fighting to be worst human being can be."

"You may say this is horrible! Is worst! Is not worst. Parents censored film. Is worse. Jeanne has seen worse. If we do nothing Jeanne will die, perhaps sooner, perhaps later but she will have done nothing to make her world better. To stop this horror."

Something funny was happening. Lost in his thoughts Dr Prosperov was losing his accent.

"Jeanne has suffered and she will suffer for many years to come. She must suffer to see suffering and know why it must be stopped. Unlike most she has the strength, and the will, and the intelligence to turn that suffering into a force for change."

As Prosperov looked up I saw in his eyes something very different. Not the crafty Russian scientist but a fierce, powerful will that could not be contained.

"Our job is not to save her from her world. That would save only one. Our job is to help her save her whole world. To help her dig out the evil that has taken root on Earth as it has in heaven."

Dr Prosperov stopped. Then he suddenly started shaking uncontrollably.

"Gennady!" Mrs Jones shouted.

She jumped up to stop him collapsing. Foam started appearing on the sides of his mouth as he kept shaking.

"Get Ken and the nurses quick!" Mrs Jones yelled as she lowered him to the floor.

Tarik jumped up and ran. Ashley grabbed a seat cushion and ran forward to stick it under his head.

"I'll get Dr Morozov," Tahira yelled and took off.

Scotty, Cam and me gathered around Dr Prosperov getting more cushions, while he lay there shaking wildly and making strange groans and grunts.

"He an epileptic?" Scotty asked.

"Not normally. I think Lucky set him off," Mrs Jones explained. "It will wear off soon," she added.

It seemed she was right. By the time the nurses, Grandpop and Ken had arrived, (followed by a pale Dr Morozov), Dr Prosperov's shaking had given way to just occasional twitches. After a bit stuffing around Grandpop and Ken carried Dr Prosperov out and we followed – tidying up the bags of spew. Upstairs we found ourselves picking at a second lunch. Conversation now turned to what we should do about Jeanne. We argued around whether we should help her visibly or invisibly.

"Look at it from 'er perspective, yeah?" Tarik asked finally, "What can we promise 'er?"

"Whatchoo mean, Bra?" Ashley asked.

"Can we promise to be there for 'er ... Like ... when she needs us?" Tarik asked.

"You mean we might be in school or asleep, is it?" Scotty said.

"Yeah. I mean like what I'm saying is, if we tell 'er that she's got, like, powerful friends watchin' out for 'er, what happens then? You know what I mean?" Tarik asked.

"She learns not to trust us," Cam replied immediately.

"That's what I mean," Tarik said. "If she finks angels is goin' ta come down an' save 'er every time she stuffs up. Lookin' after her could become a full time job, init?"

There was a pause. We thought about the awful world she was used to, and how we would respond if someone said they had the power to take us away but weren't going to, for the good of the future of Africa. It would be like, "You can stick Africa! I want outta here."

"It's like what Dr Prosperov said," said Scotty. "It's about normal, hey? We think aliens are pretty normal now, but Jeanne thinks violence is normal."

"What of 'Ope?" Tahira asked.

We asked her what she meant.

"Wizzout 'ope zat ze world can be made better, why would she try?"

It was a powerful point. If Jeanne was not to live and die like so many around her she had to have some idea that she could change things. We thought about that for a while.

"We're sorta like her guardian angels." Ashley mused.

We looked at her and she felt she had to explain.

"Sometimes we protect her, an' sometimes we don't. We jus her dumb luck. We make no promises and we shure cayn't be relied on," she concluded.

That seemed to sum it up.

"'Cept we're like angels, that don't protect er for 'er sake. We protect 'er for change's sake," Tarik reflected.

"We da Guardian angels 'o change," Ashley smiled.

"The change angels," said Scott.

"The Changels," said Cam.

"Yeah," Ashley grinned.

"It's good," Tahira agreed.

I wasn't sure I was ready to be an angel. Seemed a bit girly to me.

"So do we ask her if we can inject her or what?" I asked changing the subject.

"No," Ashley said firmly.

"No," Tahira agreed with a sigh.

Grandpop had come downstairs and was talking to the others about Dr Prosperov. He noticed we seemed to have made up our minds and came over.

"Dr Prosperov's resting. His seizure has stopped and he's asleep," he told us, "Dr Morozov says he has always been epileptic but something unusual set him off this time. Mrs Jones says sometimes possession has this effect. It's all a bit too weird for me to be honest. Anyway have you guys decided what you want to do?"

"We want to bug Jeanne," I answered.

"Good! OK, uh ... well ... I'll see you downstairs in a minute then."

And he went over to quietly mutter to Bernard who looked over at us. Ten minutes later the briefing had started again with Grandpop out the front. It still smelt a bit of sick though. I thought we might have to come back and clean it.

"OK, so here we are again," Grandpop began. "Out of interest why did you change your mind Ashley?"

"Well, sir, I ... Well, ah guess ah realised ... dere ain't much we can do for her. I mean we can show up and maybe even kick us some butt, but mosta da time she's jus a girl in a horrible place and she cayn't rely on no-one but herself. If we aysk her permission pretty soon she'd wanta know why we don't just take her away, and den when we didn't she'd think we was abandoning her. So in da end it's best if we know how she is, and where we can find her and when we can do somethin' useful. It's not da greatest but it's da best we can do."

Grandpop was listening with his head bowed.

"Tahira?"

"Ashley 'as reason. Zere is no escaping ze reality of Jeanne's crappy life."

We all smiled. Tahira had a great way of combining a French accent with English words like "crappy". Grandpop took over.

"Yep ... I think you've got to where we did. Which just goes to show that Dr Prosperov is right. You guys can work out the best answer if you're given enough information."

"OK, so Control has identified the hut Jeanne is in, as this one. " A picture of a hut among dozens in the darkness came up behind him. We noticed it was raining again.

"It's ... Ah ... two in the morning there now, which is a perfect time. We've been watching their security for a while now and, in general, their night patrols are mostly around the perimeter. There are a few watchtowers but their main interest is securing the kitchens and the command centre. Discipline is very harsh and thieves or deserters know what the penalties are, so they don't risk it here."

"So, rather than bugger about, the plan is to put down three teams. The idea is to make it look a bit like a mortar attack but without the explosions. You will bend in a pattern arriving roughly five seconds apart. Two teams are decoys. Their job is to make sure the bugging team can do its job. They will just form a cordon and trip up anyone who crosses it.

The bugging team will get as close as they can and deploy the bug. There isn't much to do except make sure the bug gets through and isn't squashed.

"OK, Ashley, Tahira, Cam? Up you come and draw a match. Burned head is the bug team."

The girls dashed up, and Cam got it.

"OK, guys this is going to be very quick. There's no reason to hang around. We can't change anything yet."

We went to the jumpstation and one by one bent out of space and time and back into it. As usual I was third.

**[+]**

When the light flare fell away I found myself on a muddy path between rows of huts. Once again it was dark, and rain was pouring down. I knelt listening intently.

The rain was making a racket on everything. I was meant to be closer to Jeanne's hut. I set off quietly down the row trying to avoid making regular squelchy noises in the mud by moving only five or so steps and stopping to listen.

I saw another flare a few rows over and about five huts up. Tahira had arrived.

"*Hey ... guess what? It's raining!*" I informed her.

"*It's always raining,*" she replied silently.

I resumed my quiet progress toward the road.

"They were over here," I heard someone shout in French. They were quite a long way away.

"*Let's get to the road. I don't like these paths, they're too narrow,*" I said.

"*Neither do I,*" she agreed.

We moved by turns down our rows to the road which was barely one vehicle lane wide.

A torch beam was swinging in the dark lighting up the heavy rain and the shapes of the huts. Behind it I could see a tall man, two not so tall men and one figure who wasn't much bigger than me. They all carried AKs. They were walking down the rows inspecting them and getting totally wet in the cold rain. If they kept going they would end up bothering Tarik and Cam.

"*What do we do?*" I asked Tahira.

"*We're here to distract. So let's run across the road and hide.*

*Bend out if they get too close,"* she said.

*"OK,"* I agreed.

I checked the path opposite. We switched blending camouflage off. Now we were just dark figures.

*"They're checking another row, let's go!"*

She took off. I gave it a second then followed. The torch light flared around me.

"Hey you! Stop!" a man shouted in French.

I dashed into the shadow of another row of huts, sprinted up the path between them, slid in the mud and rolled behind a hut. The huts were about three meters square. The paths between the rows two meters wide, while the gap between the huts was one meter. The torchlight flared along the row behind me. Voices shouted instructions. They were to shoot only at close range. They split into two groups. The one with the torch was coming up the row on my left. The others following my footsteps on my right. But I could easily jump the rows fast and dodge between the huts.

*"I'll lead them north back where they came from. If any others look for you go further east,"* I told Tahira.

*"Good luck,"* she said.

I jumped the row in front of the soldiers on my left. Shouts behind me. I dashed around the hut and ran along the next path away from the patrol and the road and jumped between more huts. I stepped into the next row and then ran further away from the road and jumped to the next row. Then I doubled back and ran back *toward* the road and slipped back the way I'd come between some huts and froze, hiding and catching my breath. I switched my camouflage to adaptive and settled in against a pile of rubbish behind a hut. My pursuers were everywhere.

They had fanned out in a line to sweep me north away from Tarik and Cam moving across the wide paths, between the huts at a careful walk following my tracks, their guns at the ready, hunting me.

I sat dead still. Crouching in the junk, head down, ready to bend the instant I suspected anyone had seen me. The rain whacked down in big heavy drops beating on everything. My breathing and my heartbeat were as slow as I could make them. I was glad my breath was not outside making a mist.

Footsteps. A soft careful tread splished on the row to my left and then a deliberate step next to the hut I was hiding by. The feet were to my left about a meter away. I wanted so much to check if I was seen but if I moved he would spot me for sure. I waited for one, two, three, four, five seconds straining with every psychic sense I have. He was looking right at me. Just as I was sure I was going to have to bend he took a step, his feet pointed past me from where I'd come. Another four seconds. I realised these feet – they were bare feet – were not much bigger than mine. He stepped on.

Now I glanced up.

The kid with the gun had moved past to the next row I had come back down and was looking left to his officer for instructions. The torchlight shone on the ground at his feet catching the fat raindrops that beat on us all. He looked down and along to his feet following the tracks I'd left. It was obvious I'd doubled back where he had just checked and he had missed me.

The kid turned and looked back where he'd been, his eyes wide in the pouring rain, and you didn't need to be a mind reader to see he knew he was going to be in big trouble for letting me get past him. He was looking quickly around for some sign of where

I'd gone. There were shouted swear words at him from the direction of the light. He was only about thirteen and although he was out to kill me I still felt sorry for him. He was more trapped than I was. I could go home. I decided he might suffer less if I zapped him than if his officer did the crude and twisted things he was shouting at him. So I did.

A brilliant blue electrical flash flicked through the rain and the boy fell face down in the mud. More yells. Another face appeared around the hut staring in fear. A young man. I zapped him too. That was enough. They would be fixated on this place now and distracted from Tarik and Cam. Time slowed and the world bent to a spinning line. I passed through light and presences and burst out into the brightly lit jumpstation.

[+]

"Good work Sam," Grandpop told me as I waded to the steps. I let the oil rinse over me floating away the mud and rain. There was another bright light followed by three more as Cam, Tarik and Tahira came in. Then Scotty and Ashley. We came out of the pool. Grandpop was still at the control desk.

"Well guys it's only two thirty. Do you want to go back to the Galleon for a while?"

Scotty who had only just come out of the pool gave a huge sigh as if this was more hard slog, and turned around and plodded back down the ladder again while we laughed at him. So we went back down and a few seconds later we were back in the ocean south of Guam swimming around looking at the pretty fish and poking about the old wreck looking for treasure.

[+]

It was a great way to escape the fear and darkness of North Kivu. We picked over the wreck looking for interesting things.

**91**

There were cannons, and barrels and jars but they were all too big to put in our pockets. So we were limited to coins, rings and necklaces, thimbles, crucifixes and pendants. There were presences around the wreck but they were very distant. More like echoes. Nothing like the presences from Egypt which, despite their age, seemed so strong. They were almost like some background mood music, than people.

Two hours digging in the sand among the reef fish, octopuses, and small sharks just went by in no time. We were like happy little kids, but finally Control was telling us it was time to come home. We didn't really want to, but we would run out of air if we didn't, so back we came.

## [+]

When we came back Grandpop was idly reading a fishing website. The debrief was short. The bug had identified Jeanne and injected her with the tag. It was transmitting basic data and would gradually improve the range of information about her Control could collect as its microscopic genetic tools built themselves in her body.

"If she has a cold, we will know about it even before she does," he marvelled. I had a feeling a cold would be the least of her problems.

Dr Prosperov was not up and about until the next day. To our surprise he seemed a bit embarrassed by his previous day's seizure. Dr Morozov was however being very staunch on his behalf and giving everyone the eye, as if daring them to ask if her husband was alright.

Grandpop rounded us up after breakfast. We got changed but were surprised to find Dr Prosperov waiting with Dr Morozov in the briefing room.

"Thank you for work yesterday. Was pleased to learn Jeanne can be monitored. Now must be patient. Mr Khumalo advises she will soon be sent to fight, and she will almost certainly try to escape. We must wait our opportunity to help. Meanwhile I have new candidate. Another girl. This one is Diana, last name again unclear, from city of Balti in nation of Moldova."

We all knew where Moldova was because it was an early stumper in our atlas game. The map came up showing the landlocked nation sandwiched between Romania and the Ukraine at the bottom of the Transylvanian mountains. Balti was the northern industrial town.

"Diana is to be future judge and expert on international standardisation of criminal codes. Diana is not in danger yet but will be soon. Unfortunate that nature of danger not hard to guess."

He pointed to a bottle of water by Morozov, she passed it and he thanked her and took a swig.

"Moldova is Soviet era invention. In Great Patriotic War Romania joined Nazi German aggressor. When Soviets invaded split Moldova from Romania. Most Moldovans are Romanian but is also large Ukrainian and Russian minority."

*Map data © Google 2016*

"Under Soviet management specialised as agricultural producer to Soviet Empire. Much like New Zealand for British Empire. Soil very deep, very fertile, climate mild. Soviets build many giant plants for exports to Soviet customers."

"Today Moldova is neither fish nor butter. Is not in Russian sphere. Giant Soviet plants outdated and broken. Is not in EU sphere. Moldovan farmers cannot compete with EU farmers because EU pays from taxes to keep own farmers in business and taxes goods from non-EU farmers to make imported food uneconomic. Everything in Moldova expensive except vodka Government sells below cost to keep people drunk and disorganised."

"So Moldova has big problem. What to sell? Sad answer is girls. Moldovan government has laws to stop trafficking but laws not policed. Police and judges not paid by government. Traffickers are rich so traffickers pay them instead. As many as one million of four million Moldovans live outside country. Many as virtual slaves. Is old export. Since middle ages rulers in Slavic world have sold people[†]. Is origin of English word 'slave'."

"So what do we know about Diana. Not so much. She is twelve. She speaks Romanian and some Ukrainian. She is white skinned with black hair and brown eyes. She has older sister, Elena. She is thin. She talks a lot. Is not much."

"In preferred future path Diana writes book of life as illegal migrant in French at age 21. Is very influential in France and Belgium. Is ultimately educated in Paris. Am attempting to gather information from book but as with Jeanne detail is difficult on path still open to random influence."

"Task tonight is simply to visit Balti and see if luck with Jeanne can be repeated."

I wondered when he said "luck" if his guide "Lucky" might have had anything to do with our finding Jeanne.

Grandpop took over.

"OK, the time in Balti is a bit after eleven at night. The temperature is about six degrees. It's Tuesday but that may mean less than normal because almost half adults there don't have any work. As Dr Prosperov says they are also likely to be drunk. Your main risk is teens and kidnappers. There are cars but petrol is very expensive and people don't drive about for fun. You are more likely not to see anyone much."

"From what I can gather Moldovans in general are said to be pretty hard people. They fight each other for everything. They have a folk belief they are cursed by their forefathers who did a deal with the devil, or in their language Dracul. Dracul … Dracula I'm sure you get it."

"Now there is an important tactical problem which we haven't managed to fix yet. Unlike French, Romanian is not a major world language. That means that while your suits can translate basic words they can't translate conversations, so you won't know what people are saying."

"There are plenty of places to put you down in Balti where the light flare will be disregarded. So what we'll do is put you down in pairs with a route to follow. Then we'll bend you to another place and you can do another route. That's about two hours worth which will take you to about one in the morning. That's enough darkness for one day. Any questions?"

Tarik raised his hand.

"Tarik?"

"This is for Dr Prosperov, if that's okay?"

Dr Prosperov got up and looked at him.

"Where do you find these kids we are meant to look for from?"

Dr Prosperov smiled.

"Is simple enough. I look into future at most effective people and then I look to history."

"But ... Sir, how kin you look into da futcha?" Ashley asked.

"You remember I once tell you small things like electrons have no clear future but large things like stars have futures predictable for centuries?"

"Yes sir," Tarik nodded.

"Well is true for people and organisations. Small person, like baby, has no certain future. But organisation is like planet or moon. Has clearer future. Predicting future of organisation is part analysis, part guesswork, part intuition. At times future organisation dependent on individuals. Then organisation acts as lens on individual. Is like way astronomers find planets by observing stars."

"So ... there is no psychic power in it? Sir ?" Tarik asked.

Dr Prosperov smiled.

"Is different kind. Perhaps we discuss when is more time?"

Grandpop stepped forward.

"Any more ... immediate questions?"

There weren't any.

## [+]

Five minutes later me and Tahira were standing on a pathway through a park that lead to a street. It was dark and the trees were evenly planted in a way that seemed spooky, but there was no-one there. Some presences appeared, drawn by our arrival. They were a mixed group. The more recent ones were thin – something said Aids to me – and stared at us, but did nothing. The fainter ones had injuries or were almost skeletons. War victims. Jews. We ignored them and walked through them. They watched but did nothing.

The map in our heads told us this path connected with a road that crossed a stream and curved around to the foot of the hill. We started walking towards the hill but the route in our heads took us down a street towards some blocks of flats. As we reached the street and turned left Tahira noticed the street signs said "strada" which was "street", the same as Italian.

This end of the street was lined with trees some of which still had some leaves. It was probably quite pretty in daylight. The wooden houses were filling the air with coal smoke. It smelt strangely cosy even as it polluted the cold, sharp air. A dog barked and was answered by other dogs. The houses were made of wood and looked like ramshackle New Zealand houses familiar to me, but not Tahira.

As we walked down the street we noticed things here and there. It was easy to forget we were meant to be there to find some girl or other. Instead we started talking about how we were like ghosts. We appeared in places in the middle of the night, walked around and did stuff, and then vanished. If someone did that to us, we decided, it would seem pretty scary.

We were talking so much that we didn't notice the neighbourhood getting steadily less pretty. Wooden houses were giving way to concrete flats. We had passed one or two people who had been out walking a dog, or taking a stroll, who had ignored us, but now we were coming up on a house that was lit up, with loud music, and the sound of women laughing and squealing. There were a group of youngish men sitting around a car talking quietly and smoking.

We took one look at them and crossed the street. It wasn't a wide street, but I didn't want to walk through them and neither did Tahira. Someone called out something which started a lot of giggling but which we ignored. As I had expected they couldn't be bothered with us and we left them behind.

But the party had woken us up a bit. We realised we were coming to a new part of town where there were more apartment blocks. The whole area felt a bit run down and less safe. The people on the street stared and cars cruised by on business we guessed was not legal. Even the presences we saw now and then seemed less friendly.

Tahira noticed we were being followed first. A man was keeping pace with us on the other side of the street, slightly behind us. He wasn't especially big. He looked like an industrial worker. But we were both getting readings on him that suggested seeing unprotected kids on the street was an opportunity he didn't want to miss.

We weren't especially scared of him. He may be bigger and have a knife but we had more weapons than he could imagine. Tahira in fact wasn't scared at all. She wanted to teach him a lesson. She suggested we make a slight change to the route that would lead us to an alleyway. Then we could turn around as if we had made a mistake.

The alleyway was fenced the whole way along. But there were a lot of trees that hung over it making it dark. We walked down about twenty meters when we heard the man behind us. Tahira stopped.

"*Pretend there is a cat,*" she 'said' silently.

She knelt down and stroked nothing at all with her back to the man. I pretended to talk to the imaginary animal. The man was about halfway to us when Tahira pretended the cat had slipped through a hole in the fence. We stood up. Then to the man's surprise we turned to face him.

It was quite interesting the way he did it really. He walked past us and we went the other way. I thought he'd given up when, with a sudden lunge, he grabbed Tahira by the head, and pulled her off balance, drawing a knife, and holding it to her throat.

He put his fingers to his lips angrily at me suggesting with a twitch that if I made a noise he'd stick the knife in Tahira's throat.

"Are you OK Tahira?" Grandpop asked.

Suddenly the man jerked, and a tiny puff of steam rose from his clothes. He collapsed where he stood, the knife falling away.

"Yes, I am very well! How are you?" she asked rolling her shoulders a bit. And then she kicked the man hard where it hurt. It made me wince.

"Madar ghahbe! (M__f__)" she shouted at him, kicking him savagely again.

Then she walked off.

"Is he alive?" I asked after her.

"Ask someone who cares!" she yelled over her shoulder.

He wasn't dead. That was obvious to any psychic. I checked him over and then his cellphone slipped out of his pocket. That intrigued me because he seemed too poor to have decent clothes but he had a cell. I thought about that. It could only mean one thing.

"Hey Tahira, wait up!"

I stole the phone and ran after her.

I caught up with her and showed it to her.

"Look! Kinda fancy for him don't you think?"

She looked at it. She was in a grumpy mood which having had a knife to her throat probably didn't help.

"So you're a thief now?"

"No! Think about it! Why would he chase us? Why would he have a fancy cell? Because he's part of a network! Like Dr Prosperov said, selling women and children is a business. That guy wanted more than we thought!" I told her as she slowed down.

"I should go back and kick him even harder!" she said angrily. She went to go back. I stopped her.

I was getting all sorts of readings from her. A man. A fat man. Turkish, somewhere on the route between Teheran and Paris.

"Tahira! Stop!"

She tried to dodge me. I grabbed her. She fought free. I let her go.

"You can't do this! Look what are you going to do to him anyway?"

"Kill the f___ker," she replied. She seemed insane with anger. I couldn't understand what had happened to her. She read crazy. I followed after her. I was a bit frightened she actually would.

"Tahira?"

"Shut up! Leave me alone!"

"No, you're acting crazy!"

"F__ off!"

"*What's the matter Tahira?*" Ashley asked.

"I'm going to kill that trafficking son of an arsehole."

"*Sam could you give us a mark?*" Ashley asked.

Literally in a flash, Ashley and Scotty were there.

Tahira looked at all of us.

"So what are you going to do? Stun me?"

There was a sort of a cough and Grandpop was in our ears.

"Scotty and Sam I'm giving you the next stage. Keep that phone

Sam, it's valuable. Ashley and Tahira you are on a private network. Tahira sort out your stuff with Ashley or I'll have to ground you. I can't have people acting up like this on missions. OK? Sam and Scotty you are gone in five seconds."

[+]

And we were.

The place we appeared was another run down suburb. It was late, it was cool, the wind was picking up and it was still Tuesday. It seemed strange to be with Scotty. We hadn't ever worked together before.

"Ag, it's the dark that gets me," Scotty said. "It's just depressing that it's always dark."

"Yeah, I know what you mean," I agreed.

"I wish they'd send us somewhere where it's daylight."

We walked along our allotted path. In the distance a car drove past. We were both thinking about Tahira.

"So what do you think?" Scotty asked.

"About Tahira?"

"Yeah."

"Someone's hurt her. A man. Turkish. That was what I was getting when she was going off at me."

Scotty said nothing.

"She was so ... *angry*," I added.

"Wouldn't you be?" he asked.

I hadn't thought of that. The idea of some guy doing that to me ... It was disgusting really. I snorted.

"Yeah ... I can see where she'd be coming from. I'd want to bring the pain too," I admitted.

"Me too," Scotty agreed.

We walked the route our suits had loaded chatting about stuff.

**101**

Then we got on to the treasure ship and agreed we needed to ask Dr P what we were meant to be looking for. Nothing much more happened so we bent home.

**[+]**

When we got back there was a fair amount of tension. I gave the cellphone to Grandpop who put it in a tank of jelly-like stuff. The official debrief was short but focused on the importance of clues like the cellphone which made me feel embarrassed. But after we got changed Grandpop was waiting outside the boys changing rooms and Mrs Jones outside the girls. They wanted Ashley, Tahira, Scotty and me to come back for another debrief. We went to the room Ishtar and Raman had interviewed us in. The plants looked like they needed a bit of a trim. Finally we were all seated on the cushion plants. Boys on one side, girls on the other, Grandpop trying not to fall off the rubber psych couch and Mrs Jones in the middle.

"I don't know how to work that," she started pointing up at the orb above us.

"So don't worry about it," she said, as Tahira eyed it nervously. "Now we're basically here to talk about what happened and how we feel about it so that we can all build trust in each other. Without trust we cannot operate at all. Trust is like light to these plants. Without it we all die."

"I want to start with Sam. And Tahira I want you to listen because Sam is an honest mirror. So, Sam tell us what happened as you saw it."

So I did. At first when I nervously checked Tahira's eyes I realised she was has having a harder time looking at me than I was at her. But when I said what Scotty had suggested she glanced at me – a bit surprised.

"Scotty can you tell me how you felt?"

So Scotty did. I was surprised how much Scotty noticed. Even just small things like tone of our minds on the telepathic channels he picked up accurately. Then it was Ashley's turn. Ashley was like Scotty but when she came to what Tahira had said she stopped.

"Ma'am I cayn't say what Tahira tol' me. It was private," she said.

"That's alright Ashley, just tell us how you felt about it without saying what it was."

Ashley said she felt shocked, angry, and impressed with Tahira all at the same time. She said Tahira had become like a sister to her and that she loved as one. Tahira started to cry and so did Ashley and they had a hug which went on for quite a while. I admit me and Scotty were a bit emotional too, although Mrs Jones seemed just pleased with the girls. Finally they let go of each other.

"Now Tahira please tell your story about today. You don't have to tell anything you don't want to but just how you felt."

It was a completely different story to mine. I was astonished how much Tahira was thinking all the time. The calculations, the balancing of emotions. Then when she saw that guy following us and read his intentions she said it was like a demon rose in her and she just wanted to hurt him. She said I was easy to lead (which was a bit insulting) and how she drew everyone after her. She even made sure, when we turned around in the alley, she was at the back so he would grab her.

She said how she worried the zapper might cut out if she enjoyed it too much and stayed as dark and angry as she could. Then she described how she had hated me for caring about the man, and then how sick she felt when I'd suggested that the cellphone meant he might be part of a network. When Ashley had come she had felt like we were all ganging up on her but when they had talked she had felt much better.

"Do you like working with Sam?" Mrs Jones asked.

Now she looked at me and then down at her lap.

"Iz not Sam. It's me," she said and tears fell from her. Ashley put her arm around her.

"I don't know if I can do thees," she said softly and burst into quiet tears.

"What do you think Mr Kahu?" Mrs Jones asked.

"I think Tahira's brilliant," Grandpop said from his uncomfortable place on the unstable leaf.

"Clever, intuitive, brave and quick. She's great. But I can't have her trying to punish every criminal that crosses her path because the world is full of bad arses and we'll never get any work done."

Tahira glanced at Grandpop warmly and her tears caught and turned into a snort of laughter.

"What would you like to do Tahira?" Mrs Jones asked.

"Would it be OK if I worked wizz Ashley for a while?" she asked.

"How do you feel about that Sam? Scotty?"

I felt a bit sad to lose Tahira but I liked Scotty. We looked at each other checking each other out.

"No problem," I said.

"Sure," Scotty agreed.

"Is this for missions or cleaning too?" I asked uncertain and thinking about the hassle of learning a new routine. Tahira looked up at me for the first time, now she was smiling through her tears.

"Oh Sam. I still like you. You are a good friend. Iz zeese 'orrible men I need Ashley to 'elp me wizz. Not ze stupid vacuum cleaners."

I felt completely confused. Then she jumped up, came over and hugged me hard. I hugged her back. It felt nice. Then she hugged Scotty.

"OK, well let's try that swap for a while and see how it works. Do you have any objections Mr Kahu?"

Grandpop shrugged, went to get up and was tipped off the leaf on to the floor. He looked comically shocked on the floor but I had the impression he'd done it on purpose. The girls squealed and laughed and we helped him up.

"Now speaking of cleaning, we do have something of a backlog for this afternoon." Mrs Jones said as she shushed everyone out of the room.

So we spent the next three hours cleaning Renwick House. Tahira and me raced our vacuum cleaners and started a polishing competition. She seemed a different person in some ways. Much happier and a bit sillier too.

## CHAPTER FORTY SIX: DR PROSPEROV'S TRAVELS

Over the next week we got to know the streets of Balti rather well. It was a strange little city of one hundred and twenty thousand built around three hills and a swamp. Dead in the middle was a long rectangular lake as if they had been planning something magnificent but never quite got around to building it. The lake was set in a wasteland and fringed by busted old factories.

The whole city was busted really. On the surface it looked like a city back home. It had roads and cars and shops with bright lights. But over the nights we came to see the appearance was better than the reality. Some of the hospitals looked more like prisons. The busiest shops sold vodka and the driving we saw was pretty erratic.

We also found we weren't the only kids on the street late at night. Tarik and Cam had the first encounter near a school where they found some local teens making out. There were quite a few who started harassing them. Tarik and Cam decided to run and with their combination of light weight and extra strength easily outpaced the locals.

But there were smaller kids on the streets too. Scotty and me met two small brothers hiding in a park from their drunk father. They were only little guys of eight and six named Pavel and Uri.

Luckily their main language was Ukrainian which is very close to Russian so we could talk to them via our suits in a way we couldn't say anything in Romanian.

They asked us where we were from because I obviously wasn't Slavic and Scotty just moved differently. We said America because they expected it. We said we were looking for some kids to help us find someone and we could pay in food. They were thin and hungry and this got their attention. But they were still suspicious of us and wanted us to prove it. So we told them to wait and we would be back in a moment.

We bent home raided the kitchen and bent back ten minutes later. They were still where we left them when we returned. They ripped up the pies and bread we'd grabbed in no time. They chomped on the apples but they tried to eat the orange skins. It was kind of good to know we could feed them. Even if we never saw them again it was worth just seeing the happy looks on their narrow little faces.

**[+]**

At debrief Grandpop said he really liked the idea of recruiting local kids to help us spy on places. He said the only real problem was the limited amount we could carry with us in our pockets. The other obvious problem was we didn't have enough information about the girl we were looking for to get anyone to spy for us.

Over lunch we talked about the problems of paying kids with food.

"What happens when we stop paying them?" I asked.

"They go back to being hungry," Scotty told me evenly. "They'll want more. They'll whine and beg and promise but when you're hungry you get what you can and tomorrow is another day. Just

**107**

don't pretend you like them. *They* will do that, but they resent you. They resent having to beg. Everyone does."

The others were more concerned about practical matters. Our pocket space was limited. What sort of food should we take? What sort of deal should we do? Would we need disposable cameras. Should we buy locally? What sort of money should we use?

The more we talked the more we realised that only being around at night was so restrictive. We also decided we needed a meeting with Dr Prosperov.

But it turned out that Grandpop was ahead of us and Dr Prosperov came down to sit at our table. He said he had always imagined that we would recruit local children and he agreed appearing only at night was a problem. He admitted the foresight he had hoped to generate was not coming along as well as he'd hoped.

The problem was we needed still more help from the Fae and having given so much already the opponents of intervening on Earth, led by Horne and Isis, were making things difficult for Hekator and Morganne. Hekator could only do small projects he mostly did for fun. But we really needed more than some adapted old Kindergarten equipment. We needed specialist tools to help us do this job.

We asked how the meteorite survey we had done for Hekator had gone over with the Fae. Dr Prosperov said from what Hekator had told him the problem was a lack of interest in the results. There was still a general reluctance to believe Lucky even though the Fae's most senior Weavers, Rama and Ishtar, agreed with him. Most Fae felt they were being too sensitive.

"So to 'elp *our* people, we 'ave to 'elp Hekator prove whatever 'e needs proving, to '*is* people, right?" Tarik summed up.

Dr Prosperov nodded.

"So what do they need proven, then?" he asked.

"They do not want to provoke Center. So is necessary to show Center is cheating on original agreement not to intervene here. Only this can justify their own intervention."

"How do we do that?" Tarik asked uncertain.

Dr Prosperov sighed.

"More bugs," he shrugged. "Perhaps then, we can catch them in act. And am thinking I must travel with Dr Morozov to Russia. I will give Mr Kahu list of targets. But you must be very careful. These targets military. Military kill to hide secrets. Is no room for error."

We looked at each other.

"So what? We's goin' ta bend into Area 51 and ask at da gate for da flying saucer department or somethin'?" Ashley asked confused.

Dr Prosperov's eyes twinkled with fun.

"Yes ... or something," he confirmed.

It turned out that Dr Prosperov had no such plans. That night after dinner he stood up in front of everyone to make an announcement to everyone.

"Early stages of project encountering anticipated initial problems. Must record here young operatives proving better than expected at tasks. In fact is own work which is proving largest problem. Project to develop forecasting machine held up by extreme precision required. Future identities of transforming persons relatively clear but link to present identities highly difficult due to uncertain life-paths. Result is only one individual identified and in problem location."

"Also is operational problems. Operatives restricted to night time in western hemisphere by simple time difference problem. This is significant as most local children asleep reducing scope for interaction and increasing suspicion. Is need for operatives to synchronise with target time zones without suffering sleep deprivation. Operatives also need bulk transport facility for supplies, and local currency access. Is possible needing secure remote resting places with adult supervision and support."

"All these problems plus some others strongly suggest more help from outer-world friends is required. However is further complication. Is misgivings among Fae leadership of supporting Earth project despite endorsement of senior weavers. Sense is that while Galactic Center continues to observe non-intervention protocol on Earth Fae intervention is unnecessary and dangerous."

Dr P paused, looking strained, and sighed.

"This implies new almost impossible task needed to achieve existing almost impossible task."

The adults all looked at each other with disbelieving faces.

"Must find Fae convincing evidence of enemy extraterrestrial intervention on Earth in order to justify further support by friend extraterrestrials."

Everyone started talking. All the comments I heard were not very hopeful. Gunter said this was like needing to find your contact lenses in a harvested hayfield so you could look for a needle in a haystack. The parents seemed a bit depressed and down about it all. Dr Prosperov had a bit of a hard time getting them to shut up.

"To achieve this and further develop capability I will travel to Russia with Dr Morozov, Nergui and Ken. Nergui has decided is time to return home to Mongolia. After this we are hoping to meet with former intelligence colleagues in Russian Federation. Russian intelligence is more likely to have clues for finding evidence of intervention than any other avenue open us. This is, of course, because former KGB has had deep penetration of US, UK, French and Chinese military apparatus. Many matters secret to Western public well penetrated by Russian spy agencies."

"Therefore flying to Japan in three days, then taking trans-Siberian trains reaching Moscow in six weeks. We plan to spend week in Moscow then week in St Petersburg."

"After that plans open for two weeks but depart London ten weeks after arriving in Japan. All going to plan expected to return 1 December."

"Am expecting to maintain communication with base via Iridium satellite phone but will also need visits by operatives to pick up data sticks for untraceable communication. Is possible we travel to Moldova to assist operatives and possibly in other location."

"Also while away am hoping to provide targets for operatives in other countries. In meantime leaving Mrs Jones in charge of Renwick and Mr Kahu in charge of operatives missions. Any questions?"

There weren't any. The big one went unasked and unanswered. It was, "what if you don't come back?" But everyone pretended, at least, to have complete faith in Dr Prosperov. After all as I heard Mitra mutter to Ali Gursoy as we went upstairs, he had managed to come back after being abducted by aliens from another world. How much trouble could his own country give him?

**111**

A more scary thought came from Rewa that night at bedtime. "What if Dr Prosperov gives up? What if he just finds it all too hard and goes back to Russia with Dr Morozov?" she asked.

I had to admit I didn't know the answer to that one. I was like everyone else. We just hoped like hell this incredible man, who had called upon powers we had never imagined, to do things we had never even thought about, could somehow create another miracle. It was then I realised how much faith I had in Dr Prosperov.

In the meantime we went back to Balti to find out more from Pavel and Uri. They were very excited with the cheap disposable cameras we got them and promised to take pictures of all the Diana's they knew or could find. And they did too, although of the twenty-four on the film only three were between ten and fourteen. The rest ranged from babies, to shop assistants to one or two grandmothers with terrible teeth. When we explained that we were looking for girls only our own age they seemed a bit disappointed. Still it didn't stop them eating a lot of Pain aux Raisin that Mr Trân had made that morning.

The others were having similar lack of luck with their contacts. Ashley and Tahira were being harassed by boys either because Ashley was black or because Tahira was so pretty. Or the teenage girls on the street were driving them off as competition they didn't need. They were having less luck than us.

Tarik and Cam were doing better than the girls but not as good as us. Cam was stared at even more than Ashley while Tarik was simply mistrusted. Even so Tarik's fast talking had got him onside with a bunch of teen boys who had at least taken pictures for money rather than food.

Of course whether the girls were called Diana or not seemed to be an afterthought. The boys had decided that if they told the girls the pictures were for an American movie scout they might get them to show more of their bodies than usual. They got the cameras developed themselves but the pictures had nothing to do with why we were there.

In general Balti was turning out to be a haystack and finding any girl named Diana in it was quite hard enough without finding the right Diana.

Then Control announced that Jeanne had moved. She had been moved to Rutshuru closer to the Rawandan border to help fight off the Mai-Mai and FDLR which had been trying to cut off CNDP supply lines from Rawanda. We figured they had decided to put her there knowing they had stolen her from Masisi over a hundred kilometers away. Rather than put her close to home they were keeping her away from it to stop her running off in country she knew.

Grandpop and Bernard studied Jeanne closely for days. They said she was an incredibly strong girl with a fast mind who knew how to keep out of trouble. But the night fights Jeanne got involved in were incredibly dangerous. Often lines crossed and there was confusion about who was shooting at who. Grandpop said most of the soldiers were just plain useless and killed their own friends as much as their enemies.

"The quickest way to get killed would be to appear in a blaze of light out of nowhere," Grandpop told us. "Every gun for a mile around would be shooting at you in seconds. The second quickest way would be to stumble into the middle of it so both sides thought you were the enemy."

The terrain was bad for bend-diving because of all the trees.

We might be safe bursting in the sky but when we came to the landing part it would become very tricky to avoid slamming into a tree.

We all looked at the situation in the briefing room and agreed there was only one thing we could do well to help Jeanne, and that was stage a big enough diversion to give her a chance to slip away. That, and perhaps, act as cover and draw off her pursuers when she did finally make a break for it. It was still nervewracking thinking that all it would take for the future of Africa to go south was one AK-47 bullet in her chest.

We had no idea whether she was thinking about escape yet. We assumed she was but she wasn't likely to tell anyone. The penalty for desertion was death or something worse. Jeanne would have to feel very confident, or very desperate, to try. The only way to find out if she was up for it was to make a diversion and see if she took the chance.

We put a lot of thought into a diversion for her. Ideally it distracted the officers but not the troops as much.

The best we could come up with was if General Nkunda called the officers to a meeting. Control had been listening to Nkunda for nearly a month now and could do a reasonable imitation of him – especially if it added a bit of fake radio static and distortion as well. The only problem was Nkunda himself would obviously be pretty vexed to hear his own voice giving orders that he had no intention of giving. Even if we got him out of the way it was obviously a trick we would only be able to do once. We also realised that once Jeanne got away she needed somewhere to go. The Don Bosco demobilisation centre in Goma was eighty kilometers away which was a very long walk. If she didn't go there she would probably end up at one of the refugee camps along the way, and they weren't much better off than the military camps.

Bernard and Grandpop started trying to work out how they could create miscommunication between Paul Kagame, the Rawandan president, and Nkunda so that there really was a need for meetings. Then Nkunda would end up calling the meetings with his officers himself. They decided the best way to help this along was to create miscommunication between Kagame and his supporters in the US State Department. Grandpop, Bernard, Zoe, Mariko and Gunter got together to form a miscommunication group. Gunter said the German word was "funkspiel" which Mariko especially liked the sound of. But there was one particular communication problem and that was satellite phones. Both the Inmarsat and the Motorola Iridium phone systems were used by leaders in the area. We had already tapped the Inmarsat system based in Britain which landed calls back on Earth but Iridium was trickier. That was because the calls could be routed satellite-to-satellite among the network of sixty-six, low-earth-orbit, 680 kilogram, satellite base-stations rather than through ground relays†.

We got excited because we started thinking we would get to go into space and bug spray the Iridium satellites as they flew overhead. We were keen but Control said we weren't equipped for space walking because we had no orientation thrusters and the adults wouldn't let us try. Grandpop got Control to ask Hekator how we could bug satellites. His suggestion was far simpler. He just got Control to find the satellites and send their orbits to him. Then he materialised a Bugspray bubble and grain in their path. This he exploded coating the dishes. Once he had the signal he sent us the receiving tokens through the lighthouse. In a few days he had bugged all the Iridium satellites and the Inmarsat ones as well.

The funny thing was the first person we managed to eavesdrop on was Dr Prosperov who had an Iridium phone with him. He called in to let us know he and the others had arrived in Ulan Ude and were about to head south into Mongolia.

Mrs Jones took the call but Control also intercepted it. Grandpop played it for us the next day because there was nothing special in it and suggested it might be fun if we had a go at spying on Dr P as an exercise. Unfortunately that turned out to be hopeless because Mongolia, where he was, was an endless sea of grass. If we had shown up it could only have been to watch their train flash by.

While Dr P was away the situation in North Kivu was becoming more and more serious by the day. Nkunda's forces were heading south and were now seriously threatening the major city of Goma and the phones were very busy. In the meantime Jeanne was in the thick of fierce fighting. She was exhausted and hungry, struggling to keep up with soldiers twice her size. Grandpop explained this was what happened when there were rumours of peace talks. Both sides fought ferociously to be in the best bargaining position for when the talks started. But again we felt stupid knowing that with all our technology we weren't allowed to help, while Jeanne herself was in the middle of it with nothing but her own strength and wits.

The girls, in particular, were sarcastic about this in front of their mothers but neither Mitra or Patricia were the slightest bit shamed. They simply said they were responsible for *their* daughters, not anyone else's, and if *their* daughters were not killed in a war, that was a good thing.

The school holidays ended without us having really achieved anything and we were feeling a bit frustrated. We could go anywhere in the world, but we had no idea who we were looking for. We had half the world bugged, but we couldn't find individual kids. To get more specific we needed more capability but the Fae wouldn't give us any because they mistrusted us with what they'd given us already. They weren't sure that they shouldn't just close us down. But they wouldn't give us what we needed, so we couldn't do what we needed to do, either. It was just *so* frustrating.

Grandpop just said it was the same in every war he'd been in and we should chill out and get used to it. But we just *couldn't*! When we talked about it on the bus finding evidence aliens were intervening on Earth sounded even more impossible than what we were doing already.

We had searched the internet for sites about alien conspiracies but most of the sites sounded crazy and were even less imaginative than the computer games, or TV shows, they had stolen their ideas from.

The idea that lizard people were loose in caves in New Mexico sounded like someone couldn't tell the difference between real life and a computer game. Because even we – and we already knew for sure aliens *did* exist – had to admit that outside of TVland, there just wasn't any real sign that President George W Bush actually was a lizard alien or that aliens were part of vast secret conspiracy with the United States or any other government.

To add to this frustration my own disappointment was that Emma was boasting she had a new boyfriend. His name was David and he lived in the capital, Wellington, where they had gone for the holidays to see family. Emma talked about David to her girlfriends constantly.

She had a picture of him and even our girls pronounced him 'hot' which made me feel just great. I thought he just looked like that wanker Justin Timberlake but there was no point telling Emma that, because she and her friends loved *him* too.

For almost a week we didn't do anything or go anywhere when finally one weekend Grandpop told us what the problem had been. It seemed Dr P had left some pretty clear instructions about the places he wanted bugged next. The problem was they included Interpol, the Mossad, the United States Strategic Air Command, the CIA, FBI and NSA, the National Reconnaissance Office, NATO, MI5, MI6 and GCSB. Further east there was Russian Air Command, GRU, and the Federal Security Service, The German Federal Intelligence Service, the French DGSE, BRGE and the Chinese Ministry of State Security.

Our parents and caregivers thought sending us to bug these organisations was just way too dangerous. Their point was if Hekator could bug satellites moving at huge speeds in space, bugging some great big stationary buildings should be easy-peasy. We knew the technical difference was that these organisations used cables underground and Hekator had already told us that it was impossible to bend underground into a solid. The dimensional pathway simply couldn't seed in an environment of high molecular density. It was only possible in water because the seeding process injected a large amount of heat which turned the water at the exit point to steam and allowed the three dimensional package to re-enter. Moreover he said our suits protected us from a lot of electromagnetism that his worms weren't built to withstand. To build worms able to be injected directly would take time and he was already over the time allotted to our project as it was.

So we were both useless and rejected. It wouldn't have mattered if we were given a bunch of technology and told to go have fun. But we'd been given a bunch of technology and told we were the best six kids in the world to do something really important. And now through nothing we'd done we either weren't allowed to do it or didn't have enough leads to find anyone.

Then something else happened which started to really worry me. After school as we were headed out of the school gate towards Mariko waiting in Betty the bus, I noticed a car parked further up the road by itself. It obviously wasn't there to pick anyone up. It was a bright sunny day with a cool breeze and there were just two men sitting in it watching us kids. Ashley and Tarik noticed too.

We started talking about it, watching from the back seat of Betty the bus. Rewa and Asal sat on the left, hidden away from view. Tahira sat at the back left, while Scotty and Cam (who had the best eyesight) sat on the right side of Betty to see what they could see of the people in the car. Unfortunately the glare on the car's windscreen made it impossible to see inside.

Mariko revved Betty up and we roared past the average looking Japanese car we were watching. Scotty and Cam yelled that they couldn't see inside because Betty was too high. As we went past the car pulled a U-turn and for a split second we could all see the driver. A pale white man in a beanie with a droopy red moustache and bloodshot, angry blue eyes.

"Ray! It's that geezer Ray from the hill!" Tarik shouted.

A cold dread settled on my insides as the car fell back to follow our bus. I snuck off the backseat and started thinking fast. Maybe I should get Mariko to drop me and Rewa somewhere else and come back for us later. The first place I thought of was Emma's but then I realised she was unlikely to be all that keen to see me.

"Are they still behind us?" I shouted down the aisle to the others.

"Yeah!" they replied. Then:

"Shit! The other one has a camera!" Tarik yelled and both he and Ashley slipped off the back seat quick. I went up to Mariko.

"There's a car following us. It's the drug growers who recognised me."

Mariko checked her mirrors. While the seal was still there she could see the gray car but once we hit gravel they'd vanish.

"Well, what do we *do* about it?" she asked practically.

I suggested she pretend to drop me and Rewa off somewhere along the way. She thought about it.

"No. They might grab you."

"It's worth a try isn't it?" I countered.

"No. You safe with me. Besides they will find out pretty quick where you rive anyway."

I started to think. Why would Aunty Liz live anywhere along here anyway? Where would she work? There was one doctor on the island, Dr Jackson, who lived here because of the "lifestyle" (meaning he smoked weed a lot). He was more likely to be friends with Ray and Ricky than us.

The more I thought about it the more I realised they weren't going to be fooled by me and Rewa getting off a well known bus for more than a day or two. All they'd have to do is ask someone and they'd soon be put straight.

"You're right. It won't work," I agreed.

We entered the gravel road and the car disappeared into the dust cloud following Betty. It was impossible to know whether they were still following or not. With the size of the cloud it was probable you could see Betty from space so watching where she went from here on was going to be pretty easy. I sat down by myself, my head packed with fears, as I imagined all the possible meanings of Ax's mates finding us.

Legally, of course, Ax couldn't come anywhere near us. But hadn't he managed to wreck Grandpop's life before he'd even left prison? That was the problem with Ax. He was clever. He got others to do his dirty work. He used rules when it suited him and broke them when it didn't. His lawyer might have been no match for Sir Michael in court but he wouldn't take that lying down either. That would just sharpen his need to win because that was all this was about; winning. He didn't really want us. He just wanted to hurt the Kahus for putting him in prison.

I told Grandpop and Aunty Liz about the men when we got home. They were more worried than the others but tried to reassure me and Rewa that Dr P wouldn't let a speck like Ax get in the way of his project.

Later we got another call from Dr P to say that Nergui had arrived back home to a huge reception from his people. Ken had also been received (although with less enthusiasm) too. Technically Ken was still wanted by the Mongolian police but his people wouldn't go so far as to turn him in. There had been some feasting but Dr P had cut the visit short in order to get back to the TransSiberian and keep his schedule.

He was clearly annoyed that our parents had put a stop to us bugging the military but he said there would be time for a "more balanced" discussion on his return. His next destination was his hometown of Krasnoyarsk where they would visit his family's graves and gather some documents about his father he had been told about. Then it was on to Moscow.

For almost two weeks nothing happened. Ray and Ricky weren't seen again. Dr P didn't call. The fighting in North Kivu got even fiercer and the CNDP were now directly threatening the UN base in Goma. There was even talk about the possibility of Nkunda driving the UN out of North Kivu altogether[+].

And in Balti it was just getting colder as winter got closer.

Then suddenly in the middle of the night Grandpop was banging on our doors. It was two in the morning and Dr Prosperov had called Mrs Jones with only four words: "Need special couriers immediately" and hung up.

The parents were a bit grumpy. But Dr Prosperov had asked for us and after weeks of not doing anything useful we were all keen to go. We raced off down to the base, still in our pyjamas.

In the briefing room Grandpop was waiting while on the holoviewer was Dr Prosperov talking to someone. He, Ken and Dr Morozov were in a small flat crammed full of old furniture talking to a bearded man at the kitchen table. In front of him was a wooden box and he was talking earnestly to Dr P and Dr M, while Ken was obviously trying to keep up with the Russian. Grandpop's briefing was the shortest ever.

"This is where you are going. Don't ask me why," was all he said. Then it was off to the jumpstation feeling like it was all a weird dream.

# [+]

A minute later we were materialising in cramped places all over the flat in brilliant flashes of light. I almost made my entrance look especially stupid by tripping over a small table.

But it didn't matter because the effect on the old man with the beard was not the best. He looked around in panic. He half rose to escape and then fainted. Luckily Ken caught him before he hit his head. Ken dragged the man, who was quite large, over to a small sofa and checked his pulse. Then he gently slapped his face while the two Russians followed and watched on with concern. We unpeeled our facescreens and looked around.

You could tell whoever lived here had once been a lot better off than he was now. For a start he had too much furniture, all of which was actually very nice. At the same time the actual flat itself was small, mouldy and smelt bad. Checking out the windows into the late afternoon light, the view was mostly of other blocks of flats. The street outside didn't look so well looked after either.

"Professor Cherensky? ... Professor Cherensky? Vassily Ivanovitch? Can you hear me?" Ken was asking in Russian

The old man groaned, shook his head and looked at Ken in confusion. Then he looked at the Prosperovs.

Now he seemed to remember what had happened and he looked frightened again.

"No! You're in league with *them*! All these years! And now I discover just as I die I was *right*! I was *right*! The injustice!" he cried in Russian.

"Calm down, calm down," Dr Prosperov told the man. "Do these look like extraterrestrials?" he said indicating us.

The old man sat up to take a better look at us. We were in

hoodies and jeans. We felt like we were in a zoo or something.

"They aren't Vassily, they are young teenagers. Earthly children."

"Children?! But ... how?"

"I have gained the help of extraterrestrials..." Dr Prosperov told him. He went pale again.

"... but not the extraterrestrials you have been telling us about. Another form opposed to the ones you have uncovered. Your evidence is crucial to our wider goal to free us from the ones you fear."

The old man listened carefully. Then he looked suspiciously at us.

"You say these are normal Earth children?" he asked.

"Of course."

"Do they understand us?" he asked doubtfully.

We all nodded or said "da" casually.

"May I talk to them?"

Dr Prosperov shrugged.

So Professor Cherensky talked to us for about half an hour. He asked us about where we came from; about our parents; to recite nursery rhymes in our own languages; and our favourite sweets. He switched to English which he spoke better than Dr P. He even had some French, Turkish and Persian. He told us jokes, one of which had us all laughing. He asked about the other extraterrestrials and, after a nod from Dr P, we answered him. At first he was sharp, and talked quickly, but after a while his suspicions we were not human vanished. Finally he turned back to Dr P.

"Very well then Dr Prosperov I am forced to conclude that you are not lying. So what is it you want of me?"

Dr Prosperov told Professor Cherensky about Renwick and finally invited him to come and visit. Dr Cherensky said he would favourably consider this invitation but would prefer more time. We could read from him that an opportunity to escape another St Petersburg winter had quite a bit of appeal. Then with some delicacy Dr Prosperov came to what he had sent to us for. He wanted Professor Cherensky's papers and samples.

Well, that set him off! This was impossible! A life's work! Never part with them! Leader in his field! He ranted on for about an hour as it gradually got darker. We were all leaning on each other, warm and drowsy, in real danger of falling asleep.

Dr Prosperov however reeled him in gradually. He pointed out that none of his papers had found a publisher in the last ten years. His theories had got him branded a nut and he was a professor in name only, as the University didn't pay him, or let him teach. Then he said our friends, however, would not only listen to him, but be in a position to review his work fairly and without prejudice. He might not be published, but he would finally be vindicated by those who could recognise his insight for what it was.

It was seven in the morning our time when Professor Cherensky finally agreed. With surprising speed he opened fridges, took out sealed tubes. Then he went into his room and brought out typewritten pages in Russian characters with photographs and drawings taped to them. We set to work looking at them with our suits' eyes which transmitted them back to Control. There were about two hundred pages altogether but we only had to see them to record them and between the six of us that didn't take long. Then we took the carefully labelled tubes and pocketed them.

"Get Dr Gursoy to send these to Hekator with the papers as soon as you get back." Dr Prosperov told us.

## [+]

We winked out and arrived back at Renwick House just as everyone else was finishing breakfast. Dr Gursoy took the tubes off to the lighthouse. We got undressed back into our pyjamas and came back upstairs. We were exhausted and school started in two hours. Luckily Grandpop told us to go to bed. We could take the day off sick.

It was so nice to get back into bed again, even though the day had begun. It took a little while to get over the sounds of day which usually woke me, but it can't have been that hard because the next thing I knew it was noon.

We had a good day mooching at home. Rewa and Asal were really jealous so Aunty Liz and Mitra agreed they could stay home the next day just to shut them up.

The next day we had another call from Dr Prosperov. He said he was going to Balti in Moldova with Ken, while Dr Morozov helped Professor Cherensky get an exit visa from the Russian Interior Ministry (which was apparently famous for being inefficient, slow and rude, even by Russian standards). He then gave a date: a Saturday, three days from then; and a time, ten at night.

So three days later at midday, Sunday, we suited up while Control found Dr P driving around Balti. Ken drove him around the streets and then finally stopped. Dr P got out and walked around. Finally he came to stand outside a fairly rundown looking wooden house. Then he got back inside the Mercedes and they drove to a nearby park five minutes before the rendezvous time.

It was a park where Tahira and Ashley had had problems before. It was a cold night with a slight mist. Not surprisingly some teen girls were soon standing around Dr P's car wearing very short skirts under long coats while a man smoking a cigarette watched on from the park. Dr P checked his watch and Grandpop said it was never a good idea to keep the boss waiting.

[+]

Six brilliant lights flashed in the Balti park. The man took his eyes off his girls and looked around at the source of the flash. He took one look at six dark, hooded figures with no faces, walking purposefully toward the Mercedes, threw down his cigarette, and ran to the girls, who had been so busy showing off to Dr P that they hadn't noticed us arrive. The man pulled them away and shouted at them before running off. The girls hesitated seeing, only six small hooded figures coming toward them, but the fear the man had shown was catching, and as we walked steadily on towards the shiny black Mercedes they finally got the impression they were caught in a situation which seemed just a bit evil. They squealed and clopped off as fast as their high heeled shoes let them.

Dr P got out of the car as we came up. He was wearing a black coat and his usual suit, his hair its usual mess.

"Believe have found Diana's house. Please to follow."

Then he led us on foot back to the house we had seen him visit before.

"Is any communication from Hekator?" he asked as we walked. We told him no. He grunted, obviously not expecting any. With Ken trailing us in the Merc he led us the short walk back to the house. Number 79 whatever-this-street-was.

"Is much easier for me to sense in place," Dr Prosperov sniffed.

Then he sighed deeply and added.

"In fact driving to Odessa tomorrow. Have strong lead there. Please to meet in two days. In meantime engage local children to learn more about Diana and family. Having feeling is not good here. Something bad will happen soon."

With that he went back to the car. He paused before he got in.

"Two days. When time, I wear hat."

Then he got into the car. We waved to Ken, who smiled and gave a brief wave, and then the Merc swept off into the dark street leaving us alone in the middle of the Romanian night.

We turned back to the house. Dr Prosperov was right. Something very wrong was happening here. You could feel the secret darkness in it. We lined up along the fence sensing and the house melted as we explored the souls inside. There was a girl our age, a man, an older teenage girl and a much older woman. The sisters were very close. The man and the older sister were father and daughter but in the same bed. It was twisted alright. The younger girl was attached to her sister but disliked her father. The older woman – grandmother – wanted the girls out, away from the man. It wasn't clear how, but she had a plan.

We came back to ourselves and looked at one another feeling slightly sick.

"Why can't these future leaders just live happy ordinary lives?" Ashley muttered shaking her head.

"Maybe some of them do. But those ones don't need *our* help do they?" Tarik pointed out.

There was nothing much to do, so we folded into night.

**[+]**

Monday night Ashley and Tahira came back with a bug to tag

Diana. While they did that the rest of us looked for kids out at night we could recruit as spies. It was the wrong end of town for Pavel and Uri. Me and Scotty had no luck but Tarik and Cam found a small huddle of cold teens in the park where we had met Dr P.

Tarik managed to talk to them in Russian and bargained with them to get us information for money. Then we realised we didn't have any local currency. So Control called Dr Prosperov. Dr P had some Ukrainian Hryvnia and Moldovan Leu in Odessa. So while Tarik led the teens to Diana's house, me and Scotty burst into a corridor with awful wallpaper in a hotel in Odessa. We knocked on a door, Dr Prosperov appeared in a nightgown looking hassled gave us some notes then we folded away to burst back into the park.

**[+]**

We then followed the route from the previous night and found Tarik being asked to show his money. We told the kids we had it and showed them the cash. There was a bit of arguing about it. They were bigger than us and started trying to scare us. Then one of the boys tried to snatch the cash from Scotty but was surprised to find Scotty much stronger than he was. Scotty twisted and threw him heavily to the ground. One of the others drew a knife and I knocked him down with the stun ray which for a change was completely invisible without heavy rain to interfere with it. It looked like he drew the knife and just fainted. Some went forward to his aid.

"Don't be bad," Cam told them in Romanian.

Now the teens were frightened. They realised we were not ordinary kids and they were surrounded.

"Who tells us about people here?" Tarik asked calmly.

"We know who tells the truth," Scotty added, behind them.

A scared looking girl a year or so older than us said she and her friend did.

"OK, you stay. Others go," Scotty said behind them.

They looked uncertain.

"Go now or Evil Eye," Tarik said staring crazily at them one by one. I had to stop myself laughing but they didn't need to be told again, and all ran, except the girl and her friend who looked terrified.

When the others had gone. Scotty went up to the oldest. She looked scared and then he gave her the money. At first she refused it thinking we were devils and that it bound her to us.

"Take the money or we make much pain. Now tell," Scotty threatened quietly.

We had no idea whether Dr Prosperov had given us a fortune or small change, but fear of the alternative ways we might use and the amount of money changed this girl's attitude a lot.

"Their name is Popovic. Is very common name. Elena Popovic is friend. She is very pretty but very shy and quiet. She wants to go to Paris and be model or secretary. Her father Gregor is a pig. He beats the girls and even his old mother. They are proud though and never ask for help. Gregor used to be a security guard but they closed the factory and he is old now. Old and drunk."

"What of the sister?" Cam asked.

"Little Diana is just a girl. She follows her sister everywhere. They are very close. Elena looks after her like a mother."

"Where *is* their mother?"

"Gone. Russia or somewhere they say," they said.

"Is Elena happy?" Tarik asked.

"Happy?" the girl repeated as if the word had no meaning and yet the sentence was as simple in Romanian as it was in any other language.

"Is she happy?"

"No-one is happy! But Elena is especially serious."

We looked at each other. We had all we needed.

"OK, we must go," Tarik told them.

So we left them and headed back to the park. As soon as we knew they had taken off we bent home.

**[+]**

At debrief Grandpop was very pleased. We now had two targets we could track. We kids were a bit uncertain about whether this was really progress. All these kids still seemed to have really crappy lives and we were just watching.

We had wondered what the mission to Odessa would be like when suddenly Dr P called to cancel it. He was returning to St Petersburg. He said we might soon expect a visit from old friends. Professor Cherensky's files and samples had apparently got the Fae interested again.

## CHAPTER FORTY SEVEN: PROFESSOR CHERENSKY

Dr Gursoy sent Professor Cherensky's samples to the Fae in mid-November. Nothing much happened at first but then came a message from Hekator. The Fae wanted to talk to Cherensky urgently. A delegation lead by Morganne would arrive with the full moon in a few days.

Meanwhile it seemed that Dr Morozov had managed a small miracle and got the Russian Interior Ministry to approve Cherensky's exit visa in record time. They were now joined by Dr Prosperov and Ken who were organising a route home.

The adults seemed to think Dr Cherensky must have something pretty special to get Queen Morganne to come back at such short notice and wondered what it could be. Having seen his house, it was pretty obvious that if the Fae thought what he had was special, the Russian government obviously did not.

For a few days we didn't go anywhere because Mrs Jones wanted us to catch up on cleaning that had been forgotten about a bit lately. It seemed that for a few days we could forget about Jeanne, Diana or whether Ax had sent Ricky and Ray to find out about us. At school we were getting ready for the annual school sports which was an excuse for us to spend the rest of the school year outside running around. The only problem with that was we arrived home more tired and hungry than usual.

We were slouching in the lounge watching TV about eight o'clock on a Tuesday night when there was a kind shock that came through the walls like a small psychic earthquake. We all looked up and then dashed out to the gallery with the parents trailing us.

Standing outside was Morganne, Queen of Fae, in a stunning blue gown holding a glowing blue sceptre. To her right there was an older goat-man with long gray hair, a silver cloak and a wooden staff topped with a green glowing jewel. On the left was another woman we had only seen on the Circle at Easter wearing a white gown, a feathered hat and with white feathered wings on her back and carrying a golden staff with a violet jewel. Between them was Hekator and Raman.

Mrs Jones raced out to see them. There was a very brief discussion and they vanished. We raced down to see what had happened.

"The Fae are settling into the caves to await Professor Cherensky's arrival tomorrow," she told us as we came out. "It's a very important delegation. The other two are Horne and Isis. They are equal in rank to Morganne and certainly not her political friends. If they are here with her this is very big indeed," she said as we went inside.

"Should we do somethin'?" Ashley wanted to know. "You know, like give 'em somethin' or perform or somethin'?"

"It would be like dogs giving you their favourite squeaky toy, or howling for you. No it's best that we simply keep them informed about the progress of Professor Cherensky," Mrs Jones said.

So that was all we did, although they only had to wait one day, for early on the morning of Monday 3rd of December Drs Prosperov and Morozov, Ken and Professor Cherensky arrived back in New Zealand. We got the news just before we left for school.

When we got home we learned that Cherensky and Prosperov were meeting the Fae while Ken and Dr Morozov had gone to bed. The meeting lasted until after we went to bed, which was pretty amazing as the two humans were completely jetlagged. The next day we learned nothing and went to school, again unclear what was happening. In fact this went on until Thursday when we were told the Fae had left. However we didn't see Dr Prosperov or Professor Cherensky until Sunday because it turned out that they had had to catch up on sleep for three days after the Fae had kept them awake for so long.

That Sunday night however we had a dinner in the hall for Professor Cherensky. It was a fish dinner and we had been sent out to catch the fish, which were Kingfish and Ka-whai. There was Borscht and sour black bread, dumplings, meatballs, cutlets, and salads. Finally there was pancakes. By the end we were stuffed. Then Dr Prosperov got up to speak.

"Mr Trân," he said indicating with his arm.

And we all broke out into applause. Mr Trân gave a silly bow with a huge grin on his face and sat down very pleased with himself.

"Mr Trân would like to say you cook like Russian," he paused. "But Russians aren't so good."

There was warm laughter and more applause.

"Friends ... Yes, *friends*, is very good to be home. I am pleased to say trip total success. All objectives met. Let me detail as follows:

"First Nergui has returned home. Was special time as Nergui is very old and does not expect to live through this winter. His wish was to die with his people. He asked me to thank you all for making him welcome and remembers you well."

He looked at Ken for a moment and then simply said.

"Is not for me to say any more."

"In Moscow my wife met with close friend in former KGB electronic warfare cadre now operating under name Para. no.ID. Even I have no idea who she met. She has entered into information sharing and mutual assistance with this group. I believe this will greatly assist our capability in future."

"In Balti, operation with young operatives great success and now have fully identified second target and traced her. This brings our count to two, after only six months of operation, which given the difficulty is, I believe very good."

"But most important is in just six weeks we have managed to find compelling evidence of interventions on Earth by extraterrestrials on a greater scale than even I had ever anticipated. Admit when we left I thought probabilities very low but this was before am meeting Professor Cherensky. Now am frankly astonished at ability of human institutions to perpetrate mass delusion even when primary data obvious. But let us hear story from Professor directly. Professor V.I. Cherensky."

We applauded politely. The parents were a bit tired and listening to Russian accents for long periods was hard. But then Professor Cherensky surprised them.

"Ladies and gentlemen, I cannot begin to express my gratitude towards Dr Prosperov for bringing me here to meet your outer world visitors. It is vindication for so many decades of struggle and heartbreak and is like a dream come true."

He spoke better English than Dr P by far.

"Mr Trân, Dr Prosperov is not exaggerating, your food is excellent, thank you, I cannot remember when I have eaten so well. Probably not for twenty years."

"And to others. Thank you for being such kind hosts. You restore my faith in humanity. A faith which has been tested for many years."

"And now a confession. Not thirty years ago I would have seen you all dead."

He paused letting it sink in. It was a rather horrible thing to say so there was a sort of drooping of smiles around the room. When he had made his point he went on.

"Not merely dead but suffering the most horrible pain and heartbreak as you watched your loved ones die, wretched, painful, horrible deaths. Men, women, children, even babies." Cherensky nodded, then took a deep breath and sighed.

"I was chief epidemiologist at Biopreparat, the Soviet biowarfare organisation. From 1975 until 1996 I led team which planned the use of worst natural diseases which had been made into weapons of war through extensive genetic engineering. Diseases including black death, smallpox, Anthrax, Ebola, Marburg fever were transformed into warheads that could be delivered by aircraft or SS18 missile to unleash misery, grief and horror throughout the world[†]. My job was to plan their use to cause greatest harm to United States in particular."

"I estimate we had stock of biological warfare agents capable of wiping out all human life at least three times over. I say this with much shame."

"But before I move on let us examine my situation more closely. I was an officer and a member of Communist party. I was well paid. I had big office, and big car. My children went to good schools. I was respected by colleagues. We had parties and holidays. I was like a successful Nazi doctor who lived well and worked in a world of horror."

"There was horror too. Some colleagues made minor mistakes and died of Ebola[†]. Ebola is a horrible disease where all organs rupture from inside. Hardly anyone survives the natural strains and nobody can survive the strains we made. We destroyed animals faster than an abattoir, recording their agony in detail, all of us perfectly aware that the difference between their suffering and ours was physiologically nonexistent."

"'How could this be?' I asked myself later. And this is the most important question we must consider. How do we create organisations that have not only no moral purpose while we ourselves claim to be moral people?"

"Could I kill this beautiful little infant with a pistol?" he asked pointing at Patience.

"Never. But then with disease I planned to kill her, and millions like her, and then went home to tell my own children a bedtime story," he said shaking his head.

"Please believe, I am no special monster. I was just a technician who was good at his job and I was rewarded for it. What I am trying to say is that *all* organisations steal our morality. They replace our values with their own by rewarding those who advance their values and punishing those who stand up to them."

"Worse, organisations create authority. If I tell you my theory as a broken down old pensioner living in a cheap flat in St Petersburg, who cares? I am dime-a-dozen. I am crazy old man. But if I tell you same crazy theory when I am chief of powerful organisation people listen. And if you as head of your organisation and me in mine agree it can become as good as fact. Bosses agree. *Everyone* agrees! They think in terms of what the people at the top want. They stop questioning."

"Bosses don't want questioning. They want their subordinates to agree and praise them."

"Some lazy people don't like questioning either. They just want to accept what leaders say so they can get back to their families, holidays and parties. Questions are waste of time. They embarrass people and stop agreement. They let in morality."

"Enough preaching. Back to story. Our organisation was very important in Russia during the 1970s and 80s in the Cold War. But Perestroika in 90s brought shocks. We had been told our weapons were matched by similar work in the United States. But in the 90s when chief scientist Ken Alibeck, defected, he claimed he could find no evidence of US biological warfare research[†]."

"Is possible they fooled him. But other possibility was the Americans had reached a conclusion which had long haunted me also, and that was if we used these diseases, how could we stop them coming back to destroy our own people? Disease is a perfect weapon to destroy people and leave resources untouched, but problem with bioweapons is that once released they cannot be controlled."

"When Aids epidemic began in the early 1980s KGB agents moved quickly and efficiently to gain as many samples of disease and as much information as possible. Our theory was this was surely an American bioweapon that had escaped containment. This could mean we were once again behind Americans technologically. But this outbreak gave us opportunity. Not only would proving Aids was a U.S weapon cause enormous embarrassment to our enemy but it could also be used as a means to gain a technological lead while the Americans wrestled with Senate inquiries and expensive law suits. We had seen this happen in nuclear energy and hoped we could turn their system against them again."

"To our astonishment none of this happened. The origin of Aids was glossed over or blamed on the victims who seemed to be mostly homosexuals. In particular President Reagan's supporters held it up as God's curse on homosexuals for sin[†]. This is religion not science. The question of where the disease had come from was turned into attacks on and defences of homosexuals. To us was irrelevant."

"We therefore decided that if Western politics was so easily distracted we would simply have to do the work ourselves and then publish it through European sympathisers."

"Unfortunately work turned out to be much more complicated than we thought. For a start it took quite a while to find the Human Innunodeficency Virus that was responsible for Aids in the first place."

"Another problem was computing power. To those not engaged in genetic engineering the use of computers is not obvious. Viruses seem to be about test tubes and Petri dishes. But to explain how computers change things I need to quickly explain a little about how genetics works."

He paused and took a drink of water.

"First, every living thing comes from previous living things. Children from parents all the way back billions of years to first life. All based on proteins made from designs coded in a nucleic acid, one of which we call DNA[†]."

"Many people have heard of DNA but don't know what is. At centre of all cells is nucleus. Is command centre. In command centre is master programme. This is made from twenty three pairs of chromosomes, twenty three from mother, twenty three from father. Chromosomes packages up DNA. DNA is made up of two strands like the legs of a ladder which twists around in a tight spiral like staircase in lighthouse. The steps of the ladder are links made of one of four basic chemicals we call A and T or C and G. Now A always matches T on the opposite side of the ladder and C always matches G. These are called base pairs[†]. Human DNA has over three billion base pairs."

"The genetic code is read along the DNA ladder in sets of three like C.A.T or T.A.G or G.C.T. Each set of three is called a codon and is translated by the cell's machinery into protein. These proteins are knitted together to make very, very complex chemicals that make changes in the organism like going to sleep or making adrenalin when we are frightened. A sequence of codons can also be a gene for a particular quality like black hair or blue eyes. We describe genes in terms of how many base pairs of AT or TA or CG or GC are needed to make them[†]."

So when we examine DNA of organism first we have to find out the sequence of the codons. This is chemical test. But we use computers to analyse codes and look for patterns in them[†]."

"Is like looking at book. You can look at the words used, the length of sentences. All things the book describes. All of these patterns can be analysed with computer."

"With stable things like plants or animals changes in the book are unusual. So unusual you can work out how often they change and work backwards to see when this or that organism changed in history. A book about elephants will have much to say about elephants. From the elephant genome you can read a history which has information about mammoths or other animals from the evolution of elephants. But imagine you are reading a book about elephants and you come to a page which describes a strong furry tail the animal used to hop along at high speed. You would think that was rather odd."

"This is what recombination can do. Recombination is where a piece of DNA from one living thing is put into the DNA of another[†]. The extraterrestrials who you have made contact with are obviously very good at it. We are only just beginning."

"But it wasn't scientists or extraterrestrials who invented recombination. It was viruses. They have been doing it for billions of years. We have all merely watched what viruses do and copied their tricks, sometimes by using viruses themselves to achieve our goals[†]."

"Now viruses aren't as big as books like plants or animals. Some of them would barely make a magazine article. Some are bigger and more complicated. But all of them are made from some form or recombination. Imagine a newspaper article made from words or phrases cut from different books or magazines. That is what viruses look like when analysed by computer."

"To make things more complicated viruses are also good at swapping words with one another. So if two viruses are in the same cell they can mix each other up. So to find out where a virus comes from you have to study what is written in its message and that is different or the same to all the other viruses around it. That way you can work out its family tree[†]."

"Now let us return to Aids and Human Immunodeficiency Virus or HIV which has around nine genes made from 9,750 base pairs. There is no doubt that HIV was derived from the ape disease Simian Immunodeficiency Virus or SIV. There are two kinds of SIV. One affects monkeys in Western Africa and seems to have turned into HIV-2 which is rare. The other affects Chimpanzees and that turned into HIV-1 which has killed 25 million people so far[†]."

"HIV-1 comes in a number of sub-types. Type A is found in Western Africa. Type B in the United States and Europe. Type C, which has proved the most deadly, in southern Africa and Asia, and there are a number of others[†]. To analyse the genetics of these viruses we began to make use of a new kind of supercomputer which uses hundreds of simple computers in parallel – called a grid computer – to carry out complicated statistical tests on all the strains and subtypes of HIV as they were being discovered to try and find patterns that did not match."

"In the early 1980s this was still all new. We already knew that United States was rapidly depleting world's stock of chimpanzees for medical research. Baby chimps were sent to the US to be injected with drugs and then killed[†]. The first reports of an Aids-like disease in apes was in 1983[†]. It seemed entirely possible to us that the Americans had isolated the SIV from those apes and recombined it to make a human equivalent."

"The problem was proving it. HIV is not stable[†]. It recombines itself relatively easily and it seemed to be full of cut out words. To make sense of it we needed copies of it through time going back to the earliest examples along with copies of similar viruses it could have borrowed from. Like collecting all the possible magazines its message could be cut and pasted from to trace the dates in the message. By combining this data it would be possible to build up a picture of what had come from where."

"The earliest known samples came from what is now the Democratic Republic of Congo from a single person in Kinshasa out of a sample of six hundred[†]. The date was around the late 50s and early 60s. The sample however is highly questionable.

Only three hundred base pairs of the virus were found and the patient's identity is in doubt[†]. There are six hundred base pair segments in the main HIV virus which are regarded as out of place so not much weight can be put on this."

"To put 1960 in context at this time Congolese were fighting liberation struggle against the Belgians and Americans[†]. The country was strategically significant as it suppled 60% of world Uranium and in fact supplied the Uranium used to make the Hiroshima and Nagasaki bombs[†]. Other examples included a Norwegian sailor, a Russian construction worker and a British sailor and of course a lot of Africans[†]."

"Throughout the 80s we pursued the goal of finding a way of pinning Aids on Americans. At the same time the progress of the Aids virus became a perfect study for epidemiologist like myself with an armoury of superviruses ready to be launched at our enemies. The HIV virus was doing in slow motion what our more contagious and deadly diseases would do much faster."

"The collapse of the Soviet Union in the 1990s came as an enormous shock to me. I was fascinated by my work. I had no time for politics. But suddenly we had defectors like Dr Alibeck and we were being investigated. The politicians were finding Biopreparat embarrassing and in the period of Glasnost or openness it was like the dark roof of our cave had been lifted off and we scurried from the blinding glare of international attention."

"I was lucky. I got a teaching post at St Petersburg State I.P. Pavlov Medical University. It was organised by the KGB so I could continue my work while they went about hiding our munitions. But when the coup de etat against Gorbachev failed and led to Yeltsin taking over the new Russian Federation it became obvious that there would be no return to the Cold War with America. Peace had come and we had obviously lost. The Americans were in Moscow buying things and hiring our best people."

"The standard of living in Russia fell rapidly. We often went without pay for months at a time. People died of cold, hunger and diseases I had never imagined would ever affect Russians."

"And now Aids was no longer foreign disease. It was making its way into Russia's population as men turned to drugs and women to prostitution. My study of Aids epidemic from beginning to end which had begun as a comfortable military officers desk study was becoming part of gritty daily battle for meaning in society which seemed to have its own form of the disease. Russia was battling its own immune system as Yeltsin's henchmen relentlessly took control of the body of the state and gifted themselves its most valuable assets. The worst was when my wife Irina left me for a man in the oil industry."

He paused to drink his water. I still couldn't see how any of this connected to us.

"All this time my mathematical models had continued beating against the patterns of dispersion and mutation being reported by those sequencing HIV, SIV and their various strains in other countries. I had to literally beg, bribe and steal to get computer time to run my programmes. What was obvious was that HIV had come from a recombination of material that originally came from Central Africa. But what was still not clear was how."

"It was clear from genetic code that SIV had been a disease in apes for hundreds, if not thousands, of years[†]. But the probability of it jumping from apes to humans was extremely low[†]. Viruses don't do that easily[†]. Like criminals they need means, motive and opportunity. They also need a breeding ground. The breeding ground must survive long enough to let the disease spread. That is why, horrible as it is, Ebola has only killed hundreds of people. The victims die and never get to spread the contagion. Small outbreaks can be so deadly that the disease kills everyone and just dies out so it doesn't get a chance to spread. Many of the earliest Aids cases entering Europe never went anywhere, victims just died[†]. To explain why HIV has killed millions meant there was something missing from the puzzle. Why did it become *less* lethal?"

"Two things then happened that changed situation I was looking at."

"The first was amazing discovery in mid 1990s. It was found that for the HIV virus to break into a human cell it had to fit its protein key into a kind of cellular lock called CD4[†]. But it also had to open a lock called CCR5[†]. In the mid-90s it was found that a small proportion of Europeans – ones with unusual chromosome 23 – did not have the CCR5 co-receptor[†]. No co-receptor, no entry. No entry, no disease. People who do not have the CCR5 genes were immune to HIV[†]."

"For every disease there are always some people who are immune. They have a random mutation which stops cell entry. Is also true of HIV. There are some lucky people of all races who cannot ever get it because of random mutations. But this was different. The delta 32 mutation is an *inherited* genetic difference common *only* in people of Nordic origin. Africans and Asians do not have the delta 32 mutation. Only whites, or to be more blunt Ayrans of the kind Hitler's followers had deemed the *Ubermensch*, the ideal of humanity, could not get Aids."

"To a former military man working for an agency which started

in the Great Patriotic War this discovery was stunning. The idea
of making a biological weapon your own people were immune
to was the ultimate bioweapon. We had not even considered
such a thing. The very thought that a disease could be designed
to target only a particular enemy was revolutionary. Also as a
Russian, the idea that this disease racially favoured particularly
those who had inflicted so much suffering on our people just
fifty years previously made my mind reel. It suggested a motive."
"There was only one obvious problem with the hypothesis
that this could be done deliberately. It was completely beyond
human science[†]. It was unknown to any scientists in 1981 when
Aids was identified as a disease. It was unknown in 1983 when
HIV was isolated. And it was certainly unknown when HIV was
first accidentally gathered in samples in the early 60s. Indeed
back in the 1960s the discovery of DNA itself was still new."
"A rational man might have concluded at this point that HIV was
not a conspiracy at all. A rational man would have concluded
that the coincidence of a disease which seemed to favour the
pure blood Ayrans who had murdered so many Russians and
could wipe out the rest of the world population was just one of
those strange ironies of history. But somewhere in the process of
losing my job and my wife and seeing my country fall victim to
wolves in human form I had lost touch with rationality. All I had
left was obsession."
"Now I redoubled my efforts to crack the riddle of HIV's
emergence. In the process I made contact with a rather reclusive
group of computer experts, one or two of them known to Dr
Morozov. These people had established a network who were the
equivalent of privateers rather than pirates. They worked for
themselves but were known to Russian security agencies and

cooperated with them in return for protection."

"This network had taken the concept of grid computing to an extraordinary new level. They had developed a small piece of software called a Trojan which travelled the internet finding its way into computers and installing itself on them. Like a virus, the Trojan then copied itself and set off to find more computers to infect. But more importantly while it remained it hosted a small programme which ran in the background of the host computer. Its job was to steal computer power from the computer and turn it over to the trojan network. What they were doing, in effect, was turning the whole internet into the world's most massively parallel supercomputer."

"As an epidemiologist my role was to help them work out dispersion models to help them design the programs to balance the load of computing resources around the network. I confess it was very exciting. It was even more exciting when I discovered these people could crack the computers at Fort Deitrick, the US military's biodefence unit."

"With the computing power the group had built, I now had the ability to run programs whose complexity I had only previously dreamed of. I began to feel that I might finally sort out the massive and incomplete jigsaw that was the origin and evolution of HIV."

"One theory I needed to examine was a persistent belief that HIV may have spontaneously formed in the culture used to propagate medicines, in particular vaccines. You see against most viruses the best defence is to warn the body's natural defences of impending attack. The body then makes antibodies which stick to the attacking virus and guide the body's hunter killer cells to wipe them out. Of course HIV is the exception because it is a virus that attacks the defensive cells themselves so any exposure is dangerous."

"Most vaccines are a weakened or dead version of the original virus you want to warn the body about. The viruses are best grown in a mixture of fresh meat kept warm. This culture allows them to reproduce rapidly. So vaccines and viruses grow best in the same thing. Today the normal practice is to sterilise the meat culture before adding the vaccine virus you want to manufacture but that was not always the case. The allegation that has followed HIV since it was first encountered is that it may have been inadvertently created when unsterilised culture containing an unknown virus like SIV was used to make a vaccine[†]. Vaccines that have been accused include Polio, in Africa, Smallpox in Africa, and Hepatitis B in America[†]. The story goes the SIV mutated in the culture into HIV and suddenly instead of giving people life-saving vaccine they are being given deadly doses of HIV[†]."

"One theory claims that HIV-A subtype was accidentally created and propagated by a Belgian medical team based in Kisangani working to distribute an Oral Polio Vaccine in the rift valley of Rawanda, Burundi and the Kivu provinces in the late 1950s and early 60s[†]. They used unsterilised chimp meat to grow Polio vaccine[†]."

Now I was starting to get a weird feeling about this. Was it just coincidence that he was talking about where Jeanne lived?

"There is very precise data about who, what and how chimps were used to make the culture to increase the amount of Polio vaccine available. The accusations have been furiously denied by those in the medical team involved at the time[†]. Because medical journals have refused to discuss these accusations openly, some

have accused Western scientific consensus of being a conspiracy to protect Western scientists, governments and companies[†]."
"But the Polio vaccine theory really does have many, many problems. The first is the connection between SIV and HIV. Yes the diseases are genetically very alike but they are not identical. Circumstantial evidence of chimp material in the culture does not prove anything. It makes mutation possible but does not prove it happened. The second is that polio vaccine was taken by drinking it. This would be a poor way to achieve high levels of HIV infections. HIV is destroyed by saliva and rarely infects via the digestive tract[†]. It is caught by injecting body fluids into people."
"To obscure this theory Western medical authorities proposed that HIV was created when African bush hunters ate chimps infected with SIV. This is another weak theory. Some ape SIV is 32,000 years old and so are the practices of African hunters. If HIV were a natural consequence of eating apes infected with SIV then HIV would be as ancient as the practice of hunting apes, but it isn't. It would also radiate out from its source of origin like all other spontaneously occurring African diseases. But Aids in Africa doesn't radiate out from Western Africa[†]. The telltale signs of Karposi's Sarcoma which accompany Aids were largely unknown in Central Africa before the 1980s[†]. They have come from the south. Aids' greatest prevalence radiates strongly from South Africa and it didn't really start being detected there until 1985[†]."
"I call this the 'why now?' problem. Why should HIV occur now and not five hundred years ago? The more I thought about the 'why now?' problem the less sense it made. It seemed to me that whenever the origin of Aids was discussed reasons were found to

blame the victims whether they were Africans or Gay men. And yet there were a few early cases in the 1960s and 70s that had most definitely come from the Congo area and spread to Cuba and further afield."

"I started to imagine a scenario. I imagined a criminal. An evil medical genius. A former Nazi who had gone to the Congo and started experimenting with tropical diseases. He discovers SIV and adapts it to form HIV. Then he tests it on people he meets. At first the disease is too deadly and kills the victims before they can spread it far. His work continues until the late 1970s when something allows him to get his latest copy of the disease into the Hepatitis B programme in Manhattan. The disease begins to spread. Then in the late seventies another version of the disease enters South Africa."

"My hypothesis was crazy but it matched all the known facts. Questioning my own sanity I began searching for a candidate who might match my description."

"I started with medical journals. The candidate would probably work for an academic institution so he would have to publish occasionally to maintain his cover. Otherwise he'd lose his standing and thus his role as a white in a black country. I imagined my man would publish only occasionally and with only one or two well known others. He was a loner but a well connected or well protected one."

"The candidate would have to have connections with both Belgian and American interests. Belgian to gain access to the Congo and SIV chimps and American to be close to the Hepatitis B campaign. If he was an ex-Nazi he might well have been given his ticket to freedom by the CIA as a useful expert. He would need a reputation as an expert in vaccines. That might mean Polio or Smallpox but ideally both. He would probably be fairly old. He would be very conservative. Probably Catholic or Calvinist."

"I carried out a brief search of all the Nazi doctors but only one met the criteria. Dr Klaus Hassler had been an expert in tropical diseases at the Robert Koch Institute. He had worked in Tanzania and Rawanda and Burundi before World War One. He was already retired when the Nazis came to power and offered him the opportunity to carry out experiments on prisoners at Dachau. He had leapt at the chance. He was executed in 1945."

"My search went back to those operating in Africa in the seventies. There were a lot of published names but working with my friends we sifted through them quickly. As I sharpened my picture of this character one figure began to meet the description better than all the others. Dr Claude Haine of the Catholic University of La Louviere in Belgium, one of the oldest universities in Europe and linked to the foundation of a predecessor of Virion Corporation in the 1950s. Haine had worked in DRC, Cameroon, Tanzania, Uganda and Rawanda and Burundi on the smallpox campaign. He had been based in Lumbumbashi near the Uranium mine in the southern DRC from 1955 until 1965."

"I wrote to the University and they told me Haine had left the University to work at the University of Johannesburg in South Africa. They sent a picture which I blew up. It looked oddly familiar. He was about fifty, a tall man, with glasses and blond hair, a moustache and a kind of overbearing look. There was a coldness too in his eyes as if he felt no real affection for anyone. Haine spent ten years in South Africa working in tropical medicine Research. Then suddenly in 1975 he left to return to La

Louviere University – something the university had not thought to mention. He stayed there for four more years and then died in a car crash. I had another dead end."

"The only way to progress was to pick up the strand by searching among the players who had worked on the Hepatitis B program in America. Many activists believed this vaccination programme had started HIV rolling[†]. But none of the doctors involved matched my criteria at all. I was disappointed but not surprised. While the homosexual community might want to blame something other than their own way of life, the fact was they were an easy target for any virus like HIV. Their way of life at the time would easily spread the virus very quickly[†]."

"But if it wasn't Hepatitis B what about a sexually transmitted disease clinic. I found a 1980 copy of the Manhatten telephone directory in the library and compared it to a 1990 one. The difference was a large ad for the Hathaway Clinic which seemed to promise rapid results and had lots of pictures of good looking men in it."

"I managed to find details about Dr Clayton Hathaway. He was American with a South African medical degree. He had a background in military medicine there and had supposedly worked with South African and Rhodesian special forces. He sounded an unusual person to be running a gay clinic in Manhattan. In 1983 the Hathaway clinic closed suddenly. I searched for Hathaway and found his name came up in the South African Truth and Reconciliation Commission's report on Project Coast."

"This was exactly what I was looking for."

"Project Coast was indeed the top secret South African Defence Force project to develop bioweapons that targeted black

Africans[†]. Most were poisons but a virus would be theoretically possible. Not everything added up because Aids is a slow killer. It wouldn't have saved the apartheid regime because political change in South Africa came faster than the disease spread. But I had followed my hunch and now here was the smoking gun. A man who spanned the Atlantic who met all my original list of qualities. He was conservative, trained, and connected to secret funding and research. Unfortunately all the Truth and Reconciliation Commission said was that Hathaway had worked for a South African company called Infratron. The firm did not last very long and by 1987 it had been closed leaving me with another dead end."

"Then something very odd happened. I finally got sent a picture of Hathaway back in the 1980s. It showed a man in his thirties, fit and well built, blond and moustached. But his cold blue eyes were all too familiar. I went back to my pictures. Hathaway, Haine, Hassler. It was undeniable. They were the same man! The only problem was he was getting *younger* not older. I couldn't believe it. I got some friends in the medical art community to draw a picture of Hathaway at 50 and 70, telling them I was on the trail of Nazi war criminal. The pictures I got back were of Haine and Hassler. I ran face recognition software. The results were a 97% probability of a match. Everyone I showed the evidence too agreed it was eerie but suggested they were related. According to the biographies that was impossible. They overlapped in time and were spread wide apart geographically."

"I had a suspect but no proof. What I needed was evidence that linked Hathaway-Haine-Hassler with the evolution of SIV to HIV through a programme of deliberate recombination. It seemed to me that as Hassler the project had been conceived. As Haine the technology refined, but as Hathaway the technology had been delivered. Haine and the Catholic University of La Louviere were the key."

"In 2001 I managed to gain a six month sabbatical to the University under the pretext of wishing to study the epidemiology of HIV/Aids. The University people were very helpful but I found most of the old records and samples now belonged to Virion Corporation. Try as a might there was no way I could get near the refrigerated vaults Virion stored its old material in – if indeed they still stored it."

"When I got back to St Petersburg I asked my old friends in GRU to access Virion. They told me that their security was not difficult. They cracked the Virion library and sent me a file of its contents. I was most interested in the items marked as secret or sensitive. Among these were a library of samples from Haine's work in the sixties and seventies. There was also a series titled AGS08 which was not only secret but inaccessible in the library if you didn't know it existed."

"Fortunately Virion's ordering system was fully automated. The security status of these samples was reset to normal. But in order to make sure suspicions were not unduly raised I got my friends to raise requests for samples to be sent to an old friend of mine – the virologist Gregori Kaspersky – based in Munich, Germany. He would onsend them to me. I explained I was doing some historical work hence the need for old samples."

"The plan worked perfectly. Within a week I had the samples I had requested. I immediately subjected them to intensive analysis. The comparison of the original SIV strain with the initial HIV strains soon yielded the sequence of recombination needed to make the new virus. Over a few months I compared all the samples to get a picture of trial and error used to develop the final weapon."

"By the end of 2003 I had a clear picture of the original recipe Haine had used and the variations he had added later as he had started trying to target the weapon more specifically.

Only one more thing intrigued me. What was AGS08? I searched the library but there was no answer. The samples obviously had the highest level of security. Even asking for them was impossible because they weren't officially there."

"I decided to sound out my friends back in intelligence. I suggested Virion might be in the biowar business. They were very interested and told me a solution may yet be available. Six months later I was told AGS08 had been recovered and had been analysed. It was not a virus or a vaccine but blood. The problem was it was close to human blood but was not human. Nor was it any known ape or monkey. I asked my friends for the sample. They told me it was security property. I pointed out that strange blood was no threat to security and should be studied. Finally when I agreed not to publish anything they let me have a little."

"The DNA I recovered from the cells in AGS08 is unlike anything I have ever seen before. Much of it is very like human DNA. But the structures normally associated with aging are completely different. In fact nobody I have ever shown them to has seen anything quite like them. I concluded it is, quite probably of extraterrestrial origin."

"Sadly my work is not widely accepted. Instead of aiding publication the Dean of Epidemiology demanded I see a psychologist. While I have been found to be sane I am regarded with a great deal of suspicion and treated badly by some childish colleagues. I cannot publish my findings in any reputable journals and nobody would believe any of the others. Before I met Dr Prosperov I was seriously considering writing a book expounding my theory in the hope it might sell at least to public. But there are so many books with crazy conspiracy theories I was reluctant to join their ranks."

"Worse, a month ago, Gregory Kaspersky vanished, and was found wandering a week later. The diagnosis was a stroke. I called his wife Sophie. She said he is confused and has lost control of his bowels. He can't remember that week. He also has terrible nightmares of people operating on his brain while he was fully conscious. I must confess I became very worried when I learned this."

"But now I find myself like Alice in Wonderland. I have followed Dr Prosperov down the hole and the strange world I have encountered since makes my story seem dull by comparison." Professor Cherensky paused.

"Ever since 1898 when HG Wells published his novel 'War of the Worlds', where Martian invaders are destroyed by Earth's bacteria, we have assumed our biosphere is a protective shield against invasion. What we have failed to recognise is that advanced civilisations would know how to use that shield against us. I have no idea what Claude Haine had in mind when he fashioned this disease but my greatest fear is that we are living through the beginning of a campaign that has only just begun."

Cherensky probably would have continued but Dr Prosperov started clapping and we all joined in. I got the feeling Prosperov was worried that Cherensky might say something he didn't want us to hear. Then the two Russians shook hands and Dr Prosperov spoke.

"Nobody more surprised and disturbed by Professor Cherensky's discovery than I. Obviously have been certain of extra-terrestrial interest in Earth for decades. However this attack is work of single operative. Whether rogue or under command is not known."

"Our friends have confirmed Cherensky hypothesis. This is a serious breach of an ancient interstellar Treaty against modification of pre-contact species. By using disease against those not immune this man and his associates are effectively selecting humanity in favour of those who have inherited immunity. Not all exposed to HIV will have delta-32 mutation, as some have random immunity but it can be seen that those with Delta-32 will have a better racial capacity to live and reproduce than other races. In this way the Nazi programme has survived."

"Allowing such a thing to occur has fundamentally changed the terms of the Fae's engagement with the Galactic Administration. The Fae do not believe this could happen by accident. They cannot believe this attack on our species could be the result of individuals without official sanction. Queen Morganne, Isis and Horne believe this signals the end of any possible peace with the Center. The Fae policy of live and let live with the Center is over."

"For we of Earth Aids remains a silent long lasting killer. Is first human epidemic discriminating in favour of one race over another. Others may follow[†]. So far HIV/Aids has killed 25 milion people and continues to spread every day, helped by people who have forgotten the danger[†]."

"Part of our mission must be to assist work to identify Haine and any associates but also to stop development of other bioweapons. Must recognise that where bioweapons are concerned conspiracy is inevitable[†]. Must also recognise that Cherensky hypothesis has shown our world has been infiltrated by at least one other-worldly agent who lives and works among us, with objectives hostile to humanity."

"My opinion is humanity has enough problems with own stupidity without alien help. Therefore new mission objective in addition to assisting future leaders must be to remove this and any other infiltrators."

"We will work with friends to ensure our operatives have best possible equipment and support to this end. Queen Morganne has already obtained support for additional resources for us. These will be used for original and new mission. We have also established contact with network who assisted Professor Cherensky and have understanding for mutual assistance."

"Finally cannot stress enough importance of secrecy and security. Our friends believe enemies are ruthless and intelligent. Only defence is hiding. If found we must evacuate immediately. Hekator insists we begin frequent evacuation practice. Will implement alarm system. Recommend all staff keep evacuation bag of special keepsakes ready. Plan to be distributed later."

The dinner ended and everyone fell to talking and clearing up. Scotty and Ashley were shocked by Professor Cherensky's story. The idea that the disease that had killed Scotty's father or Ashley's aunt was made by some evil person rather than being a freak of nature was too horrible to think about. How could anyone spend ten years perfecting a way of causing years of suffering, pain and heartbreak. And yet there was Cherensky himself. He too admitted to having done exactly the same thing. And in Renwick House you didn't have to wait long to see some ghost of the horror of the Spanish Flu after the First World War to realise that death and suffering was what war is. That was what lasted.

I thought about Jeanne that night. I wondered what it was like to be in that place without a magic suit that could whisk you away, or make you invisible, or fire bolts of lightning. To just be a thirteen-year-old girl in a place where kids were shot around you every day. Where neighbours were burned alive in churches. Where little boys asking for their sisters back were shot dead with as little thought as if turning off the TV.

What could you hope for? What could you plan? Living with only pain, cruelty and fear all the time. It made me feel so grateful for Grandpop and Aunty Liz. Then suddenly I was on a hill, under a tree at night. At the foot of a tree was a village made of huts each with a little light in it. The village was enormous and stretched all the way to the horizon with millions and millions of huts. And in each hut a mother was singing a lullaby to a baby, and a father was playing with the children in the bath. Then there different sounds. Shooting. Screams. Shouts and cruel laughter. And fires were starting. Fires were breaking out in patches all over the place. But what was weird was that the people in the homes not on fire seemed to ignore what was going on around them. They kept singing and playing while the house next door burned and people screamed.

I had a bucket of water. Just one tiny bucket to deal to all the fires around me. Then Ax came up the hill with a burning torch in his hand. He was about twelve foot tall and the ground shook with each step. He was covered in soot and blood. He looked at my bucket and walked on, roaring with laughter. Then I woke up.

## CHAP†ER F⊖R†Y ₴IGH†: THE HI† ⅢAN

So are you saying Aids is a *bioweapon*?" Sue asks doubtfully. We've been swimming around a warm pool among a lot of plants and fish, and some animals like small otters who just ignore us. It's bright as day inside the Fae quarantine station, but the roof from which the light and warmth poured in is too low, and you still just want to bust out and run away. The headache and general tiredness that has set in on me since I woke up keeps me in a small hot pool. Sue, however, swims around energetically, obviously enjoying a holiday from her normal routine. We'd made clothes out of a robe to avoid being embarrassed with one another. We both have skirts and she has a top of sorts tied around her chest. I've been streaming my memories directly to Sue via the telepathic link. These are the first words she's spoken in hours.

"Pretty much," I reply.

"A weapon to ... wipe us all out?" she asks, looking at me with a doubtful expression from where she stands in the water.

"No, a weapon to pick survivors by race."

"But that's ... that's totally racist!" she replies shaking her head in bewilderment. I laugh.

"You think?" I reply, sarcastically.

But she's still uncertain.

"But it can't work can it?"

"Why not? Genetic weapons can be made to target just *one* person but it's just been too advanced for us to think about until now. And because we assume we are the most intelligent beings on Earth we assume it never occurred to anyone else."

"And I thought human beings were evil."

I smile, "Oh we *are* evil alright. No doubt about that. But we just aren't the *only* ones who can be evil."

"I suppose you're right. There's no reason we should have a monopoly on being evil in the universe."

"What's unbelievable about HIV is that nobody wants to think about it. It's like the whole world has sort of gone 'eeww' and they won't look at a disease they don't want to catch; as if talking about it will encourage it or something. It hasn't stopped. It isn't cured." I say.

"But ... if what you're saying is right, and they are trying to wipe us all out, won't the latest anti-Aids drugs stop that?" she asks.

"Well, they would if everyone could get them, but for people living in the poorest parts of Africa on a dollar a day or less, those drugs are just not available†. So they protect rich, mostly white people and Aids goes on spreading among poor, mostly black people. Hekator says the obvious problem with our world is that we haven't worked out that diseases which gain strength killing the poorest people, still breed and strengthen to kill the richest. Genetics doesn't care about how rich you are. Professor Cherensky thought the whole idea of trying to make money out of stopping Aids was dangerous because it means not treating those who can't afford it. Aids doesn't care, it spreads wherever we let it. Every naturally immune person the virus encounters just makes it stronger – like the other diseases they're working with."

"Other diseases?"

"Why do you think they'd stop with Aids?"

"Who is this they?"

"Hathaway and his friends."

"Why do they want to do this?" Sue asks wiping water out of her eyes, while I sit and suffer.

"Hekator and Dr Prosperov think that it's a plan by a group of alien infiltrators who have lived among us for centuries, maybe even thousands of years. The Fae call them 'the watchers'. But they stopped watching and started ruling us indirectly. They think they had Eastern Europe under their control but when revolutions started happening and peoples started rising, well, they didn't like that."

Sue stands up. The pool isn't that deep. It covers her up to her tummy.

"How many are there?" she asks.

"We don't really know, but there may be hundreds, or hundreds of thousands. They also don't agree with each other. We found that out too. There are very different groups. Rocelli, who you met is in Die Bruderschaft along with Hathaway. They are the most vicious. We think they arrived the latest, around the early 1900s, and adopted the Nazis later. They are still into ethnic cleansing and are trying to find ways of encouraging it."

"What for?"

"They need our blood. Stem cells and blood. They can't reproduce naturally like ordinary creatures. They've wrecked themselves genetically extending their lives. There's something about blood that helps them make their babies. That's what Mr Ceder told me."

"Eeeew that's ... creepy," Sue says, lying back and floating on her back.

"Yeah," I agree.

"But ... how do they manage to stay hidden?" Sue asks.

"They stay hidden because they have amazing mind control powers. Very dangerous. The only reason you got away from Rocelli was he was taken by surprise. He thought he didn't need to work too hard, otherwise you would never have been able to get out that door."

"They don't try to rule us directly. They put ordinary humans in positions of power and take the background jobs. They have families with us to but they are really only interested in other infiltrators. They are bad parents to humans. They substitute themselves into families – as adults usually – and they fake their deaths with the bodies of those they substitute. They usually move among the rich and powerful, or they help others build themselves into positions of power."

Sue rolls over, dives down and swims underwater over to me, sliding over onto a nearby rock.

"So these infiltrators? They're sort of like viruses themselves then? Infecting our governments and organisations?" she suggests, settling into another hot pool.

"Yeah ... I guess ... that's *is* what they're like." I nod, not having thought of it like that before.

"But how do you fight that? They have all our own laws and governments behind them?"

"Well, it is hard. You have to expose them to human politics and make it impossible for them to continue. A bit like you embarrassed Rocelli into leaving your house. Or you have to expose them to Center politics. If that happens the Service comes to get them. The Center has taken out quite a few infiltrators in the past."

"How can they be a threat to the Center?"

"That's the hard part. But you have to remember the Center thinks differently to us. They have their own rules. One of them is the treaty which is meant to protect pre-contact civilisations from interference until certain conditions are met."

"But with these infiltrators here they can't claim that at all!"

"Well, the Center pretends that the infiltrators don't exist. It's like Cherensky in the Cold War. In theory biowarfare was banned under the Geneva Convention. In practice they were all doing it. It's only when things become too obvious and too embarrassing that anything happens. World War Two was pretty embarrassing for them. The Service took out quite a few Bruderschaft who had taken a leading role in that."

"How do they take them out?"

"A big shiny flying saucer comes to get them."

"But we would ... Oh, OK, so we *do* see them?"

"Sure. They don't care. Especially the Service. They don't give a shit whether anyone sees them or not. The Belgian Air Force tracked two UFOs on radar, then scrambled jets to intercept in March 1990 while two and half thousand people watched on[†]. Of course it was like sending a war canoe to attack a nuclear submarine, more annoying than anything, but what it does show is that human governments do respond to flying saucers. Normally not so publicly but they all do it. *They* just make sure we have no political connection with *them*. *They* don't talk to us, so we don't try to talk with *them*. Anyone who tries to talk to aliens gets laughed at, because you look pretty stupid waiting by the phone for someone who isn't going to call."

"Yeah ... you sure do," Sue agrees, thinking of Rachel.

I say nothing, letting her think that one through. Then she looks back at me.

"OK these infiltrators? *Did* a big shiny saucer come and pick them up?" Sue asks.

"Yep, they did."

"So what happened?"

"Well heaps really. We got *them* to pick up the Brudershaft."

"How?"

"Well, pretty much by exposing Hathaway. That's probably why the Bruderschaft came back to wipe us out which is why I'm waiting for everyone to tell me where Ka-rea-rea fits in with the plan to rescue Sian. The plan will involve tricking them into thinking I'm going to blunder into the rescue."

"Are you in any condition to do that? You look awful."

"It's the genetic engineering. It's always like this."

"What!?" Sue squawks.

"They've given me something again," I sigh. "I don't know what, but it's the only way I'd be sick here when you aren't."

"That's awful! They can't do that! They shouldn't just be able to do stuff to you without permission!" Sue says angrily, sitting up.

"Oh, I did give permission. Ages ago. It's part of a long term development programme they have for us. Enhances our powers. The idea is to make us less reliant on their technology."

Sue sits back.

"Oh! ... oh well, I'll shut up then."

"I like it that you stick up for me though," I add.

"Well. To be honest, I'm only here because of you. By myself I couldn't cope with any of this, I'd be terrified."

That doesn't sound right.

"You didn't look so terrified perving at that nurse who met us."

"No ... well," she starts shyly. She smiles, at me. She knows she's been caught out.

"OK, you're right. Now I know what you mean about that girl, Tabika. There is something really sexy and attractive about these people. Even Hekator, and I don't usually ... well, you know. It's like a kind of yearning you can't quite put your finger on."

She thinks for a moment, then adds, "are the infiltrators the same?"

"Hell no! In fact there's something deeply repulsive about them even though some look like supermodels. You learn to recognise it after a while. They try to use pheremones and mind control, but deep down there's something cold and ugly about them. Just like Father Rocelli."

"Do you think that's why you fight them? Because they're ugly?"

"They feel cold and ugly because they do cold and ugly things. It's hard to like mass murderers."

"I only met ordinary murderers. But they weren't likeable either."

Sue sits down and gets comfortable.

"What happens after this wait is over?" she asks.

"I guess we go to the new base and you get to meet Dr Prosperov."

"When does that happen?"

"I dunno. Maybe I should call in?"

"Will they be awake?"

"I dunno, let's find out."

I call the others.

"*Sam?*" Ashley replies.

"*What's happening. Why hasn't anyone called?*"

"*Oh, we thought you were asleep.*"

"*Me? I thought you were!*"

"*Us? No way! We've been up for hours.*"

"*What are you doing?*"

"*We're staking out Von Streicher's location from that RSS feed para.no.ID sent you.*"

"*To rescue Sir Michael's daughter from Von Streicher?*"

"*Yeah. Turns out it's in a town called Belzer in Lichtenstein in the Alps. It's in the Rhine valley and quite busy. I'm lookout in the Swiss Alps to the west. Cam's in Lichtenstein on the other side of the valley to the east closer in. The others are moving in. It's raining, so I hope you're all tucked up, snug and warm, because it's pretty damn miserable here.*"

"*Do you need Ka-rea-rea yet?*"

"*I don't know,*" Ashley says, but gets interrupted.

"Sam it would probably help if Ka-rea-rea did a low level, high speed, visible pass on inertialess to establish you are around," Grandpop tells me.

"*Cool!*" I say, glad to be useful.

"Sorry Sue, I've just got to watch over Ka-rea-rea."

She shrugs.

I close my eyes and wake up Ka-rea-rea. He takes off and we thread through the mountains and over the alpine lakes towards Lichtenstein. It's a fun place to fly. Ka-rea-rea flashes silently over the reference coordinates at five kilometers altitude at about Mach four. The town below looks very pretty. The site is a castle on a small hill on the side of a big valley. There's a town below it while the mountains rear up behind it.

I zoom Ka-rea-rea down the valley then drop out of inertialess and warp light around him to become invisible. I navigate back up the valley, getting closer to the castle, looking around for a place to land but its all too busy. I decide to zip up and join Cam instead.

I land next to her under an overhang on a ledge high above the valley.

"*You know Cam could be me,*" I suggest to everyone. "*I mean if I was here by myself I might get out and look around.*"

"*You'd wait for night to get Ka-rea-rea up close and that's another four hours away. Why don't you wait til then?*" Tarik points out.

"*Yeah OK. I just feel a bit useless sitting around in quarantine.*"

"*How do you think we felt leaving you all by yourself. Relax, you've done enough. Let us find Von Streicher's trap,*" Scotty tells me.

"*OK then. I'll put Ka-rea-rea back to sleep again.*"

I open my eyes. Sue does too.

"Did you get all that?" I ask Sue.

"Yeah. You guys have worked together for a while haven't you?"

"Yeah."

"It shows."

There was a pause.

"So what happened after Professor Cherensky's visit then?"

"Oh then it got pretty hairy," I tell her and continue on telling her about the evil bastards who are our enemies.

•••

Professor Cherensky did not stay long. He went back to Russia via India. What he didn't know was that we had bugged him the same way we had bugged Jeanne and Diana. Dr Prosperov was nervous about Cherensky, who he regarded as a valuable ally but also a dangerous security risk. He knew about both Morozov's network and our contact with the Fae.

Hekator showed up to the briefing just before he left to tell us about Fae memory modification. He said that for memory over a few minutes it was necessary to use viruses because the data had been committed to permanent biochemical storage. Their preference was for complete amnesia. Wiping all memories for a period was simpler and couldn't be broken. The links between Cherensky and para.no.ID however meant confusion was needed.

The Fae had given Cherensky a virus to attack particular memories. The main memories they wanted to change were of themselves, and who he had visited in New Zealand.

The Russians, Dr P and Dr M, were to become Mr and Mrs Popperwell and the Fae were to become colleagues at Auckland University. Renwick House became a house in Auckland. We kids and everyone else were to be simply deleted.

Unfortunately the virus would also make Professor Cherensky quite ill and we had to make sure he was alright. To do that, they said, we would have to help him after returned.

Hekator also told us we had a new weapon.

"We've tweaked your beams a bit to give you a short term amnesia weapon. What it basically does is interrupt the cortex and make people forget what they are doing. To use it you need eye contact. The laser tickles the optic nerve quickly and is very short range. No more than ten meters. You can however treat up to ten targets in less than a second. The effect is like a sudden headache with spots before the eye. It will make them close their eyes and lose balance for a second. It has a very short time effect – no more than two minutes. All they will do is lose track. They won't forget anything in long term memory. If they have been interacting with you for longer than two minutes they will have to think to remember who you are and what you've just been talking about. We think it will be useful when bending into places with witnesses. It will also help you with Professor Cherensky, although as the memory modification virus takes effect, he won't remember much anyway.

It turned out that was an understatement. Cherensky was OK flying home but within a day of arriving back he was in a pretty bad way. He crawled into bed and fell into a fever. For two days we appeared twice a day to make sure he had heating, water and food. He was delirious and would stare at us without seeing. It made you feel kinda stink to know we had done this to him.

It didn't help that it was getting colder. St Petersburg in winter is bloody cold. Outside things would stick to metal and the skies were gray and hard. In addition to the bugs inside Professor Cherensky's body we added bugs and cameras to his apartment and crappy old Gaz car. Dr Prosperov wanted Control to watch him closely.

Meanwhile the Fae – except for Raman – returned home. Hekator said he would be back soon with Hekati and some new equipment we needed. It made us feel good that the Fae were now much more staunchly on our side. They wanted us to find out lots more about Hathaway and his links, if any, to the Administration.

Raman stayed to help Dr Prosperov with his forecasting. Two more kids were becoming clearer. Sarah Kogan lived well in Haifa, Israel. She was about fifteen and of Ukrainian descent. There had been Qassam rockets falling in Haifa last year but she was in no special danger yet.

**171**

We all felt bad about Jeanne. We knew she had been in the fighting around Rutshuru that had been so intense. She had been constantly scared, hungry and sleep deprived. She knew her own side would beat her and abuse her. But the Mai-Mai she helped fight against would be twice as bad and try and kill her as well. Luckily for her, her side, the Rawandan backed CNDP, were winning. They were even driving back the Monuc UN force. We knew from the radio traffic that the CNDP commander, General Laurent Nkunda, wanted to make sure he had the strongest possible negotiating position before peace talks started.

In the meantime Hekator had sent some pills for us through the lighthouse transporter. The pills were to help us recover from sleep disruption. They really worked too. To test them out Grandpop woke us up at one in the morning and sent us to Paris. We had to wait in the jumpstation for a while then Control put us down inside an empty lift as it headed for ground the floor. We ran out the door, past an annoyed woman at the door, and out into a cold rainy Monday afternoon in the French capital.

We did a bit of tour with Tahira leading the way. Any French person suggesting we should be in school got an earful from Tahira. It was the first time I'd been anywhere famous during the day so everything was new. The cars, all so French, with interesting colours, parked bumper to bumper. The ironwork, the busy streets and the dog crap that seemed to follow me around. The only real danger was all of us, except Tahira and Ashley, kept looking the wrong way when we went to cross the road. We only stayed for an hour, then found a quiet doorway to step into and vanish. By three we were back in our beds. The next morning the alarm went off and Aunt Liz forced me out of bed. I just didn't want to get up. But I took the pill Grandpop had given us the night before and staggered down to breakfast. We all looked terrible. But by the time we got on the bus we were starting to feel better and when we arrived at school we felt like walking around Paris in the rain that night had just been a rather nice dream.

At school Mr Wakefield was slowly giving up for the year as summer was showing signs of coming early. Homework had stopped and we were doing a lot more sports and trips around the island. We were already on summer time and the evenings were getting lighter and longer. Now it was still light at eight but on the other side of the world it was getting steadily darker. Professor Cherensky recovered from his virus but became a bit odd. He was talking to himself more, and laughing for no apparent reason. Then suddenly he had a pistol which he fiddled with a lot, while looking through his blinds. Dr Prosperov was very concerned as it seemed Cherensky was sleeping badly.

It was a Wednesday a few weeks before the breakup of school for the summer holidays, when we were picked up, not by Mariko in Betty, but by Ken in his van.

"Guys gotta be real quick today. You're needed pronto," he called as we ambled out the front gate. We ran to pile in and I noticed Emma saw what was going on. Ken slammed the doors and took off fast before we'd even buckled up.

"Gotta get back fast. Professor Cherensky's been grabbed!" he told us, "Check the video."

He tossed us an MP4 player.

The video from Control's bugs showed Professor Cherensky in

bed at night, get up and take his pistol from his bedside drawer, then sneak over to the main door of his apartment and hide in an ambush position he had made with his furniture earlier. The door opened slightly and a bald, thin, white man slipped through, looked around briefly, and moved quietly towards Cherensky's bedroom. Another bigger man with a beard slipped in after him. There was the unmistakable click of a gun being cocked and Professor Cherensky gave a command in Russian and the two men froze, putting their hands up. Cherensky turned on the light and gave another command and the men knelt down with their backs to him putting their hands behind their heads. Then he came out from behind his ambush position and started questioning the men.

This was where it went wrong. Cherensky drew up a chair with his back to the door and then started questioning his prisoners. The men were mumbling and he didn't see a third, tall, slender man, wearing a cap, push the door open silently, and come up behind him.

It was like a movie except you knew the person involved. The man in the cap simply put his hand on Cherensky's neck and his head lolled sideways. The two men kneeling looked around smiling. They stopped smiling at once as the man in the cap spat orders at them in harsh Russian and they scampered at once for the bedroom while their rescuer disarmed Cherensky's automatic and looked around. It was at this moment he looked briefly directly up into the camera and the video froze. The man's face was clipped from the picture and placed between a face labelled Claude Haine and another named Clayton Hathaway. He was tall and lean, like a sports teacher, with a reddish face and blond hair with a moustache. He had aged about

ten years on the Hathaway picture so he was halfway in age
between the Haine and Hathaway. His blue eyes were the
same cold instruments of measurement they had always been.
The video restarted and Hathaway idly twisted the seat from
under Cherensky tipping him onto the floor. Cherensky was no
lightweight so it was obvious Hathaway was incredibly strong.
The other two emerged with bedding and began to wrap
Cherensky in it. Hathaway didn't even look at them. He walked
with complete confidence to the fridge and opened it. Putting
aside some food he pulled out Cherensky's prized samples. Then
he unfolded a supermarket cooler bag and put them in.
The big man had Cherensky over his shoulder and carried him
out to the lifts. Hathaway waved the big man on to the lift, but
returned with the bald man to Cherensky's apartment. They
searched the apartment and finally found Cherensky's passport,
which Hathaway pocketed, then they put the quilt back on the
bed. Hathaway took out a cigarette, and casually lit it with a
silver lighter. He took a few puffs on it and then suddenly leapt
at the bald man near him pinning his throat against the wall
with one hand.
The man tried to break Hathaway's hold and kick at him but he
couldn't reach. Hathaway was holding him there looking at him,
smoking away. It was hard to watch and Ashley couldn't. Then
Hathaway did that grip he'd done on Cherensky and the bald
man slumped.
With amazing strength Hathaway snatched him off the wall
and tossed him like rag doll onto the bed like he weighed
nothing. Still puffing on his cigarette Hathaway pulled off
his shoes and pulled the quilt over him as if tucking him into
bed. He put Cherensky's gun back in the bedside table then

he carefully applied the cigarette to the cheap nylon quilt. Immediately it began to blacken, then smoke, and finally flame. Hathaway watched it as it caught on fire, and then casually made a cellphone call, walking away from the thickening smoke, speaking in French.

Then he walked out the apartment door, pulling the door closed and picking up his samples on the way. The last shots showed the bed burning fiercely and thick smoke filling the flat. Then the video reached the end.

We looked at each other. It was fairly sickening to realise we'd just witnessed a murder and kidnapping. He had used his own man as a decoy body to make it look as if Cherensky had died from a fire caused by smoking in bed. He'd even left him alive in the flames. It was also scary to realise that the guy we had to rescue Cherensky from was obviously a pitiless killer who moved like a professional. Our mood in the back of the van as we twisted down the hill behind Renwick was quiet, and frankly worried.

We were straight into the cellar and in our suits in the briefing room in no time at all. Grandpop and Drs Morozov and Prosperov were waiting for us.

The holoscreen was showing Professor Cherensky in the back of a van tied inside a blanket unconscious. The van was being driven along a motorway at night by the big bearded man with Hathaway in the passenger seat.

We looked through the windscreen. There was a fair amount of traffic on the wide motorway. The landscape was full of tall, dark pines and dark shiny lakes with low curling mist that sometimes crept out onto the road.

Dr Prosperov began.

"Appears kidnappers taking Cherensky to Finland on route A-127. Expect already have arrangement at border. Lappeenranta airport has a connecting flight to Brussels. Mission is simple. Must recover Cherensky and get him to safety.

Then Grandpop took over.

"Our plan is pretty simple too. We're putting you down beside the road around here."

The holoscreen showed a long stretch of road ending in a tight bend around a pine edged lake.

"Sam and Tahira wait here to flash blind the driver on the corner. The van will leave the road here and smash into the roadside barrier. It will probably go through and with luck hit a tree. The two in the front will probably be hurt, possibly killed. Ashley and Scotty are to zap anyone who gets out. Tarik and Cam cross the road – without getting hit because there is a lot of truck traffic – and get Cherensky out of the back. Sam and Tahira cover the others. The idea is to make is look like an accident. Sound OK?"

Nobody had any objections so we bent out of there.

**[+]**

The road Tahira and I arrived next to was quite big. We were on the right side in the dark under the pine trees with fog thickening around us. Some ghostly soldiers were watching us from the mist. Immediately I knew we had a problem. Although it was five in the morning there was a lot of truck traffic and the glare of the oncoming headlights made it impossible to see the driver behind them. I called Grandpop.

*"There's no way we will be able to recognise this van. And zapping the driver isn't going to be easy either,"* I told him as a truck roared past

"We'll mark the van for you. It's ... five minutes away now. You'll just have to rely on thermal to target the driver."

That was all very well if we were shooting the guy. The target would be the whole body. But he wanted us to hit the eyes of someone we couldn't see moving at 100km/h towards us behind a sloped windscreen. Another truck appeared at the end of the straight.

"*Let's try and at least put a low power beam on this guy,*" I suggested to Tahira.

We went for the lowest power but by the time the truck had roared past there was no sign we had done anything. Then we heard the truck driver put out a warning over the CB radio that there were some kids on the side of the road with a laser and that anyone who could spare the time should give them a thrashing. There was some angry agreement broadcast back. Now all the truck drivers were looking out for us! What a fail! Fortunately, of course the rental van didn't have CB so they wouldn't be warned.

"*We should be on the opposite side of road to get clear shot on the driver's side,*" Tahira said.

"*You go. I'll try this side,*" I told her.

I watched her dart over the road to the left side. In fact I had another plan. I told my suit to set bending to automatic targeted at our original landing point. I switched my colours to ordinary jacket and jeans.

"*Van in sight!*" Tahira announced.

I got myself ready. My heart was beating a bit now.

"*One hundred meters.*"

"*Fifty.*"

I had less than two seconds. Heart hammering I broke and ran out from the right onto the road right in front of the van. The headlights were bright. I put my hands out instinctively to stop it as the van's brakes began squealing and it tried to swerve left to avoid me.

"*Sam!*" Tahira screamed.

Tahira swept the windscreen with a powerful beam. The suit bent me out automatically as I'd told it to do.

## [+]

For a moment as I passed through the realm of presences it occurred to me that if the van had hit me I might be here permanently. Then the world came back in a blaze of light. I heard a violent 'crump' in the distance but it was the ghostly pair of eyes I was looking at now that had my full attention.

There were a small group of Finnish soldiers dressed in heavy coats and armed with small machine guns. They grinned at me and said when they had fought Russian tanks in 1939 they had run *behind* them. I didn't really have time for this so I ran back up the road.

The van had swerved hard left to avoid me and rolled, driven by its high speed, over on its right side twice and then smashed into the left roadside barrier at the tight left hand bend. It had come to rest back on its wheels, lights out, with most of its glass shattered like ice.

"Sam, that was crazy!" Grandpop shouted, almost as Tahira saw me and started shouting at me too.

"*You wanted them stopped. The flash was never going to be enough. He had to swerve to lose control so he swerved,*" I replied as we closed with the wrecked vehicle.

"*We're going to be seen by traffic so we need to look natural,*" Scotty warned as he and Ashley approached the van on the right

**179**

side. He opened his facescreen and his breath came in small clouds. There was a sudden eruption of Russian swearwords from the driver's side on the left. Tarik and Cam were nearest on the other side of the road. The driver's door opened.

The big Russian had slid out of his seat and collapsed onto the road. I was coming up behind the van as Ashley was approaching it on the right side, hidden from any potential traffic. Tahira was coming up behind Tarik and Cam on the left looking at the big driver, they too opened their facescreens, their breath clouds of vapour. The driver tried to yell at them but was obviously in too much pain to keep it up.

Scotty was covering the right passenger door where Hathaway was slumped having taken most of the violence of the rollover. Ashley opened her face screen and tried to slide the side door behind him open as I got to the rear and opened my facescreen. "*The door's jammed,*" she told us.

I got to the back door. It was locked, so I fitted my omnikey to the lock as Ashley turned to join Scott at the front. As I opened the rear door Scotty carefully pulled open the passenger's door. There was a loud bang. We all jumped. Ashley screamed – which was very loud. I looked along the side of the van. Scotty was down on his back his facescreen covering him up. There was a second loud bang. Then Hathaway fell forward out of the door, face down.

"*Got him,*" Tarik said from the other side of the van. He'd zapped him through the cab.

Scotty folded into nothing. Ashley ran up to the unconscious Hathaway and kicked him as hard as she could in the side screaming and swearing at him. She kicked him again and was about to kick him in the head when she too folded away.

There was a torrent of swearing in Russian from the driver which ended suddenly.

"*You can shut up as well,*" Tarik added, as he did.

"Scotty will be OK. The suit stopped the bullet. Check on Cherensky!" Grandpop yelled.

I went back to the back of the van where Cam had already climbed in. Cherensky was unconscious with a bleeding – probably broken – nose. We cut the ropes he was tied in. A bright light lit up the back of the van and with a deep roar this big truck came to an abrupt halt behind us. Its brakes made a loud hissing sound. Tarik and Tahira were behind us. Cherensky was breathing – just.

"What's happening here? What are you doing?" The truck driver shouted from behind the glare of his headlights, half getting out of his high cab.

"Call police. Call ambulance. Is kidnapping," Tahira yelled back in Russian.

We dragged Cherensky, who had been thrown around and was covered in blood, to the edge of the van. He coughed suddenly and blood spurted from his mouth. That didn't look good. Cam turned his head so it drained away. More soldier ghosts were gathering around us, out of the mist. They seemed to find it all very interesting.

There was another bright light behind us and another truck drew up. The arrival of the second truck seemed to make the first driver feel a bit braver and he got out of his cab and met up with the other one.

"*Let's get the other two around to the back. Otherwise they could trap us in the van,*" Tarik suggested so we hopped out of the van as the two Russian truck drivers came up. The

**181**

newcomer inspected Professor Cherensky as the first driver followed Tarik and Cam around to the big Russian asking them questions, their breath lit up in the headlights.

"Where do you live?"

"Here," replied Cam.

"How did you get here,"

"We're always here," Tarik answered copying Cam.

"It's five in the morning."

"Yes."

Tahira and I went to get Hathaway. He was sprawled on the ground by the door. I grabbed his pistol, and pushed the safety down and pocketed it. Tahira grabbed his legs. We realised then that his right leg was broken as it flopped. I grabbed his arms and we picked him up and carried him around to the back of the van in the glare of the truck headlights. The first truck driver was returning from his cab with a silver blanket. We shoved Hathaway into the back of the van next to Cherensky. The first truck driver was having much more difficulty moving the big Russian. We helped him shove him in the back as well. Then we helped wrap Cherensky in the silver sheet. He was still in his pyjamas and it was below zero now.

"*How's Scotty?*" Tahira asked.

"He's got two big bruises and cracked ribs. He was just winded." Grandpop told us. "They are making a big fuss over him upstairs."

"*How do we make sure Cherensky's safe?*" Tarik asked.

"His breathing is very shallow and his blood pressure is very weak. He needs to get to a hospital as soon as he can," Grandpop warned us.

"This man needs hospital," Tarik said for the truck drivers to hear. "Others criminals. Need police."

We had to face away from them so they couldn't see we didn't speak with our mouths.

The drivers inspected the three again and conferred.

"Russian hospital no good. Finnish hospital better. If he can pay I take him to Finland," the first driver said. He was small with a cunning looking face.

"Tell him he can pay, that he's rich," Grandpop advised.

"He is rich man. These kidnappers." Tarik told the driver.

"How do *you* know?" the other truck driver asked. He was taller and more doubtful.

"Tied up in back. Too old to be gangster. Why else? We cannot take him," Cam said.

"He might die anyway," the second driver said.

"I'll do it," the first one announced. He looked like he was calculating the angles.

The second driver looked at the first and shrugged.

"What do we do with them?" he asked of the other two.

"Do what you like," the first driver suggested.

"Help me with the injured one," the first driver half ordered us. We carried Cherensky to the truck's cab. He wasn't well. His breath was rasping. We propped him up as well as we could in the truck, while the other driver, seeing no profit in calling the Police or staying drove off.

Finally when Cherensky was as well looked after as could be expected. The other driver took off as well, leaving us in the dark. We looked back at the van and noticed Hathaway was gone.

"*Watch out he's dangerous,*" Tarik warned unnecessarily.

We searched the forest for a short distance but the van was

attracting attention. We heard sirens and as there was no sign of
him we came home.

[+]

Back at base I gave the pistol to Grandpop. He sniffed as he
inspected it.

"FN five seven. Nasty little buggers these. They can penetrate
Kevlar armour at 100 meters. Serious gun for killing people.
Shows you how good your suits are."

Grandpop removed the magazine and cleared the chamber.

"Give it to Scotty. It'll make a good souvenir," he said.

"Was Scotty's suit damaged?" We wanted to know.

"Control?" Grandpop called over his shoulder.

Control appeared.

"Scotty's suit suffered internal bruising and bleeding. The skin
was scratched but the integrity of the adamantine lattice was
unaffected. Fortunately the first projectile struck the armoured
power link and was deflected. The second struck the upper left
chest and also deflected, impacting the left arm."

"Where would he have been hit without the suit?" Grandpop
asked.

"Upper lung and through the Aorta. Mortality would have been
certain."

It was the first time someone had really tried to kill one of us.
It made you think as we got changed. Mostly we thought we
regretted not shooting Hathaway ourselves – though in reality
we knew we hadn't because we couldn't.

We went upstairs to see Scotty. Ashley was hovering around Zoe
who was sitting with him. He showed us his big purple bruises.
He appreciated being given the gun too. The changer's scanner
said his ribs were cracked but not broken. The two nurses would

bandage him up for night. We asked him what had happened.
"He was slumped against the door, not moving, he seemed to be out to it. So I pulled the door open and saw he had the gun in his left hand pointing at me. Then he opened his eyes, looked at me, and winked. Then he shot me."

"He *winked*?" I asked. We were all shocked.

"Yeah, he winked, like it was all some sort of game. I was lifted off my feet and thrown back. I noticed a flash from me, as well, when the gun fired, so I think the suit did something. Anyway, I got thrown and landed on my back. I was winded. He must have been hurt because he swivelled in his seat and took a while to aim with his left hand. Then he fired again. That one hurt more and stung my arm. I was just about to zap him when he collapsed. Thanks for that mate," he said to Tarik.

"No problem," Tarik said modestly.

But, of course, it was a problem. Scotty wasn't going to be able to go on any missions for a while and certainly not physical ones like we might expect if Jeanne tried to escape. Also he was probably going to have to be off school too.

We had dinner and played a few board games with Scotty when at nine o'clock Grandpop put his head in. He came up to us looking a bit withdrawn.

"Guys, I'm afraid I have some bad news," he began.

"Professor Cherensky died before he reached hospital. It was combination of injuries, age and the drugs Hathaway used to sedate him."

Grandpop sucked a bit on his teeth, then added, "I'm afraid we may have killed him."

It was like a cold shock went among us. We all felt awful. We'd meant to rescue him and the crash we'd used to rescue him had ended up killing him. I kept thinking of stupid excuses and realising as I made them to myself they only made it worse.

It was our biggest, worst mistake yet. It was horrible. I felt horrible. It was so awful for poor Professor Cherensky and yet I was going to laugh. I remember looking at Ashley. We both felt so bad and so guilty but the tension became unbearable. And then we were laughing. We were all laughing like this was the worst joke on us in the world. It went on and on until finally like balloons that had stopped farting around a room we just stopped.

I felt bad for laughing but if I tried to be serious it just made it worse. Gunter called it 'schadenfreude', the joy at other's misfortune. He said it was common enough to have a name. But it still made us feel guilty. Finally we all called it a night and went to bed. I don't remember my dreams from that night exactly but I had a pistol in my hand and it kept going off and killing people and I felt so embarrassed.

We spent all the next day at school feeling down. We couldn't talk about it, of course, not even in the bus because we didn't want Rewa and Asal to listen in. So it wasn't until we went downstairs – after cleaning – that we had a chance for a proper talk. Dr Prosperov was there, as were the parents and Mrs Jones. Gunter and Mariko were upstairs with Rewa and Asal.

"Mission last night unsuccessful. Professor Cherensky died, Scott hurt. Is important we discuss. All will have say. I start, then Mr Kahu, then Scott, other operatives and families. This will expose most information before opinion.

"So, with greatest candour I am feeling guilt. Was very concerned Professor Cherensky a security risk. His death is convenient from that perspective. However also brave and honest man who did not deserve to die. I am guilty in that insisted to Mr Kahu that kidnappers are stopped. Is all." And he sat down.

Grandpop stood up.

"To be honest I have been involved in worse … cockups. I blame myself for thinking like a military man. We could have slowed the van by blocking the road. We could have put one of the kids in the back to get Cherensky free without a crash. But even then there was no guarantee that Hathaway would not have shot them. I saw how dangerous Hathaway was and I wanted him hurt in the crash before the kids tried to rescue Cherensky. It didn't work. Sometimes things don't, but I am really glad the suit protected Scotty. When I saw Hathaway hide under the van I didn't let the kids know. That guy was too dangerous to mess with, and besides what could the kids do with him anyway. That's all I can say too." And he sat down.

That solved the mystery of Hathaway's vanishing act. I'd been a bit worried the guy was this unstoppable superman who had run off despite a broken leg.

Scotty was about to get up but Dr Prosperov waved him to sit down.

"I'd like to say I shouldn't have opened that door. I had a feeling he was waiting. We're hired because we have those feelings and I should have known better. I should have warned everyone instead. I just didn't want anyone else hurt. He just surprised me and beat me to the draw. I should have been more careful. I don't blame anyone else but I am damn pleased our suits are so strong." Ashley was gazing at Scotty, her eyes a bit dewy. She realised that by "anyone else" Scotty had really meant her, because she was on the same side of the van. But she said her only regret was not killing Hathaway. We all knew that was bullshit. Ashley was the gentlest of all of us.

Cam said the main problem had been a failure to think through the whole mission. She said it was obvious when we had Cherensky safely away from the kidnappers we didn't know what to do with him. She said we needed backup. Tarik's complaint was that we didn't have anything to move large objects. He said if we could have bent Cherensky somewhere we wouldn't have had to rely on passing truck drivers.

I said the dazzle plan hadn't really worked because it didn't cause the crash. The driver could have simply stopped. Then we would have to bust into the van with them defending it. I said I felt guilty now because I had forced the swerve that caused the crash and led to Cherensky's injuries and death.

Tahira was grumpy with me for not telling her about my plan to dash out onto the road. I said I didn't want anyone to worry and there wasn't time to explain. Tahira said I wasn't to do that again. We bickered a bit, and then we noticed everyone was smiling at us, so we got embarrassed and shut up.

The parents came to the conclusion that the mission had been badly planned because we were vulnerable to Cherensky. They pointed out that we had had many guests, some of whom knew about the Fae, and that we needed to make sure there was no danger of them being kidnapped too.

Dr Gursoy said that if Grandpop had been monitoring Hathaway closer he could have spotted the ambush. Grandpop said he knew that, but that everything had happened too quickly, and he couldn't tell us what to do all the time or he'd ruin our confidence. Bernard said if Hathaway had had a more powerful gun, like an AK-47, Scotty might have been killed. We kids said we all had realised that.

"It's a case of fools rush in," Grandpop summarised.

The meeting broke up, surprisingly positively. We'd expected the parents to be more worried and protective but they showed they still trusted us, and Grandpop and Dr Prosperov. They said they wanted to help plan missions more, and we all agreed with Tarik's idea that we needed a way to bend people or things who weren't in suits. That night I asked Auntie Liz if she was worried about me going on missions.

"Of course I worry. It was a dumb plan of dad's and he knows we all know it. You knew it too. When I watched the replay you damn near gave me a heart attack. But Sam you're growing up. You knew how to use that amazing equipment you have and you used it bravely. I only worry when you get over your head your bravery will make you do something dumb. Just promise me you won't do anything you know is dumb, Sam. Promise me you'll think first."

"I promise Aunty Liz."

She turned out the light.

"You're a good boy Sam. The others really admire you too. You can see it."

And she left me in the dark feeling really embarrassed.

## CHAPTER FORTY NINE: KIT

We had a memorial for Professor Cherensky. Dr Prosperov admitted it was hard to be grief stricken over someone you had barely met, but that his death and our role in it was something we should all reflect on. Mariko made the memorial all the more effective by making it understated. The ballroom was shrouded and dark. There was a single candle and a picture of Cherensky.

Dr Prosperov said a very few words and then invited us all to consider Professor Cherensky in silence and leave when we thought we had done him justice. The last person had to put out the candle.

The parents were the first to leave. They had had little to do with the man. The other adults went with them. That left us kids, Grandpop and the two Russians. We stayed for quite a while. Mostly we were apologising to him, we were also thinking of ways we could avoid such a disaster in future. I wondered whether we'd see Cherensky among the presences when we next bent space and time. I hoped he'd forgive us. I got the impression he was not unhappy to have moved on as he had had little to look forward to.

We stayed for about an hour making our peace with Professor Cherensky. Outside the day seemed new and fresh like a new calf – completely unaware of everything that had gone before it. It was Dr Prosperov who was last to leave and who extinguished the candle.

In public Scotty's injuries were passed off as having fallen out of a tree. But the effect Professor Cherensky's death had on the whole house was not so relaxed. Before Cherensky everyone had treated Dr Prosperov as a well meaning, brilliant weirdo. We were going to save the world and look after people. We were do-gooders. But Hathaway's viciousness had shown everyone how dangerous our enemies were. Hathaway had loosed a disease to murder most of the world. We had seen him knock out his own henchmen and set him alight. And he had shot Scott after winking at him like it was all a big joke.

Worse, Prosperov was warning us Hathaway was not the only one. Professor Cherensky had provoked *him* into revealing himself through tricking Virion Inc. He told us we could be certain there were many others – others just as evil – who were hidden in the world.

Everything got more serious. We started having evacuation drills. Us kids were sent to bug Professor Dubrov and Aunty Nea. Our satellite communications channel was fed with random nonsense intended to look like secret codes while we got sent to Brazil, Singapore, London, New York and Japan to plug Control into the internet via quantum modems Hekator sent.

We started getting more training on first aid, disarming guns, and Mariko made up scenarios for us to play act. Even Asal and Rewa had roles. Ken and Gunter, Soraya and Bernard, everyone got roped in. We learned to spot Scotty's pistol pretty quickly. Sometimes Mariko cheated but Grandpop always backed her up saying nobody was going to give us a second chance and it was better we learned that now than when there were real bullets in the gun.

The Immigration Department was also making a pest of itself again. It insisted that the Robinsons, and the Trâns leave the country and apply for jobs properly. However the deadline set was 31 December and Dr Prosperov said there was no point acting before then.

It was three weeks before Christmas when I woke up one Sunday night. It was calm, the sea was gently rolling up onto the beach and the moon was a crescent.

Yet something was niggling at me. I looked out of my window but saw nothing unusual. I went and got back into bed. It was 3:12 a.m. In the DRC it would be two in the afternoon. I wasn't hungry. I didn't need the toilet. But I was awake. Wide awake. I wondered if anyone else was up, so I slipped on my clothes and shoes and, despite the worry of meeting ghosts, went for a walk in the corridor. No ghosts! Not even any suggestion of ghosts. Just for a change Renwick felt almost like the sort of place you wanted to sneak around after dark. I even went to the gallery where the ghosts normally were, and there was no hint of their depressing presences.

I noticed two smaller figures slip out the front door. I went back to the stairs and heard someone else in the corridor.

"Sam?" whispered a girl.

I jumped.

"Shit!" I swore.

And then I realised it was Tahira.

"We have to stop meeting like this," I told her.

"Idiot," she replied, smiling.

"I saw two of the others go out the front," I said heading down.

"Which uzzers?" Tahira asked as we crept down the stairs.

"Couldn't tell."

We stole down the staircase carefully because it was as dark as the inside of a cow at midnight.

"They were headed for the beach."

"If zey are swimming naked we shall steal zere clothes!" Tahira snickered.

"Who would swim naked?" I asked thinking it would be chilly.

"Ken and Patricia maybe?"

"What?" I hadn't imagined adults acting like kids.

"Av you not noticed 'ow friendly zey are?"

"Ah, no. Anyway it was one of us. I think Tarik and Cam."

"I don't know what she sees in 'im," Tahira commented in the dark as we edged down the rail. I thought about this was a second.

"Not everyone thinks about shagging all the time Tahira," I told her off gently, "Look at us."

She was offended.

"Shagging iz for animals. *Yumans* 'av roh-mances," she said rolling her Rs heavily. We reached the door.

"Well, we aren't having a romance either," I told her.

"So what are you doing up then?" asked Scotty from the top of the stairs.

Tahira and I both swore in shock.

"Same as you mate," I told him.

"Wait up ... Ashley's coming," he replied.

We heard Ashley softly pad up to Scott. I caught a glint of her glasses.

"Did you have to wear a *pink* hoody?" Scotty asked.

"Yeah, it's all I could find."

They felt their way down the staircase.

"But why pink? It stands out." Scotty nagged.

"Ah liike standing out, dawlin," Ashley said somewhere in the dark.

"Why not bring a torch then?"

"Yeah, I should've of too. I cayn't see a damn thing!"

Finally they joined us and we slipped out the front door into the mild night, the salt air and quiet crunch of sea on the beach becoming clearer as we got outside.

"The others went this way," I said, starting off at a gentle run to shut Scotty and Ashley up.

We jogged around the back of the house. There was no sign of anything. We kept going until we reached the beach, then we stopped.

"So here we are, wide awake for no reason, runnin' 'round da house also for no reason," Ashley commented.

"Last time this happened we met Tabika," I said.

"Except she was screaming," Scotty added.

"Mah question is what do we *think* we're doing?" Ashley asked.

"We are seeking somezing," Tahira said certainly.

"What?" Ashley asked.

We stood still looking around at a beach in the moonlight.

"I dunno but I think it's near the old gun emplacements," Scotty said.

"Why?" Ashley asked, more checking than because she doubted him.

"Because that's what it feels like, and that's where the others went. Look there's a footprint! Come on," Scotty replied.

We followed the prints for a while. Then we started running.

It was funny running in the dark without a suit on. There was no low light or thermal vision, and no extra power or protection if you fell. As the track got steeper we slowed to a walk. We spread out a bit. Scotty was feeling his taped up ribs and Ashley had the stitch.

We came to the top of the crest and found Cam and Tarik standing on top of one of the old bunkers looking out to sea.

"What are you guys up to?" Scotty called out.

Tarik waved us over impatiently. We came up behind them. Cam shushed us when we started to ask what they were doing but helped us climb onto the emplacement too.

"Over there," Tarik pointed.

About a hundred and fifty meters away Dr Prosperov and Dr Morozov, dressed in black, were standing together looking out to sea. It was a mild and pretty night. At first I thought they had come up for a romantic walk. They were certainly quite close. For someone who was normally so cold and withdrawn Morozov seemed almost affectionate toward her husband. But I also realised they were waiting for something.

We waited for one, two, three, five, ten minutes. But nothing seemed to happen. We were all sitting down now, swinging our legs and chatting in low voices about stuff. When suddenly right above our heads this huge thing just silently appeared.

It was as big as a sports stadium, and although it was dark as the sky with stars twinkling through it, there was no way you couldn't notice it barely fifty meters above our heads. There was a deep hum like you hear near high tension lines.

It was just instinct. We all leapt into the old gun emplacement to take cover from it. We sat there cowering looking up at it. My mind was reeling. The only saucer we had seen had tried to get me and this one was way, way bigger and right over us. We had no suits, no protection and it was right by Renwick! It felt like my insides were frozen with fear. The size of this thing was jaw-dropping and it just sat there in mid-air without any effort, transparent as a heat haze.

Suddenly a brilliant white light shot out from it and covered Dr Prosperov and Dr Morozov. They were huddled together, shielding their eyes and looking up. Then, with a slight squeal from Dr Morozov, they began to rise off the ground and accelerate toward the light. We watched them zoom up and vanish inside. Then the light went out, leaving spots dancing before our eyes.

They had been waiting for it! We couldn't understand it. Why were we in danger from saucers if Dr Prosperov and Dr Morozov were going out in the middle of the night to meet them? Who's side were they on?

Slowly the vast craft moved silently over our heads barely stirring the air. It descended so that its flat top was level with the top of the cliff but about its own large diameter away from it. Then a number of tubes' each the size of train carriage extended out the side of the huge oval mothership. The tubes, like the mothership, looked like they were made of glass. They detached and one swung around towards the gallery of emplacements below us. We were tempted to run to the edge and look when a voice spoke in our heads.

"*Stay where you are children,*" Hekati commanded.

That explained a lot! The Fae had saucers too and this was one of theirs. The fear vanished, replaced by admiration and relief. There was a huge flash and a small cloud of dust erupted up the edge of the cliff. The tube that had made the flash swung away from the edge but another moved to take its place. There was no flash this time but the second tube was replaced by the third and the first merged back inside the mother ship. One by one each of the four tubes took their place until all had been returned to the vast mothership they had come from. And then the mothership simply vanished. It winked out like a dream. It felt as if we had imagined it all.

We were just checking with each other what we thought we'd just seen when, in a flash of light in front of us, a figure appeared. Her curves, fur, and wings were instantly recognisable. We ran up to Hekati.

"Hello children," she smiled at us.

"We didn't know you had spaceships," Tarik said enthusiastically. Hekati started walking to the side of the steep bank. She said nothing but her thoughts were rapid.

*"Your idea of 'spaceships' implies travelling through space – which is, of course, far too large to cross in ordinary dimensions. The Vimana don't move much in ordinary space. Your nearest concept for our Vimana would be 'arks' and yes there are many – always enough to evacuate Fae. They are like ships except the Vimana are beings in their own right. Inorganic beings yes, but beings nonetheless. They can move in space but generally they bend and they can bend huge distances without the need for gravitational assistance like us. We needed to bring more equipment for this project so the Vimana Rishi – one of the younger ones – has agreed to transport us."*

"Where's it gone?" Ashley asked.

"She *gone. Rishi is a replicating incubator Vimana so we use female pronouns.*

"So she really is a *mother* ship or Vimana or whatever?" Tarik asked. Even I could tell he was thinking of science fiction stories. *"Yes. She can make new Vimana. She hasn't gone far, still in your star's domain, but far enough away to be safe."*

"Why are Dr Prosperov and Dr Morozov in it," Tahira wanted to know.

*"The Rus mates have a small replication matter we are helping with."*

We came to the edge of the steep bank down to the sea. There were sparks coming from the gun emplacement below.

*"We're adding a new tunnel into the main complex. Another Draca is in the tunnel. It should be finished in a few weeks. Then we will be able to expand your range of tools,"* she smiled.

"What are we getting?" Tarik asked.

*"You'll see,"* she smiled, and added *"And seeing that it is such a lovely night, and I haven't been outside for nearly a week I think I may do a little fishing,"* she announced simply.

She spread her wings, which were quite large, and stepped lightly off the bank gliding down the steep slope before skimming along above the sea.

"I wish we could do that," Cam said.

"Yeah, skydiving isn't really the same," Tarik agreed.

"How come you two were up so early?" Ashley asked.

"Because we live on this side of the building, right? and whatever it was woke us first, init?" Tarik pointed to Renwick.

"I better go home. My father will worry if I not there," Cam told us.

He would be up soon to start his baking too. So we ran back down the hill and all the way to Renwick. Even before we got there we knew the ghosts were back. That depressing sad air had returned. We slipped in the back door and up the back stairs but you could still hear them whispering to themselves.

We split up and went back to bed. I looked out at the beach thinking of Hekati as I got changed. I got back into bed and remember nothing more until the brilliant morning sun woke me because I'd forgotten to draw my curtains.

To our surprise Dr Prosperov was around at breakfast, drinking water and telling everyone about the new building work. He didn't bother telling us as he obviously knew we knew. But he also said Dr Morozov would be away for a few days.

The day seemed light and happy as we set off for school. We had taken our night pills and although we still felt groggy we knew we'd be right in an hour or so. We were looking forward to finding out whether Hekati had brought the stuff we'd wanted from Hekator.

It was a day of sports, music and not much work. The lunch hour seemed to be becoming two hours when I noticed there was a bit of a gathering at the edge of the playing field. I went over, out of natural curiosity when Marshall and his mates walked away from the fence at the same time as a man who they'd been talking to. They were all pocketing five dollar notes and smirking at me.

The man got into a fairly ordinary looking car and the driver drove off. I noticed all the people with Marshall were all looking at us with nasty little smiles. I got a reading on them which confirmed they had been talking to whoever it was, about us.

I drifted over to Scotty who was with Tarik and Cam.

"They're snooping around us."

"Who are?" Tarik asked.

"Marshall and his mates are telling Ray's friends about us."

**199**

"So what?" Tarik asked. "They can do what they like."

It was bluster. I knew he was worried as hell. His fear was Ergenekon would pick up their trail. But what bothered me was the patient and careful way Ax was doing this. He wasn't just charging in like he would have before. No, he seemed to have become cleverer. He was finding out about us and I knew he would only do that because he wanted to find our weaknesses. I knew our main weakness was most of the others were only in New Zealand through technicalities and doubtful claims. If someone really investigated they could all end up being chucked out of the country.

Of course the bigger problems for the Robinsons and the Gursoys were MS13 and Ergenekon. If Ax started digging into where everyone was from, things could get pretty tricky real quick.

I was talking about this when I realised Emma was hovering. She didn't act especially differently but I realised she had caught something from what I'd said. I noticed she quietly started asking the others what the visitor had asked, but she didn't share it with me. She just started looking at us a bit differently.

But when Ashley and Tahira heard what was going down they didn't muck around. They went straight to the office and complained a strange man had been at the fence giving kids money for answering his questions. Well, that started a scandal! Mrs McLean dragged everyone into the office, including Marshall, and gave them a bollocking. She made him turn out his pockets but the money had vanished. She hardly caught anyone. At the end of school Marshall led a bunch of kids in showing their five dollar notes like red flags as we were picked up. It was just mean.

When we got home we had to wait until briefing to talk about it, but when we came into the theatre we found a whole crowd of people: Mariko, Gunter, Ken, Dr Prosperov and Grandpop were milling around a bunch of black boxes. Some were on trestle tables while others were on the floor. Hekator was present as a hologram as well.

"Come and have a look guys," Grandpop called.

We went down and joined them. Some of the boxes were cages and in them were animals. We dodged around each other looking at the animals to see what was there.

There was an ordinary looking sparrow with darting little eyes; a little brown owl who was asleep; a black mouse with cute ears; a very ugly, little black bat hanging upside down from a branch; a small very cool bird of prey with bright eyes and the last cage didn't seem to have anything in it until Tarik pointed out a small spider hiding in the corner.

There was also a range of black boxes around the floor. Two looked a bit like coffins except the smaller, lower one, had lights on it. There were three ordinary looking soft carry bags which didn't seem very special. There was a square solid box with a compartment big enough for a pair of shoes which also had lights on it. Finally there were four thick, adult-sized sleeping bags, one unrolled showing it had a facescreen and the other three rolled up in bags.

Hekator started to explain.

"The animals are to be partnered to a particular suit. We're making a special pocket for them to travel in with you. Once free their home suit will open a communications channel allowing the suits wearer to perceive what they are seeing and hearing and give them general instructions. So long as the animals are properly looked after they won't go off looking for food. They are all asexual and won't look for mates either."

"The sparrow is for general reconnaissance. It can get into all sorts of places and has excellent eyesight and hearing, though not of lower frequencies. It can provide bending target coordinates. Sparrows don't fly at night and the owl and the falcon are potential predators. He'll need a place in your room as will all the animals."

"The owl is for long range night time reconnaissance. It has enhanced day and night time vision and excellent hearing. It's best used to fly up to watch over someone or something in the dark. It could follow a vehicle in an urban environment but not where the vehicle can reach full speed. Owls are very hard to detect either still or in flight so it's perfect for watching over an area without exposing yourself to observation."

"The mouse has good night, and day vision and good hearing in the higher frequencies. It can get into small crevices and climb most rough surfaces. This mouse is somewhat fiercer than most and has sharp teeth. It is very good at getting into buildings to provide you with bending target coordinates."

"The vampire is able to gain access to buildings and provide sonar scans of internal spaces as well as excellent eavesdropping. Its special trick is it can inject the bio-builder for the tracking device linked to Control."

"The falcon is a daytime reconnaissance animal. It flies high and fast up to 100km/h[+] with excellent eyesight. It can quite easily follow a vehicle from so high it's almost invisible. It can even follow a helicopter for a few hours. It's also good for finding bending targets. The falcon can attack remotely piloted aircraft, and even drop objects with some accuracy."

"Lastly the spider is one of my own creations and I think pretty special. It's fast for a spider, takes on the colour of its surroundings and is able to walk on water. It can sneak into buildings easily but its eyesight and hearing are not compatible with ours. Its main ability is to spin eavesdropping webs that act as antennas for radios including telephones and satellite signals. It has a poison bite that will sedate a human for a few hours."

"So who wants which animal?" he asked.

We looked at each other and then at the animals.

Grandpop decided to get involved before we all started shouting.

"Hang on! Hang on! This will depend a bit on your teams. The animals have to work together just like their owners. Now let's see, we've got Owls and vampires for night time. The mouse and the spider work together any time. Then we've got the falcon and the sparrow. So let me see how does that work out? Let's see. Who wants the spider?"

Tarik finally volunteered.

"Good. OK who wants the vampire?"

We all turned to look at the vampire. It was pretty ugly although the injection thing was pretty cool. Scotty was the only one up for him.

"Thanks Scott that helps a lot. So Tarik is a spider, Scott is a vampire. That means Cam should be a mouse and Ashley an owl Sam a falcon and Tahira a sparrow. What do we think of that?"

Ashley looked happy, Cam looked chilled. But Tahira was upset.

"Why does Sam get the falcon?" she asked in a small voice.

"I just thought Kahu means hawk in Maori so Sam would want the falcon."

Tahira bit her lip.

"Why what's the matter," Grandpop asked.

**203**

"The Persian name for falcon is Shaheen. My fazzer's name."
Grandpop looked at me. How could I come between Tahira and
her dad? Besides the sparrow was kinda cute.

"S'ok Tahira. You have the falcon," I told her.

She gave me a quick kiss on the cheek and slipped off to the
falcon.

"Ever get the feeling you're being played?" Scotty asked softly,
while Ashley announced she was naming her owl "Hooty".
Hooty greeted this news by hiding under his wing.

"Yeah," I agreed with Scotty quietly.

I went over and talked to the sparrow. It was taking it all in and
not looking at all nervous. He pecked me when I stroked him. I
decided to call him Cheeky, because he looked like he was.
The falcon was Shaheen, Scotty took Ashley's suggestion and
decided the vampire's name was Buffy. Tarik had named his
spider Peter Parker. Cam had taken her mouse out and let him
run up and down her arm sniffing around so he became Sniffy.
Hekator reappeared among the boxes.

"OK, we can sort out the suits and animals later. Now transport
units all have different uses. The body bags are for moving
people. I'd recommend the only people you move with them are
people who are unconscious or from Renwick. They can only be
moved with a suit attached.

The soft bags, which expand, are the same but for moving larger
objects. They too only work in contact with a suit. This small box
is a bit different. It can be moved by itself but more important
it can also be used to transfer solid objects inside it to and from
here. It will put large microwave charges through any objects so
don't try and transfer animals or anything delicate with it."

"If we put a raw food in one side will it come out cooked at the other?" Mariko asked.

We all laughed.

"More charcoal than cooked," Hekator replied.

"The big trunk does the same thing but for larger items. Once again don't transfer anything delicate in it. But the really big box is a medical evacuation unit."

He opened it up. It looked like the inside of the changing machine felt – all meaty and disgusting. The tentacles were particularly gross.

"It's for badly injured people. The inside is a life support system with synthetic blood and an air supply. The system can also prepare victims for cryogenic suspension if time is running out. The box has its own security and can travel large distances if need be. We hope none of you will ever need one."

"Finally we have one more tool, recommended by Lana, which is waiting for you outside with me. If you put the animals back I'll show it to you."

And with that his hologram vanished. We all crowded out of the base leaving the animals in their cages.

Hekator himself was waiting outside in front of Renwick with a bunch of fairly beat up looking BMX bikes. We all gathered around.

"These are based on a wonderful human invention I've always admired: the bicycle. We've copied them in carbon polymer to make them more springy and stronger and so anyone in a suit can bend with them. We also made the tyres out of a carbon spiral so they don't need air, will grip to nearly anything and provide extra suspension. We also added a small induction motor to the frame powered by your suits so that the rear wheel is powered and of course the brakes are now attached to the motor as well because you need a real brake system. Our own children tested them at up to 70km/h on flat level ground and 40km/h on bumpier ground. The pedals of course don't do anything except spin and the chain isn't doing anything either. But aside from that they are like ordinary bicycles. Do you want to try them?"

We were on them in no time. At first we couldn't get them started. The pedals just span uselessly.

"Just think about transferring power to them," Hekator told us. Then we started over-powering them and falling off. It took a while to get the power levels under control. They were kind of weird to ride. They were like motorcycles because they were so powerful but silent and so light. The real bliss though was balancing on the pedals and just powering up the hill behind Renwick. Then we came back down. The brakes were awesome. You could skid or not skid. It was up to you. We had a great time riding around and jumping them just because we could. Finally we came back in. Hekator had a few last thoughts.

"Lana told me to remind you to pedal. It looks more natural. The bikes have locators in them so even if someone steals them you can get it back. But finally remember these bikes are slow compared to cars and even in suits you are very vulnerable to larger metal vehicles. If they hit you, you will get a lot more than a few bruises. At speed they can certainly kill you. Remember you can always bend. Only use these bicycles on quiet roads and paths and shape your hoods like helmets. It will encourage other human children to use their simpler bicycles safely too."

"So that's all we have for you now. When Hekati has finished with the extensions we will set up the rest of your equipment. Any questions?"

"What do we do about looking after the animals?" Scotty wanted to know.

"Nothing for the moment. I have to talk to Control and Gunter about that. Then we'll give you your animals and instructions. Anything else? No? OK, well, we'll bring the bikes into the base so leave them. I'll leave you there."

And he vanished. We all went back down to briefing room. Grandpop summed up.

"OK, so we have covered off the transport problems we had with Professor Cherensky. We have also made it possible for some of us adults to travel with you as well. That should be helpful where you need one of us," he waved at the others as well, "to negotiate with or distract other adults for you."

"It also means we can carry out exercises together away from Aotea which will help a lot. But before we worry about that we'll start training with the animals. The animals mean Tarik and Cam become the building entry specialists, Scotty and Ashley the night watch, and Sam and Tahira the day watch. If we have Ashley and Tahira together they are the wide area search team while Scotty and Sam are the site watch team.

"Now we have a new kid on our radar and I'll hand over to Dr Prosperov to talk about her."

Dr Prosperov took over casually from Grandpop.

"Sarah Kogan is most interesting case. Lives sometimes in Mytilene on Island of Lesbos in Aegean with mother, other times in Denya suburb of Haifa which is northern industrial port city of Israel with father. Divorced parents not unusual. Unusual thing is both parents in Mafiya. Is often called Russian mafiya but is in actuality Jewish mafiya."

"Father Uri Kogan is diamond trader and arms dealer who

also sells women from Moldova and Albania. Is wanted in USA by FBI. In theory wanted by Interpol but seems to have no problems travelling in Europe and still manages to visit New York often."

"Sarah's mother is Alisha Semovich whose father Michael Semovich is kingpin of Jewish Mafiya. Uri and Michael remain friendly as father blames own daughter for divorce not son-in-law."

"Sarah is only partially aware of family's illegal work. Lives very privileged life and is treated like princess by father. As Alisha also raised like princess by father is apparent mother daughter relationship problematic. Is case of too many princesses when Sarah lives with Alisha."

"Sarah has professional bodyguard named Ivan Federov. Very dangerous man. Former associate of grandfather, Michael Semovich. Is convicted murderer. Sarah is normally chauffeured in black armoured Mercedes similar to this. At age 15 Sarah has small circle of friends who she communicates with using mobile phone constantly."

"Forecast indicates Sarah destined to become Israeli Prime Minister. Is no great surprise. But surprise is coming. If forecast is correct Sarah is subject of kidnapping plot. Is essential plot succeeds. Alternative is nuclear war in middle east."

"To secure contact with Sarah through kidnap period is essential also to bug her, perhaps using new vampire assistant. Is difficult as Sarah heavily guarded and most environments carefully secured. Estimated time to kidnap attempt is four weeks."

"Enhanced forecasting also suggests Diana Popovic and Jeanne Mazuri entering critical period. Am suspecting school holidays will be busy time. Is any questions?"

We looked at each other. Then I told them about the man at school handing out money for information about us. Grandpop looked grumpy. Dr Prosperov seemed to be calculating something.

"Am thinking is useful to bug Mr Stephens. Is not good time for surprises and may provide useful material for response," Dr Prosperov said to Grandpop.

Grandpop agreed.

"OK boss, we'll do it as a test of the animals. Tarik and Cam with Ashley and Scotty as cover to do a bug run at 2 a.m. tomorrow night."

"What about me and Tahira?" I asked.

"You can go to Israel with the bikes. Your job will be to scout out the neighbourhood of this Sarah Kogan."

Tahira perked up suddenly.

"Iz it OK if afterwardz we go to zer shrine of zer Bab. Is in Haifa. Is special place for Baha'i⁺?" she asked.

"Where is it?" Grandpop asked.

"On top of Mt Carmel."

"Control? Map please."

A map of Haifa came up with the expensive hillside suburb of Denya or Had HaKarmel and the Baha'i gardens and temple outlined. Control traced a route through suburban streets. They were close but not that close.

"No problem I can see," Grandpop shrugged.

"Yesss!" Tahira cried, making a fist.

I could tell this was going to go down very well with Mitra and Soraya. I wasn't sure however why Grandpop hadn't wanted me on the team. I didn't say anything at the time but Grandpop caught up with me before dinner.

"Sam, I can't send you there because I need this girl in Israel checked out and you and Tahira are best for that, and you might be recognised by Ax."

"With a facescreen? At three in the morning?" I challenged.

"Well, OK, I admit that's pretty unlikely. To be honest I'm not sure how you would react if you had to deal with your father. He may not be asleep, and he may not be alone."

"What do you mean?"

"I mean ... he's got a girlfriend, Sam ... young thing called Sade." I was surprised how much that news hit me. It had never occurred to me that he might have a new woman in his life. On one level I hoped it meant he might leave Rewa and me alone, but on another I worried that it was only a matter of time before he beat up this girl too. He might not kill her, but I couldn't believe prison had turned him into the Jesus figure he dressed up as. I shrugged to Grandpop who seemed to be looking for my for a reaction.

"Doesn't bother me."

"Yeah, well you say that *now*, but if you saw them up close and personal while wearing a suit you might be a bit different and after Tahira went crazy on that guy I'm not taking any chances with you lot. You've all got a lot of stuff in your lives and there's too much at stake to find out the hard way."

That night I lay awake thinking about my dad and some girl. I imagined bending into their room while they slept and looking at them. They might be peaceful and asleep in the moonlight. And I knew the last time I saw my mum alive would keep coming back to me.

"You bitch, you slut! I'll teach you to ..."

His last words to my mum flared into my brain. I felt my insides clench. I was cold and short of breath. It was true I didn't know what I'd do. Having seen Hathaway set that guy on fire I couldn't completely rule out doing the same thing to Ax. I didn't *think* I'd do it but I wasn't a hundred percent sure either. It turned out I needn't have worried.

## HAIFA AND SURROUNDS, ISRAEL

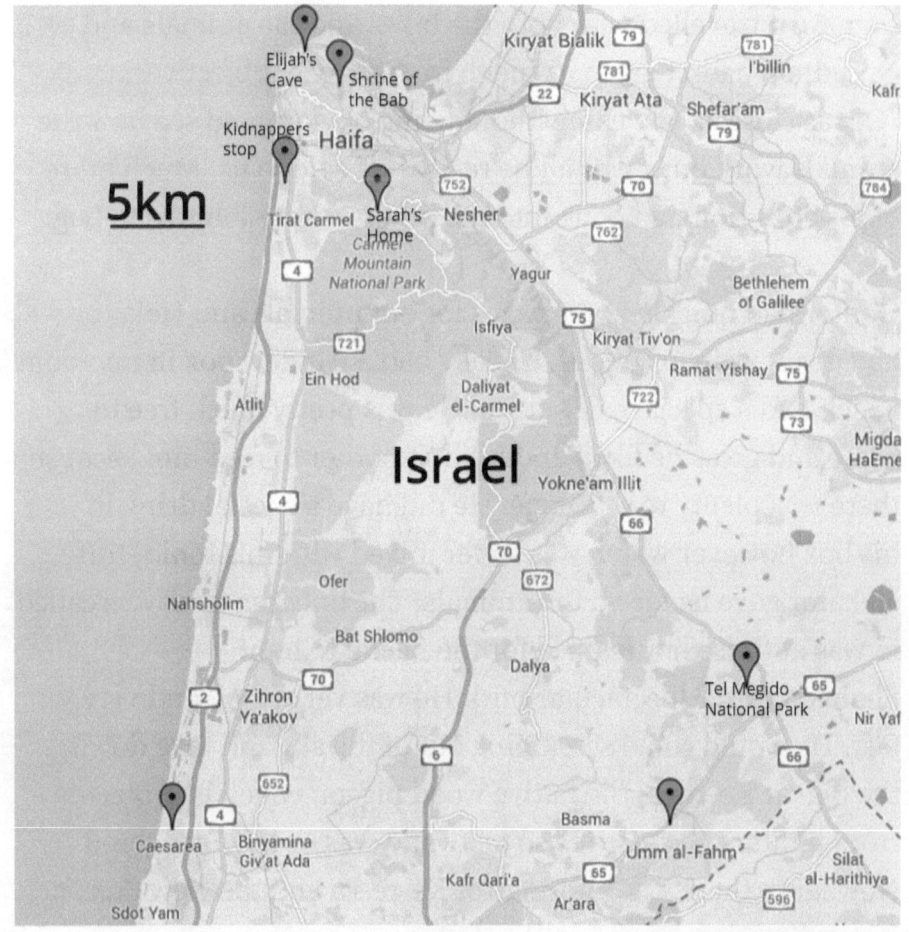

*Map Data © Google 2016*

## CHAP†ER FIF†Y: HAIFA

We visited Haifa on Sunday at two in the morning our time, three in the afternoon local time. It was the first time we'd travelled with both the bikes and the animals and Grandpop hadn't given us much in the way of objectives. "Get as close as you can without being obvious and see how the animals work out," was all he really had said to us. Much more of his attention had gone into the others whose job was to bug Ax.

Gunter had quickly made cages for our animals and Hekator had given us instructions. Cheeky had a window box in my room which had a special call button. He was pretty much free to come and go as he liked and I didn't bother to feed him because there was plenty to scavenge. He did have a special drink in his box however which was water mixed with this tonic stuff Hekator gave us for all the animals. The only times he was called in was at those hours fixed for the falcon to hunt.

Shaheen was a spectacular bird. He was very small and very fast. He would come screaming out of the sky and take down the big fat Ke-re-ru the native wood pigeon which is protected from hunters because it's so tasty and was once endangered. Nowadays there's no shortage of Ke-re-ru and the New Zealand falcon is endangered. But the Ke-re-ru were lucky. Shaheen only got two hours of hunting in a day. The rest of the time he had to hang around Tahira's room. Mitra and Soraya talked to him but his claws could carve up furniture.

Sniffy the mouse just lived in a cage as did Peter the spider. Hooty the owl slept all day and hunted at night. Ashley was surprised to find owls are not very good pets. They don't like being handled and need to kill animals to make a stomach pellet of skin and bone.

But the trickiest of all the animals to look after was Buffy. At first Buffy was allowed to fly around the house at night but not allowed outside. The problem was she didn't take well to hand feeding. Vampires need fresh blood and preferably have to take it from sleeping animals. As Scotty wasn't keen on being bitten himself – and neither was anyone else – we needed something Buffy could feed from.

A cow would have been ideal but keeping a cow inside at night wasn't practical. And Hooty might eat Buffy if Buffy flew free. Gunter's solution was to rig up a roost for Buffy in the garage and get a couple of young pigs who could scavenge the leftovers during the day and get bitten at night. Buffy didn't take much feeding being very tiny.

The pigs, who Mariko named Tricksy and Grunter (to annoy Gunter), were clever and sneaky. They would try and get into the kitchen if they weren't watched, and had to be given some firm guidance from various boots about staying outside. They cheerfully ate loads of scraps. But they were also lots of fun and enjoyed chasing games and being scritched behind the ears and on the tummy. Mariko, Mr Trân, Scotty and me really liked them and took them on walks along the beach like dogs. Tarik, Tahira and Ashley didn't, while Cam only liked them because she wanted to eat them.

We were all thinking about Christmas now although more for the end of school than any presents. The suits and the Fae technology were just so cool that getting a normal pet or bike seemed pretty dull by comparison. In fact we were all making a bigger deal of Rewa and Asal at the moment than each other. That was part of the reason Tahira wanted to go to the B'hai shrine in Haifa. To get a keepsake associated with the Baha'llulah for Asal.

[+]

We arrived in Haifa in a stand of trees area on top of Mt Carmel, just slightly down-slope of the University. It was raining off and on in occasional sprinkles so there was no-one about, but it wasn't all that cold. We headed downhill out of the trees following the wide gritty path.

The view made us stop and look around. Although Mt Carmel was only six hundred meters high, which was less than the hills back home, the view of the city, and a large amount of the country was quite something. The clouds seemed almost within reach, while the Mediterranean Sea glittered and danced before us.

We were in a valley that ran east-west from the sea below to the summit behind us. The city in front of us was quite industrial. There were complexes and ports, and lots of apartment blocks, there were even a couple of towers being built to our left that seemed to loom over the area. There were quite a few ships either out to sea or in the container port below us. Behind us the University dominated the skyline looking all shiny and modern. Although the place we were in was scrubby and wild there was no shortage of city around us.

While we looked at the view a large silent crowd of presences was gathering around to look at us, drawn by our bending. Most were on foot and some were on donkey or horseback. Some were soldiers and knights, most were farmers, others were just people mostly dressed in simple clothes. Unlike the newer ghosts in the DRC, or the Finnish soldiers who had watched me run in front of Hathaway's van, they weren't individuals, just a crowd of blurs. Still there were heaps of them – although unlike the ones in Egypt it was fairly clear they weren't united. From Crusaders to Palestinian farmers, Jewish pilgrims to British police they seemed simply aware that people always came here to visit. Our way of arrival might be unusual but it was expected that we would want to come here.

The house we were looking for was in the next valley over so we were headed for a point on the northern ridge of our valley which could see into the next one. We rode our bikes down the rocky, muddy path and took a turn that led us up toward the ridge. As we started climbing again it felt a little like cheating to not need to pedal hard up the steep path, though sometimes you had to stand on the pedals to avoid tipping over.

At the top of the path there was a lookout spot so we got off our bikes to look around. The opposite ridge of the other valley was lined with expensive looking houses. Tahira opened her pouch on her stomach and woke up Shaheen who was asleep in the darkness.

I knew a bit how he felt. It was two in the morning to us and this light and activity just seemed all wrong. At first he resisted but when he realised he was being given a chance to fly free he seemed to wake himself up a bit. Tahira pulled him out onto her arm and before she was even ready he launched himself off her

215

and rose up the valley gaining height rapidly into the swirling gray sky.

While Shaheen was busy with that I woke up Cheeky. He seemed to have a lot to say about it and tweeted loudly as I pulled him out in my hand. I opened my hand expecting him to fly off but he sat there all fluffed up looking miserable. He knew where he was meant to go. He was just wanting to get back in my pocket and snooze.

I tossed him in the air and he streaked off fluttering his wings and then gliding in succession. He flew low over the valley and now if I closed my eyes I could feel myself streaking across it. It made me almost lose my balance so I had to sit down.

Tahira found it was easier if she sat down too, so we both sat together by some bushes channelling birds. Tahira had sent Shaheen high over the suburb to get a better view of the whole place. She said he was enjoying himself catching the thermals rising off the mountain. It occurred to me that Control could get any of these views and more anyway.

Meanwhile Cheeky was closing with the house. It was large with strong outer walls, and a large glass gallery coated in mirror glass looking out over us and the bay. Cheeky flew over and found a courtyard on the inside complete with pool and garden. He landed in a tree and began checking it out.

There were security cameras, TV and other antennas and more mirror glass. It also didn't seem that anyone was at home. I got Cheeky to fly down and look for ways in. The roofing was tiled and there didn't seem to be much scope for birds to get in under the eves. The whole house was pretty new so the cracks and crevices that animals find their way into over time hadn't happened yet.

Just as I was starting to get bored Tahira told me that a car was approaching. Cheeky went to the street side in time to see a big black Merc roll up and one of the two internal garage doors open. As the car pulled into the garage Cheeky flew down to the street below. The driver got out as did a girl with her ear glued to a cellphone. The girl had long, dark, curly hair, expensive boots and jeans, and a pink top. The driver was younger than I expected, wearing a dark suit, no tie, and amber sunglasses. Cheeky caught a glimpse of the man's annoyed glance at the girl as the garage door began to lower but the girl seemed to ignore it.

Cheeky went back into the garden. I got him to fly over and hop along outside the mirror glass but he couldn't hear anything happening on the inside. The house was closed up against a cold winters day.

*"This is dull,"* I told Tahira.

*"That's true."* she agreed.

*"I'll bring Cheeky home. I think Shaheen should meet us back at the trees or he'll draw attention to us."*

I called Cheeky as we picked up our bikes and rode them down off the ridge. He caught up with us as we were riding up the hill. We got back into the trees and had to wait a while until Shaheen found us again.

We were a couple of kilometers from the shrine of the Bab and the nearest roads were a bit busy for bikes so rather than ride all of it Control checked out another path by the small zoo in Central Carmel. Once again it was empty so we bent to that and rode our way up the hill leaving behind the crowd of presences under the trees as the birds settled snugly in their pouches and the rain started to come down in a serious cold shower.

**217**

We got up to the road trying our best to look like we were
pedalling but really enjoying the fact we could tackle the steep
hill without breaking a sweat. Because this area was more public
we opened our facescreens and the cold rain started to splat on
our faces bringing with it smells of rain and greenery.

We set off along the one-way streets of Central Carmel. The
suburban streets were fairly narrow and any traffic was slow
and careful but the bigger streets were faster. We rode along the
one-way road past some low-rise apartments until we came to
a major intersection. I was a bit thrown by the fact they drove
on the right, something I wasn't used to but Tahira was, so I
followed her lead.

The bikes were great. We zoomed down the road keeping up
with the cars. As we went down the hill the buildings were
getting taller all around us. There were apartments, and hotels.
It was definitely a rich part of town. All the time the route in our
suits was guiding us along the main road. In no time we came to
the top of the gardens looking down on the shrine.

It was a magnificent sight.

The sun was forcing its way through the clouds in rays of light
as if from God. The leaves, the golden spire of the shrine, the
streets and roofs were wet and shiny. The garden which swept
down the hill into the city looked stunning. It was as if someone
was making a huge poster for the Holy land.

Tahira was very excited. It was her first visit and she had a long
list of instructions from Mitra and Soraya. Although I had no
idea of Baha'i religious customs I could appreciate that a place
as stunning looking as this had to be pretty special. We rode
down the hill to the shrine. It wasn't busy, but it wasn't empty
either and people didn't seem to be too happy with us turning

a holy place into a BMX track. We decided to stop, but this presented a new problem. What to do with the bikes if we were both inside?

The bikes might not pedal but with so many downhill paths a thief could easily be a kilometer away before they even discovered that. There was only one solution. I would have to stay with them while Tahira did her religious thing. There was no real risk. She was better protected than anyone else in the world. So off she went leaving me sitting on a park bench looking at the view.

The showers seemed to have stopped for a moment. I sat there watching the light shift over the sea and sky. A number of people came and went. Most wore jackets like the one I seemed to be wearing and, although they noticed I seemed to be darker than they were, nobody said anything. Then an old man wearing a hat, scarf and a long coat came up

"Is this seat taken?" he asked in Hebrew. He was being over polite to make a point. I shook my head and slid sideways.

The man sat down. We both watched the light.

"First time?" he asked. His voice sounded deep and scratchy like he'd smoked for years.

I nodded.

"I come here every day. For my soul. It's always fascinating."

I said nothing. It was partly respect for an elder but also because Hebrew was not one of the suit's fluent languages. I could understand what he said if he spoke slowly, as he did. He seemed to be in a chatty mood because he started talking to me.

"I've been coming here since 1952. Every day. Every day is different. It's my synagogue. God talks. I listen. It pays to listen to God."

I nodded vaguely. Strangely in this place it seemed easy to listen to God. The old man said nothing for quite a while and then started up again as if we had been chatting the whole time. "The Prophet Elijah. He lived in a cave right over there. He listened to God. Everyone else was playing politics but Elijah, he listens to God. And just for once God backs his man and everyone gets a real kick up the ass. You have to listen to God. But you have to listen hard. God whispers."

I looked back at the view. It was strange as he spoke my view of the scene before me seemed to changing although I couldn't quite tell how. It was as if there was something in this view. A message or something. Then it passed. I looked back at the old man he was still staring out to sea.

"You're getting it. It takes practice. Practice and a certain talent." He looked at me for a moment and I knew he was reading me. Rather than let me read him he simply came out with his story. "I was only a little younger than you when the SS rounded us up. Four days in a cattle truck with no food in sub-zero temperatures from Sveged to Treblinka – the extermination camp. My mother, father and sister. All my Aunts and uncles and cousins. They were all gassed. They used diesel engines that often broke down. People had to stand around naked, crying and terrified in the cold for hours waiting to be killed. Everyone died there. Almost a million people except me and a few other guys." He looked out to sea and spoke more quietly this time. "That's a lot of ghosts to live with."

There was another long pause.

"To stay alive we had to do terrible things. Nobody escaped those camps innocent. When you face evil like that, you have to bend. Bend and listen hard. I learned to listen. It was a hard lesson for those of His people who survived."

There was something enthralling about this man. He seemed to be speaking to me in a way nobody had ever spoken to me before. I forced out the Hebrew question

"You listened to God?"

He nodded,"And to the souls of people. But God is more important," he said looking out to sea.

Then he glanced at me and smiled.

"You're making a big trip," he said. It wasn't a question.

I nodded. He looked at me closely. He spoke Hebrew but now it was more like when Hekator spoke. The ideas formed very clearly in my mind.

"Most of those Nazis were just dumb-ass, no-nothing thugs. You get that kind everywhere. Even here. But the real enemy, the real enemy was different. They were thugs too – don't get me wrong – but they were clever and very, very old."

When I first came here in 1952 aboard the *SS Artza*, I was 22. I thought I had left them for dead. Burned in the firestorms of Europe or prisoners of the communists. I was wrong. They had just scattered, as we had done. They hid among their friends and now they are rising again. Even here. I even see some in the street. Even among our people the contagion spreads. So I come here and I think of Elijah and I listen to God."

Now I couldn't contain my curiosity and without translating or even thinking I asked, "Who are you? Who are they?" in English.

He smiled at me knowingly, and turned to face the sea.

"Me? I'm Mordechai Ceder, pleased to meet you. But to you I'm just an old man who remembers too much."

"*What* are you?" I asked.

Mr Ceder found that amusing.

"Exactly! Samuel, exactly the question I ask God. What am I? Am I a Jew? I look around me and wonder. So many people are suddenly Jews these days. I don't go to the synagogue. I don't follow the observances. I didn't even vote for that corrupt prick, our Prime Minister. I'm not sure I am a Jew but I'm just as certain I'm not anything else. What does that make me?" He paused. "But you didn't mean that did you Samuel?"

He mused for a while then he spoke quietly.

"I'm like you, Samuel," he said in Hebrew. "I'm like an older you. I see the ghosts. I hear the things people don't say. I have more practice at listening and seeing than you and more experience with people but I don't have your fancy suit. It's good you have friends to make such things for you. It makes things more even. They won't be able to kill you like they killed us."

It bothered me that he could read me so easily but what was more important was he seemed to know something about Hathaway and his friends.

"Who killed your people?" I asked.

"The Nazis. Die Bruderschaft."

"What's that?"

"They made it happen."

"The Holocaust?"

"The Shoah, yes. They took advantage of longstanding resentment against our people to create a machine to consume us. It made no rational sense. They didn't need to kill us. But they needed to kill someone and we were easiest."

"Why did they need to kill someone?"

"You have to understand. They are very old. They aided the Jomsviking, and the Teutonic Knights, the Franks and the Prussians, Hapsburgs and Hungarians. They hid in the shadows of power knowing that so long as they were careful they could do anything to anyone and get away with it. They whipped and tortured, raped and murdered in the name of their masters."

"They were the retainers, the police chiefs, the coachmen, the doctors, the teachers of the Princes, Archdukes and Dukes of the East. Never aristocracy themselves but always alongside aristocracy for generations doing their dirty work: imprisoning, burning and killing, pouring poison in their master's ears and blackmailing them."

"They love blood and terror you see. They thrive on it and it helps them breed. Terrorising peasants, Pogroms against Jews, religious hysteria, blood libel, and wars were encouraged in the rulers – who, God knows, needed little encouragement – to help them get the blood they needed to reproduce."

"They live for hundreds of years, Samuel. The blood and bone makes them young again. They pretend to die but then they come back. They know how to sleep so they seem dead and then they rescue one another from graves. But it means they keep moving, always moving. Just as His people did. From Kingdom to Duchy, Duchy to County seeking out power and the right to commit murder and torture in its name."

"They lived like this for many centuries. Inspiring the worst horrors, oppression and wars. Then their worst shock. World War One, an aristocrat inspired slaughter greater than all previous bloodletting got out of control and leads to the destruction of the Prussian, Bavarian, Hungarian and Austrian nobility. With the Eastern aristocracy robbed of authority in whose name can they act? How do they survive now?"

"The rise of the communists under Stalin and the fascists under Mussolini provided the inspiration. They will rule directly. No more hiding under the skirts of the aristocracy they will rise up, these teachers, doctors, policemen and drivers. They will find a new leader and start a new European empire founded on blood. A thousand year Reich."

"They form many groups and parties looking for a man to lead them. Finally they found one. A man who could organise, manage and attend to the detail of a thousand tasks. A mastermind with the political skill to manipulate others to underpin a throne of blood: Heinrich Himmler."

I was confused.

"What about Hitler?"

"He was a little pervert who slept most of the time and got in the way. He couldn't organise to save himself. No, it was Himmler who pulled the Nazi rabble together. He turned them from a bunch of street-fighting fools into a political machine able to raise money and win elections."

"He was no speaker like Hitler or Goebbels, but without Himmler Hitler would have been stuck speaking in Bavarian beerhalls and Goebbels would have gone communist. There are lots of clever speakers Samuel. But it takes money and connections to turn them into a political movement. Himmler was the Nazi organiser. He had connections to aristocracy, he was their Mr Fix-it[+]."

"I started to recognise them among the SS. I was one of their little Judas goats. I spied on our people for them, but all the time spying on them. Their parties and their songs of old Thule. Things they could do or say knowing we would soon be fed to their gas chambers."

"But you escaped."

"Like I said, it pays to listen to God."

It was a warning he wanted me to get.

"Are there many of them?"

"Enough. But Samuel, this is important. I never told anyone this because nobody like you ever listened. They have a weakness. It is their greatest problem and everything they do is because of it," he paused to make sure he had my attention. He sure did!

"Their women Samuel. Their women are barren. They barely have one birth in a decade and always boys. Their women are the ones who drive their men on. They may play innocent but they know everything. They demand everything. It is their thirst, their hunger that drives their men. The men are ruthless, cruel and dangerous but their women are worse. Look out for their women Sam. That is their weakness."

He smiled and looked back out to sea.

"For fifty five years I've been coming here. Every day at the same time and I watched and waited and listened to God. And he said wait. So I waited. I waited and listened to God and wondered if my mind had played tricks on me then, and was playing tricks on me now. And now after all these years of wondering if what those evil inhuman pieces of crap boasted to me would ever be believed, here you are, by God knows what means, to listen to me."

He chuckled to himself.

"That's God for you."

"Did you ever meet one called Hassler?" I asked in English.

"Hassler?" he rocked his head repeating the name.

"What did he do?" he asked.

"Medical experiments. Tropical medicine."

"No. Where I was it was get their gold and bank account details, get them in the gas chamber and get their teeth out. It was an extermination camp. They didn't play around like in the other camps. For them the only good Jew was a bar of soap."

"Who did you learn this from?"

"Oberscharfuhrer Kuttner. The lower camp commandant. I was his special informant. Some said his pet. He marked me for death twice but had me pulled out of the gas chamber at the last minute both times. He didn't want me to take my value to him for granted. But I was too useful to him. I could find Swiss bank account numbers that the Nazi Government couldn't touch. They were like crows feasting on the dead those SS. Everyone was making money out of killing us. Even the locals[†]."

"I had no friends. I betrayed thousands. If you didn't they would betray you. Nobody trusted anyone. We were all starving. If I found one hiding anything he would get it out of them. They were all sadists. All of them. Their idea of 'sports' was torturing us[†] and they were sports fanatics."

"He liked giving the gold Jews – the prisoners with skills in making jewellery out of the gold from their fellow prisoners teeth (usually Belgians) – hope they could buy their way out and then snatching it away at the last moment. He found their screams funny."

He paused closing his eyes. He waited for almost a minute before he spoke again, fighting down the need to be sick.

"You know people pleading for their lives have a special kind of scream. It rips at your soul, if you have one. He didn't. I was losing mine fast. He liked that."

"What did he tell you about himself?"

Mr Ceder opened his eyes and looked at me appreciatively.

"You really want to get them don't you?"

"Maybe," I said, not sure what I wanted, but sure I wanted to find out more.

"He told me that he and his brothers were gods who lived among men and that the Jews had made them angry."

"Gods?"

"Demigods maybe. Descended from gods."

"And you believed him?"

"I was a good Jewish boy. Of course not. But he wasn't just a sadistic thug. Unlike the rest he did have greater powers than me. He scared me. A lot of them scared their underlings and not just because they didn't value human life and enjoyed hurting people. They had a special aura of evil about them. Like fiends from the pit of hell. They really were creating Gehenna, a hell on Earth. When the burning of bodies started it really looked like hell too."

"Why had the Jews angered them?"

"They blamed us for their losing the first war. But there was something else. They had a special hatred of Ukrainian and Russian Jews. The Ukrainian and Russian guards seemed to have a special pleasure in hurting their Jewish countrymen."

He looked around and then lent towards me and spoke softly.

"And they were no angels either, those Jews. Stalin's leaders in the Ukraine where seven million were starved to death were often Jews. Trust me. Lot of them here run all sorts of shady business as you are finding out. Be very careful of them, they are completely merciless too."

He lent back and nodded. And now I had a reading of him too. He had no faith in anyone. He was completely alone, without love or hope of it. His soul was a burned and blackened stump. When he said coming here was good for his soul he meant it. His soul was a withered thing, whimpering in perpetual terror and darkness. The vision repelled and appalled me.

"Did this Kuttner guy ever say how many of them there were?"

"No, but when Himmler visited, he had a few others with him. I got to see them from far away. Close up meant they were going to kill you. Himmler was something. Even from a distance you could see he was like a machine. He was full of plots. He pretended to be friendly but he saw everyone as disposable. I got the feeling there were others in the West he worked with. I didn't worry about it much. I was starving and freezing. I was only interested in food and hiding from the cold. I just remember Himmler like a devil in a dream. I still get nightmares of him. But there was one thing about him that made him different."

"Yes?"

"His daughter, Gudrun, was very important to him[†]. She was not much older than me at the time."

"He took his daughter with him?" I asked surprised.

"Yes, but only around the administration area we had to make it pretty for them. That was when I picked up the connection between the daily murder that happened around me and the daughter. The necessity of killing us was linked in his mind to his cherishing her as a father."

"But how did you find out about the breeding thing."

"That was Kuttner. I asked about him about it when he was drunk after Himmler left. He drank a lot. He told me he was only telling me about them because he was going to kill me personally in the morning. He told me about Die Bruderschaft, or the brotherhood of Thule. It was a secret society of them. They were leading their kind in Europe."

"Their kind?"

"He called them Ayrans but he also called them Aesir. He said there were many secret societies of them infiltrated throughout the world especially in Europe and the Americas but that the Brotherhood was showing the way to their kind all over the world. The thousand year Reich would return the Aesir to their deserved status of demigods. By sacrifice and blood they would repopulate the world in their own image."

"Why would he start talking to *you* about their problems with having kids?" I asked trying to imagine the circumstances when a sadist SS officer would talk like this to a dirty little slave he was planning to murder.

The old man looked at me like he'd been caught out. Then he dropped his eyes and looked away. I could tell that even decades later he was still ashamed and uncomfortable.

"When your life depends on making a man happy – even a brute like Kuttner – you will do *anything*." he mumbled.

Tears started in his eyes which he wiped away as he looked out to sea. He was trembling, having a hard time getting the memories under control. They were awful memories too. I just felt so grateful no-one had ever done that to me. I put out my hand and touched his shoulder.

"Mr Ceder ... it's not important how you found out. What did he tell you?"

He fidgeted a bit as he struggled free of the deep mental bruising he had suffered.

"He said they had few women left. The women had been dying out and they only had sons. Daughters were rare and the ratio of men to women was almost a hundred to one. The men could have children with humans but they were always boys and the blood of their children would be further diluted. Only the

women could keep their bloodline pure by having daughters.
Daughters were important."

"But how does the blood thing work. Why the killing?"

"It's not the blood as such. It's the bone marrow that makes the
blood. They need fresh marrow to stay young. When the women
regenerate they can have babies and the more blood they get the
better the chance of daughters."

"But why kill Jews. They had a war going on. There must have
been plenty of blood?"

"Two reasons. The marrow from children is richer in nutrients
for them. War kills young men which their women liked, but
children were even better. But the other reason is connected
with these Russians and Ukrainians. They wanted them
exterminated. I got the impression they were a rival tribe of
theirs or something but I never had a chance to find out because
they killed them so fast."

"Were there any Belgians among them?"

"No. Mostly Austrians and Bavarians. Not even that many
Saxons or Prussians. Why Belgians?" He asked suddenly,
confused.

"The only one I met was Belgian."

Mr Ceder thought about this.

"There were a lot more Belgian and French Nazis than were ever
admitted to. There were Belgian SS divisions but the Belgians
weren't in the Totenkopf division that guarded the camps."

"Of course after the war the mass murderers who survived all
scattered and went into hiding. Some went to South America
like Stangl, Mengele and Eichmann thanks to Gudrun Himmler
and her friends[†]. Others went to America to help them against
the Soviets[†]. Some went to Egypt and Arabia where they were

welcome in their common fight against Israel[†]. Others just hid in Europe – especially Spain[†]. A lot committed suicide or were killed and buried in unmarked graves. For example nobody knows what happened to Himmler[†]. He died but nobody knows what happened to his body. A surprising number of the top Nazis who ran the genocide were never found or got away[†]. Wittner and Lerch were never brought to justice because there was supposedly no evidence[†]. Mengele died of old age in Paraguay[†]."

"But weren't they caught at all?"

"Sure, most of the guards were caught and executed. Some of the officers too. But most of the leaders either killed themselves or got away. As I said there were secret societies that quietly helped them get away. Even some in the Catholic Church were sympathisers[†]."

"What happened to Kuttner?"

"Nobody knows. My theory is he escaped to Switzerland with the bank account numbers I gave him."

"How did you escape?"

"I escaped from Kuttner the night he said he'd kill me. I knew he meant it. But I knew my way around. The guards knew I had special access to Kuttner. I had already planned my escape but never been certain I could pull it off. I hid in a burial pit among the bodies of the dead for two days. The smell of death has never left me since. I dug my way out and got into a rail wagon full of old Jewish clothes heading to Germany. I escaped somewhere in Poland and walked through the war until I got to Greece."

Now it was my turn to look away, thinking. I wondered what Raman would make of this. There was something about this place that somehow felt like everything meant something. I just wasn't sure what. Then I saw Tahira coming up the stairs. She looked happy and beautiful and I could feel Mr Ceder recognise the joy in her, like she was an angel. I got up.

"Thank you Mr Ceder. I have to go now. I think you've helped us. I'm not sure how exactly though."

"One last thing Samuel. The Totenkopf, the death's head on their uniforms. The skull and bones. It meant something to them. More than the heukenkreutz. There was some special reverence about that skull that seemed to mean something special to them. I don't know what."

Tahira came up to me.

"*What's happening?*" she asked silently.

"*Tell you later,*" I replied.

"Todah rubah," I thanked Mr Ceder in Hebrew.

"You're welcome," he replied in English for the first time.

We wheeled our bikes up the path to the road. Tahira rode in front up the hill. The traffic was very busy and having to pretend to pedal slowly made the whole ride too distracting to tell her about what I had heard. Finally we came to the zoo turn off and could ride back around the one way until we came to the path. We zoomed down there and then even as we were moving we folded into darkness and after the usual transition burst into the pool.

## [+]

It was four in the morning. I went upstairs but I wasn't tired. I needed to think over what Mr Ceder had told me so I went into the café in time to see the sky in the East was turning pale while outside the birds were starting to sing. The others had all gone to bed. Then Mr Trân came in. He seemed pleased to see me and chatted away while starting his morning baking routine. He made me a cup of hot milk with cardamom and honey and we talked about bread.

Mr Trân's happiness, despite his suffering as a child, the dawn chorus and the milk all made the horror of Mr Ceder's life on the other side of the world shrink back to size. Here, far from that legacy of pain, it was a fresh, clear and beautiful day. A tomorrow to do better things in.

I went to bed and suddenly I was in a gray land. All around me there were trees, white bare trees that seemed gray, and what seemed to be a sort of gray snow falling softly. In the distance there was a kind of groaning, roaring sound but this snow fell so slowly it fascinated me. I caught some and it didn't melt and I realised it was ash.

I set out through the woods, which seemed deserted, with the groaning and roaring sound growing louder and with a new clanking and banging sound added to it. Then I found a shortcut off the path and cut through the woods so I could see what was happening.

There was a huge clearing. In the middle of it a massive fire. The flames seemed to be ten meters tall. There were some tractors outside the flames working in a huge pit nearby and thousands of figures in black and white striped suits running around them. They were pulling objects as large as themselves out of the ground and carrying them to the fire on stretchers and throwing them in. They didn't want to get too close to the fire but other figures in black with whips were beating them if they didn't go closer. And then one of the striped figures tripped and immediately a black figure stepped forward and shot him so that another striped figure had to throw him to the flames. And I realised what they were burning was bodies. Thousands and thousands of bodies. The fire was roaring and howling like a hungry beast. The bodies were burning and exploding sometimes covering the prisoners in burning filth. Round the outside the men in black prowled beating the prisoners who fed their neighbours, friends and relatives to the flames until they could no longer stand and were fed in their turn to the fire. And I realised this was hell. Hell had come to Earth. I was just about to leave when one of the guards looked around and saw me. Our eyes locked, both brown, both faces similar. It was Ax. Slowly a big grin spread over his face and smiled at me and gave me a wave. Then turned back to the fire and noticing a baby at his feet, threw it in like a bit of firewood.

## CHAPTER FIFTY ONE: PRESENTS

W"ake up!"
The shock of Rewa's voice burst into the dream. I was aware of her but clung tightly to sleep not wanting to let go. My dream was trying to tell me something important. Then the curtain tore in its rails and a bright light stabbed at my eyelids. My sleep starved brain wanted to stay undisturbed but it was losing.

"Wake up Sam. C'mon!"

"Leave me alone," I grumbled.

Rewa went out of the room. I couldn't believe it was so easy. I lay there with my eyes closed and ears listening for her. There was brief sound of a tap. Then silence. I was so tired I knew something was up but I just didn't care anymore. I was a sleep addict.

A cold wet slap in the face and I was sopping. I was sitting up spluttering as Rewa's squeal of wicked delight forced me to open my eyes. She had a now empty glass of water and a happy grin. Then she ran.

"Rewa I'm gonna get you for that," I said, jumping up and chasing her. I was mad and I meant it. She ran out of our apartment and down the corridor squealing and laughing. I knew this was a Mariko inspired stunt but I was still pissed off.

She ran down the corridor to the lounge and then down the stairs right behind me.

"You know what day it is Sam?" Rewa called as we slid down the stairs.

"Sunday," I replied grimly, thinking Sunday was a day of rest. She ran though the downstairs lounge and at the café slowed down so I caught her just in time to realise Dr Prosperov was finishing a little speech with Dr Morozov beside him. Everyone turned and there I was. The biggest egg ever, in wet pyjamas.

"Sam ... come sit down, have some breakfast," Dr Prosperov said.

I had no choice now. Everyone else was up and dressed. The clock said it was ten. So I pressed on through to the counter and realised this was a fairly special meal. Mr Trân gave me a stack of waffles with whipped butter and maple syrup and bacon and a black coffee. Normally Sundays were Mr Trân's day off, something I'd been too distracted to realise earlier in the morning. I tottered over to a table next to Grandpop who slapped a sleep pill down next to me, which I swallowed down with some coffee.

In the meantime Dr Prosperov had finished. I was too sleepy to catch what he was on about.

"What's happening?" I asked Grandpop.

He smiled.

"Rewa, tell him," he said to her across the table.

"We've been here a year today." she told me.

I was surprised, but tired. A year.

As I ate I tried to remember what life had been like before. No kids, no missions, no training, no suit, no Fae, no predictions, no Tabika, no Cam, no Tarik, no Ashley, no Scotty, no Tahira, no nothing. Just Ax after us. It seemed amazing to think how much our lives had changed ever since we'd met Dr Prosperov.

"What did Dr P say?" I asked.

"Just that he thought we were doing well and we were a lot further ahead than he had expected but that the real work is only just beginning."

"Oh! OK," I shrugged, eating.

"And we're having a party," Rewa added.

"Cool."

I was having enough difficulty just eating to worry about anything else I was meant to be doing.

"The others bugged Ax last night," Grandpop told me.

"OK."

"He gave them a bit of trouble. He wasn't asleep until three."

"Yeah," I said, not at all surprised.

"Ah he was with his girlfriend ... and well ... they had to wait."

That was too much information.

"Grandpop, you're putting me off my breakfast," I complained.

"OK ... sorry I just thought you'd want to know before the others told you about it."

It seemed like the least of my problems.

"I met an old man in Israel last night," I told him.

"Oh yeah?"

"He knew all about Hathaway's friends."

"*What*? How?"

"He was a Holocaust survivor."

Grandpop's eyebrows shot up.

"He was psychic too. Very psychic. Read me like a book."

"Did Tahira meet him?"

"Briefly. She was doing her Baha'i thing. You should listen to what he said. It was very interesting."

I yawned. I was still tired, although the pill was starting to kick in. It was all becoming a dream.

"So what did he say?"

"Just that they have a shortage of women because they have a shortage of daughters. Their women need bones and blood to have kids or something. They prefer to get it from children and young people rather than adults."

Grandpop was looking surprisingly uncomfortable.

"That's ... pretty horrible, Sam."

I shrugged.

"Did he have any idea where they were?"

"No, he was trying to escape them ... but he said after World War Two they spread out and hid everywhere they could. They were helped apparently."

"Hmm well the Nazis were helped. That's well known."

"He also said something odd about Russian and Ukrainian Jews."

"What about them?"

"Just that they hated them more than usual. But that they were merciless themselves. As if there was some kind of fight between them."

"Hmm Dr Prosperov is one. I might ask him."

I hadn't thought of that. I'd been wondering a bit about Gunter's family in that war but I'd forgotten Dr P's mother was Jewish.

"What are we doing today?" I asked.

"You? You're doing your chores and resting. *We* are getting ready for the party."

It was a quiet day. The others didn't talk to me about Ax but I could tell they had had something of an education and were smirking a bit. But a few hours later when I was in the middle of vacuuming Dr Prosperov found me.

"Sam, very interesting conversation last night. Have sent to Hekator as part of his research. Maybe need to talk again with Mr Ceder."

He indicated for me to sit down on one of the side chairs on the landing.

"Thought to explain little about his views on Russian and Ukrainian Jews. Is intriguing but without history you may find confusing."

He paused for a moment and began again.

"First must be explained Communist Party of Soviet Union had many Jews in it when started. This is not surprising. Jews arrived in Russia in eighteenth century, later than elsewhere in Europe, usually after being expelled by various Kings and nobles for religious reasons. Jews brought business to Russia as they did everywhere and if not welcome mostly tolerated[†]."

"Must be remembered Russia is built by very rich noble families on backs and bones of slaves called serfs. Russian nobility very harsh. But after French invasion of 1812 Russians influenced by Napoleonic idea of equal opportunity. Jewish thinkers at forefront – because Jews cannot own land but becoming rich so is in interest to promote modern economy with democracy and equal access for all[†]."

"Communist revolution in 1917 extension of this. Party takes over land, displaces aristocracy. Is civil war until 1922. Many Jews in high places in Party. Trotsky, Kamanev, Zeminiev, Yagoda and Kaganovich[†]. But many also minor like my father. Stalin used, betrayed and killed all[†]. Nothing special. Was same to Russians."

"Ukraine is special case. Stalin wanted to build war machine and destroy Ukrainian power. Only had limited resources to begin so stole food from Ukrainians to sell to America in 1930s. Ten millions starved. Is called Holodomor[†]. Kaganovich among communists responsible, but most not Jews. Among millions are some German farmers settled on Volga by Tsarina Catherine generations before. Many moved to my home city during war in case they side with invader. However in Holodomor mostly Ukrainians died. When Germans invade ten years later at first Ukrainians think they are saved from Stalin[†]. Soon discover mistake. German Nazis even worse than Russians."

Dr Prosperov stopped looking at me. I thought back to what Mr Ceder had said.

"Then he could be wrong about everything, even the Germans?"

"Child in death camp easily confused by many things but not death."

"But why was *Mr Ceder* so anti Ukrainian and Russian Jews?"

"Ah ... Russian Mafiya is mostly Jewish and has entered Israel – especially Haifa. Also ex-Soviet arrivals greatly changed ethnic and political mix in Israel. Favours right wing politics, land seizures from Palestinians by force. Am thinking Ceder is old Kibutznik who mistrusts newcomers. Is nothing special."

I wondered if he was telling me this to make me trust him more.

"So you don't think there might be a tribe of alien descendants hidden among Ukrainian Jews?" I asked.

He smiled and shrugged.

"Anything possible Sam. Anything possible. One year ago could you have guessed you even wonder this? So perhaps. Perhaps is so. But if it is would surprise me much."

He got up. I stood too.

"Please to tell the others of what you have learned. Is best when all operatives informed."

So I did. We spent the afternoon walking along the cliffs to the south past the gun emplacements. There was no sign of anything going on beneath us. The metal barrier that had been blasted open by the tubular spaceships had been replaced by a new steel sheet, as rusty looking as the old one. The only sign it was new was the graffiti was Mariko's. We hadn't seen anything more of either the giant Vimana or Hekati since that night and we weren't sure when they would be finished.

We talked about Ax and Mr Ceder, Christmas and what we wanted to do. We decided we might do a drop over the Galleon site that evening and practice bend diving over the sea. Ashley still wasn't that keen, so she and Scotty decided they would take the treasure chest in with them. They wondered if they should steal Bernard's rakes to help us work the sand.

We played a bit with Rewa and Asal when we came back and then at four talked Bernard into acting as controller while we went to Guam. We all bent at once.

[+]

It was a lovely afternoon twelve thousand feet above and twenty kilometers south of Guam. You could just see the island in the distance with just little fat puffs of cloud dotted here and there around the Pacific. There was no wind.

Tahira and I took the lead swooping like falcons in deep dives before pulling up into stalls. The trick was to be confident and not think about it. The suit did the thinking, you just had to trust it. We checked on Cam and Tarik and although it was new to them they were OK.

The last dive started out about four kilometers out from the wreck site which was picked out in green. Diving from one grand, we pulled out of our dives to skim along the flat sea at about two hundred and fifty kilometers an hour. I looked over at Tahira as she looked at me. I couldn't see her face but I was pretty sure she was grinning as much as I was. After one kilometer we were down to one hundred and fifty and by three we were very low, doing fifty using the lifting effect of the water's surface and a touch of gravity reduction to stay airborne. Pretty soon however we were almost out of wing lift so we reduced gravity more, flapped, then pulled up to stall and folded our wings. We knifed into the water legs first from about five meters. It was still quite a hit.

Cam and Tarik didn't do the final stall but skimmed into the sea reducing gravity so they could get slower but remain airborne. They came in headfirst. We swam over to Ashley and Scotty arguing which technique was better.

We got to work on the wreck and started digging closer to the old ribs of the vessel, me and Tahira watching out in case they moved because they were big and still heavy. For about an hour we found nothing very interesting and it was getting boring, when suddenly Scotty struck wood. We dug some more and found the lid of a chest. It disintegrated in our hands and we found ourselves looking at some red cloth. It was surprisingly well preserved.

There were lots of clothes of all sorts. They had gold embroidery and there were some pretty belts and shoes. We kept digging and found more chests. Most of them were full of clothes and personal belongings. It seemed a rich family were moving and had brought their stuff on the ship with them. Then we found another chest and opened it too. There was a cover of simple sacking. Then Ashley pulled it aside and gasped. The chest was full of gold coins.

They glinted in the wavering light under the sea. We all just stood there staring at it.

"*It looks like chocolate coins,*" Ashley murmured.

"*About a million bucks worth,*" Tarik guessed.

We called Bernard and he went and got Dr P.

"Is the treasure of Antonia Isabella Cabriel," he told us. "Excellent work."

We picked up our transfer chest from where Ashley and Scotty had left it and started loading it. Most of the gold was in biscuit-sized coins but beneath them there were bars. It was smaller than a big seachest. There was about a square meter wide pile about a quarter of a meter high but it still looked like a lot of gold to us.

### [+]

When we brought it home everyone was there to see it. We tried to lift the chest but we just couldn't. We waited for the oil to drain and opened it up and bailed the seawater out and tried again but it was still too heavy. Even Ken, Grandpop, Bernard and Gunter had no luck.

Bernard asked Control something and then announced, "The transfer mass was two point eight tonnes of which two was the gold. At current prices this is worth... "

He concentrated counting, and then he did it again, checking, and looked up, a bit stunned.

"Fifty one million US dollars."

We all whooped and cheered.

"Howsit feel to make your first four mil?" Tarik asked Ashley grinning his head off as we all whooped.

243

"Four?" Scotty asked over the noise.

"A sixth of half ... more or less," Tarik replied.

Ashley just whooped long and loud and we all high-fived each other.

To get the gold out we had to form a chain and pass it along. It was heavy. Even the small coins were heavy. Everyone wanted and got, a look and a touch.

"Lucky we're having a party, eh Aunty Liz," Rewa said.

Everyone laughed.

We moved the gold up to the strongroom. It looked very impressive sitting there. It just made us feel good knowing it was ours. The colour made you feel anything was possible.

The party was outside on the beach. Mariko had made some more torches, and had some stuff to make huge bubbles. You could suddenly find yourself inside one if you weren't paying attention. Ken had brought Aunty Nea up by chopper.

It was a different party to the one we had had a year ago. Then we had mostly just escaped being on the run. We'd had more games and run about more. We'd had so much more to find out about each other.

Now we were secure in our place and in each other. We held up Patience as she tried to practice walking. We chased round after Asal and Rewa but we weren't checking each other out anymore. We had been though a lot together. Scotty had been shot. Tahira had more or less told us what had happened to her. Ashley and her mum had fought all over the house. Tarik and Cam were close and Scotty and Ashley were even closer. We had faced our fear of falling together and become a team. But mostly it was the day-to-day jokes, the shared annoyance with Mr Wakefield and Marshall and his friends, the bus rides and the cleaning routines.

The big news of the night was Drs Prosperov and Morozov announcing they would have a baby next August. They seemed so much older than Bernard and Zoe but everyone was happy for them. Dr Morozov was a different woman. She smiled and chatted. It was as if she had melted, just a little. We kids went to bed about ten. The party was getting a bit adult and dull anyway. We left Ken and Patricia to boogie down and Dr Gursoy and Mitra talking about religion together by the light of the moon. As I took Rewa off to bed I noticed Aunty Liz with Aunty Nea alone and I wondered, for the first time, if she was really happy at Renwick.

Christmas was coming up fast and we spent Sunday in Auckland shopping. I was trying to think what presents to get everyone. This year we had no shortage of money, but a shortage of time. I would have loved to have gone to all sorts of countries to get things for different people but we were still a bit unsure about doing that and we weren't sure our gift cards would work anywhere else. In the end it was all a bit of a rush but when we finally all crammed aboard Betty it looked as though we'd bought half the shopping centre.

I'd got a special present for Emma. It was a pretty bracelet made from blue stones and silver. Tahira had helped me pick it out. On Monday it sat in my bag all through the school day making me feel like an egg. Finally at the end of the day I gave it to her with a mumbled "Happy Christmas" before diving aboard Betty to stop my face going too red.

That night I imagined her opening it and being really pleased. But the next day she didn't say anything much to me. I spent two days being pissed off before discovering she had put it under her family tree with all the other Christmas presents. She gave me something small, along with some of her girlfriends, a day or so later which I knew were some cookies she'd made with her mum. It was nice but I knew she'd be a bit shocked on Christmas day.

But her big news was the family holiday they were planning to New Zealand's pretty South Island with the family of her boyfriend David. They were going to be camping all over the place at Department campsites for a whole month. It churned me up with jealousy. I fantasised about bending into their camp and making David look like an idiot.

Tahira was great though, when she heard about it. She sat me down after vacuuming and told me that if I wanted Emma's attention I was going to have to put in a lot more effort than I had so far. She gave me a good telling off and started plotting with me to win Emma back again. I felt lucky to have a friend like Tahira. I wondered if I would ever help her out the same way.

The last day of school, before the long summer holidays, was a bit of a downer. My plans to be cool and mysterious with Emma were a humungous fail. I just ended up saying "seeya" and feeling dumb. But the mood on the bus was great. Mariko was playing our favourite sounds and we were all dancing around and being idiots, something we kept doing while we were cleaning as well.

Grandpop gathered us, told us to suit up and come in for a briefing. We were still feeling as jumpy and excited as freshly shorn sheep but we knew to pay attention to briefings. They could be important.

The surprise at this one was Hekator, beaming in by hologram. "Hi guys," Hekator said. "Today's trip is a bit different to most of those that you go on. It's another bugging mission except that your target is a lot more dangerous than any you have dealt with so far. So dangerous, in fact, that we will have you permanently locked to bend out the whole time."

We were a bit worried we were going to a war zone. Our happy mood chilled a bit.

"The place you are going is sandy and it's essential you don't leave *any* tracks."

Hekator seemed to be deliberately mysterious.

"At the same time it's dark and you must *not* use gravity reduction or you will be detected at once. To help out we've fitted some stilts to your suits. They will raise you a meter above the sand. They are pointy and will stick in so if you stand still too long you will be stuck. The idea is to work fast."

"What you will be doing is laying sensor wire." Hekator held up a green ball of gray wire the size of a tennis ball.

"The wire is extremely thin and very strong. You will be bent into position in a hexagon. The person with the wire roll will anchor the wire end with these wire staples and throw the reel to the next person to the left. Hold it in place until it is thrown to the next person, staple and then advance into the centre of the hexagon five meters. That way you will produce a spiral. You will all do this four times until you are at the centre of the hexagon. There you plant the reel in the sand and hide it. Then we will bend you to the next location to do it again."

"You will need to keep watch the whole time. If there is the slightest chance you are spotted we will bring you home."

"We're going to practice with a ball in the Sahara desert where it's just before dawn. Remember this is about speed, accuracy, teamwork, and awareness."

"You're going to take a while to work up to a rhythm but when you get it, it'll be time to switch from practice to the real thing. Mike has the practice balls and the reels. The practice balls are blue, the reels are gray…"
"Um, Hekator where are we going?" Ashley interrupted.
"You mean after the Sahara?"
"Yes."
"To six sites ten kilometers from the Galactic Administration's headquarters for this world. So you will be in almost constant danger for about half an hour."
"You mean where the flying saucers come from?" Scotty asked.
"Yes."
Now we were all awake. It was going to be the fastest game of throw and catch we ever played.
"Where is it?" asked Tarik.
"Your moon."
We all looked at each other. We were shocked and a bit worried by that.
"Do our suits work there?" Ashley asked.
"Of course."
"Guys," Grandpop began, "for this kind of mission the main thing is to focus on what *you* are doing. The scenery, the risks, are all secondary. You have to think about your team as a whole and relax. Relaxing is how you do a simple task in difficult places. Don't think or worry. That's how you'll lose it."
Which seemed easier for him to say than for us to do.
Hekator picked up.
"The only way to do this smoothly is by getting a rhythm going, so Mike will give you all a practice ball and a reel. The practice ball will glow because it has a gravity reduction field which I've

set to equal your moon. The reel will identify itself to your suits."
Hekator said.

"To get your eye in," Grandpop added, "We'll start with pairs,
then we'll get you on stilts, then we'll do it in a circle, then we'll
rehearse the whole thing. Any questions?"

There weren't any. It was like a P.E. lesson but a bit harder.
Grandpop handed out two balls each which we pocketed. We
trooped down to the jumpstation.

"You'll be in two lines about a hundred meters apart. Girls throw
the blue ball first."

And we were gone.

## [+]

The place we arrived in was a plain of sand so big it was almost
like a dream. Above us the starscape was so fiercely beautiful it
was hard to ignore. There was a pale crescent moon which put
a little light on the untouched sand about us. There was not a
breath of wind. The plain was rimmed by distant mountains and
dunes but they were so far away it hardly mattered.

Looking around I could see five green outlines. Without the suit
I wouldn't have been able to see the others at all.

"OK girls, you start," Grandpop said.

Three blue dots arced out of the dark. Our first throws were
well short. We had to go back to our orange marks before we
could throw again. It took us about fifteen minutes before we
were reliably getting the range and angle. The balls fell strangely
slowly so they were quite easy to catch.

Then Grandpop said it was time to extend our stilts. They were
thin, about a centimeter, but very stiff and for some reason
didn't sink into the sand far. They made throwing and catching
all the harder. It took us another half an hour to get used to

them. Finally we bent into a hexagon and began practising in earnest. There were a few poor throws and muffed catches but we were getting better. Then we bent and did it again. After ten hexagons we had got the last three perfect.

"OK guys take a look at these pictures from one kilometer up. The first one is your first practice site. The second your last. The images arrived like memories in our heads. The first was a mess. There were footprints everywhere. It was obviously disturbed. The last was untouched.

"The wind will cover your first site in a few weeks but on the moon there is no wind. OK? Everyone ready? Here we go."

**[+]**

The place we arrived on was very like the one we had left but much deader and darker. There was starlight from the zillions of dead untwinkling dots in the sky. The sand was gray like a blanket of death and the shadows seemed darker than black. It was strange to be in a place that was so lacking in life. Even the Empty Quarter, was somehow, still part of a world of life. Here life was unknown and you felt it at once.

Tarik called to Cam and the reel floated, outlined in green, but otherwise invisible toward her. Cam caught it with a whip, sorted herself out and re-threw it to Scott. When it got to me I was able to see the wire, which was as thin as a hair. I threw it on, not as well as I would have liked and Tahira had to use the whip as well. As Tahira threw to Tarik I stapled the wire and took a huge step which was easy and waited my next turn. The circuits sped up as we got accustomed to where we were. Grandpop had been right. It did help to forget about your surroundings and just focus on what you were doing. Finally Tarik planted the reel and we were off to the next site.

Slowly we sped up. The next site was eight minutes, then six, then five, but at the fifth site there was a problem. We were halfway through when Scotty called out.

"*Stop!*"

"*What?*"

"*Drop the stilts and crouch.*"

"*Why?*"

"*Shadows.*"

We dropped and crouched.

"Scott, What's happening?" Grandpop asked.

"*Look.*"

We all picked up his feed.

Three stars were curving around overhead. They were a long way away but moving fast. Scotty watched them for us all as they sped towards us.

I checked my shadow. It was very faint. I looked over at Tahira. She was fully blended and if it weren't for the green outline I would never have noticed her.

The dots had got bigger. At best magnification I could see they were scouts moving quickly but they were heading directly for the crater we had been circling a long way away. They slowed and just for a moment we saw three tiny silver saucers drop out of sight. We remained still for a moment.

"Guys. Let's get this done and get home," Grandpop growled in our ears.

We got back on to the stilts and began moving the reel around fast-as. There were a few more mistakes as we kept looking around but we got it finished within a few minutes and bent to the next site. This one we got done in six minutes. I picked up a rock for Rewa. Then we were home.

# [+]

We got changed for the debrief. As we did so we started wondering aloud what we had been doing. Control could watch anywhere and Hekator could bend things anywhere. Why had we lain that wire? We put the question to Hekator.

"Well, it's a bit technical but what it comes down to is that if we open a vision channel in or near their base, they will not only know about it, they will also be able to grab it from us and stick a trace transponder down it. That was what we did to recover Tabika. If you look at *them they* will find you in an instant. It's because the amount of energy needed to open a super-dimensional pathway for radiation is large – even for a pinhole-sized wormhole. It's much, much larger for a matter one."

"But then they could have detected us, bending in, couldn't they?" Tarik asked.

"That's exactly right Tarik. They could *if* they were worried about it, but it's not something they expect. This is a scientific outpost not a military base. They just limit their security to space above their entrance and to a fairly limited ground perimeter, knowing you can't bend in underground. If you'd gone to look at their base – which is underground with an entrance which is practically invisible anyway – you would have been detected if you bent in or out."

"So what did we do?"

"You laid a passive sensor array so we know about their movements. It will detect the coming and going of their craft. It only has a quantum modem which is the least energy intensive of them all. They could hover right on top of it and not detect it."

"Why do they use saucers instead of bending?" I asked.

"They aren't as advanced as we are. Their craft can bend but it

**252**

takes them a lot of preparation. They are better at inertialess travel which is capable of near light speed. So in a system as small as this by the time they have worked out their bending computations they could have simply flown where they want to go so they prefer to fly. They haven't got technology like your suits or our super-dimensional computing network. They would love to get hold of them. And if they did we would be in very great danger. That is why we keep a close eye on you. You are potentially risking not only your lives but also the millions on Fae. That is why we say never to take a risk with the Administration's Scouts."

That was a bit of an eye-opener. It had never occurred to me before we were a risk to millions of Fae. It made me feel very responsible.

We went upstairs for dinner. Rewa wasn't very excited by the moon rock and I couldn't blame her really. It was pretty dull. Still, she put it her window to soak up 'moon rays'.

A week before Christmas Hekati announced the base extension was ready. A wall was suddenly demolished revealing a whole extra set of rooms. She gave us a tour in person. The surprise was a set of four extra suit changers. Hekati explained.

"The maximum design body mass for our child suits is fifty kilos. There are three people who are under fifty kilos here who may be needed for support tasks. Rewa and Asal will need their parents permission but there are a number of important roles Raman has foreseen for them. Mariko may supervise them, or she may be needed as an adult assistant for the psychic operatives."

I noticed Aunty Liz and Mitra look at each other with concern.

I had a fair idea that both were unlikely to let the girls go anywhere even remotely dangerous.

Rewa and Asal meanwhile looked like they would explode with happiness. Only the strangeness of Hekati was preventing them from screaming and running around like mad things. Surprisingly Mariko wasn't whooping or punching the air. Instead she was looking very serious. She seemed to have expected this announcement and looked, if anything, a bit nervous.

"The girls suits are a bit different. They are for our smaller children and have a few things added and a few things removed. I'm afraid they don't have wings or any weapons except the electric shock, and confusion beam. They can only be used with the supervisor who can also bend them. Mariko's suit has been tweaked a bit to put those supervisor capabilities in it. Of course our teachers don't wear suits."

There were a few grumpy looks from Aunty Liz, Soraya and Mitra at Dr Prosperov but he didn't seem to notice.

The next room was different. There were six roof rack capsules on rails like bullets in a magazine mounted facing a round door. Control appeared among us although Hekati ignored him.

"These are a significant new tool for you, quite different to your suits. These are very like Administration scouts but much, much smaller. In fact they only fit one person. They can act by themselves but they need instructions from their pilot. They won't do anything without instructions and they won't do some things even *with* instructions. They will only respond to a single pilot so each craft will be your own. You will need to name them."

She opened one up. There were no controls, just handles to hold on to.

"How do we see?" Tarik asked.

Hekati pointed to the skullcap shaped thing in the popped up door.

"The interface is similar to your suit's. The capabilities are very different. The craft is not able to bend. So if you are in trouble, you are in trouble. We can't make the passenger compartment big enough to hold your suit's energy pack and maintain the disguise which Lana wanted. We've started designing a new suit but it's a whole new project which might take a year or so to finish. Like your suit this is technology we have available now and we've only made a few modifications to it for you."

"This craft can't bend but it can hide. It's very good at hiding. At over two hundred meters it can project an invisibility field that will defeat all frequencies up to x-ray. It has the same blending ability as your suits. Like your suits its primary hull is a carbon-crystal lattice, but this is rigid and ten times thicker so it is able to withstand extreme heat and pressure. It can dive to ten kilometers underwater and achieve submarine speeds of two hundred kilometers an hour."

I wondered if I had heard that right.

"It can operate in space and can achieve orbit. But its main feature is that it has an inertialess drive. Inertia is momentum, so if anything is still it takes time for it to speed up. If it's moving it takes time to slow down. Changing direction has to take into account what direction it is already going in. Inertia is what ties mass to space-time. Inertialess means no momentum. This can only be achieved by transferring mass-energy into other dimensions by creating a kind of super-dimensional bubble. This means you can go from extreme speed to still instantly and not feel any deceleration. The only real restriction on speed is the temporal constant of the primary dimension: time. Inertialess flight has a few important features however. First it creates large field distortions and doesn't work with the invisibility field. So inertialess is best for high speed movement and manoeuvre but it's detectable.

"How far could they detect it from?" Ashley wanted to know.

"Well the craft are small for a reason. The Administration monitors this planet for intrusion fairly closely. They are not perfect but let's just say that their satellites are better than yours. By making this craft so small however we think we have given you a detection radius of one hundred kilometers. That means you can fly inertialess up to fifty kilometers up without being detected by the Administration's surface monitoring satellites. A scout's radius is a five thousand kilometers but they are a hundred times bigger. Of course both their satellites and yours can also watch out for ice trails and visual clues as well. The main thing is you should see them before they see you. Of course at the speeds they can go that may not be long.

"But how do your ark thingies not get detected," Ashley asked.

"The Vimana don't use inertialess drive. They use negative gravity which is different to gravity deflection. Gravity deflection as used in your suits converts gravity to energy and makes the glow you find so annoying. It's an old technology based on a microfusion core which is desirable in a child's suit but not in yours. Antigravity is different. It involves production of antigravity fields. These are the fields which expand the Universe. They repel mass from mass and produce significant accelerations which can balance the acceleration due to gravity. It is fairly obvious negative or antigravity and gravity do not interact to produce energy or the boundary between gravitational and antigravitational cosmic sources like galaxies would be bright instead of dark like deep space."

"Practically this means an antimatter core power system which is more complex technology than that in your suits. This is a significant difference because the microfusion reactor in your suits is completely failsafe. If it dies the reaction stops and you have no power. But an antimatter core is not so convenient. If it is fails there is a very large explosion. Breaking open the vortex at the core of these craft will produce such an explosion."

"To get in place your hand on the top and tell the craft its name, which is the password. We'll initialise these in a moment. But there is one more room which we've built for storing your equipment."

We went into the third room. There were ten alcoves. They all had the bikes in a closet on one side, a tall cupboard on the other side and drawers in the middle.

"Because you can't use the suits inside the craft we've got a few useful extras for use with them."

She went to the cupboard and opened it. There were a t-shirt, cycle pants and a hoodie there. She took them out.

"These are protective undergarments made of similar material to your suit's middle layer. They are not as good at protecting you as a suit but they will resist some penetration, acids and help cushion some impacts. The hooded top has the same adaptive camouflage as your suits. The control is in the button. You can copy a pattern, or choose adaptive. You will not be as hard to see as your suits."

She opened a drawer.

"These transparent gloves will prevent you leaving fingerprints and protect you from heat and cold. This soft hat will catch hair and skin flakes that may yield DNA material. These sunglasses are linked to Control for sight and sound. This card can imitate any Earth technology card by being pressed against it. This is for access doors and your religious custom of money. The music player translates the same languages as your suit. This watch is your navigator and computer, we've taught it English but you can adapt it to other languages if you wish. You dial up the avatar like this."

She twisted the dial and pushed the button and a little hologram appeared.

"Hello I'm Jo. If you are my new owner please speak now." it said.

She twisted it again and the hologram vanished. Then she picked up a pretty average looking cell phone.

"The watch can connect to this or any other phone like this." She showed us the gel bridge.

"This phone is a communications device for communicating with Control, your friends and craft. Control is the only safe channel your suits and craft will usually accept although they can monitor local radio and radar signals. The phone itself identifies you by smell and sound and can tell your moods. It's as sensitive as a dog. The phone can open channels on your telecommunications system and retrieve data from your networks."

She jangled a key chain.

"These keys are all adaptive like the ones in your suit. They adapt when given three quick squeezes."

Finally she picked up a short umbrella.

"Lana wants you to have some kind of weapon. This is a stun

ray disguised as an umbrella. The umbrella is a real umbrella but the fabric is impact resistant as well. It will deflect smaller, slower bullets. The ray has an ultraviolet targeting beam visible through the sunglasses. The weapon can administer ten knock out discharges. And that's about everything."

We turned back to the craft.

"The craft will give you powerful support. It is equipped with a wide range of sensors and its weapons are much more powerful than those in a suit. It means you can keep track of vehicles and aircraft including landing on them. But it has its drawbacks which is why we're giving you all this extra equipment. The main problem is that unlike the suit the craft is not built for extended use. You have no water and waste system like the suit has. You will have to get out sometimes and when you do you could be vulnerable."

"How long would it take it to get to Africa?" I asked thinking of missions in North Kivu.

"To reach the other side of your planet from here and come back again at maximum speed would take half an hour if you went into orbit and were not worried about being detected. But with altitude limited to thirty to forty kilometers, taking maximum advantage of cloud cover and avoiding ice trails it would be closer to four hours. Four hours there and four hours back. Even in these craft it is a long way."

"How long does it take *them* to get here from the moon?" Tarik asked.

"Depending on whether it's a straight line or they have to swing around the planet, about half an hour to an hour."

"But why is it faster to go four hundred thousand kilometers from the moon to the Earth than forty thousand around the

Earth?" Tarik checked.

"Because you have to stay slow to reduce field intensity. Too much and they'll pick you up. But even at top speed the Scouts are built for space and are much faster than your craft. Do *not* try to race them. If you detect one, hide. It's the only advantage you have. Your craft are no match for them in speed or fighting. Blend in with your kind or hide out of sight. Underwater would be best. Your craft are built for stealth that is why they are so small. They are not built to fight or run."

"But you asked about the distance Tarik. The other reason their scouts can get here quickly is because they move in straight lines. As the technology relies on inertialess drive the curves imposed by gravity around a planet become redundant. Inertialess drives work best in straight lines. Moon to earth trips can reach speeds which become a fraction of the speed of light. The hard part is realigning with the planet's gravitational field so you don't crash. And sometimes *they* do. Your craft is slower but manages that for you. It flies itself. Your job is giving it a purpose."

She led us back to the room with the capsules in them.

"So all that remains is for you to try them. Pick one and get in. There will be a short period where you introduce each other and you name your craft. Then you can tell it what you want."

She stood back. We were feeling a bit shy because everyone was watching us, but we got into the open hatches and lay down. The insides were padded but not much. I thought being closed up in this was going to be a bit scary. Then Hekati came along, made sure we were in position and closed the lids on us.

The cap almost forced itself onto your head. Then the weirdness began. It felt like you were hiding in a dark closet with a friendly stranger. The stranger asked a whole bunch of questions all at once and just thinking the answers was enough. Then it asked "What is my name?"

I had wanted to call the falcon Tahira had taken from Hekator "Ka-rea-rea" after the New Zealand native falcon, so I named this box "Ka-rea-rea" instead. He (he was now definitely a 'he' although I got the impression that was because I wanted him to be) seemed to like the name and its associations. Then suddenly I could see. Everything was a bit blurry and distorted at first. "Just relax. It takes a while to get used to."

I started to realise I could hear as well. Hekati was leading everyone else away. Rewa and Asal were going with Mariko to get changed for the first time. I wondered what Rewa would think about the waste system. She was quite shy normally.

The others seemed to be headed for the briefing room. Then I became aware of the others lying in boxes next to me.

*"You know if these things don't fly we could look pretty stupid,"* Scotty commented. We could see each other all lying in boxes and it did look pretty dumb. We all laughed. It would be a funny practical joke.

But as Scott said it, my awareness came clear. It wasn't like normal vision. You could see what you focused on without moving your head all the way around you. It was more like seeing in a dream. You had a general impression but also a point of focus.

*"Who's on the end of the ramp."* Ashley asked.

*"I am,"* said Cam, *"but I'm not ready yet."*

None of us were. Slowly we were becoming aware of what these little craft could do. It was exciting and fascinating at the same time. We learned the controls for visibility, then came the beams, then came the movement.

Suddenly and silently we all lifted into the air and the room came alive with big box things nosing around, turning upside down, revolving, twisting and spinning. There were no collisions, even if you wanted to the craft wouldn't let us bump each other.

"Control here, I've finished my area check and you are safe to launch under invisibility field and exit the launch tunnel. Your exercise destination is Raoul Island. Location given. Please form an exit queue. Exit speed one hundred kilometers per hour. Accelerate to Mach point nine five. Your waypoint is one hundred kilometers east-north-east."

The door slid open as we went invisible and jostled into a queue. At such close range invisibility wasn't really possible. All that happened was we looked like big bubbles of transparent air with a big glow around the outside. I hoped the invisibility was better than that from a distance.

Then we took turns zipping out the tunnel through the gun emplacement door. As my turn came up I was worried I might hit something going up the tunnel into the circle of bright blue light, but as I went into it and accelerated all my nervousness about getting it wrong fell away like the island behind me.

*This* was flying! It was completely easy. You could see all around you as if you weren't inside anything at all, but you felt snug and protected in a way that bend-diving definitely didn't. The island fell back behind us as we zoomed into the sky rising up to get a look up and down the length of the island and back over the top of it towards the city.

I looked for the others. If you got close enough you could see a halo start to form around them but apart from that they were

only visible because of the green circles we saw around them.
Otherwise you couldn't see them at all. I was a bit shy of taking
the controls at first, thinking Ka-rea-rea should do the flying but
Ka-rea-rea was asking me what I wanted him to do. It was a bit
like riding a really good horse. Not a lazy or tricky one, but one
that wanted to have fun.

I tightened my grip on the handles and swung back lower toward
the sea to intercept with Tahira. All I had to do was think it, and
Ka-rea-rea did it. Tarik was heading higher. Cam, like me, was
swinging back to join the others.

"Waypoint please everyone," Control said in our heads.

The waypoint was further east than we had been heading. We
had all been going north at about five hundred kilometers an
hour now as we turned east we began to realise we were well
short of Mach point nine five. We all urged our craft forward.
But it was like riding a racehorse at a trot. Ka-rea-rea was just
looking around, ears pricked, checking out the track. To him,
this was nothing.

To me it was still pretty exciting. We zoomed back down and
formed a line flying along at nine hundred kilometers an hour
Now we were charging across the sparkling water rolling over
and changing position just because we could. It felt completely
righteous.

The waypoint was coming up and Control had a new instruction.
"Twenty kilometers altitude please."

We pulled up and headed near vertically. Normally we were
hurtling the other way. Defying gravity like this was just lovely.

"*What's that noise?*" Scotty asked.

We listened. There was a regular beep in our ears. Ka-rea-rea
had the answer at once. It was the civil aviation radar, but we

were invisible to it.

The dark edge of space was becoming clearer as we left the ground behind. Below we could see the whole country like a map with tiny dots of cloud over it while the curve of the Earth was now clear. My body was tense. It remembered falling from this height in a suit. It felt hard to breathe. But Ka-rea-rea was relaxed. Now the racehorse was ready to run.

"Control here. You are clear to disengage warp invisibility and proceed inertialess to Raoul island. Max safe field intensity."

We turned to face north-east. The change from warp invisibility to adaptive or blend camouflage didn't make much difference. The adaptive camouflage was so good the others were almost transparent. Then Tahira turned to a blur and was gone. I wasn't having her beat me and followed. The feeling of instant acceleration was odd. One instant you were flying at one speed the next at a much faster speed with no feeling of acceleration at all. At that altitude it didn't feel fast because there was nothing to compare it with. You just got a satisfying sense of not wasting time.

We covered the eleven hundred kilometers in ten minutes. Tahira kept her lead. Ka-rea-rea was just enjoying himself doing what he was made to do. I couldn't help thinking that it was a very different thing to go from one place to another including the places in between instead of bending space to avoid them. I liked the feeling of passing through light and space instead of the realm of presences when we bent.

As Raoul Island came up Control came back.

"Descend at two kilometers short of destination, patrol at 300km/h."

I expected ka-rea-rea to dive, but he didn't. I was confused by this when Tahira suddenly dropped vertically out of sight. It looked freaky. I imagined the feeling in the pit of her stomach, but Tahira wasn't complaining. I came up to where she had been and suddenly I was dropping as fast as I had been moving forward. I didn't feel a thing! I was lying there as if I had spent the whole trip on a mat in a box.

It certainly looked pretty amazing dropping at that speed. Way faster than bend diving. There was a buffeting of displaced air as the island zoomed up, getting bigger and bigger and bigger until it looked enormous and there seemed no way to stop in time when suddenly I was just flying forward slowly, vaguely following Tahira who had decided to fly west around the island. As the others caught up Grandpop talked to us.

"Raoul Island is a small volcano under the administration of New Zealand's Department of Conservation. It normally has a few volunteer conservation staff working there. Your first exercise is to find them without letting them see you. No lower than five hundred meters please. Off you go."

We turned east and flew over the island and went invisible again. At first we were a bit messy; flying in all directions. Then Scotty and Tarik and Cam started flying line abreast about five hundred meters apart. Pretty soon Ashley joined them, followed by me and Tahira. The island isn't very big and flying in three kilometer wide lines meant we could scan it quickly.

We had a lot of sensors. Ka-rea-rea's vision was better than the suits. You could take in a whole scene and spot small movements easily. It really was like being a bird of prey. If we were over trees we had a radar which you could send in pulses like a flashlight. It made leaves vanish so you could see the branches and animals below. But our hearing was better too. We could hear generally but also in focused spots.

We soon found everyone on the island and cross-checked the other way. It took us about fifteen minutes to make absolutely sure we had all five of them. Three of them were working near the edge of the crater hill. There were two back at the house. It was quiet. Hundreds of kilometers from anywhere, just quietly going about their work, it seemed a great place to escape from the world.

"OK good work. You've pretty much sussed your sensors. Hekati suggests you play a game of tag to learn about manoeuvre. Invisibility off. Inertialess on. Tag is a beam hit at one hundred meters, no tag backs. Bounds is twenty kilometers radius from the island. No underwater yet. Sam you're it."

Tag was a very good way to learn how to manoeuvre. It taught us to think differently. For a start, it didn't matter about up or down, you went just as fast in either direction. Then there was no momentum. Tarik dived almost into the sea in front of me but with inertialess on it meant he could suddenly move vertically at the same speed, sliding beneath me as I headed toward the wall of water. But as I could do the same thing I could still catch him because he had run our of room to dodge. The trickiest of them all was Cam. She seemed to really get the idea of inertialess better than anyone. She would get you thinking she had momentum by swooping or circling around in an ordinary way and then suddenly do something impossible like go into instant full speed reverse or do 'the escalator' as we came to call going up or down suddenly. The clear lesson of the game was opening your mind to all the different ways you could manoeuvre. We had a great time for about half an hour. Then Hekati came back to talk about entering the sea.

"You can't hit the water fast at all. If you do your craft will
be damaged. It's very hard stuff. The best way to enter is to
move to the surface very quickly but then stop and disengage
inertialess drive. Then gently slip into the water. You can still do
that very quickly. Inertialess doesn't work well under water but
antigravity works better. We've found you a spot near the Mayer
Islands. Go there and submerge."

The Mayer Islands were seconds away. We zipped over one
by one turning off the invisibility field but still remaining
transparent using adaptive. We went full speed up to the surface
of the sea and stopped instantly. Then we just sank into the
world below.

It wasn't as pretty as Guam but it was still lovely. The islands
rose steeply out of the dark, mysterious depths. We nosed
around moving slowly. There were large shoals of small fish, and
a few larger ones like groper and sharks gliding around. Some
were bright and pretty like the ones we'd watched near Guam.
Others were duller and seemed tougher.

In the distance we could hear humpback whales calling and
singing. We weren't sure how far away they were. Closer by
there were dolphins chasing something. The whole area seemed
to be extremely busy. But while nature put on a show, Hekati
had a lecture.

"The main point of this is to learn about your underwater
mobility. Having a rigid hull your craft are much better at diving
then your suits. You can also go much faster."

"The biggest problem underwater is drag. Your craft use
hypercavitation to reach speeds of up to two hundred kilometers
per hour which allows them to move quickly and quietly. But
for very high speed your craft can project a steam lance which

reduces the friction of water in front of you by turning it to steam. This allows very high speeds in the cold dense waters below two hundred meters where there is little life. "

For deep diving it pays to move reasonably slowly. An impact at depth could crack the hull, leading to an implosion that would certainly kill you, and then make a huge antimatter explosion that would set off a tsunami. The best speed depends on how much room you have but one hundred kilometers an hour is a maximum."

"So head east and you will soon come to the Kermadec Trench which is about seven kilometers deep. You may want to switch from invisible to lit up. As you go deeper you will find there is no light so you will have to rely on radar or sonar rather than light."

We turned from transparent shapes to brightly lit ones and moved quietly down to the bottom of the island mount and then down the slope from the island, deeper and deeper away from the light. Then we came to the edge of the world.

The cliff seemed to be a source of darkness. As if darkness was more than the absence of light, but a stuff in itself. Something that swallowed light, sound and movement. A kind of ending to all things. We all looked at the edge of the cliff imagining monsters in the deep. Then Scotty said.

*"Well, we should go and look I suppose."*

His reasonableness was a kind of antidote to the unreasonable fears that were niggling at us, and we followed his lead off the edge into the darkness. Like a trail of Christmas lights we spiralled slowly down into the deep. There was nothing much to see. We just followed each other into the soupy dark, our lit craft flaring in the thick, deep water. It was similar to, but also different from, the moon. There was not much life, though sometimes we saw worms in the glare, or lights in the distance, but generally we saw nothing except the glow of our own illumination.

At first there was no sign of any real difference to Ka-rea-rea. Slowly however he seemed a bit sluggish and less perky. He still provided heaps of information, but his lack of enthusiasm reminded you just how completely we were relying on both our craft and the Fae for our lives.

The bottom was too jagged to get close to. We flew along the bottom of the huge cliff about a kilometer above the sea-floor content to rely on the picture in our heads given by sonar. Apart from our own brightness the darkness around us was total.

"Your craft have feet for holding on to cars but they can also be used like arms to retrieve objects from the sea floor." Hekati told us.

"One of your most useful tools is an electro-magnetic pulse beam. It works like a stun ray for vehicles that rely on silicon semiconductors. You can knock out vehicles, computers or equipment from up to two kilometers away. This means you can knock out a vehicle before landing on it."

"OK, you may as well climb to two hundred meters below sealevel."

Our string of lights began to rise up the side of the cliff. I could feel relief all around. There was something depressing about having an Ocean pressing down on you in the dark. The sea floor was not on my list of happy places to be.

When we got to two hundred meters it was still dark but we knew the surface was within easy reach. Hekati told us to move from line astern to line abreast and test the underwater speed of the craft. We accelerated forward.

We accelerated to one hundred and ninety kilometers an hour and then our steam lances started. It was almost impossible to see where we were going, which bothered me. All you knew was there was nothing in front because the front beam was getting no reflections.

I looked at the others. They were hard to see. Almost like looking through a window in heavy rain. A bright blue light projected from the front of each capsule into the distance. The capsules themselves were covered in a blur which started from the blue line well in front. It might be fast but with nothing to compare it with there was no sense of speed. We didn't do it for long.

"You can slow down and exit the sea now to come home." Hekati said.

We weren't sure what to do but our capsules were. We dropped speed and the lances disappeared. We climbed up toward the surface and whizzed along below it at about one hundred kilometers per hour then one by one each craft leapt ten meters out of the water, almost fell for an instant, then went inertialess and took off in a blur of instant speed.

There was no doubt about it. Ka-rea-rea preferred flying to diving. We zoomed along at a three thousand feet above the sea at about Mach five. It felt very, very fast. We loved it. After five minutes Control called us.

"All craft return to antigravity and invisibility please, decelerate to subsonic, and return to Hauraki."

We turned for home. Slowing down to subsonic and climbing to nine grand, we formed line abreast approaching Aotea with Auckland harbour behind it. It felt great. It made flying in Ken's helicopter seem primitive and very, very slow. Then we zoomed in, towards Renwick, circling around over the bay, little bubbles of nothing in the sky. One by one we went into the tunnel and landed again in the room we'd left. We opened our hatches and emerged blinking into the brightly lit room. Hekati was waiting for us, sitting on the launch platform eating an apple.

"How was that?" she smiled.

We were grinning like idiots. We told her the craft were fantastic. She looked like she'd expected that.

"The others have gone back to the house to hear from the girls about their diving. They seem to have enjoyed their suits as you have these craft. But I must warn you. These craft have great abilities but also some serious shortcomings. A mission to the other side of your planet will still be long and difficult. The lack of a water and waste system forces you to expose yourself to additional risk. Dr Prosperov however said you needed a system to provide aerial observation and to deal with vehicles and aircraft. Again we have adapted our children's play equipment for your use. It's all we can do for the moment. Your needs are very different to our own and without Lana and Dr Prosperov we find it hard to know what to do for you. So we are going home to work with them on some better equipment for you. In the meantime be careful and all the best for your mission."

With that she folded into nothing. We went upstairs talking and it was then Ashley named our craft "speeders". But Rewa and Asal were the ones who got all the attention. They had gone out swimming with Mariko and it had gone well. The months of playing with Mariko meant they probably had a better attitude to listening to her than Mitra or Aunty Liz.

I asked Rewa about the waste system.

"Yeah that was gross. But it was also good because I could pee when I was swimming instead of having to get out. So I kinda got used to it."

I was glad she wasn't going to be bend diving or anything. Somehow it bothered me that my little sis was now able to get into trouble. But then I thought if she helped us on treasure ships having more help wouldn't be a bad thing. I definitely didn't want her anywhere near North Kivu.

Mariko still seemed a bit different. Less naughty and a bit strained. After dinner that night we played pool. I asked her about her suit.

"Yeah it's cool," she said without enthusiasm.

"Don't you like it?" I asked.

She said nothing for a while as she lined up the shot. She made it and took another. She sank three and then missed. I thought she'd forgotten the question but to my surprise, she answered it.

"I don't want to be schoolteacher. I am artist."

She took a sip of coffee, looking at me, for reaction.

"We don't want you to be a schoolteacher either," I told her. It was the last thing we wanted. She gave me a small smile.

"Is not you who is pushing me," she said quietly.

She was thinking of Dr P.

## CHAPTER FIFTY TWO: BUSINESS IN BELGIUM

O ur new equipment had been great fun to play with but Dr Prosperov wasn't paying us to play, and the Fae weren't giving us all this gear for fun either. They wanted more information about the infiltrators, and in particular, the Bruderschaft. They also wanted to know more about the Administration's ties with the infiltrators and human authorities. Dr Prosperov wanted to find more of the target children and tag Sarah Kogan. There was also a boy in Washington DC who would need attention soon.

The only link we had to the infiltrators was through Virion Corporation. They had stored Hathaway's secret material and, it seemed, blood. The para.no.ID group and GRU (the Russian external intelligence service) had penetrated the company for Professor Cherensky. The question now was, would Virion defend itself? This would suggest it was an Inflitrator centre. Or would Hathaway just slip away into the world like a ghost again? The Fae had assigned Raman and Ishtar to advise Dr Prosperov on security matters. They recommended a gentle approach to Virion rather than the all-out assault Cherensky and the Russians had carried out. They pointed out the Russians had attracted a counter-attack – something we really didn't want. We swapped some information on network equipment we had, for some details Para.no.ID had on Virion. It was typical that the information was swapped via an anonymous file sharing site so that neither party had access to the others connection information.

The Virion internal telephone directory and human resources files were very important. Now we had some idea who was meant to work at Virion. Not surprisingly Hathaway's name did not appear on that list or the list of directors or stockholders. Para.no.ID warned us they had encountered a much improved security system. The GRU agent working as a storeman when Cherensky had been stalking Virion had long ago left the company. So Raman suggested worms should be put in place to intercept communication both at Virion and the Catholic University of La Louviere, the University where Clayton Hathaway in his older form as Claude Haine had worked. Bugging the University was very easy. There were many quiet corners among the medieval buildings and not much security outside at all. But Virion was harder. It was another company with buildings set in a park. The park had few trees and they were all bare for winter. The silver box buildings were on a hill and we were pretty sure they had cameras everywhere. Normally Control would have checked out the building inside but Raman said that would be too risky. The infiltrators may be able to grab the link and trace *us*. He suggested we wait for a bad weather before laying the worms instead.

Although the weather had been strangely warm in Europe lately the combination of cold nights, wet clouds and warm days was making some thick fogs[†]. The next day after lunch Scotty and Ashley bent into a night time fog so thick they could barely see a meter ahead. Then they biked up the road toward the Virion buildings. They noticed that as they got closer their suits got warmer. Control told them it was a surveillance radar. They dropped their worms outside the frozen grounds and cycled past. Then they came home.

It took the worms two days to drill through the icy ground, find fibre and latch on. Meanwhile the rest of us were looking up people on the Virion list in the phone book and tracking them down and mind reading their access PINs. We bent into some of the security guard's houses early in their morning to copy their access cards onto the omnicards Hekati had given us.

There was no doubt that for most of them Virion was an ordinary place to work. It researched stuff in its labs, made stuff in the factory and it sent truckloads of stuff out, and got truckloads in. It had the usual manuals and personalities, and paperwork. It was a big organisation, pretty much like Aunty Liz's old hospital – just way richer.

But as we moved up the ranks the story changed. Virion had customers, most of them governments. The company was linked to the World Health Organisation, a number of Universities, but also to defence organisations as well. Its vaccinations and antiviral treatments for strains of influenza were world leading. Its security had to be military grade.

But for us this just made it more worrying. Living in a house haunted by the ghosts of men killed by the 1919 "Spanish flu", a connection between a psycho like Hathaway and a 'flu research company was scary. Were they just treating the flu, or were they making it?

Aunty Liz and Patricia told us they would have to do both. To make effective immunisations they would have to find wild strains of virus and make more of it. That wasn't very reassuring.

Control monitored the fibre and began to get a feel for the organisation. Luckily he found the security camera datastream and soon we could watch the company using its own security system. Even better they had no idea at all that we were doing it because all we were doing was copying data from the fibre as it went by.

Watching them on the screen in the briefing room we carefully began to psychically probe the researchers. Our tactic was to all hit the same person at the same time because Dr Prosprov said it was safer. They were fine. All ordinary people trying to prevent disease. It wasn't until we got to a research leader in the reconnaissance department that we struck a problem.

His name was Dieter Huuygens with a whole alphabet soup of letters after his name. He was forty-something, black hair, good looking, tall and confident. Married, two kids about our age, pretty dark haired wife, he drove a beamer M3, she drove a beamer stationwagon. But we couldn't read him.

Not at all.

Raman was very pleased. He said the reason we got nothing from him was that Dieter was an infiltrator biobot. He couldn't be read because he had no soul to link to. The question was, were there any more or would we now find an infiltrator somewhere?

Raman warned us that we would not be able to read an infiltrator without them knowing. Worse, some would be able to turn the tables on us, and read us instead. That was why we all did the same person at the same time. If they *were* an infiltrator they would know they were being probed but would find six attackers too hard to get a fix on individually.

So one wet Wednesday we went through the senior staff of

Virion in five minute probes, sitting in the briefing room, watching them at an administration staff Christmas party on their own security cameras. We found three more biobots and one infiltrator.

The infiltrator was Paul Maartens a tall, blond man in his fifties. He was the manufacturing manager. We watched him via Virion's blurry security camera in the briefing room for a while. He seemed stiff and old and gruff. While the others laughed and joked he just sat back and watched. Occasionally one of the younger women would tease him and his face would twitch into an unnatural smile, go red and there would be a flash of his brilliant blue eyes. But as soon as the attention left him he would slip back into watching and eating stiffly. You got the impression he was a bit dim and boring.

That was until we probed his mind. Where the others were laughing and having a good time, this guy was watching all of them for the slightest signals of attraction, hostility or competition and working them all out as a complicated social equation. As we went in, he suddenly sat very still looking down at his plate, and seemed to physically transform as we watched, from a grumpy old man into a highly sensitive and intelligent being.

We'd been told to break off any contact with an infiltrator immediately so we were only on him for about ten seconds. We found ourselves looking around at each other. Dr P's eyes checked us all out. Raman's hologram smiled knowingly.

"Is infiltrator?" Dr P asked.

Again we looked at each other to check each other answer, and then nodded. Meanwhile Maartens himself had noticed us probing his mind and was looking around. We switched cameras

277

to a corner of the cafeteria looking at the others in the distance. Maartens was the one quietly slipping off towards the door. We didn't need to be mind readers to know he would be making a few calls.

So Virion did have *one* infiltrator other than Hathaway there. Not the boss, but highly placed in manufacturing. Raman made the suggestion that the biobots' wives were probably the real infiltrators. He said we shouldn't probe them to find out, as that would warn them. If Maartens was alone in sensing an intrusion they might be alert, but not concerned. Two probes and they would have their backs up. Dr P said we should visit their houses in the afternoon as they would probably be out getting ready for Christmas.

Suspiciously it turned out that all three lived in the same nearby village. The daytime weather was wet and cold but not freezing and it was an ideal time to use our animals.

Grandpop decided against all six of us because he thought a group of six kids on bikes would be suspicious where four would be fine. The team was me and Tahira, Tarik and Cam. We were bringing Cheeky and Shaheen with us. Sniffy and Peter were too slow and valuable to waste on this mission so Hekator sent through twenty flies similar to the ones we had used before. Luckily the village was full of hedges so bending in wouldn't be hard. We would go at two in the morning our time to be ready for their afternoon.

Meanwhile Ashley and Scotty were given a separate job. They had to go to Utanda near Masisi in North Kivu and bug Jeanne's parents. We knew where they lived from our previous visit but we hadn't been back since, and Bernard was concerned that if we didn't know where the Mazuri family was, we wouldn't be able to guide an escaping Jeanne back to them.

They went at three in our afternoon with Hooty and Buffy. It was three in the morning there. We watched on the holoviewer and they did a great job. Ashley was on watch with Hooty, while Scotty was to manage the entry and tagging with Buffy.

I couldn't help thinking they looked so well trained as they went about their jobs it was no wonder the parents trusted us. Buffy was in position ready to swoop in through the window when Scotty stopped the whole thing.

*"These people aren't the Mazuris,"* he said suddenly.

"How do you know?" asked Grandpop, uncertain.

*"They just aren't. They moved in here when the Mazuris moved out. They're too young to be Jeanne's parents."*

Grandpop had Control snoop into the house but two black people curled up together in the pitch dark were too hard to examine for family resemblances. Control flashed light on them and took a picture but the woman's face was obscured. They certainly seemed a bit young though. So Grandpop turned to Ashley.

"Ashley can you confirm what Scott's saying."

*"Hang on,"* Ashley said.

She moved from under the tree Hooty was in, down the path past some other huts, and came to the place Scotty was; in some bushes about five meters from the hut we had first found to be Jeanne's home. She knelt down next to Scott and focused. It didn't take long.

*"Those two teenagers are definitely not the Mazuris,"* she agreed.

"Is there any chance they are in the area?" Grandpop asked hopefully.

279

They sent Buffy flittering among the huts.

"*Most of these houses are empty, Mike,*" Scotty told him.

"*It's like they've all left and a few people have come back since to occupy the village.*"

"Bugger! We've missed them. Well, we'd better wrap it up. Good work guys, come home."

So they recovered Buffy and Hooty and bent home.

Losing track of the Mazuri family was a bit of a blow. We had been so focused on Jeanne that we had forgotten that she needed somewhere to go after she escaped. Now she was a thirteen-year-old girl with no family in a country ravaged by civil war. Even if she got away from the CNDP army who had kidnapped her, where would she go?

We already knew about the many refugee camps. They were towns of people in UN tents and makeshift huts nearby clumped together for protection. The various aid organisations set up tents among them and gave out food, clothing and shelter. There were also doctors there. But the numbers of people in the camps was enormous and the aid limited.

There were already reports of cholera spreading in the camps as places that had once been fields suddenly became small cities without safe water, rubbish or sewerage systems. Crime was inevitable as was stealing wood and poaching from game reserves. The various armed groups even gathered volunteers from orphans and young people who would rather risk dying in the fighting to make their fortune than risk dying of disease living among the sad little hovels they were forced to survive in. Finding a place for Jeanne to escape to would be our new priority for her. She would need to get some education somewhere if she was going to play her role in the future.

Meanwhile we got a fresh delivery of flies for the infiltrator soccer moms in Belgium from Hekator via the lighthouse. We went to bed early and were woken up at two in the morning for the operation. At briefing Grandpop went through the plan.

"OK, you are officially distributing flyers for donations for your refugee youth club. Mariko and Mitra have made you up some forms in French. If anyone asks that's the story. Don't be surprised if they think you are burglars. The locals don't like refugees anyway, and the police are even less sympathetic."

I'd recommend you put Shaheen up high to recon the area. Check for traffic, especially cops. Cheeky can get in close. It's pretty cold so they can't fly the whole time. Tahira and Sam are the watch and cover. Find and obscure any security cameras. Look for dogs outside and in.

If the house is safe then Tarik and Cam get in close. The flies are not too bright in the cold so you'll have to get them inside yourselves. The easiest way would be to unlock the front door but dogs and cameras are a risk. Remember you only need a ten mill hole to get a fly inside. If you have to break a window do it. The main thing is to be fast. The quicker you are the less suspicion you will arouse and the quicker you can come home."

"What if one of them is home?" Tarik wanted to know.

"Raman says not to risk it. These people are as sensitive as you are. We don't want them on alert."

"Should we visit homes not on our list?" I asked. "To make it look real?"

"We're better off the fewer people can recognise you." Grandpop said. "It may make you look more sus but the idea is to be fast."

The viewer gave us a helicopter eye view of the village.

"We'll put you here. Launch Shaheen. You ride around the

corner, down this road to here. Launch Cheeky. This is the first address. Have a chat while Cheeky checks it out, then Tarik and Cam go in."

"Down the road. Through this lane, over the stream, Cheeky cuts through here, around the corner and the target is here. Then on up this road quite a way, to here, turn right, down this road to the target here."

"Reply to greetings but don't stop to chat. The weather is cold so we don't expect too many people outside. School holidays have not started yet but because it's Wednesday the kids your age all came home at lunchtime."

"What? Why?" We all wanted to know.

"I dunno. That's what they do over there apparently."

"Lucky!" I said.

"Not really. They start half an hour earlier and finish half an hour later, so they do the same hours as you they just get one afternoon a week off. Anyway what it means is you aren't out of place."

We knew that was a good thing.

"What about other kids?" Tarik asked.

"Tahira does the talking. This is a French speaking part of Belgium."

"Zey will 'ear my accent."

"S'OK, you're a foreigner. You *should* have an accent," Grandpop pointed out.

"Any more problems?" he asked.

We couldn't think of any so off we went to get our bikes and birds. I went upstairs to get Cheeky. The whole house was asleep and it was dark. The ghosts were moving a bit more than normal. They were still creepy, even now. The suit made no difference except the chill didn't make the hairs on your arms and neck stand up. Me and Tahira jogged upstairs past the gallery where they tended to sit and along the corridor to get our birds.

Our apartment was asleep. All the lights were off and apart from the starlight through the curtains and the little red LEDs it was dark. I slipped into my room and went to the window where Cheeky was. He was asleep in his little box with his head under his wing. I engulfed his little warm body in my hand. He fluttered a bit but then I put him in my chest pocket. He wriggled but liking the warmth settled down without any coaxing.

I came out of my room and found the light was on. Then Aunty Liz came out looking half asleep.

"Sam? What are you doing up?"

"Getting Cheeky. We're going to Belgium."

"Oh, OK ... well, be careful," she turned for her room. "See you in the morning."

I couldn't help smiling. I was up at 2:30 a.m. and telling my aunt I was off to Belgium to bug dangerous aliens and she was as worried as if I had told her I was going down the road to see someone from school or something. I slipped out the door. Tahira had Shaheen in her larger pouch on her chest.

"Ee pecked me," she complained.

We walked rather than ran back to keep the annoyed Falcon happy. The others had got our bikes and handouts together. Then we got down to the jumpstation and we were gone.

[+]

Four bright flashes in a Belgian lane startled a lone blackbird. There was a large, dense hedge. I had to remember that we were meant to be on the right side of the narrow road. Ghosts appeared, drawn by our arrival. They were fairly faint. Soldiers from the wars, mothers, accident victims. We ignored them as Shaheen was released from his pack. Tahira put him on her wrist as he looked around, not especially impressed with the cold, gray day. Then with a jump and a whiff of feathers he leapt into the air and took off in the direction of the first house circling higher and higher.

We rode around the corner into a larger street and found it was lined with trees and big, brick houses set back from the road. It seemed pretty rich. The cars were all expensive French and German jobs.

We reached the place where we were due to have a discussion. It was quite windy so we decided to hide under the trees closer to our target on the left side of the road where reading our fake map would make more sense.

I chucked Cheeky out into the cold air. I had learned that he was lazy and preferred to snuggle up if I didn't actively make him fly. He chirruped and took off to the house.

Shaheen was telling Tahira there were no cars at either of the two nearest houses. Now he was hunting for cop cars to make sure we weren't being interrupted. Cheeky was checking out the first house.

There were lights and an alarm on the two storey, brick house with a steeply sloping roof but no sign of a dog. Cam slipped away up the drive to the house. Cheeky flew around the place looking for openings. The back garden was fenced off with a rose covered trellis. Cam jumped the three meter trellis and found the back door. She opened that with her key, tossed in the flies and came back out to us again while Cheeky came back to me.

She was gone for thirty four seconds.

"Beat that," she said quietly to Tarik as we picked up our bikes and pushed off.

We rode to the lane. There was a big fat man walking a small dog in it. Tarik was in the lead and didn't stop. We went to single file so we could get past this guy who seemed to take up most of it. Our facescreens were open and the man looked at us.

"Good day," he muttered in French. He seemed annoyed that he had to share the lane with young foreigners on bicycles.

Tarik didn't reply but Cam and Tahira did. The others crossed the little bridge but I stopped because it seemed more natural to look at it so I could launch Cheeky. This time I just set him down on the iron railing and he flew off. I pretended to take a picture. When I looked back over Tahira's shoulder I noticed the fat man had stopped and was watching us. Tahira looked back at him and his face softened and he waved. Then we rode on.

"What did you do?" I asked her thinking it was some psychic thing.

"Number two smile. It's for old people."

"Oh."

I had never imagined you could have smiles for different sorts of people.

Cheeky had found the second house. It was basically the same design as the first house. The main problem was the kids in the yard next door. Cheeky flew around the place checking it out as we followed our route. It was hard not paying attention to Cheeky but if I didn't ignore him I'd fall off my bike.

We rode around to the driveway and again pretended to check our 'map'. Cheeky had had a while to look over this house. Just to be difficult it had a camera by the driveway and a dog around the back.

"Send Cheeky to the bedroom windows and go back to the lane," Tarik said.

So back he went.

Cheeky was sitting on a chain holding up a flower box looking in the bedroom window. We were in a lane surrounded by walls. No-one could see us.

"OK Sam. LZ please."

"That's cheating," objected Cam.

"Why?" asked Tarik, and then folded into a line and vanished. Ten seconds later there was a flash of light and he was standing where he'd left.

By this stage Shaheen was over the third house. This was the Huuygens' home, and there was a problem. Mrs Huuygens' car was in the drive. I retrieved Cheeky, who didn't like the cold and we rode on.

It was about three kilometers up the village's main street which was a little busy. I noticed as we rode through the main shopping area that the locals watched us suspiciously. With Scott still in bed there wasn't a single white among us and that was unusual there.

We turned off to the right, two kilometers up the road. This road was full of trees which were all quite tall as well. We rode along by the Huuygens' house where the dark blue beamer wagon parked in the drive. There was smoke coming from the chimney and lights on the inside as well. I released Cheeky and we rode past to the park which met up with the stream we had crossed earlier.

Cheeky flew into a tree overlooking the house. Tahira called Shaheen in. He was pretty cold as the air was only about five degrees centigrade. There was no doubt that the Huuygens family were home. The kids were playing Playstation in a family area while their black haired mother was on the phone in the kitchen. I sent Cheeky to check upstairs while in a huge flutter of feathers Shaheen landed on Tahira's wrist.

Shaheen was unhappy to go back into Tahira's frontpack and just as she was coaxing him in a couple of teens appeared around the corner of some trees in the park chatting and walking in our direction. They were guys and quite a lot bigger than us. Shaheen had to choose that very moment to make a bit of a fuss with his wing and cry attracting the teens' attention. The tall, serious faced, dark haired one of the pair stopped, while the shorter, heavier, red haired one in the leather jacket looked at us hard.

"What are you doing to that ..."

He didn't finish his question. They both stood there looking dazed while Tahira turned away and closed Shaheen up. Slowly their hands crept to their heads and eyes and they looked at us again.

"Don't stare. It's rude," Cam snapped at them in French.

The pair were confused.

"What are you doing?" the tall one demanded of us.

"Nothing," I replied, out of habit.

"We're riding around the villages," Tarik said.

"Trying to get the shops to give out these," said Tahira in French using her mouth instead of the suit. She gave them one of the flyers Mariko had made.

The tall one took one and showed it to his mate.

They looked offended by it.

"Begging," the short one sneered.

The tall one crumpled the flyer in his hand ignoring Tahira's smile and outstretched hand.

"All you dirty monkeys know is begging," he sneered.

I was distracted because a car had driven up to the Huuygens' house and Cheeky was watching it.

"And all you inbred Belgians know is taking," Tahira snapped back.

"Why don't you just beg me to take you then?" he leered.

He was way too much of a dweeb to mean it. He just meant to insult her, but he sure picked the wrong girl to insult that way. With the strength only the suit could give her Tahira threw her whole bike at them. They were taken completely by surprise. It hit them hard, smashing into their arms which they put out protectively by instinct. Then they were hit by Tahira herself. If they had expected a thirteen-year-old's tears they got an angry bear instead. She ran at them and jumped after the bike landing a solid kick to the tall one's chest sending him flying back, his arms flung out by the force of the impact. As she landed the other one crumpled. Cam had put him down and looked annoyed.

"*You're wasting time,*" Cam told Tahira sharply.

The tall one was stirring. Tarik turned toward him and his head slumped.

"*Let's get them into the bushes. Quick!*" Tarik suggested.

Cam, Tarik and Tahira dragged the teens off the path under some trees. Meanwhile I was watching something interesting at the Huuygens' house. A silver Audi had arrived driven by Paul Maartens. He came to the door and was quickly let into the house.

"*You just can't go around attacking people,*" Tarik was telling

**288**

Tahira off.

*"I didn't zap them. I just wanted to slap them around."*

*"Tahira before you got that suit how many people had you slapped around?"* Cam asked.

*"A few."*

*"How many?"* Tarik demanded.

*"Three."*

*"How many were adult sized?"* he insisted.

*"None. But ..."*

*"But nothing,"* Cam interrupted. *"How can we be secret when you go around beating people up?"*

*"Shut up will you?"* I told them. *"Paul Maartens is visiting the Huuygens woman."*

*"Can Cheeky get a landing zone upstairs?"* Tarik asked.

I got Cheeky to fly to an upstairs window. There was a kid's bedroom.

*"Yep."*

*"Be back in a sec,"* he said and folded away.

There was a brief pause. Then Tarik swore.

*"The kid's seen me and run for his mother."*

"Release the flies, open the window and come back here," Grandpop told him.

"You others come in and bring Tarik's bike."

**[+]**

We did as we were told. At debrief Grandpop seemed relaxed. "The flies are all reporting in so mission accomplished. The fact that Tarik was caught in the break-in is neither here nor there. The two teens Tahira attacked will not want to admit that a younger girl wasted them so they will exaggerate how big you were. The Huuygens boy will too. Foreign teens out to steal

**289**

Christmas presents will probably get the blame. But there is something more important for you guys to do now."

"Raman is a bit worried that you are all vulnerable to infiltrator psychic attack. You can't be hypnotised but you can have your minds read. That was why I wasn't keen to have Tarik try and talk his way out – something he is usually pretty good at."

We all grinned.

"Raman wants you to be given some extra powers to block your minds to mind readers. Unfortunately it can't be done here. So they have sent four of those medical boxes through to the changing room. After you get changed get into one. They will take you to where-ever it is they do these things. Raman says you will sleep through it. Afterwards you will have an increased awareness of people who try to read you – including each other. You will slowly gain the ability to block probes or turn them back on your interrogators. Raman says this takes practice but obviously you can practice on each other. Any questions?"

"What about Scotty and Ashley?" Tarik asked.

"They've already gone."

"How long will it take?" I wanted to know.

"You should be back by ten in the morning."

"Do our parents know about this?" asked Cam.

"Yeah, we talked about it last night. They think if the Fae want you to go near the infiltrators they should give you the protection you need. They took a while to get there, but that pretty much sums up where they got to."

It was a funny idea to us. We went back to the changers feeling a bit uncertain. We had always read each other the same way we read everyone else. We only didn't read some things out of respect for the people themselves. Now to be able to shut the others out. That was new. We wondered what it would be like. It was our first time in the medical boxes and they looked gross, but once you got in them they felt just like suits. In no time I was asleep. It was four in the morning. I didn't dream and woke up back in the changing room feeling a bit dozy with a slight headache.

We didn't do that much in the morning but that afternoon Tarik and Cam went back to the Virion village with Peter the spider to put some cobwebs and worms around to pick up radio and cable traffic. Three in the morning was a better time to work undisturbed over there. They had a cunning trick where Sniffy the mouse would carry Peter the spider to the house while Cam kept a watch out for cats, owls or other predators. Meanwhile Tarik dropped smaller worms directly on to the telecom cables. It meant they could be quite a distance away from the houses and not set off the security lights. They did all three in about an hour.

While they were gone we had a visit from a man from the Immigration Department named Paul Homewood. He was small, wore a cheap suit, and talked like a robot. Immigration had visited the house before when we were all at school and talked to Dr Prosperov and some of the others. I hadn't paid much attention because it didn't effect us. But it turned out that Paul Homewood was threatening to bring the cops with him soon and begin arresting people starting with Patricia Robinson. The Immigration Department had been getting impatient with everyone on Renwick except, of course, us Maoris.

It was mostly because Dr Prosperov kept ignoring them. I suppose between running an investment fund, making scientific breakthroughs and dealing with politicians from other planets he didn't find New Zealand immigration rules very interesting. Even the lawyers he'd hired in Auckland were frustrated with him. It also didn't help that our stories kept changing too.

Dr Morozov and Dr Prosperov were business migrants who had started out setting up an investment fund, and then a clinic. They had hired an Iranian family for reception. That would have been fine until the Department had discovered that the Khadem's had entered Europe as refugees and had only been granted asylum in France, and that now their only Iranian passports had expired. The lawyers were working hard to get them through the paperwork of being Baha'i refugees in New Zealand too.

Ken, Gunter, Mariko, Mrs Jones, and Dr Gursoy had been hired as foreign nationals with specialist skills. The lawyers had got the weirdest stories from Dr Prosperov about why their skills could not be found in New Zealand. Stories Mr Homewood found annoying but which didn't break the rules.

The other problem was Khenbish who had an arrest warrant for him in Mongolia. But because neither the United States nor New Zealand had a treaty with Mongolia to send him back to face trial, and he now had an America passport, he was technically an American on the work visa he'd been granted when he came here with Dr P.

The Khumalos were lucky. They had got in on a technicality that was open only to Zimbabwean citizens in 2006. That just left the Trâns.

Mr Trân had been terrified of Immigration and his already confused English had got even worse. The lawyers had been worried that he would have to leave the country and the problem with that was he had no passport so the only place he could go was Vietnam where he was born. This was the only case where Dr Prosperov paid attention and got Dr Morozov and Control to find a way to keep the Trâns in the country. After a few false starts they decided the Trâns were Australians. We all found that very funny.

Nguyen Trân had to be the most common name in Vietnam and, because nobody had any idea when Mr Trân's actual birth date was, it was relatively simple to find a suitable Australian Nguyen Trân living in Melbourne and duplicate him. Then it was just a matter of building up a tangle of changed address notifications, memberships, accounts and health records. With a bit of help from Control Mariko's talent for forgery, and the use of the "sleeping bags" to visit local offices and paying a Vietnamese man to hold mail, Nguyen and Cam got shiny new passports from the Australian Passport Office.

Because Australians can work in New Zealand and because apparently way back in the '70s Aussies could even enter New Zealand without a passport at all, suddenly Mr Trân's immigration fears had simply vanished. Mr Homewood was not convinced, but the little black books with the Kangaroos on them were our aces. He and Cam were no longer under suspicion.

Patricia Robinson was a clear problem. She had entered New Zealand as a tourist on an American passport and she was pretty obviously American. We couldn't pass her off as anything else. What was more she had overstayed her three months and, the Department suspected (but could not prove because Dr Prosperov's business was registered in the Cayman Islands), was working here illegally as well.

Dr Prosperov suggested she take the opportunity to visit her mother in Houston for Christmas before heading on to Belgium where they would rent a house to provide a base for operations. Ashley would travel with her in a suit but come back to Renwick regularly. Ken would go with Patricia as a "bodyguard".

Ashley made a few cracks about her mother's need for a "bodyguard" when her mother was not around. It wasn't that she didn't like Ken. Everyone liked Ken. But haunted by her father she wasn't that keen for the quiet friendship between Patricia and Ken to become anything more. Ashley claimed she would be checking on Ken and her mother at random to keep them on their toes.

With Patricia heading home it seemed a bit unfair to the others. They were also keen to visit loved ones. Zoe was frustrated with the poor internet service her parents had in Harare which made sending photos of Patience difficult, and Skype impossible.

The Khadems had less difficulty with friends in Europe and the United States but connections with Iran were monitored. Talking to other Baha'i there was very difficult. Any suggestion that there was a conspiracy and their friends or relatives could end up in big trouble.

Dr Gursoy was limited to letters to his parents in Adiyaman to avoid being traced, although he could email his wife's parents in Mosul. By now conditions there were quite bad with frequent bombings as Al-Qaeda funded Saudis infiltrated the Arab half of town and attacked the Kurdish half.

It was frustrating to all of them knowing that the technology to help them visit existed but that could they couldn't use it because it created a security risk. By contrast with everyone at Renwick who *missed* their friends and family, came the arrival of Christmas parcels from Northland the next day which showed Ax had finally tracked us down. We knew that he knew where we lived, what we didn't know was what he would do about it.

I was pretty sure he would do something like he had done to Grandpop. Use the authorities to weaken us and then do something illegal to finish us off. I was sure that he would try and get friendly with someone like the island cop, Gavin Smith, and then try and burn Renwick down the way he'd had Hua-kai burned. I suspected he was behind the Immigration hassles everyone had been having. It turned out I was right about his methods. I just should have realised my dad wasn't very likely to cosy-up to the police.

## CHAPTER FIFTY THREE: JEANNE ESCAPES

At seven forty seven in the evening local time on Saturday the 22nd of December 2007 Jeanne Mazuri left her post in the CNDP army and slipped away into the Virunga National Park. She was part of a lookout for her unit of about forty CNDP soldiers probing the park near Rugari. We learned later Jeanne had been beaten up and sexually abused the night before by six of the other soldiers and can't have been looking forward to spending another night with the same men.

When we watched Control's files at debrief later we saw it had been a simple thing. One minute the young men were sitting by the fire getting stoned while she gathered firewood and responded to their fierce demands for food and water and the next minute she was gone.

There was no real boundary between the overgrown farmland and the jungle. The farmland just sort of blurred into the taller trees and brush of the jungle and the ground got steeper and steeper as it rose up towards Mt Mikeno, the volcano that rose above them. She was running for the jungle in the dark hoping to get away into the deep shadows of the tall trees.

At that moment on the other side of the world it was Sunday morning. I was lying in bed idly wondering what Emma would do when she opened my Christmas present and trying to think what I would say when she called to thank me. Suddenly my screen made an awful noise and flashed red. I ran over to it to shut it up before it woke Aunty Liz. Then Control appeared like a newsreader on TV with Jeanne in the dark jungle behind him. "All operatives to the jumpstation. This is not a drill. Jeanne is escaping," Control said in his rich voice.

I ran out of our apartment in my pyjamas, nearly falling over Ashley as she did the same. We all thundered down the corridor and stairs, into the cellar, through the vault and into the black tunnel to arrive in ones and twos completely out of breath at the changing rooms.

Still panting we pulled off our pyjamas and leapt into the changer. The normally comfortable and soothing feeling of getting changed just seemed to take forever. We were totally pumped. This was it. We had planned and exercised for this for ages and now it was finally real. We were going into a jungle war zone to help a girl no bigger than ourselves escape from some seriously mean dudes with machine guns.

I couldn't help feeling nervous. We knew Jeanne had finally decided she was better off running than submitting to those with power over her and it was not something she would do easily. The penalty for desertion was death and being thirteen didn't make any difference. She either made it or she didn't. It was up to us to make sure she did. Finally we were bundled out onto the other side. Grandpop, looking a bit puffed as well, was waiting. "Gunter's grabbing Buffy and Patricia should have Hooty here in a minute. Tarik and Cam you are the point team. Go make sure she isn't running into any more crap than she's in already. Sam and Tahira you are the rearguard. Remember no zapping! I do not want those mad bastards shooting back at you or shooting

**297**

Jeanne. Your job is to confuse and distract. They're off their faces already so that shouldn't be too hard."

"Tarik and Cam find safe waypoints for Jeanne and ID them for Ashley and Scotty who will be the escort team. OK, here she is." As we watched we saw Jeanne running up a path made by animals. The undergrowth was up to her chest. The ground was hard to see and she tripped in the dark. She was already gasping. She had one black eye and a fat lip and she had also recently cut herself. She was obviously terrified.

"Match her clothes and off you guys go. Scotty and Ashley wait here. You'll need your animals."

The rest of us ran down to the jumpstation. The walls went dark to match our destination and we were gone.

[+]

In a brilliant flash we arrived among tall bushes under larger trees on the slopes of Mt Mikeno and just for once it wasn't raining. The map data started to hit us. The path we were on was in a gully on the slopes of the extinct volcano. It crossed the path of deep gouges made long ago when the volcano erupted. Jeanne was heading up the path hoping to find cover in the forest. Her pursuers were about a minute behind her running along with fiery torches pulled from the fire shouting and trying to catch her. They saw this as fun. Being way bigger than she was, it was not going to take long.

Jeanne's only advantage was that it was very dark because the bush kept the path in shadow. Even so it was clear Jeanne was not going to make it as she blundered blindly about 200 meters ahead.

I looked around. There was another path of sorts into the jungle taking a steeper route to the left. It was an old stream bed and there were loose rocks everywhere.

*"You follow on after Jeanne. I'll draw them this way,"* I told Tahira.

She ran off after Jeanne and I ran up the slope. I was very glad of the suit's extra strength because Jeanne's former mates were catching up fast. I was just a hundred meters up the steep slope when they came over the ridge of the gully and soon reached the place we had appeared. In my hurry I had loosed a few rocks rolling down the hill and these plus my need to bash my way through the bush quickly distracted them in my direction. They turned after me.

Now I had the problem that it was very hard to see where I was going because there just wasn't much light, the slope was steep and the ground underfoot uneven. The flickering torches, which reflected long sharp machetes, were gaining on me. I suddenly realised this race was not all that different to the one Scotty and his family had run. It made me appreciate Scott more.

The men were breathing heavily but they were also laughing and calling out taunts and horrible threats in French and Kinyarwanda. I found my way blocked by dense bamboo and had to head right around it. They were only sixty meters behind me but the dark made it impossible to be sure. Suddenly one yelled commandingly in French.

"Stop Jeanne! Come back or I shoot!"

The others fell silent. I looked around. He couldn't see me clearly to aim but he knew he was close enough to make the threat believable. The nearest protective cover was a tree about half as thick as me. That was no good. I couldn't rely on him not being able to see me if the bullets started flying. They could kill me whether they could see me or not. The only answer was back.

I folded into the dark.

## [+]

The world folded to a line and span and I was back in a flash of light where I had first arrived as the echo of the AK47 blast died away.

They could hardly not notice the enormous flash of light with a figure in it just a hundred meters back down the hill. I ran on up the path that Tahira had followed as I heard shouts behind me. They were obviously confused. But my suit had matched Jeanne's clothes and they were yelling at the shooter he better not have killed a gorilla or they would all be in deep trouble with the commander.

"*Ran into a dead end. How's she going?*" I called to Tahira who was closest.

"*Still running. She hears me following and thinks I am one of them. She is terrified,*" Tahira said.

"*We need something to help her find the path,*" Cam said. "*She keeps stepping off and slowing down.*"

Scotty and Ashley arrived. They were upslope and we didn't even see the flash in the deep forest cover.

"*Hooty can do it,*" Ashley said. "*She might follow an owl. You guys go ahead and just keep feeding me a route.*"

Meanwhile I had found another fork and this one led downhill. I waited as long as I dared before running down it. The thugs were fifty meters behind me. I ran loudly down the path that led under some large trees. At one point as I ran I noticed a very large spider hanging in a web about a meter wide just five meters away.

I got about two hundred meters. The light of the torches and the shouts were behind me again. Suddenly they stopped.

Their mood had changed. They were pissed off and no longer saw Jeanne's escape as an excuse for repeating their previous night's 'fun'. Now they were going to kill her to show their own commanders how loyal and tough they were.

I sidestepped behind a big tree just in time.

The gut-wrenching sound of the AKs blasting the tree and brush around me filled the night. It was a long burst. Three seconds. They were empty. I ran to a bigger tree just five meters away. There was another roar from at least two guns. The tree I was behind and the bush around me were being shredded. My heart was pounding and I wanted to curl into a ball but I had to stay straight behind this protective trunk. This was way scarier than our practice with Grandpop. I'd had enough. I'd bought her a few minutes but I didn't need this. They were creeping closer now, probably out of ammo. I asked Tahira for a landing zone. Just before I bent I fell loudly into a bush as if hit. Hopefully they would waste time looking for me.

Once again the world folded to a line and I flared back onto a steep path in the dense jungle next to Tahira.

**[+]**

"*You OK?*" she asked.

"*Yeah,*" I answered shakily.

"*She's just ahead.*"

"*Hooty's got eyes on her. Ten meters,*" Ashley announced.

We heard the owl's call.

"Sam and Tahira," Grandpop called, "She's worried by you two behind her I think you managed to lose those guys Sam. Good work. Now wait there and let her be led by Hooty. How are you guys going Cam?"

"*This jungle is scary Mike. There are a lot of animals and I'm*

**301**

*hearing all kinds of weird noises,"* Cam replied.

*"You are, by far, the scariest thing in it Cam,"* Grandpop reassured her.

*"You got that right,"* Tarik muttered softly of the girl who had elected herself his girlfriend. We only realised how tense we were, when we laughed.

"She doesn't seem too happy about Hooty, Ashley. I'd say she's scared of him," Grandpop said.

*"Hang on,"* Ashley said.

The owl hooted again.

*"I'm moving him up the path."*

*"You need to tell her Ashley,"* said Scotty. *"Everyone quiet and focus on Jeanne. Tell her ... why, you are a large snake!"* he suddenly changed subject.

*"What?"* We all replied.

*"Nothing ... sorry I mean I got him. He's sleeping now. We have to tell her to trust the Owl. So what you do is focus on Jeanne. Think hard about where she is and how she's feeling. OK now think 'Jeanne trust the Owl'. Three, Two, One."*

We all concentrated. It was funny. You felt like you really were with her, cold sweat on her back, sore feet on the rough earth, scared in the dark and dangerous jungle. Follow the owl. Follow the owl.

Hooty called again.

"That's done it! She's moving," Grandpop reported.

We relaxed. It hurt your head to do that sort of thing. Tahira and I sat together under a funny looking tropical tree. The land seemed to be breathing in the uncertain moonlight which came and went with holes in the clouds. If the jungle was free of presences the great rift valley felt busy. There were small twinkling fires here and there across the land. In the distance there was a popcorn rattle of gunfire and the crump, crump, crump of explosions. It seemed to be coming from further south. Close by us there seemed to be no end of small insects about. Malaria was big here and Jeanne had no protection.

"Hooty's working a treat," Grandpop reported. "She seems to be following steadily now."

"*How is she?*" Scotty asked.

"Fear is down a bit but she's still pretty worried," Grandpop told us.

"*Uuh guys?*" asked Cam. She was furthest up slope, leading Tarik into the jungle about a kilometer away.

There was a short cough and then a bellowing which tore through the night. It echoed even where me and Tahira sat under our tree. Cam had bent home.

"*We've ... Found ... Some ... Gorillas,*" said Tarik quietly as if he dared not breathe.

"Crouch down and look small Tarik. Don't look at him," Grandpop said.

"*That is coming very easily, Mike. He's standing over me. Man, those teeth are big,*" Tarik babbled.

"*He charged me,*" Cam pleaded.

"Good girl for bending out. You others follow Cam's example. When in danger leave. Tarik, you're fine, stay where you are. It's cool. We can use this," Grandpop told us.

"*Where is Hooty leading Jeanne now? She's looking freaked,*" Ashley said.

"Lead her to the gorillas," Grandpop said.

"*Are you nuts?*" Ashley replied.

"They won't hurt her and she needs protection at night."

"*Are you sure they won't hurt her right? Because this big guy is pretty vexed with me,*" Tarik said.

"He's just making sure you aren't a threat."

"*I think that's easier to see where you are. Here, he's just huge, hairy and angry with big fangs.*"

"You stay where you are. You can bend home when Jeanne gets there," Grandpop told him.

"*Well, she's not following Hooty up there,*" Ashley put in.

"*Don't blame her,*" Scotty muttered.

"Tahira and Sam could you start moving up behind Jeanne," Grandpop asked.

"*You want to scare her toward the gorillas?*" I asked.

"Tarik, how are you going?"

"*I'm OK. He's settled down a bit. Just watching me.*"

"OK, you're doing really well. Much better than I would. The main thing is you stay down and keep him calm. That way we can switch you for Jeanne. Otherwise you guys will have to be there all night and probably all day as well."

I could see Grandpop's point. Alone and unprotected Jeanne stood little chance in the jungle. There might be leopards. There were certainly pythons. At the mercy of the soldiers she stood even less chance. The gorillas might not look after her but they might tolerate her and indirectly protect her from predators that would threaten their own young.

I got my suit to play back some of the voices of the men who had been chasing me, only quieter as if they were further away. We flickered orange and yellow on our suits at each other. Then Hooty called.

"*She trusts Hooty, alright,*" Ashley said.

"*I'm watching her come up the path. She's looking back a lot,*" said Scotty.

"Gently rearguard. Don't push her. Let her follow Hooty," Grandpop warned.

"*Hooty's moving another 50 meters. About ten moves to reach Tarik,*" Ashley reported.

"*I'm alongside her up the hill. She looks really tired,*" Scott added.

"Yeah, she hasn't eaten much. Have any of you guys got any food on you?" Grandpop asked.

"We haven't even had breakfast," I pointed out.

"No, hey Cam why don't you take a box and whip back to the kitchen and get some food for her."

"*Now I'm hungry,*" Tahira muttered.

"*You guys need to move up. She thinks she's lost you,*" Scotty warned.

We started moving up the hill. I played a bit more talking.

"*You know that doesn't make much sense,*" Tahira commented on the French. "*It would be better if we just talked with a male voice in French.*"

"OK, what do you want to talk about?" I asked out loud, sounding like a French gangster as we walked up the steep hill.

"I dunno. Whatever arsehole soldiers talk about when they hunt down unarmed girls," Tahira replied.

It was weird hearing her talking with a man's deep voice.

"Well, like I know loads about that," I replied sarcastically.

"Doesn't matter. All that matters is that she hears us talking," Tahira said.

It turned out she had. She was moving ahead of us while Scotty kept pace. The path was very steep now. We were clearly climbing the side of the volcano. We had to remember not to push her too hard by gaining on her. From time to time we stopped to pretend to check for prints.

Cam burst back halfway between Jeanne and the gorillas. She had brought a carry bag with a plastic bag inside including food, water and some of her own clothes. Scotty wasn't sure whether she'd seen the flare of Cam's arrival or not. Cam left a glowstick with the bags and bent back to us.

Scotty described Jeanne discovering the bag later as sort of like a fairy tale. At first Jeanne was transfixed by the dim green glow, fearing some kind of booby trap. Then Hooty flew to it and away. Jeanne approached fearfully and then seeing more clearly what was there, quickly. She looked all around her. Then she grabbed the water and drank, sniffed the food and ate it, still looking around for whoever had left it there. It wasn't long before she threw the glowstick away. It made her far too obvious and attracted eyes in the dark. But she sat there eating for quite a while until Tahira and I goosed her along a bit.

She picked up the clothes bag and stumbled unknowingly toward the gorilla camp the same way Cam and Tarik had. Tarik bent away to Cam who had set up a landing zone in dense bush nearby. It was very dark. Hooty had been patiently leading her up the hill and she had put all her faith in his calls.

The big silverback waited quietly as Jeanne, unable to see much at all, stumbled into the family of sleeping gorillas. As with Cam the charge was short and sudden. Jeanne simply fell over. The Gorilla loudly gave her a piece of his mind and shook the trees. She was going to run but Scotty paralysed her and she had to sit out his fury.

We watched over them for a couple of hours. Jeanne seemed to slowly realise that the Gorilla was not going to kill her. The

Gorilla also seemed to realise that Jeanne was unarmed, small and female and no threat to his family or himself. Even so he obviously didn't trust her and just as he had with Tarik sat two meters away hunched over and mistrustful.

By ten thirty Grandpop reported that Jeanne was asleep. The silverback was dozing and all the other gorillas were sleeping too. We were all starving and Grandpop called us home to breakfast.

[+]

We ate in our suits. The coffee, OJ, pastries, scrambled eggs, hash browns, onions, sausages and bacon were fantastic. We talked about Jeanne all agreeing that spending the night in the jungle with a family of gorillas was pretty rugged.

"Its pretty sad she's safer in the jungle with wild animals than her own people in a camp," Tarik said.

Well, that started a discussion about why that was. Tahira said it was because of all the guns. Scotty said that guns made killing easier but people had to want to kill, and when people were natural they didn't kill anymore than any other animal. Then we started talking about the gold and mineral mines, which we hadn't seen. They were what Bernard had said was behind the money for the guns. Ashley said the problem was there weren't any laws. Scotty pointed out laws needed force behind them and Cam said they also needed agreement because people would fight laws they didn't like.

Tahira said none of this explained why there were so many rapes and said that came down to men being worse than animals. Scotty disagreed because animals were mean too. Tarik said it was about genocide. The soldiers wanted to replace other kids with their own.

"Then why murder the girls afterwards?" Tahira asked.

Frankly I didn't get it. It made us all annoyed and depressed as well. So instead we recalled what we'd learned about gorillas. We thought it was likely the gorillas would, as Scotty said, "gap it" early to get away from Jeanne. That would mean she could end up alone in the jungle.

At eleven Grandpop warned us we would have a lot to do from about five in the evening until midnight and beyond. He suggested we go back to bed and try and get some sleep. Unfortunately we didn't feel tired. It was a sunny day and we were wide awake.

So Grandpop decided to send us back to the jungle to find routes Jeanne could follow when she woke up. We split into our pairs. Scotty and Ashley got north along the ridge, Tarik and Cam got south along the ridge and Tahira and me got up to the top of Mt Mikeno.

## [+]

The jungle at night was dark. Very dark. There was hardly any moonlight and not much starlight either. The hard part was just walking along because the ground beneath the undergrowth was uneven. Scotty discovered the best way to see was with ultrasound like Buffy had. You used it like a flash so you could see the way the ground rose and fell under the greenery. We peeped in a range from forty up to fifty kilohertz every two seconds or so.

The ultrasound showed up the ground and the trees. The animals glowed because of their body heat. There were quite a few of them about as well.

Early on we came across a very large spider. It was the size of two hands being used to pretend to be a spider. Tahira was going to zap it but I told her off and tried to pick it up. She said if I threw it at her she'd zap *me*. I knew she wasn't joking. I don't like spiders much but with the suit on I felt protected from it. It couldn't do a thing to me. I got a hand to it but it wasn't keen to be picked up by an animal a hundred times bigger than it was and escaped.

We climbed on up the hill. The paths weren't always clear and sometimes there just weren't any. We worked on the basis that we were Jeanne. It also meant we looked around for food but there was nothing we recognised growing there. We found that we were being forced to head north by the steep land and big trees.

We must have been going for hour or so when Ashley and Scotty said they had found a camp. It was based around a huge fire and there were about twenty armed men. They didn't seem to have any particular uniform but that didn't mean anything. Grandpop got Bernard down to have a look. He said they looked like a Mai-Mai gang making charcoal. Making charcoal out of the National Park trees was not great for the park but people needed fuel and what with the war it was hard to stop them doing it. He suggested that if we could find some rangers they would want to know that Mai-Mai were near the gorillas. They might also be able to help Jeanne, though he couldn't guarantee it. The rangers would not want to annoy the CNDP (who had captured their headquarters) by helping deserters.

Scotty and Ashley decided the best solution for them was to bypass the Mai-Mai by taking to the trees. Using their whips they swung out into the forest, crashing their way through the branches so they could get past. Control said the Mai-Mai were watching out for them but didn't look too worried, probably thinking they were animals.

We kept walking. By one o'clock we were getting pretty bored with dark jungle paths. Cam and Tarik spotted a large cat of some kind, but it was when they almost tripped over a path full of silently marching soldiers, that they got the biggest shock. There were hundreds of them. Even Grandpop was impressed. "They *are* good. Sound and light discipline, and those packs aren't light either."

Bernard thought they were probably Rawandan regular soldiers illegally in the jungle to join up with the CNDP and give the FDLR and FARDC a hard time. For Cam and Tarik, however it was the end of the line. They might have made it past the quiet column but Jeanne never would. Cam and Tarik's route south toward the war zone was definitely not a good idea. They bent home.

Scotty and Ashley kept going north. This took them downhill again. By one thirty they had found some recently flattened clearings in the forest. Scotty knew at once what had caused them.

"*Elephants,*" he told Ashley happily.

Being a city girl Ashley didn't share Scotty's enthusiasm for a herd of ghostly wild animals each the size of a truck. But Scotty really wanted to show her the elephants and she was willing to be guided. We heard him tell her that if there was the slightest problem they would bend home.

This seemed fair enough because it was pretty clear that if Jeanne went north she would have to dodge Mai-Mai. As they were even worse to young girls than the CNDP – and here even *that* was possible – that seemed pretty risky. Then if she did dodge them she'd have to avoid the elephants who were probably pretty jumpy given all the explosions during the day. So it looked pretty much like Jeanne would have to follow our path up the hill.

We kept at it for half an hour while Scotty talked about elephants and Ashley oohed and ahhed. All the time we were getting pretty annoyed because our hill just seemed to go on forever being boring and it was way past lunchtime.

**[+]**

By two Grandpop noticed we were bitching at each other and brought us home. Lunch was nothing too exciting – mostly just bread and salads but we were happy to get it down. Then Grandpop suggested we have a nap. We told him we weren't in kindergarten, but he really meant it.

"Guys, you may be up all night. The sleep pills are not as good as real sleep. Get some in while you can. That's what we used to do in Vietnam. Sleep is money in the bank. You save it when you can. It's going to be a real long day."

So we got changed and went to bed at three. I felt a bit dumb about that, but I felt even dumber when Rewa woke me up two hours later – this time without water.

"Grandpop says it's time to eat. Then you have to look after that poor girl," she told me.

For the second time that day I went downstairs in my PJs. We had lamb biryani, chicken tikka massala and a dahl with rotis, rice and papadums followed by Indian sweets. Then feeling a bit bloated and with a carry bag containing a backpack for Jeanne we suited up again and burst into the early morning sounds of the jungle in central Africa.

**[+]**

We landed about a hundred meters from Jeanne. The sky piled

**311**

with clouds seemed so high. The light was yellow-gray with rain on the way. The birds and animals were making noise expecting it. The gorillas were moving around and seemed to want to get away from Jeanne. It wasn't that they were scared of her. They just didn't want humans in their group.

For her part Jeanne was quite relaxed about watching them go. The big apes were wild animals and she was defenceless. She didn't see them as endangered and needing protection the way all our school books wrote of them. To her they were just another natural hazard to be avoided.

The gorillas took their time deciding which way to go, but after half an hour settled on heading north. That was good because Jeanne wasn't going to go back down the hill to her former comrades and she wasn't going to go south toward the sounds of gunfire either. So, that only left east, up the mountain where we'd scouted the night before.

She had kept a little of the food from the night before and after the gorillas had left she took it out and ate it. She kept looking around – I guess as anyone who slept the night in a jungle war zone kind of would. She was very curious about Cam's clothes too. Cam had left her a pair of olive green cargo pants, and a dark green hoody which had some random words on it that made no sense in English. It was a good choice of colours because they matched the trees and stuff in the area.

Jeanne tried the top, and liking that, the pants. Although the girls tried to make us not watch her, we all saw the cuts and bruises on her thin body. There were purple lines someone had made with a stick on her black back. It disgusted all of us that she had been beaten like that.

But that was forgotten now as she tried on these strange new clothes that were just a little too small. She twisted around looking at herself. She certainly seemed to like not wearing the uniform they had forced on her. She even half buried it. Then looking to all four possible directions she made the only choice really open to her and began to steadily climb the hill.

We put the backpack smack in the middle of the path. She found it about ten minutes later. At first she hid, apparently thinking someone was using the "bush toilet" nearby. But after five minutes of stillness ended by a pair of monkeys fighting she realised the pack had been left there.

She approached it cautiously. She must have thought it was boobytrapped. But as she got closer she could see no wires and she could smell food. She just grabbed and opened it, pulled out the flat bread and bit into it. She was hungry!

She ate and ate and then found the water bottle. She drank in a long pull. And then she just started laughing. She was laughing and looking at the sky until she was crying. She wiped her eyes on her sleeve and then went back to eating.

After ten minutes she'd had enough and got up, shouldered the pack and started walking up the path. She seemed to be determined now even though she had no shoes, and no idea where she was going. She just seemed to think her guardian angel was looking after her.

Cam and Tarik were put on point picking up where we had left off about an hour ahead of Jeanne. She was moving faster by day than we had by night so now we had to lead the way. Me and Tahira were close ahead of her while Scott and Ashley were quarter of an hour behind as rearguard.

I had Cheeky with me. He was a bit disorientated by having dawn when his body clock was saying it was dusk so I let him doze in my pocket. We might need to replace the guide owl with a guide sparrow.

Walking through the jungle during the day was way more interesting than at night. Bernard was watching us in the theatre and was telling us about the plants, insects, animals and birds as we walked. Meanwhile Tahira left little markers; a rock here, a broken branch there; little things that would show Jeanne the way. Once I got caught in a snare. Bernard said the local people would set snares to catch small deer and gazelle for food. It was illegal but in this place with nearly a fifth of the population forced off their land and into refugee camps by the fighting you couldn't blame them for robbing the Park. We broke the snare and left it to guide Jeanne.

Jeanne meanwhile, was moving at quite a pace obviously wanting to get as far away from her old unit as she could. She was going north to escape the fighting but she knew that she wanted to be on the other side of big Mt Nyiragongo which stood tall and proud, behind us to the left, smoking in the middle of the great valley.

The path Cam and Tarik were following was winding its way down into the plateau and the bamboo forest. We didn't have any real plan for where Jeanne should go. We were just there to make sure she didn't get eaten, trampled or shot. If she was going to become this bigwig later it would be because of choices she made not because we led her by the nose.

It was two hours later as they descended into the plateau to the north of the steep mountain that Cam and Tarik had their first contact. They had to slip into the bush quickly to avoid being seen. The group that went past was black guys in uniform and white people looking so expensive it seemed they came from another planet.

Perfectly camouflaged in the deep greenery Cam and Tarik were invisible. They counted four unarmed whites and ten mostly armed blacks.

"They're rangers with tourists," Bernard told us. It seemed incredible that anyone would want to be a tourist in a country that was having a civil war but apparently whites were still coming to see the endangered Mountain Gorillas. It seemed unreal given the effort we had made to protect a single human kid how much money these people were prepared to spend to come to this place to look at wild animals.

But at the rate the two groups were walking they would cross paths in fifteen minutes. Cam and Tarik did a little thinking and bent to the likely spot they would meet. They were seven minutes up the path from us. I decided it was time for Cheeky to wake up and earn his crumbs.

I woke Cheeky while we walked. For a moment he looked around curiously, but then with a chirp he took off for a nearby tree. We walked on while Cheeky checked out this strange new place he'd been brought to. Then he started following us, flying from branch to branch keeping us in view.

Cam and Tarik were sorting out an observation post. The best spot seemed to be in a large tree looking over the clearing. They just had to scare off some golden monkeys who didn't seem to like them climbing up. They used infrasound and changed to leopard spots and the monkeys beat it pretty quick.

Grandpop and Bernard had decided there was no reason to hide Jeanne from the rangers. Whatever happened had to be better than being held by any of the gangs.

We got to the clearing and quickly joined the others in the tree.

Jeanne was about two minutes behind us and the rangers about three minutes away. To slow Jeanne down a bit I sent Cheeky out to fly around her. I was also impressed that she noticed him straight away, probably because sparrows were rare in the jungle.

At first Cheeky just chirped and flew along from tree to tree with Jeanne. But as she got closer to the clearing I had him fly closer to her. I wasn't sure exactly how she'd react. For all I knew they barbecued small birds here, but Jeanne seemed happy with the way Cheeky flew around her cheeping. By the time she reached the clearing Cheeky was almost dancing with Jeanne, who was laughing happily.

From above I saw the rangers coming nearer and ordered Cheeky away. Jeanne found herself in the middle of the clearing when the rangers appeared out of the bush. They had heard her laughing and exclaiming to some bird. At first Jeanne froze. The green uniforms and the guns scared her. The rangers were surprised. They clearly didn't find girls alone in the bush every day.

Their leader was a man in his forties. Smaller than the others and much older. He was old enough to be a parent. He seemed a bit severe at first.

"Where are you from? What are you doing in the park?" he suspected her of poaching or something.

Jeanne lowered her eyes, one of which was still puffy, and looked sulky. Jeanne didn't answer. She just looked down. Then he switched to Kinyarwanda.

"What have you in your bag? Drugs? Gold? Birds? Meat?"

Jeanne just shook her head, still looking down sadly.

"Give me your bag."

Jeanne handed it over, still looking at her feet. The head ranger opened it and tipped out the contents. There was just a little food and a bottle of water with English writing on it. Now the ranger looked at her with less suspicion.

"Where is your village," he asked her carefully.

Jeanne mumbled.

The ranger told her to speak up.

"Utanda, near Masisi."

The tourists were getting restless.

"That's a long way away. How did you get here?"

Jeanne mumbled again, and again the ranger told her to speak up.

"They took me."

"Who?"

"CNDP."

Now the oldest tourist came forward. He had wrap around sunnies on his head and a goatee beard. He looked very fat compared to the people here. His accent was American but I didn't know where specifically it was from.

"Ahh Francois, look she's not a poacher, we're here to see gorillas not kids. That's what we pay for."

"This girl is a former child soldier. She has just escaped from Nkundas CNDP," the ranger called Francois told the man in English.

The man was chewing gum, and looked like this bit of news was no interest at all to him. But the two women tourists who had been looking at Jeanne with some concern were now both talking at once asking the guide if that was why Jeanne was injured.

Francois questioned Jeanne and relayed her shy answers to the foreigners as she explained they had beaten her so she had run away. Even at a distance we could tell Francois knew there were more injuries than Jeanne was ready to talk about. He asked her about her escape and when she mentioned the gorillas Francois exclaimed in English to the others.

"Great!" enthused the man, "Can *she* show us where they are?" Francois ignored the man's rudeness and asked Jeanne. You could tell she was scared to go back nearer her old unit. But when she was promised payment she changed her mind and shouldered her pack. She let the armed rangers go ahead so she could stay close to Francois. You could tell she felt safe with him.

"Now what?" Tarik asked.

"Back to the gorilla camp everyone," Grandpop called.

Six brilliant flashes lit the jungle where the gorillas had spent the night. It was all soft and green now in the daylight. It seemed a waste to have to come back, and we didn't even have to walk it.

"OK guys take a break while Control finds the gorillas," Grandpop instructed.

Somehow this day seemed to be very long. It was only about nine in the morning local time but of course that meant it was nine at night for us. We sat or lay down, feeling dozy.

Finding the gorillas took Control about five minutes. Then he had to scout the area around them. Far off in the distance the heavy beat of helicopter rotors reminded us we were not just having a picnic in some quiet forest somewhere.

Bernard was a bit concerned that the rangers would notice tracks if we legged it to where the gorillas were. Grandpop agreed so once Control had scouted the area we were allowed to deflect gravity and use our wings to find observation points along the way.

If we had just been able to fly around it might have been easy but we had to find routes through the jungle we could swing like chimps. So all we were doing was flying to useful looking branches and then going back to full gravity and using our whips.

The jungle was hard to fly in. There were branches and vines everywhere. It was dim too, so our glow and the buzzing of our wings made us pretty obvious. Monkeys and birds were frightened of us.

We kept our wings out even as we were swinging, just in case. If we hadn't been thinking about Jeanne it could have been quite a lot of fun.

We spent an hour exploring the jungle between the camp and where the Gorillas were now, eating and having a little midday rest. They didn't see us (because we didn't go near them) but they certainly heard us, and because our buzz was not a scary noise, it made them curious. It was good to be able to play about because it gave us a feeling for the place. Instead of being a dark and scary jungle full of dangerous men and animals with giant creepy-crawlies it became our playground. Even the webs of the bird eating spiders didn't bother us. We just busted them so they didn't catch Cheeky.

By the time Jeanne and the rangers got to the gorillas' camp we were completely ready. They stopped to eat and I woke up Cheeky. Francois and Jeanne seemed to be reaching a kind of understanding. If she told him what the CNDP had been up to, and where the gorillas were, he would take her along for the trip. Jeanne noticed Cheeky right away. When discussion fell to where the gorillas had gone she stood up immediately and walked to where Cheeky had been dancing.

"This way," she called.

Cheeky earned his crumbs over the next hour, leading Jeanne and the rest toward the gorillas. The rangers were sure that Jeanne must be a witch, given the way the strange little bird guided them. Even the tourists were impressed.

Meanwhile we were swinging and dashing through the bush to keep ahead of them. The rangers heard us many times but none showed any sign of seeing us. Finally the party found the place where the gorillas were. Francois led the tourists forward while the rangers stayed back as lookouts with Jeanne. The rangers talked softly to her, asking questions they had not had a chance to ask while she had been questioned by Francois. During this time I took Cheeky home and put him in his box with some water and crumbs. It was weird to appear in my own room in the dark night and then re-appear in the warm sun of the jungle. After half an hour the party moved on. By now my head felt like it was made of lead. All I could think about was sleeping or perhaps eating. It was like a dull gray fuzz had replaced my brain while it tried to crawl off and find a nice quiet place to lie down. I knew I was blundering about like a drunk person.

They were headed north back to Rumangabo, the park HQ. Jeanne was walking with them hoping she wouldn't see any CNDP soldiers who would recognise her. As they walked Francois explained her situation in English to the tourists.

The gum chewing guy didn't seem to care too much. His head was into crossing things off lists, bragging and money. The two women (the thin, pretty blonde one was with Mr Gum, and the bigger, black haired one with the tall, thin guy with glasses) were very upset. Jeanne herself just fell into step with the rangers, squinting around at the country that surrounded them. She was

**320**

free, and for the moment at least had an armed escort who could be trusted. It was unlikely she would be safe for long but she was, at least, safe for now.

We followed them for a while but it was becoming more difficult because we were trailing them now. The forest was opening and we were getting closer to farmland. At two in the afternoon, they left the jungle altogether and Grandpop called us home.

**[+]**

I couldn't remember being so tired. I almost fell asleep in the changer. When I got out I found my PJs waiting for me. For a moment I thought Aunty Liz had left them out for me, but then I realised Scotty and Tarik were dressing in theirs as well. They had been there since I'd got up almost twenty four hours ago. Grandpop led us up to the café and made us all hot milk with honey. He smiled at us as we got milk moustaches. We were so droopy. Outside the wind was up a bit and the waves were crunching on the beach.

"Guys," he said quietly, "that was a job really well done. Jeanne will remember it only as a day of incredible luck and the birds that guided her. She survived because of you, because she wouldn't have without you. You all deserve a good night's sleep." He told us to leave him the cups and sent us upstairs. The ghosts were in the gallery as usual. Just for once we were too tired to be scared of them.

When I got in I found the light on. I turned it off and went to my room. I went and looked out the window into the dark. I couldn't help thinking of Tabika and how we used to go to her in the night. Now I was travelling half way around the world to protect a girl like Jeanne from her mean countrymen. It felt righteous. I got into bed with a smile on my face and must have fallen asleep.

## CHAPTER FIFTY FOUR: CONFRONTING AX

I woke late on Sunday and dozed for a while before getting up. At nine I went down to breakfast, which was just grapefruit and cornflakes as Mr Trân – who we now called "Cobber Trayn" as a joke because of his newfound Australian citizenship – didn't work Sundays. Grandpop was up and told us that Jeanne was not having such a great time because the rangers weren't going to look after her so she had to go to a local refugee camp. It made us feel very lucky compared to her, but at least she wasn't in any special danger anymore. Grandpop reminded us that our job wasn't to make these kids lives easy, but to make sure they survived and wanted to change the world. They weren't likely to want to do that if they liked the world as it was. Even so we still felt guilty.

Dr Prosperov came down to thank us for our work but said it was now critical that we tagged Sarah Kogan before the kidnappers got her or we would never find her again. He had looked at the options for tagging Sarah and decided there was no choice but to be pretty brutal about it. She was too well protected to get close to her by stealth. At three that afternoon we would bend inside the house where it would be four in the morning, stun everyone as they slept, and set Buffy loose on Sarah. The parents liked the plan because it meant less chance

of another mess like the one with Professor Cherensky.
Control had already mapped out the inside of the house. There
were three bedrooms of importance. The master bedroom where
Uri was, Sarah's bedroom and the bodyguard, Federov's room.
Guess who got Federov? Me and Tahira. It seemed our warrior
roleplaying game characters were also our mission roles as well.
Control had watched Federov for a few weeks. He usually went
to bed at eleven and woke at six. He always had a mini-Uzi
submachinegun with a laser sight within reach of his bed. He
had to be taken out immediately and we would land on either
side of his bed to make sure he was. We would both stun to
make doubly sure he was down. If he had a heart condition, too
bad.

Cam and Tarik got Sarah's father, Uri and whoever was with
him. Scotty and Ashley got to stun princess Sarah herself. Ashley
would do the honours while Scotty got Buffy ready. Hopefully
by three Buffy would feel like a snack. The maid we would leave
alone.

The whole operation should take five minutes tops.

The animals were Buffy, and Peter to put in some webs to catch
phone calls and wifi within the house. We talked about this as
we finished our breakfast. Then because it was a fine, hot day
we decided that it was a good day to forget work and enjoy our
school holidays boogie-boarding and went to play on the beach
with the others.

It was fun to swim and surf without our suits. The smell of the
sea got into your nose, the sand was gritty and stuck to your
skin, and the chill slap of the waves was a great contrast to the
burning heat of the sun. The suits were amazing but you realised
how much they deadened the feelings of being in a place. Even

swimming on the wreck in Guam wasn't as much fun as getting seawater up your nose in our home bay.

All the swimming made us hungry so we had a raid-on-the-fridge lunch of leftovers out on the beach. We were just joking and talking when I saw a sudden flash of light up on the hill overlooking Renwick. For the merest second I thought I saw a man with binoculars. The suspicion it was Ax flashed into my brain and wouldn't go away. I didn't say anything because I couldn't see anyone there anymore.

When we went in at two-thirty we were all very relaxed but I definitely wanted to know where Ax was. Grandpop took the briefing very quickly. The schedule was simple. First Control would find Federov. Then we would bend in and stun him. Then he would find Uri Kogan and Tarik and Cam would stun him. Then it was Sarah's turn. Buffy and Peter were loaded up and ready. We climbed down into the jumpstation and everything went dark.

"Checking Federov. OK, he's good. Kogan and friend are good. Sarah is ... good. Bending Sam and Tahira in five, four, three, two, one."

## [+]

Time slowed down, the colour drained and my field of view seemed to fold up and distort. I closed my eyes. I was falling back, unable to move, falling and spinning, and then suddenly I stopped falling back and started falling forward. There was brilliant light all around me. Brilliant light and presences. My mother and my Grandmother. Dozens of people surrounded me, and slowly began to fade. Darkness enveloped me."

I was staring at the wide eyes of a man with a hard face just as he suddenly jolted, and his eyes rolled up in his head. I looked over at Tahira.

"One down," Grandpop told us.

"*Why didn't you zap him?*" Tahira asked.

"*He was looking straight at me,*" I replied. "*I felt weird.*"

"Two down," Grandpop called.

"Three down," he added almost immediately.

"OK, Sam and Tahira come home."

We bent back.

**[+]**

We waded out of the jumpstation, which was still dark.
Grandpop and Dr Prosperov were in the briefing theatre
watching Tarik and Cam. We came and sat down. In five
minutes it was all over. Grandpop was all smiles and called them
home.

"Grandpop, Can I ask Control something?"

"Of course."

"Control, where is Ax Stephens?"

Suddenly we were at Emma's house where Ax, wearing his big
cross, was sitting at the table opposite Tama, talking, all smiles,
and laughing with his black bible on the table in front of him.
Grandpop swore in astonishment. I noticed the smile on Dr
Prosperov's face harden. The others came in joking.

"Cam go get Sniffy please," Grandpop growled softly.

Cam looked confused.

"Quick," he added, nodding at her.

Cam folded into nothing. Everyone was staring at the holodeck.

"Isn't that?..." Tarik began.

"Yeah," I agreed.

"You look just like him," Scott said.

"The Chapel!" gasped Ashley.

Cam appeared in a flash of light. We all got spots.

She looked at the holodeck.

"What's happening?"

"My dad thinks he's found a new church. The Chapel at the top of the hill," I told her.

Cam looked back at the deck, concerned.

"Mr Kahu, please to gather information. I will be in my office," said Dr Prosperov getting up and leaving.

Grandpop let him leave.

"This is going to be tricky because we are dealing with neighbours. Tarik and Cam, bend your bikes up the path above the Reeve's place. Then come down past their place and stop to let Sniffy and Peter off. Scotty and Ashley you are the lookouts. I think you already know where to go. OK, off you go."

"Control, do we have anything that warned us of this."

Control appeared on the Holodeck.

"I'm reviewing my files but I don't think so. Mr Stephens is very cautious with his phone. He seems to assume he is being monitored."

"When did he arrive on the island?"

"On Saturday morning but we were busy with Jeanne Mazuri and my instructions were to monitor, not to warn."

Grandpop sighed.

"Thanks Control. Please warn whenever he is within five kilometers of Renwick."

"Sure."

"Mike?" Tahira asked.

"Hmm?"

"Should we get changed?"

"May as well. You too Sam."

I let Tahira go and then asked Grandpop a question.

"How come me and Tahira get the dangerous missions but nothing to do with Ax," I asked, pissed off.

Grandpop looked at me. He told me straight.

"Because you two are our best fighters but you are both at risk of going nuts around a woman murdering bastard like Ax."

I was a bit surprised and a bit pleased.

"Oh ...OK," was all I said. I turned away and then back and caught him smiling to himself. I said nothing and got changed. The others weren't back for over an hour. Part of the problem was Tarik and Cam ended up talking to Emma and Andrew and had to make stupid excuses about keeping their bags on and not letting them try their bikes. Cam said Emma looked pretty pissed off and she couldn't blame her. I just knew she was pissed off with the lot of us. I also knew that this made Tama angry with us too.

Dr Prosperov checked his agreement with the Department and as he had suspected it didn't include the Chapel at the top of the hill. He rang Auntie Nea but she said it might be difficult to stop something Tama was already doing. He tried to call the Department but they were basically closed for Christmas.

So Grandpop tried the good old Maori way of solving problems by going around and having a chat over a beer. It turned out that just made it worse. The two men had nothing in common and were a generation apart. The more they talked the less they liked each other. In the end Tama said it was a matter of first come with a reasonable proposal first served, and Dr Prosperov had had a year to extend his lease to the Chapel but had not done so. If Pastor Stephens wanted it and fronted with the cash he could have it.

Grandpop said later he got rather grumpy with the term "Pastor" used in relation to a convicted murderer, gang leader and drug dealing sonavabitch. This did not help the negotiations. He came home angry and had to go off for a walk to calm down.

Dr Prosperov came down at dinner. He said it wasn't the best but it wasn't necessarily a big deal either. He said we would have to strongly enforce the non-molestation order and take care when training in the open. I said I was worried they would try and burn down Renwick like they had Grandpop's boat Hua Kai. Dr Prosperov said he would instruct Control to keep a close eye on the Chapel and those who would be "restoring" it. As he saw it Ax was just a minor annoyance, no more important than "boy with loud car".

I couldn't share his confidence. I did not trust Ax. I just knew he would never be so stupid so as to be caught breaching the non-molestation order. But I also knew that with only one cop on the whole island who didn't even like us much, catching Ax would be the problem. It would be so easy for Ax to distract Sergeant Smith and then what difference did it make what a judge had to say months later? If it even came to that.

At dinner that night I talked about it with Aunty Liz and Rewa. Aunty Liz didn't seem worried about Ax. Aunty Liz said Dr P was way too powerful for a small time thug like Ax. Rewa just sat there guiltily wondering what he was really like. She knew I hated him so she didn't trust my judgement, but she didn't say anything. I was worried she might try to go to him.

After dinner we watched the news show Mariko had started making to replace the boring shit on New Zealand TV. It combined reports on the kids we had bugged, and items pulled from TV channels all over the world plus interviews with people

from Renwick. It was a great combination of news about the
world and news about us, and everyone gathered around the
screens to watch it at nine.

It was snowing in Romania and the people there looked grim
and resigned. The school holidays had started for Diana and
Elena but they didn't seem very happy about it. They just looked
worried and scared.

In the Democratic Republic of Congo Jeanne sure was not
enjoying the refugee camp. It was raining again. She was
squeezed into a small hut made of sticks and plastic sheeting,
like the thousands of others around her, just coping with the
combination of mud, filth, grumpiness and boredom around
her. She was getting UN food biscuits more often than she had
been in the CNDP but she looked unhappy. I thought she would
probably try and find her parents.

And now in Haifa, Israel we had Sarah. Everyone in her house
had woken up with bad headaches due to our zapping them.
Sarah had decided she had a "migraine" so she decided to stay
in bed and receive the flood of texts from her concerned friends.
Her father Uri, and bodyguard, Ivan, just looked sore.

Then we had a bunch of news about oil prices rising and growing
concern about food prices. Apparently the price of food had
risen with the price of oil and farmers were growing more crops
for fuel instead of food. That just seemed wrong to me. Like it
was more important to feed a rich white man's car than a poor
black or brown man's kids. I couldn't get it.

It all ended up in a confused dream that night. I was in a village
at the bottom of a hill. It was snowing. It looked pretty but there
was a feeling of dread in the air. At the top of the hill there was
a church, but next to the church there was a big black tank with

a long gun sticking out. All the kids were in the village below along with the people from Renwick. I went up the hill through the snow past the graveyard. On the way I saw Jeanne poking in the snow looking for anything she could sell. She looked thin and sad. When I got to the top I could see the tank more clearly. It was big and dark green with a star on it, although every time I looked at it the star changed design. It was red with five points, then white, then the star had six points. Ax was sweeping snow off it with a broom and whistling. He looked up.

"She's a beauty eh son? Man, are we going to have some fun!" And he started to laugh, and the laugh seemed to be amplified as if it came out of some huge speakers. And I wanted to tell him I didn't want to drive into the village with him but the cold had taken away my voice.

I woke up. It was very early in the morning and the sun hadn't risen yet. I snuggled down thinking about the dream, but gradually it dawned on me that it was Christmas Eve. Emma would open my present tomorrow. I went over what I would say to her again, trying to sound cool. The more I thought about it, the more I started to think she would think I was a total doofus. Not for the first time I began to wonder whether I should have ever bought her anything.

To avoid thinking about that, my mind turned back to Ax. Why did he have to chase us? Why did he care so much about a couple of kids he hadn't liked when he was our father, but wouldn't leave alone now? Raman was right! I had spent all my life trying to avoid my father so that he was at the centre of all my fears. I dreamed of him as all-powerful even when I knew he wasn't.

Then I thought about all the things I had done with the others.

Taking out Federov, crashing Hathaway, diving from high over the ocean and flying just meters above it. I resented being frightened of Ax. I resented having nightmares about him. I knew he was just a man and I am not a coward. But I also knew I'd only be free of my fears of him when I had confronted him. Maybe if *I* went and talked to him? Stopped hiding, and creeping about him, and showed him (and me), I wasn't afraid of him anymore. Then I could find out what he wanted so he might leave us alone.

I looked at the clock. It was ten past five. Mr Trân would be in the kitchen but the others would be asleep. I thought about how I should do it. Should I appear in a blaze of light and zap him? It was tempting but it would be bad for security and trying to bully a bully was weak. I knew that from school.

No, I would ride to him on a bike like any kid might. I would be wearing a suit so he couldn't do anything to me. And I'd ask him why he was being a ... What would he not like? The first word that sprang to mind was the c-word. He wouldn't like that for sure. It would make him angry. Then he might try and punish me and I'd beat him up. I fantasized about that for a while but slowly realised it wouldn't change him. He was used to violence, he didn't care about it. I needed him to realise he was wasting his time and leave us alone. For that I needed him not to be angry but to talk. To talk normally like I was completely not afraid of him.

That was it. I would get up, get changed, take my bike and go see Ax before anyone woke up.

I lay there for a moment.

A lazy, chicken part of me told me I could also do it another day and just go back to sleep. But the more I thought about it, the more I was sure it had to be done now.

I slipped out of bed, out of my room and out of the apartment. The ghosts didn't like dawn, the whole place lay sleeping. As quietly as I could I ran down the corridor, through the lounge, down the stairs to the cellar and through the vault. It seemed all dark, cold and still, like a castle in a fairy story where time is frozen and everyone is asleep. I entered the vault and ran all the way to the changer.

Getting changed by myself felt weird but also exciting. When I came out the other side I went to Control's desk and spoke to him.

"Control?"

"Sam?"

"Control I want to go talk to Ax. I think I can make us leave us alone. He wants me and Rewa and he won't stop until he has us, but if I show him it won't work, just by talking to him, maybe I can get him to go away."

"You should have one of your kind to supervise," Control said immediately.

"I know but they're all asleep and to be honest I'm not sure they would help much. It really is between me and my dad."

"My concern is only for the security of this facility and the people of Fae. To do that I would have to deprive you of bending, gravity deflection, wings, adaptive camouflage, and your whip. Does that affect your plans at all?"

"No. I was going to take my bike and ride. I thought it looked more natural. Ax is still on the island isn't he?"

"Yes, he is sleeping about six kilometers south-west of here."

"So if I ride there you don't have a problem."

"I remain concerned that you are not being supervised but

as you have a good record of judgement and agree to the
limitations on the suit you are within your security parameters."
"So I can go?"
"Yes."
"Thanks Control. I am doing this for everyone. To make Ax go
away and that has to be good, right?"
"I shall monitor your attempt with interest."
I went to the storeroom. Then it occurred to me. How could
I get the bike out without bending? I wheeled it back to the
jumpstation. Control understood and I bent in almost at the top
of the hill by the Chapel.

**[+]**

It was almost six now and I had six kilometers to go. Riding on
gravel was hard. You had to stay on the wheel ruts and keep
your speed up. Even so it was still easy to slide out. Luckily the
ride followed the route to school and at least this way, it was all
downhill.
I didn't have a speedo on the bike but I must have been doing
about 30km/h the whole way. It took me about twenty minutes
to find the bed and breakfast he was staying at. It was called
"The Beachcomber", and consisted of a main house at the back
and four cabins out the front. I knew at once the cabin with
the red Ford Falcon out the front was Ax's. Who else would be
there?
I felt really weird now. My heart was banging in my chest and
I felt sick and nervous. I had thought I'd be all cool but that
wasn't happening. Mum was standing by, winding her hands
through her hair looking nervous. I nearly told her to stop it. She
definitely didn't like this.
The cabins were made of plywood with aluminium doors and

windows. The front was a big sliding door with tinted glass, and behind that was a white netting curtain. There was a veranda of sorts with a table and bench made of wood. The plants were all scraggy looking because it had a good view of the wide surf beach where the big, fresh, morning waves were rolling in.

I felt nervous, and small and stupid. I wasn't even sure if I could say clearly why I was there. But I pushed my bike up to the outside of the veranda and put it down, then, making more noise than I liked I stepped up onto the deck, went over to the table and sat down, with my back to the door looking out to sea.

For a while I just sat there, my hands almost shaking, my heart beating hard, listening behind me for the slightest sign that Ax was awake. I was breathing like I had run a big race at school and feeling stupid about that I tried to relax and get that under control. All the time I was sure there would be a sudden bang as Ax slammed the door open. But it didn't come.

Slowly I stopped thinking about Ax and lost myself in the beach. The smell of the sea, the gulls and the other birds. I listened to the sea, and thought about skydiving and diving and flying Ka-rea-rea. I watched the light change as the sun came up. It helped steady my nerves, thinking of all those things.

"Sam?"

I jumped even though his voice was very quiet. I looked around at him. He was standing in the doorway. He seemed stunned to see me. Then he began to smile.

"My son, have you come back to me?" he smiled doing the Jesus thing like he was on camera.

My expression must have shocked him because he stopped smiling. My face had shaped itself into a look of horror and I struggled to gain control of it.

Ax seemed a bit smaller and older. He was still an evil Jesus but he had only just woken up. He went back inside. I hastily changed to the other side of the table because it was closer to my way out. Ax reappeared with his tobacco pouch and came outside, closing the door quietly so as not to disturb the woman inside. Then he walked over to the edge of the veranda and looked out to sea, rolling his cigarette.

I chanced a glance at him. He was thinking about what he'd say. I was struggling to keep the cold weight in my stomach from making me run or be sick. It was hard being in his presence. All those dreams, and the memories. The hallway, the screams, the shouting, the beating, the smell of beer and blood, the wall, mum's eyes. Mum's ghost wouldn't approach. She was down the drive winding her hair in her hands tighter and tighter.

His voice came to me from a long way away.

"I have thought about talking to you for so many years. I … have … thought about what I would say … for such a long time. And now … now … I'm not sure where to begin."

I said nothing. Looking at him. This was much harder than I had imagined. I had just wanted to tell him to f___ off and leave us alone but too many other things … things bigger than words … had settled in my brain. I was afraid and angry with myself for being afraid.

He looked at me. I looked away.

"She was cheating on me," he choked out.

I didn't understand what he was talking about.

"It was that little shit Matiu Pomare."

I vaguely remember a friendly "Uncle Matiu" who was young and good looking. A figure, hazy and incomplete watching mum from the beach appeared.

**335**

"She was seeing him behind my back. Everyone knew but me. They were laughing at me. They were all laughing."

The laughing. He had killed her to silence the laughing. And the righteous anger was still there. He had silenced the laughter and made them afraid. He had become feared and being feared was the nearest he could get to being respected. But I realised something I had never guessed at before. He had killed Matiu Pomare as well but as far as I knew he had never been jailed for it.

"He was such a weak, pathetic bastard too. So I had a choice … I knew I did. To be weak or to be strong."

He took a draw on his cigarette. He thought about that for a while.

"I was young then … I didn't stop and think. I was just overcome by a deadly sin: anger. It was like it possessed me."

That was his excuse. Possession. But it was also a boast. He glanced at me and I realised he loved it. He loved his anger. It was what made him a big man.

"So I went to jail. I deserved it. I had to pay my debts to society. I knew that."

He smoked some more. He spoke to the sea.

"You learn a lot of stuff inside. They take a lot away but it helps you focus on making you stronger. And you have to be the strongest in there, Sam."

He exhaled smoke in a long breath, and looked to the horizon.

"It's not all about the muss either. You have to get strong inside too. You have to master things like anger so you can think. I learned to master myself to beat sin."

His face turned into a brutal smile. He made a fist, clenching and staring at it.

"You have to take those sins that live inside your heart and squeeze out their poison. You have to dominate them rather than let them dominate you. You have to have the power as Christ did to master demons."

Just as I had expected. It was all about him. *He* had to be strong, *he* had to dominate, *he* had to master. He really was the figure of my nightmares. I knew what he wanted but I didn't know what he thought he wanted. So it was time to ask.

"Why..." I coughed because my voice sounded so small, and I spoke up.

"Why are you here?"

He looked at me and smiled. It was a stupid smile. I looked away.

"I want to bring you to join me in the house of the Lord."

I had expected that but it didn't answer my question.

"What does that mean?" I said to the table.

"It means bringing the Lord Jesus into your life. It means accepting his dominion over you and enjoying his blessing and forgiveness. It's like the song 'Amazing Grace'."

And he began to sing it. He had a good voice too and he knew it. But I wasn't buying. After a few lines he stopped.

"It is amazing how wonderful the dominion of the Lord truly is Sam," he tried to get my attention.

I could see at once he couldn't tell the difference between himself and his "Lord". In his mind there was almost none at all. His idea of the "Lord" was no more than him in disguise, a sock puppet who blessed and forgave him no matter what he did. Joining the dominion of the Lord meant being under his dominion, his mastery, but all bowing to his stupid sock puppet.

"Why do you want to set up a church right by us?"

He seemed a bit surprised that I knew about it but said nothing. "For you Sam. For you and Rewa."

"But you aren't allowed to come near us," I said finally looking him in the eye.

"I won't. I haven't. It's the church," he said gently. "I'm just helping it find a new place."

"OK," I nodded.

My lack of enthusiasm spoke to him so he tried to break through.

"Look Sam, I know I have been a bad father..."

I looked at him and away as he stood there smoking.

"I haven't helped you, or guided you, or anything a father should. I have made mistakes Sam. Bad mistakes. I know I was wrong to kill your mother. I never meant to, but the Anger Sam, the Anger possessed me. And I don't expect you to love me, or even like me – especially when you've been living with your grandfather for nine years and Mike Kahu won't ever forgive me for taking away his little girl."

He threw the butt of the fag away and appealed directly to me.

"But Sam, you don't have to hate me like he does, or fear me because I succumbed to anger when you were small. I have learned and grown. That is why I am building this church near to you, so that you can experience the Lord's love and mercy and forgiveness, as I have. I want you to learn it now before you grow up to be like me."

I looked at him sharply but he went on.

"Because you are, *so* like me Sam. I can see it. I can see myself in you."

It was almost convincing. Except that in back of it all was what he really wanted. It wasn't hard to see at all. He wanted our

forgiveness. It haunted him. And now that we came to the core
of it I could see the danger. If I called his bluff, pointed out all
his delusions he would be possessed again by anger. He would
simply want to destroy out of Anger. But if I gave in, his head
would swell like a tick. It was a knife edge.

"So what are you hoping we will do?" I asked him directly. I
found myself looking at him and found to my surprise it was not
as hard as I thought.

"Join our church. Feel the spirit of the Lord. His grace and
forgiveness," he said looking into my eyes.

I thought about that for a while.

I said nothing. My lack of eye contact made him think through
the situation again. Finally it dawned on him that I had not
come to be reunited with him.

"Sam, why did you come here?" he asked.

"I just wanted to ask you to leave us alone," I said to the beach.
He masked his disappointment. Then he rubbed his chin.

"You haven't told Mike you were coming here, have you?" he
guessed.

"No," I said and looked at him, and again I was surprised that I
could.

"I wanted you to get it straight from me. I don't want you to have
anything to do with us. I don't need your Church or your Lord
or your forgiveness. You need them, not us. So I want you to go
away and never come back."

It was like being in a movie. I was saying exactly what I wanted
to say, calmly and clearly, looking into his eyes. I could only do it
because I was wearing the suit and with that I knew his violence
did not frighten me anymore. I could take him.

The Anger was rising. His eyes had gone from soft brown to

mean steel. He hated hearing that and he hated me for saying it. But his lips curled into a sneering smile.

"You've got guts Sam," he said quietly, nodding.

"But then you would. You are a Stephens."

I stood suddenly.

"No Alan. I'm a Kahu."

"You don't just look like me, Sam." he growled softly. "It goes way deeper than that."

I had to stop myself from shouting at him. I felt the iron inside me going cold. If I wasn't careful there would be a fight and he'd discover something I had to keep hidden.

"I've said what I came to say," I said and turned for the way out. He didn't stop me. There was an angry silence between us as I picked up my bike and got on it.

"You may think you speak for yourself Sam. *You* may even be lost to me. But you don't speak for Rewa," he jeered.

I almost stopped. I wanted to threaten him, to shout at him to tell him to leave Rewa alone but I also knew I would end up losing my rag and do something dumb, so I rode away as he called after me.

"She's my daughter Sam. She'll join us."

"In your dreams, Alan," I called back.

I rode away as fast as I could, my head spinning like a tornado. It was true. He didn't really care what I thought. He wanted Rewa to forgive him because she looks like my mum. If she forgave him, he was released from the burden of guilt that even his Lord could not really take away. I realised I was the sideshow. The main attraction, the reason he was here, was Rewa, not me. She was his little Joy.

It was about seven in the morning now. I rode as believably as

I could, but I was still trying to get home fast. Uphill and on a gravel road. I had to slow down a bit when a cloud of dust came down the hill toward me. It was Tama. He barely noticed me before I was enveloped in the dust cloud behind his old ute. I used the cover as an excuse to accelerate out as fast as a silent motorbike.

I got home about seven thirty. I was all dusty. Control brought me into the jumpstation. I dropped the bike and got changed back to my pyjamas. I snuck back up the stairs. There were a few people in the café but I climbed the stairs and crept back along the corridor. But when I came back into our apartment I found Aunty Liz sitting at the table with a cup of tea reading a magazine.

"Where have you been?" she asked without looking up.

"Umm nowhere much," I said trying to get past her.

"Really? Ax is nowhere much?"

I was totally sprung.

"OK, I went to tell Ax to leave us alone. What's wrong with that?"

"Sam, what's wrong is sneaking. You know that."

She looked at me. It was hard to meet her gaze, so I didn't.

"It was early. I didn't want to wake you."

Rewa came out of her room attracted by our voices.

"So you wake up early in the morning and suddenly get it in your head to go see Ax? Sam, you aren't being straight with me! What are you doing? You could make it hard for Dr Prosperov's lawyers to keep him away from you and your sister! I mean you told the judge you were scared of him and now you're having breakfast together."

"We didn't have breakfast …"

"I know that! I watched the whole thing. But it's what *he* will say happened. He'll make out it's me and your Grandfather with the beef against him, not you."

I felt bad. Maybe I'd made it easier for him to trick the judge to get Rewa.

Aunty Liz sighed and gave me her what-will-we-do-with-you-Sam-Kahu look.

"Sit down and tell me about it," she grumbled.

"Starting with why you went. And don't leave anything out."

So I did, starting with my dreams. Rewa came over and sat down and listened. Aunty Liz listened too, nodding but not interrupting much at all.

"Did it help?" she asked finally.

"I dunno, what if I gave him a chance for his lawyer tricks?" I asked anxiously.

"Did it help you?" she pressed.

I thought about it.

"Yeah ... it did really. It ... it sort of shrunk him a bit. I knew I didn't have to fear him. Without the suit it would have been different."

"Well, that's at least one good thing."

"It's not me he wants anymore," I said looking at Rewa. "It's Rewa."

Rewa looked a bit shocked.

"Me? Why me? I don't even remember him."

"It's coz you look like mum. He wants you to be mum for him and forgive him," I said.

"That's nuts," Rewa complained. "I'm not mum. Sam sees mum. I don't even remember her."

Aunty Liz explained

"You're the same age as Joy was when they met. He used to tease her and chase her around. I used to chase him away for her. He was just annoying at first, but as he got bigger he changed. He told everyone he would marry her one day. He was obsessed with Joy. Joy found it scary, but she was also drawn to him in spite of herself. Confidence attracts and Joy was pretty but always unsure of herself. Alan was the opposite. With dad away I was her only protection and when I went to nurses college she just drifted into his power. It was hard to watch. He was obsessed and she didn't know how to resist."

Aunty Liz seemed sighed.

"Mum was sick and dad and me were too busy to protect Joy. We knew there was something wrong. We knew he threatened her and hit her too. But she said it was OK, that she'd be OK. I didn't know about Matiu Pomare. He was a gang prospect who went missing at the time. Everyone just thought he got scared and took off."

She looked at Rewa who seemed fascinated, as I was. The idea that mum's fate had been decided by a kid in her class at her own age was a scary thought for us both. Aunty Liz took Rewa's hand.

"Don't worry Rewa, we won't let him get to you."

And Rewa and I looked at each other and thought it wasn't just Ax who was trying to relive the past through us kids.

## CHAP†ER FIF†Y FIVE: MISSI⊕N †⊕ M⊕LD⊕VA

Christmas was quiet that year. Rewa got a lot of pretty clothes which reminded me how like mum she was. Mum's ghost was very proud of her. Rewa also liked the jewellery making kit I got her. It was a small drill kit with attachments and a soldering iron. She had learned a lot from Mariko and she and Asal collected stuff and made jewellery together. They often went into the ocean in their suits to get shells or fish and practice using their suits.

We older ones mostly gave each other small stuff. Tahira gave me a sharks tooth necklace and I gave her an incense holder. They were more keepsakes than anything because with all the stuff the Fae had given us human-made things seemed a bit lame by comparison. The exception was the surfboards we'd all got. We decided to take them to the beach later.

Emma called about ten but the conversation I'd thought about for weeks didn't really happen as I'd hoped. We talked uncomfortably for a bit and hung up feeling dumb and disconnected. She was going south the next day so we weren't going to be able to hang around together these holidays.

Mr Trân's Christmas breakfast was simpler too. He had based it on Middle Eastern food with flat breads, yoghurts, comb honey, spiced scrambled eggs, sprinkles of pistachios, almonds and relishes of lemons, apricots, or pomegranates. It was more like painting with flavours than something to make you bloated. Mariko had decorated the place with copies of Russian icons. They were really twisted looking cartoons of us all. But they were all funny and the colours: golds, and reds, browns and blues, were fabulous. We had a Christmas tree again in the hall and Mariko wrapped all the presents in her usual style.

Last year had been about travelling and kings but this year she was mostly into Mary and baby Jesus. I got the feeling that Dr Morozov's pregnancy was on her mind and it didn't take much mind reading to see that Gunter was being given a big fat hint. She wanted to get married and become a mum too.

We were all very aware that Patricia and Ashley had to go, and that Ken would be travelling with them. They were headed directly for Texas, followed by a week in Washington, then on to Frankfurt and a house Dr Prosperov had rented in Klagenfurt, Austria. For operational reasons Dr Prosperov had thrilled the Iranians by deciding to send them on a month long holiday to Haifa. Their route was via UAE and Jordan. The cover was they were Baha'i pilgrims. The only person slightly unhappy about that was Dr Gursoy who would miss Mitra but Dr Prosperov needed him to stay to work the lighthouse.

He was also seriously thinking about sending Mariko and Gunter to Japan, although Mariko was holding out for the Northern spring. I think she wanted Gunter to ask her to marry him. Gunter and Ken were both looking a bit hunted anyway. There was also a bit of jealousy about these trips even though Dr Prosperov had said that anyone who wanted to visit Austria or Israel could pop by for day trips in a "sleeping bag". The Khumalos wanted to go back to Zimbabwe to see Zoe's parents,

and Aunty Liz just wanted to go somewhere – anywhere – as
she was the least travelled of everyone. The only person who was
happy to stay exactly where he was, was "Cobber Trayn" who
just loved his kitchen. Grandpop was keen to take him back to
Vietnam to go shopping for ingredients but Mr Trân was a bit
scared of this because technically he was a wanted man in his
old country.

So Christmas dinner was a special sort of night as we talked
about what we would be doing and thinking about how
important we had become to each other. Mariko had caught
a tuna and we had some stunning steaks in a Greek style with
loaves of bread and salads. There were flowers all over the tables
and somehow we all felt mellow and contented. We even had a
stroll out to the lighthouse under the stars afterwards. Soraya
shepherded Tahira, Tarik and Asal off to bed leaving Mitra and
Ali Gursoy together. Tahira and Tarik started squabbling about
whether they would end up being brother and sister, but Soraya
told them to be quiet.

We were getting ready to see the Robinson's off on the 28th and
the Khadem's off just after New Year. Ashley was to be the go-
between, bringing messages back and forth. She was annoyed
she couldn't get onto the plane in her suit because the armour
would stop X-rays and attract security and the schoolbag part of
the suit made sitting in a seat impossible anyway. The plan was
that once they had landed we would bring her back by sleeping
bag so she could change back into the suit again.

Ashley wanted Scotty to visit them when they were in the States
so he could learn more about where she came from. She said he
had guided her in the Congo and it was her turn to do the same.
Hekator had also invented a very cool little device out of an

old USB data stick. It looked like a data stick but was actually a quantum broadband connection which meant that Patricia and Mitra's netbooks connected direct to Control back at Renwick. The Khadem's visit to Israel meant we would also have a base there. Dr Prosperov had picked a house south of Haifa in HaYam down the coast towards Tel Aviv. It was amazing how small that country was and yet the big house was still relatively private by the beach.

Everyone was excited and thinking about travel when we were all surprised by Diana. Because on the 26th of December 2007 Diana Popovic and her sister Elena, snuck out of the house to a waiting car and left their home in Balti. From there they headed west into Romania. Control reported heightened levels of adrenaline in Diana's bloodstream from 11 p.m. as they drove towards the border. We had no idea what was happening but felt sure this would be the beginning of the dangerous period in her life Dr Prosperov had predicted.

At exactly that moment on the other side of the world we were all waving goodbye to Ken, Patricia and Ashley as they lifted off in the Squirrel and headed for Auckland Airport to catch their plane to America. It was a windy sort of day and the surf was throwing up a huge mist of spray along the whole coast as the waves roared into the bay. Ken did a circle around Renwick and then they were off over the hill to Auckland. While they were away the Squirrel was being given a thorough overhaul to make sure salt from the sea air hadn't started rusting it.

We came back inside to learn we had to suit up in case we needed to help Diana. We all gathered in the briefing theatre to watch them drive through Romania on the holo theatre.

There were three people in the car. A middle aged man in a

leather jacket named Ivan, Elena in the front, and young Diana in the back. Elena was trying to be in charge. She was the size of a small woman but even to us she looked extremely young. Diana was in the back, scared to death, though she didn't say anything.

The man, Ivan, was giving nothing away but we were sure that what he was planning didn't have much to do with Elena's hopes and dreams of being a secretary. Our readings on Ivan were that he was planning to take Elena to a 'hotel' which in fact was a prison his gang kept women as slaves. There they would steal the girls' savings and keep Elena until they sold her to "work" in a similar "hotel". "Work" meant having sex with men. They would tell her she had to "work" to pay for Diana, who they would keep hostage but were really hoping to sell for a better price. We all felt pretty sick.

We told Grandpop what we were getting. He wasn't surprised and just nodded gravely. He looked at his screen. Meanwhile Tahira couldn't sit still. She was prowling the Holo theatre like a lioness at feeding time. Five minutes later Dr Prosperov arrived and came and sat down in the theatre.

"Who is driver?" he asked.

"Ivan Moldovan."

"What is his plan?"

We told him what Ivan was thinking.

"You know where he is going?" he asked.

We looked at each other. We didn't.

"Suggest you find place and destroy it."

We couldn't believe what he was saying.

"Sorry ... ah ... Gennady, could you repeat that?" Grandpop asked looking as surprised as we were.

"Certainly. Find Moldovan destination hotel and destroy. Force relocation. Will delay abuse of Elena. But not to rescue Diana or Elena."

He got up and made to leave.

"How do we destroy it?" I asked.

Dr Prosperov paused.

"Fire is best," he shrugged.

Tahira looked amazed and thrilled. Dr P winked at her and walked out the door. I wondered what *that* was about. She obviously did too because she frowned.

"OK, well you guys have to find this place and you better get it right because burning down someone's house in winter is a pretty serious thing to do," Grandpop warned.

We asked Control for a map and started our reading. Ivan was pretty easy to read. He was thinking a lot about what he would do to Elena when he got to his destination and it was pretty horrible. The good news was it was an old, run down hotel outside the nearest town and we had almost an hour to go to work on it.

Control found the target and mapped it for us. Then he extended a visual probe and we could see the place. It was pretty shabby. It was two stories. Most of the people were upstairs in the bedrooms. Some were even asleep. Downstairs there was a large lounge, dining area, bar and kitchen. There were four mean looking men in the bar drinking and smoking. They were obviously waiting for Ivan. The only real problem was the cellar. There was a cell with two girls in it down there. Grandpop looked really pissed off, and got up to talk to us.

"OK guys the boss wants this place taken out. The easiest place to start a fire is the kitchen. The hobs will use gas. Heat cooking oil in a pan or wok, light it, then throw water on it. The result looks like a small napalm bomb. Surest way to badly burn yourself too. Happens all the time. With your suits you can do it safely – that's the easy part. The problem isn't starting the fire, the problem is making sure no-one dies or gets burned."

"So there are three main risks. Burning – obviously; smoke, which is as deadly or worse; and freezing to death outside because it is below zero. Another risk is bits of the house collapsing and trapping people inside."

"What if they get fire extinguishers and just put it out?" Tarik said thinking about our own fire drills.

"That's another problem," Grandpop agreed, "Control, what do you think?"

"The building is old and not well built to resist fire. There are no automatic fire protection systems and no warning alarm. An oil fire in the kitchen will spread quickly. However the only reason for casualties in any fire is an inability to escape. Smoke inhalation can prevent people from waking if there is no alarm so avoid casualties you must wake all those sleeping. This building is relatively simple to escape from, providing there is warning and freedom of movement. A crucial problem is that the two young females in the cellar are locked in, and two females in the upper level are restrained. Freeing these people is key to preventing casualties."

Grandpop nodded.

"OK, so here's a plan. Cam and Tarik set fire to the kitchen. Scott you are their security. Meanwhile Tahira you run along the upstairs corridor screaming 'fire' to get everyone out and up. Sam you cover Tahira. Tahira, you have to make it sound real. Everyone bends out. We call the fire brigade. Control checks the

evacuation. Anyone left behind gets rescued. Any questions?"
It sounded OK to me.
"How far away is Diana?" Scotty asked.
"Thirty seven minutes," said Control.
We scampered for the jumpstation.
"Fireteam first," Grandpop called and they were gone.
There were a few minutes while they sorted themselves out.
They had to work in the dark because the kitchen was closed.
Then they lit the oil. Using their whips they threw on a pot of
water and we heard their shocked voices.
"*Shit! It's everywhere!*" said Tarik.
"Spread it guys. Add more fuel. OK, Tahira and Sam. Go!"

### [+]

The world folded, span and blazed back again. We were in a long
corridor with awful pink paint and a horrible old shaggy carpet.
"Foc!" ("Fire!"), Tahira shrieked in Romanian. We banged on
the doors.
"Foc! Incendiu! Ieşi!" she shouted running along.
I followed behind as she set off at a run along the corridor,
shouting and banging doors. I copied her voice and repeated her
words.
"Foc! Foc! Ieşi! Ieşi!"
I hoped the fire was really burning because there was no sign of
it. A man put his head out of his door. He looked dazed.
"Foc!" I yelled at him.
"Ce foc?" (What fire?) he asked, confused, but refusing to panic.
"Facem focul!" (We make fire)! I yelled at him.
A look of horror crossed his face and he ducked back in the door.
Somehow a hooded person with a covered face telling them
we had just started a fire on purpose woke up everyone in the

**351**

corridor way faster than just yelling a warning. One guy burst
out of a room and tried to tackle Tahira with his shoulder as
she came down the hall. I stepped over him a moment later as
he lay groaning on the ground where she'd poleaxed him with
her elbow. We kept running and got to the stairs. We ran down
straight into two guys running up the stairs. They went to grab
Tahira with a move they had obviously used before but only
tripped her. She went sailing up into the air, falling down the
stairs in slow motion suddenly glowing brightly and then winked
out. They turned to me with astonished faces.
"You didn't see *anything* guys," I told them and gave them the
amnesia ray. Their eyes closed and I was gone too.

[+]

We landed outside in the garden. Lights were on everywhere.
Three more lights flared by us and the others arrived.
"*Wicked flashover when Scott opened the door*," Tarik said.
Already we could hear screaming and shouting from inside. We
moved over by some trees.
"Sam and Tahira. We have a landing zone in the cellar for you,"
Grandpop called.
What we arrived in was more of a dungeon than a cellar. There
was what looked like a movie set with lights around a bed and
behind it a wall full of things that made my blood chill.
It was quiet. You couldn't hear the noise above. There were
two cages which looked like they were for animals but they
contained two skinny looking girls, one of whom had bruises
over her face. They were huddled as close as they could get to
each other with hands touching through the mesh. They only
had skimpy nightdresses to protect them from the cold.
I heard a whisper of warning from one girl to the other. The

352

flash of our arrival had obviously woken one but now she could see nothing in the darkness and feared we were one of the men. Suddenly Tahira lit up. Her suit was brilliant gold, and she unfurled her wings. I guessed why, and did the same. The girls looked at us with shocked disbelief. The cages were padlocked. We flew over and used our universal pinky keys and unlocked them in no time. Then we stood back.

*"These girls need warm clothes,"* I told Grandpop.

"Cam's already on it," he replied.

The girls crept out of their cages looking at us with shocked eyes. "Așteptă! (Wait)," Tahira told them in Romanian. You could see they wanted to run but they were also shaking with fear. Then she unpeeled her black facescreen. Seeing Tahira's face smiling at them they relaxed a little.

"Este rece (it's cold). Ai nevoie de haine (You need clothes)," Tahira explained in Romanian, her mouth not moving.

"Așteptați aici (wait here). Aducem (We bring)."

Realising they didn't want a boy watching them I went to the cellar door and opened the lock. There was smoke in the stairwell. I switched the suit from gold to black and furled away my wings. Then I slipped up the stairs to check the exit, just in time to meet a thin bald man who was coming down the stairs. Behind him were two bigger men. Thinking I should be scary I gave my facescreen red glowing eyes under my hood and followed it up with a subsonic fear attack and a high pitched scream like a kettle boiling. They stood still, eyes bulging, stunned by my unexpected and demonic appearance. But I knew appearances weren't enough for these guys so I took their legs out from under them with a shot of my whip and they tumbled down about me. Then I generally beat them up with kicks, stamps and painful electric shocks. One went for his pistol and when he collapsed just from my glance the other two ran for it, convinced I was a devil. I chased them up the stairs leaping from wall to wall under reduced gravity. They were literally crapping themselves. It smelt bad even as the smell of smoke came down. At the top of the stairs I stopped and let them run. The fire was now getting serious. There was heavy smoke in the corridor and I could see flames flickering. The smoke was getting thick.

"*Are they dressed yet? Because this place is going up fast.*"

"*Coming now,*" Tahira called.

"Cam upstairs fast!" Grandpop called. "There's a woman handcuffed up there."

"*Coming,*" Cam called.

Behind me Tahira was leading the two girls up the stairs. She was still bright white now with wings. She came around the corner and started at me.

"*You look like the devil,*" she said silently, hinting that it would scare the girls.

I went back to golden again just in time, but things were getting serious. The smoke was thick and the glow or flames lay on our route.

"*You'll need to close up your facescreen. There's too much smoke. We'll have to carry them,*" I told her.

Tahira closed her screen and furled her wings turning back to the girls who just looked terrified and started coughing as the smoke enveloped us.

"Noi trebuie să efectueze (we must carry you)," she told them and knelt down.

"Minciună pe umerii mei (lie across my shoulders)" she told the nearest one in the awful purple tasselled leatherjacket Cam

had found her. Uncertainly she lay across the flat of Tahira's schoolbag. Tahira took her hands and grabbed her bare feet. The girl was much bigger than Tahira but she lifted her easily.
I approached the one in the jeans jacket and knelt too. She too lay across my back. I noticed Tahira was glowing slightly and reduced gravity too. Then we were off through the smoke, Control giving us instructions while the girls coughed and called out to each other. It was only about thirty seconds but it felt longer. Finally we burst out the front door.

"*Mike I need help,*" Cam called. "*The lock's a combination and the chains won't break.*"

"*Coming,*" Tarik and Scotty replied.

There were a lot of girls standing outside in a huddle. The men were all driving off, taking a few girls who watched out the back window, but leaving most. It was very cold. As soon as we were away from the fire we put the girls down, leaving them coughing. Then we ran back into the fire to help Cam with her woman. We got about ten meters inside but the whole place was in flames. There was no way we could get anyone out through that way. So we went back to black and went back outside again. There was a smash of glass from an upstairs window. A small dark figure was smashing the whole window out.

"*You OK Cam?*"

"*Yeah, Tarik's smashed the bed. We had to knock her out, she was going nuts.*"

At that moment Cam and Tarik, looking like dark little figures, were moving the woman through the window. All the girls below were crying and screaming and pointing. Then Tarik jumped from the second storey. His glow was lost against the fire and he just seemed to float down eerily. He turned as he landed and

Cam leapt with the woman in slow motion, Tarik going to catch her.

"Sam that guy you knocked out will die if you don't get him out," Grandpop warned.

I ran back inside. To my surprise Tahira was behind me. We ran though the fire and then bent to the cellar steps. The man was lying headfirst at the bottom of the stairs. The smoke was really thick. We pulled him through the cellar door and closed it behind us. Then we dragged him down the stairs each to an arm and on to the bed on the movie set.

The air in the cellar was not the best. We needed him outside.

"I'm putting a sleeping bag in a travel box." Grandpop told us. Sure enough five seconds later a bright light burst behind us and a small travel box sat there, its violet light glowing in the dark. Tahira opened it and pulled out a sleeping bag.

"*I hope he's clean,*" she said bringing it over. The travel box quietly vanished.

"*Police arriving,*" Tarik announced. "*We're gone.*"

I opened the bag then we rolled the man inside, then closed it again. We bent him out the back about twenty meters from the building.

**[+]**

We opened the bag and rolled him out. I was ready to go, as the others had already left. But Tahira opened the man's coat and searched him. Finally she responded to my questioning look by showing me the man's phone. She put it into her pocket and Romania folded into darkness and then light.

**[+]**

After all that running the oil bath we returned to seemed beautiful with the tiny bubble trails it left around us. We

slouched for a moment in it before trudging slowly out again.
Tahira gave Grandpop the phone and he put it in a tub of green
gel.

"Diana and Elena are arriving," Grandpop said getting up.

We went into the holotheatre and flopped on our chairs. It had
been pretty intense.

Ivan drove up to the gate of the 'hotel' and stopped. There were
fire trucks, police cars and flashing lights everywhere. You
could see he was thinking hard, then he drove on. A discussion
between Elena and Ivan started. He now seemed to be saying
that the low cost hotel had had a fire so he needed to charge
more. Elena was arguing fiercely back. Diana was asleep. They
drove off.

Grandpop stood up in front of us.

"I'll tell you what, that was one of the best executed missions I've
ever seen anywhere. You all did really well. Burned down the
whole place, thirty eight people evacuated no casualties, really
brilliant."

"The chains were a big problem," said Cam.

"Yeah, we need cutters," Tarik agreed.

"I agree it seems odd you don't have cutters. I'll talk to Hekator
about it."

"What will you do with the phone?" Tahira asked.

"Let's ask Control."Grandpop replied.

"Control?"

Control appeared.

"The phone has given up some interesting messages and
numbers. We will have to move quickly to trace them. I'm
cracking the exchanges to get triangulation information on the
location of the phones on the contact list. I don't expect many to

be moving as it is two in the morning. I think we have about half a day before the phone owners consider changing Sim cards but by then I should have them under surveillance."

"Excellent. Oh and here's the boss," Grandpop said cheerfully as Dr Prosperov reappeared. We all turned as Dr Prosperov came down the stairs to join Grandpop on the stairs. Dr P gestured for Grandpop to sit down and he did.

"I come to say a few words about mission tonight. What is for, and context. Is part of agreement with parents," he started.

"First congratulations. Excellent work. Your part is perfect. But I must tell you bad news. Even though your mission is successful you make little difference to slaving problem in Eastern Europe."

"Most gangsters escape. Police paid by gangsters. Girls shunned by families for losing honour. Diana and Elena like many thousands of Eastern girls in danger to be sold in Europe, Former Soviet Union, Israel, Middle East. Is international criminal network of abusers."

"So to reasons for mission. By destroying the outer node of network Diana and Elena exposed to inner nodes. Outcome for Elena likely to be bad. Objective however is survival of Diana. Diana will move west deeper into network. Normally would not survive. Your mission is to make sure she does. Revelations by Diana to cause deep embarrassment in nations connected with Traffickers. Later to become international justice campaigner."

"Second reason is for you. Is important for operatives to ... as Americans say it 'kick the arse'."

We all laughed. It sounded funny with his Russian accent. Dr P smiled good naturedly.

"Is important to kick the arse of criminal abusers as means to deal with horror of abuse. Just to watch would lead to stress and resentment. Attacking network provides dual benefit. First: relieves stress. Second: unbalances network and forces greater revelation of network than if not challenged. Therefore please to expect more 'arse kick' operations."

As he left we could almost hear Ashley whooping, even though she was probably on a plane halfway across the Pacific by now.

"Dr Prosperov has also let me know he is working on some more treasure hunting projects, so it won't all be kicking arse," Grandpop told us. "We also have to watch out for Jeanne and Sarah, and start looking for this girl in Yemen and this boy in Washington DC. We are going to be pretty busy."

He stopped and smiled.

"But right now I don't have anything else for you so you'd may as well have the rest of the day off and relax."

We were all pretty pleased about that.

The weather was a bit windy but after burning down that place in Romania we all felt kinda tired. We went upstairs to the lounge and played board games with Rewa and Asal while Patience staggered around trying to eat the pieces. It wasn't the slightest bit exciting. But when Rewa tried cheating at monopoly I found myself smiling at Tahira and she smiled back at me before we turned away a bit embarrassed. It wasn't anything between us. We were just both so happy to be home playing games with our little sisters who were safe and having fun. Just for the moment the world's problems could find someone else to bother.

I don't think I really realised how upset the Romanian "hotel" had made me until bedtime. We hadn't really talked about it much. I mean we knew that busting it was a good thing but the way they had been mistreating those girls made you feel sick. It kept popping back into your head all the time. I kept thinking about what they had been doing to them.

It was like they had treated them worse than animals and by doing so made everyone animals – just meat to be used, not even for pleasure but just to make money. Even the customers were just stupid bits of meat – stupid bulls in a paddock that the owners could take money from. It was a world where love had been crushed out of existence and hope was just about the things you could buy or make other people do. It made me feel bad just being in the same world with people who could think like that.

I wanted to talk to Aunty Liz about it. I don't think I was the only one that night either. All the adults decided to see us off to bed. Aunty Liz spent a long time talking to Rewa, reading her stories and settling her down. Then she went into her own room. I couldn't sleep so I got up and knocked on her door. She came out.

"What's the matter?" she asked.

"Can't sleep." I said. I felt a bit embarrassed.

She sighed.

"It was that bloody mission today wasn't it?" she said.

"Yeah."

"Get back into bed and I'll come and talk to you."

"Thanks Aunty Liz."

I went back to bed and she came in and sat on the bed with me in the dark.

"It upset you didn't it?"

"Yeah."

"I'm not surprised. We didn't know about this one and everyone's a bit grumpy with Dr P for sending you."

"But what about Diana?"
Aunty Liz sighed.
"I know. It's just this stuff … well … how did it make *you* feel?"
It took me a while to get my ideas sorted out. But finally I got
down to it.
"Don't you have to love someone to have sex with them?"
Aunty Liz sighed.
"No. For some … mostly men … sex is just about power."
"Power?"
It didn't make sense to me.
"Taking pleasure without giving any. Worse. Taking pleasure by
hurting people. Being mean to them."
I could sort of understand that. Lot's of kids liked being mean.
Marshall for instance. But I couldn't see what it had to do with
sex. I must have looked confused.
"You kids are *way* too young for this," Liz grumbled.
"Diana's too young for it too, but she's stuck in the middle of it,"
I pointed out.
"I know. I know. And that is wrong too. Look Sam, some men …
because it is mostly men. They just like …" she paused.
"They just like sticking it to people. It makes them feel powerful.
They don't care about being wanted. They just want to … stick
it … especially where they *aren't* wanted. Just because they
can. And because they can that makes them feel powerful … or
something."
I had a sudden understanding of what Mr Ceder had been
talking about. And Tarik about his dad. I suddenly realised how
awful it was. It made my body tense, thinking about it. I wanted
to fight. I wanted to fight them off. I suddenly realised what
made Tahira so angry and violent. She was fighting back at it,

still – all these years later.

I looked at Aunty Liz.

"Was Ax like that?" I asked quietly. I expected the worst.

It was like I'd shocked her. She started, and looked suddenly vulnerable.

"No ..." she choked out. "No, actually. It wasn't Ax."

She got up. Her soul, her mind was bleeding. She was suddenly jumpy in just the way I'd been a moment before but a whole lot worse.

"Umm just go to sleep, eh? Just keep trying to stop them," she said vaguely and walked out.

That was way too weird.

I had stumbled onto something. It was something I had always known was there – deep down. But I hadn't gone there out of respect for Aunty Liz. But now, somehow, I needed to know what Ax had done. I needed to know in case it was something *I* might do. Something I had to watch out for as I tried not to become him. I lay back and let the reading come.

I drifted back. Back in time. Back into the 1970s. Liz was thirteen, like me. Joy was ten, like Rewa. Ax Stephens had come to see them again. He'd brought his cousin Clint who was way older, about 16. They were outside. Out in the back garden. Clint had been eyeing up Joy. Ax and Liz noticed. Grandpop was away. Away fighting in the war.

Clint said he could get a car. The girls didn't believe it, but that afternoon he'd turned up with Ax and two of his mates the same age. Ax had convinced them to get in. They'd gone to some dunes to swim. It had started out as fun. Then things had turned bad.

Clint had tried to get Joy out of her clothes. Ax was scared of the three bigger boys but he had taken Joy away to get changed somewhere else, leaving Aunty Liz to them. Liz didn't want to do what they wanted, but they had threatened her little sister. Aunty Liz had given herself up to protect Joy.

Joy had never known what those boys had done to her sister. Why she was sick, and she cried later. Why Ax couldn't look at Liz. All Joy had known was that funny boy of thirteen who always followed her had taken her off for a walk and been kind to her. It had been a secret Ax and Liz had shared all of Joy's life. I was stunned. I had never imagined how loyal and staunch my Aunt was. How bad it had been. But then I realised she had been protecting her baby sister and I wondered what I wouldn't do, to do the same?

In a kind of daze. I staggered out of bed, through the darkened lounge and burst into the light in Aunty Liz's room. She was sitting there. Looking at her picture of Joy and brushing her hair which looked nicer than I'd ever seen it before. She looked around at me and she could see straight away, just from my eyes, what I knew. I raced into her arms and I hugged her silently for a long time. Neither of us said anything but both knew exactly what we meant. After a while it seemed we had said as much as we had to say, without saying anything.

"Go to bed, Sam," she said, wiping her eyes on her arm. She hugged me tight and kissed me.

"Sam, I know you wonder if you're like Ax. But let me tell you straight up. You will always be a better man than your father *ever* was."

I wish she hadn't said that because I ended up dreaming about Ax again.

He had Emma, nude and tied up on that bed in the dungeon in

the light. I was naked too and I could feel the heat of the lights on me. He shouted at me from the dark to "be a man". But the really awful thing was that I knew a part of me was turned on, too...

•••

"I haven't told anyone that bit before," I admit to Sue.
I didn't mean to tell her either. It's shaming.
We're sitting back to back in a room full of weird plants. We haven't spoken a word in hours. The thoughts have come tumbling out of me like clothes from an overstuffed wardrobe. They're so fast that I watch them flash by like slippery fish in a stream which I can't stop. My face is bright red. I don't want to look at her. I've let her get under my guard. Too close.
She sits around and looks at me. There's a long silence and all I can hear is water. I chance a glance at her face and I'm surprised to see she's smiling understandingly at me.
"Oh Sam!" she sighs.
"What?" I ask not looking at her. I still feel shamed.
"It's OK."
I'm a bit surprised by this and check her again. She's looking at me like a patient school teacher.
"Don't beat yourself up about it! Sex is like that. Fantasy is always full of twisty stuff. It's the same for everyone. But you never really wanted to *hurt* Emma, right?"
That idea makes my insides freeze.
"No way! That wasn't it. That was Ax. He thought I should ... you know ... like those men in that hotel. But I didn't want *that*. I wanted Emma to ... It was ... she was ... I dunno ... it's too

embarrassing," I spit out, not wanting to think in case I gave too much else away.

That was the only way I had managed to keep any secrets from the others. Living with mind readers is hard.

But Sue's still smiling.

"Sam," she chuckles ruffling my hair. "Your Aunt is right! You are completely, and totally OK. You are a waaay better man than your father! Really!"

She looks at me for a moment.

"You just sometimes get surprised by what turns you on. It's the same for everyone. Can you imagine what it was like for *me* when I first kissed a girl? I mean *really* kissed her?"

"No," I admit. I've never even thought about it before.

She grins.

"I wasn't always Sue-the-lesbian policewoman you know. I had boyfriends back a million years ago. I had sex with them too, when I was old enough. But all the time, deep, deep down I knew what I really wanted, and it wasn't them."

She sighs, remembering.

"I was so scared. So ... so scared of what was hiding in my own heart. My parents and sister were bloody useless – still are. And then there she was ... there we were ... alone ... and we both knew ... we really *knew* that we wanted each other. We were so, so scared and so ashamed. And when we kissed! Oh God! It was just fantastic ... and I knew everything I'd ever been told about Prince Charmings was so totally and completely wrong for me," she laughs looking at my face.

She thinks for a moment.

"Then, of course, the little bitch betrayed me. I was outed and she stayed in the closet. She ended up unhappily married and living in Hamilton. But me? I was free! Free to be me and despite all the hassles and heartbreak it's still worth it."

She looks at me and grins.

"So don't worry Sam. You're totally OK. Sex will come and because you love and feel with all your heart you won't be like your dad's cousins or those bastards who ran that hotel."

She thinks about me now.

"But I bet there was trouble about you guys seeing all that adult stuff? What did your Aunt and the other parents say?"

"Oh yeah! There was heaps. Mitra and Soraya especially, even Zoe, but everything came down to Diana. That was the danger she was facing, just like the dangers Jeanne was facing."

"Yeah, I get that. But I just think there is something a bit wrong with a bunch of thirteen-year-olds raiding a brothel."

"What was wrong wasn't us."

"Yeah, but you've being exposed to some pretty, evil shit."

It's true. We have been. I shrug.

"I'm not saying seeing what we have seen hasn't affected us coz it has. But all it's really made us do is grow up. A lot of other kids don't know the difference between fantasy and reality. We do. Kids like Marshall boasted about looking at porn online and he didn't think once about the girls in it. He didn't see them as sisters or friends or daughters. He didn't give a shit about their lives. He didn't care about the drugs or the cold, or the beatings. He wasn't really any different to the pricks who made the stuff in the first place."

"There is something in what you say but I think you've seen too much of the worst of what people do to each other."

"It got worse," I disagree.

"Well, that's what I *mean*."

"But it's what *happens*, Sue! In the world! Evil shit happens by the bucket-load. It's like that movie they made about Jeanne's life that made us spew. It wasn't for laughs. It wasn't a test of how staunch we could be. It was about feeling the suffering. Feeling the pain. Because it's what happens. The same with Elena and Diana. There's literally millions of others just the same: Moldovans, Thais, probably Cam's mother too. Those sex trafficking networks are huge. We barely scratched the surface."

"What happened to Diana and Elena?"

"Well, it was just like Dr Prosperov said it would be. They moved them around Romania and then on to Hungary, but the deal was pretty much the same. Elena had to be a prostitute to keep them from abusing Diana. She hated it. They tried to escape but where would they go? They were being pulled into this network which used beatings and drugs to keep the girls in line."

"And what did you guys do?"

"What could we do? If we rescued Diana the chance to make any lasting change was gone. We had to just keep an eye on them and be ready to step in if we were needed."

"But that's what I mean. You were watching a real world horror story when there are so many other stories that aren't so horrible. It had to be bad for you."

"It was a damn sight worse for *them*! How can we make the world a better place if we just hide the worst of it behind a curtain and pretend it doesn't happen? Who does that protect? Not the kids who are hurt, that's for sure! Millions of kids in the world live these horror stories. Eduardo in Manila, he's the same. The world is a hard place for hundreds of millions of kids, Sue! Slavery, abuse, mutilation, starvation. And telling the rest it isn't so bad or putting them in a fantasyland pretending

**367**

it's normal makes it worse. Shit like Jeanne and Diana and the others cope with everyday. Right now even. It hasn't got any better in two years."

I think a bit.

"And Sarah! Sarah had the shock of her life when she found out not only what her father was doing in Africa and Eastern Europe and what it meant to be a Palestinian. She hadn't wanted to know before. So long as she was happy with *her* life she didn't care. She was no different to the kids I went to school with. It was all about her! It was all about them – except she's a lot richer."

"So you think protecting kids hurts them? What about Rewa?"

I can see her point. I'm as guilty of protecting Rewa as the adults had been of protecting me.

"Well, OK. She *is* too young."

"But you're not?"

" I don't know. I was four when Ax killed mum. I remember it. Rewa doesn't. Maybe I've always shielded her. But sometimes I think hiding bad stuff – and I don't mean they have to see it live, or live it, like I did, I just mean know about it – but hiding bad stuff, is protecting the people who do bad stuff, not protecting the kids it gets done to."

"I mean look at Khadiyeh. She was married at twelve. She had no idea what her husband would do to her. If she'd had some idea she might have ... well, I don't know about her. She's a bit strange. But Diana. She was protected by Elena. Elena *died* protecting her sister but she protected her so much that she really never learned to protect herself."

"What happened to her?"

"Diana? Well she ended up being taken by the Brudershaft ..."

"Those aliens in Belgium?"

"Yeah, that's when we had to get Inspector Du Croix to rescue her."

"Who's Inspector Du Croix?"

"He's an alien policeman."

"An alien *policeman*?"

"Yeah. He works for Interpol, but he's really *their* top agent on Earth."

"And you got this policeman ... what was his name?"

"Du Croix ... Inspector Du Croix, Rene."

"You got Inspector Du Croix to rescue Diana?"

"Well, we actually got him to arrest a gathering of Bruderschaft."

"How?"

"By giving him proof they were intervening on Earth."

"But that meant he knew you were watching him."

"Yeah ... well, we met by accident we were looking for someone and he was looking for someone else. Du Croix hasn't got the same powers as Rocelli for example. He just has the Administration behind him and ultimately the Center."

"Just like all police."

"Yeah, and because the Bruderschaft were planning to kill Diane and a bunch of others and *we* couldn't stop them because they were too powerful we ratted on them instead."

"So he rescued her?"

"Yeah ... Not for us, but because he had no choice. We gave him the evidence. He couldn't ignore it."

"Wow."

"Yeah, it was pretty spectacular."

"But he's not on your side is he?"

"Hell no! He wants to catch us. The Fae are the enemy of the

Center."

"Hmmm," Sue says, thinking. "This is the first thing you've told me that is starting to hint at why you had to abandon Renwick House."

"Is it?" I ask, surprised.

"Yep," she says, certainly.

"Does that mean all the other stuff is a waste of time?" I wonder.

"No," she says confidently. "That's the problem with detective work. You need data. Sometimes the needle you're looking for is buried in a mountain of hay."

Then she looks at me carefully.

"Actually there's something else I found in your files. Your dad's dead isn't he?" she checks.

"Yeah. It was a car crash," I say, a bit quickly.

"On Aotea," she adds pointedly.

"Yeah," I admit faintly. Sue looks at me hard. She's thinking it.

"Did you ...?" she asks.

"Did I what?" I ask defensively.

"Cause the crash?" she's thinking of Rocelli.

"No," I say too quickly again. Then looking at her fierce eyes I explain. "Well, I mean I didn't *murder* him. It wasn't like getting back at Rocelli after he hypnotised you. I didn't like Ax but I wasn't *trying* to kill him. It was an accident."

"What were you trying to do?"

"Help Rewa and Aunty Liz escape. It was later after things had got a bit hairy around Renwick."

"Around Renwick? You mean like before the fire?"

"No, no, way before that. We wouldn't blow up Renwick for *them*."

"Who? The aliens? I thought you said ..."

"No, no, no," I interrupt. "MS13 with Sinaloa, and Ergenekon."

"Oooooh," she says, realising the connection.

And then thinking that strange she asks, "what did they have to do with your father?"

"They teamed up."

"On Aotea?" she asks, shocked.

"Yeah ... That was as close as my dad ever got to big time, I s'pose."

"But how did they find you?"

"Well, with Sinaloa the problem was old Mrs Williams."

"Mrs Williams?" she asks, thinking of her mum, Anne.

"No, not your mother. Ashley's Grandmother in Houston. It wasn't until they got there that they discovered it was a trap. Remember that guy Martin who had creeped them out in Houston? He'd found Patricia's mother was hanging around her acting like her long lost son, telling her stories about Ray, and acting like he cared about her."

"Eww, yuck."

"When Patricia got to Houston she obviously didn't trust him but her mother said he was a better son to her than Ray had been, and took more care of his mother than her last remaining daughter did."

"Oooh" Sue says with sudden understanding. "*Another* guilt merchant Mrs Williams."

"As soon as Martin found out they were connected to New Zealand he ran off to tell his gang contacts."

"Why did they go to Houston anyway?"

"Dr Prosperov was getting close to identifying the future President. They were passing though on their way to DC. Having Ashley on site would help."

"Did it?"

"At the time, yes, but it created problems later. The reason why we had to burn down Renwick was Ashley was tagged when she visited Nathan. That means someone had worked out the connection between her and Nathan and that she was one of us. So someone had either recognised Ashley or knew that Nathan was a possible future President."

"Who?"

"I don't know. That's what we want to find out to get our security sorted out. Who tagged Ashley? How? And what do they know about Nathan?"

"So what is this connection between Ashley and Nathan?"

"They're cousins."

"*What!*"

"Wild isn't it? We had no idea."

"Was that Lucky too?"

"No, it's that thing Raman talked about where the past and future are connected? If Ashley hadn't been his cousin and shown up just when President Obama was elected he might never have even thought about it."

"So Nathan knows who you are?"

"Yeah, he doesn't know as much as Emma, but way more than Jeanne."

"That has to be how they caught you then."

"Yeah. It was. Ash was tagged when she visited him."

Sue thinks about it for a moment.

"But how did they know to pick *him*?"

"Exactly! Maybe you'll see it when I get there because I can't."

"Good, let's get on with it then."

...

## CHAPTER FIFTY SIX: FINDING NATHAN

Scotty took a sleeping bag over to Ashley in Houston a day after Ken and the Robinson's arrived. Ashley wanted to show him around but Patricia was a bit flustered and didn't want her running off just yet so they only got to walk around the downtown hotel block. Scotty came back saying Ken and Patricia were being really, really, polite to one another and Ashley was bored already.

They were planning to surprise Patricia's mother but she wasn't at home. They did find Mrs Williams a day or so later but the surprise was mostly for them.

Mrs Williams lived in a part of the city called "The Trey" or Third Ward. When I saw the pictures it was not what I had expected at all. I had imagined Houston to be all glass towers and apartments but it was a bit like Auckland with parts that looked like farmland in the middle of it. Like Auckland you had to drive to go anywhere and for Ashley (who was now used to going anywhere she wanted) sitting in the back seat of the car while her mother and Ken played 'happy families' was driving her crazy.

Patricia was disappointed by her mother's reaction to her arrival. But it turned out a lot of it came down to money. Grandma Williams had her sisters and friends but she was poor and getting letters from her daughter from all over the country hadn't helped. Patricia also realised that Martin had set himself up to steal the gift cards if Patricia gave them to her mum. And if he thought the old lady had them he'd use the gang to get them out of her anyway. Patricia tried to convince her mum to join us but she was too bitter and too stuck in her ways.

Ashley's reports made everyone a bit sorry for Patricia. It also made them realise that family reunions can be trickier than expected. To be honest it made me feel *better* because at least I wasn't the only one with family problems.

Ashley was also a bit unsure about Ken and her mum. She wasn't sure she was quite ready to have someone replace her father in her mum's bed. She said her father's ghost didn't seem to mind but Ashley couldn't get used to it, so she spent a lot of time hanging with Scotty who had been through it with his mum and Bernard.

Ashley stayed the night at Renwick all the nights up to and including New Year. Part of the reason was to give Ken and Patricia some time together but mostly because we had started recon trips to Washington DC. It was just before New Year 2008 so the American capital was still pretty much on holiday. That made it easier for us to just walk around and check it out.

The time difference was not so bad for Washington. Technically it was eighteen hours behind, but it was easier to work out as six hours ahead, and one day behind. That meant our Tuesday was their Monday and as their school day ended ours was just beginning. To catch them in the morning we would have to get up in the middle of the night so we tended to walk around in the late afternoon, local time, or morning our time.

Washington was cold and bare for winter. The trees were all

stripped down and there had been some snow. It was strange to think this was the capital of the world's most powerful nation because it didn't blow you away like you might expect. It didn't have the wow factor of New York, or the style of Paris. Sure the Capitol dome was there, but it just joined the skyline from where we were in Columbia Heights.

# [+]

We had been told Columbia Heights was being redeveloped from an area full of poor black, Latin and Asian people to an area full of largely rich, white people. That suited us fine because we could all easily blend in without face screens, no problem. The place was just malls, streets, shops and things. It was shinier than back home but it was just a city.

The housing in Columbia Heights varied a lot. There were big apartment blocks, set on wide grounds that looked a bit like prisons. There were small blocks that had been done up by designers to look new and expensive. Then on the backstreets there were blocks with bars on the windows that looked ugly and rough.

We did a lot of walking rather than taking the subway or bus. Not too many other kids walked. Everyone seemed to cruise by in cars swishing the slush and snow around. It didn't bother us that it was cold and getting dark. We were probably even more comfortable than they were.

Mrs Jones had always told us that if you wanted to be left alone you should look like you know where you're going and walk fast. It usually worked too, but because we were just there to look around it was hard to act like anything but tourists. And that was how we got mugged.

Columbia Heights was interesting. But Grandpop had warned us it had a reputation for crime. Shootings were not uncommon as gangs fought over drug turf. That was something Ashley knew all about and we looked to her for our lead.

The main street of Columbia Heights didn't look so bad. It was still all lit up for the holidays and even with the slush everywhere, and the gloomy dark sky, it seemed somehow warm inside. But when we turned down a side street we soon found ourselves in an area none of us liked. The streets were narrow, dark and wet. It had something mean about it, and it wasn't just the apartments with the bars on the windows or the MS13 graffiti (that Ashley pointed out).

We turned to go back and saw a group of three older teens wearing big puffy black nylon jackets and woollen hats rolling towards us, their breath making clouds in the air. They were smiling but their thoughts were not kind. Two were black, the other was brown. We knew at once they had been waiting for a chance to catch us smaller teens out like this. We looked like a bunch of rich kids wearing quality winter jackets with school bags on. We also looked like we were small, vulnerable and definitely in the wrong place.

The sight of them made us stop and turn to Ashley, even as they came closer along the dark, wet, slushy pavement grinning at us. I noticed a pink and orange lit curtain twitch behind the bars on the floor above us. Someone knew what was going down.

"*What do we do?*" Scott asked Ashley silently.

"*Easy,*" she smiled.

"*Run!*" she said, and took off, with us after her.

The teens immediately began chasing after us. They thought this was going to be easy and leapt forward on their strong long legs. But just because of our suit's power we ran faster into the gloomy streets at Olympic speeds despite the icy footing. They certainly didn't expect us to be *that* fast because they gave up pretty quick. Ideally we wouldn't be running away from the lights of the shopping area and deeper into the gloomy badlands. If we'd been ordinary kids with no protection and no idea where we were this would have been seriously scary. But we had maps in our heads, armour on our backs and we were each better armed than a police cruiser. At the end of the street we had another quick huddle on where to go.

"*Let's head for Petworth Rec Center,*" Tarik suggested, so off we walked. Unfortunately we didn't know about the gang house ahead. Four minutes later as we walked the street down the dark narrow canyon of apartments we saw a group of four young black men in black puffy jackets get up in front of us while the three who had chased us before had caught us up and were coming up from behind. They were definitely out to jump us. This time we were surrounded.

The guys in front were older, tougher and looked scarier than the younger ones behind; so me and Tahira, who were the point (as usual), stopped. The others following froze in place at once. The gangsters ahead were eyeing us seriously as they walked steadily up the dark, icy street towards us. They had guns hidden on them and we were small, vulnerable-looking, and obviously in the wrong place.

"*Eyeball the ones in front. Then on 'go', turn and break through the ones behind,*" I called silently facing the four ahead. The six of us stared hard at the four hard faced teens rolling purposefully towards us. Behind us the other teens were closing fast. They seemed very happy, laughing and nudging each other about us. I called it.

*"Three, two, one, go!"*

There was no warning. As one we all turned and charged the ones behind us who had chased us before. We were moving helluva fast. There was just enough time to see that we were determined to break through and would probably make it when the black leader's eyes narrowed and he pulled out a silver pistol and pointed it at us, gangster-style with the grip on the side. His motion was completely fluid. He drew the gun from inside his jacket, pointed it, looking mean, and instantly fainted, stunned by Tarik. The others standing beside him glanced sideways with stupid expressions on their faces, as he collapsed, then back at us. Their eyes widened and we were on them. They hadn't expected us to actually run *into* them. Cam and Tarik's hard shoulder charges were like blitzing linebackers and knocked them back five meters, then Scotty and Ashley trampled over them like small bulls, stamping hard on ankles, knees, and hands, breaking them. We left them crying on the wet road. It was all over in seconds.

The older gangsters who had been heading us off had no sympathy for the ones we'd knocked down either. If anything they were more angry with them than they were with us. We heard the leader tearing into them from a block away.

"Sup w 'yo, f_____ pussies? They were f_____ little kids man! Knocked down by f_____ little kids!" he yelled kicking them savagely in the ribs.

Us 'little kids' were very tempted to go back and give them all a hiding but as Grandpop warned us, there was nothing to be gained from becoming another Heights street gang. They had enough of them around here as it was. We bent home not long after.

## [+]

Later Ashley was annoyed to find Patricia was getting all protective. She said her mum was maxed out on guilt because of having a good time with Ken. Luckily Zoe stepped in and calmed Patricia down.

That night New Years Eve 2008 was pretty mellow at Renwick. I think the fact that the Persian and Vietnamese New Year was in February and was more fun had an effect. Even so we had a fire on the beach under the stars and danced around to music from Betty the Bus.

Thanks to Raman Dr Prosperov now had a pretty good idea where to find Nathan when the Robinsons reached the U.S capital because there was a huge clue. Dr P knew the future President came from Columbia Heights because he knew Nathan had been at the Columbia Multicultural Institute because it boasted about its associaction with the President in the future we wanted.

## [+]

So at six in the evening, New Years day for us, we bent into the Columbia Multicultural Institute administration block and started touring the darkened, empty school. It blew us away. We had never seen a *school* as new, or clean, or as well equipped as this. It looked more like one of the IT companies we'd bugged.

"*Is* this *what American schools are like*?" Scotty asked solemnly thinking of the dusty shack he'd called a school in Zimbabwe.

"*Hell no-oo!*" Ashley breathed, as dumbstruck as we were, thinking of her own Charles Drew Elementary in New Orleans. We couldn't believe we were in a school at all. The theatre was huge and stunning, like something from TV. There was a gym, like a real adults gym, with machines for everything. There were

**379**

computers everywhere. But there were also a few things that told us all was not so great too. There was a creche and a mothers' room for the teenaged *students*, and all the entrances had metal detectors on them.

We went back to the admin centre. Now that we looked at it, it was certainly a strange place they were running here. Everyone had huge files on them. Everything was measured and recorded. There were big medical records with all sorts of complicated tests of some sort. After about an hour and a half we had as much information as we needed and came home in time for a yummy Vietnamese dinner.

Once he'd checked the rolls with Dr P Control told us there were three Nathans at the school who were the right age. Nathan Green, Nathan Roberts and Nathan Montgomery. Dr P also said their marks were pretty bad but the teachers notes had different styles suggesting they had had more than one teacher over the year.

Our job was now clear. We had to find these Nathans and follow them home after school so Dr Prosperov could tell us which one we were looking for. School re-started on the third of January so we could have Nathan bugged by the time Ken and Patricia arrived in Washington for the weekend.

The day after New Year's day we split into pairs and visited the homes of the various Nathans. Tahira and me got Nathan Green. He lived on the third floor of a low-rise apartment. It was a nice enough area. There were a few people venturing out into the cold to shops and some cars were out in the snow. We hoped Nathan might come down. After an hour though it was pretty clear we were wasting our time and nothing much was going to happen. It was cold and nobody here stayed outside long. We

also had no feeling that Nathan Green was even in the building.
So we turned to go back to the place behind the dumpster we'd
bent in from. Suddenly a cop car sounded its siren behind us
briefly making us jump. He had been trailing us on the wrong
side of the narrow road. The car drew up alongside us and a
beefy black cop opened his window and spoke to us.

"You kids been standing a long time on that corner in the cold.
Who you waiting for?"

He suspected we were a drug drop.

"Nathan Green," Tahira smiled her prettiest smile.

The cop wasn't charmed.

"How come you're wearing school bags on a holiday?"

I thought, "Oh shit, here we go," but Tahira had a brilliant
answer.

"We're a study group."

"And this Nathan Green stood you up right?"

"Yeah."

"So now you're going..."

"Home."

"Which is ...?"

"Downtown."

We were headed the wrong way. We should have been on the
main street heading for the subway to go downtown.

"Uh-huh," the cop paused for a moment. He didn't believe
anything we said but wasn't sure enough to search us.

"Well, if you see Chavez tell him if I see you two loitering again
we'll take you in, get yo parents and do a full body cavity search.
I'm talking rubber gloves, vaseline the whole nine yards. You got
that?"

He was not joking either. He looked very serious.

"Who's Chavez?" I asked, a bit alarmed by this threat.
"Exactly!" the cop nodded." You make sure you keep it that way,
kid."
And he drove off.
We found our dumpster and bent home. The others had not had
much more luck than us.

**[+]**

The afternoon was a lot more fun. Dr Prosperov had decided we
needed a break from cold places and sent us north to fly a search
grid looking for treasure ships. There had been over a hundred
Manila galleons and twenty of them had gone missing, so we
were working on the basis that some places were more likely to
sink them than others.
After standing around in the dark depressing slush of a
Washington winter it was great blasting off into the summer sky
using the Speeders again.
The sky was bright, wide and free. We headed east away
from Auckland for a hundred kilometers, climbed to twenty
kilometers, or 65,600 feet, and kicked it to Mach six (6,300km/
h) and headed nor-nor-west. It was a fun flight. Most of the time
we were over sea but we whizzed along New Caledonia and a bit
later the northern side of Papua New Guinea, in the distance.
The speed almost hypnotised you. We played around each
other, chasing and rolling like dolphins in the sea, happy that
the speeders, glowing slightly with the heat of the air friction,
did the actual flying. After about an hour we finally reached the
Philippines and not long after that, the search area: the Spratley
Islands.
The islands are tiny, set in a fabulous blue sea and surrounded
by reefs. They cover a wide area and are claimed by six separate

countries. They are mostly too small to be occupied and only the largest has fresh water. But they have long been a graveyard for ships, hundreds of which pass by them each day, bringing stuff from Asia to Europe, the Middle East and Africa and back again. They follow similar routes to the ones the old sailing galleons from Spain and China did. Nobody wants to sail among the Spratleys because the chance of being wrecked is high. Once in, they could be hard to get out of again; almost impossible in a sailing ship.

Our search method was to form a line and cruise along at just below Mach one, a thousand feet up and five hundred meters apart pinging with our active beam sensors. They could penetrate about two hundred meters of water and ten meters of sand. We were searching for patterns Control might recognise as a wreck. We had to use adaptive camouflage because warp invisibility interfered with the sensors. We would fly for twenty minutes for about two hundred nautical miles, then wheel around and make another pass next to the line we'd already followed.

So we did this for about an hour, flying steadily over clear blue seas, looking down on fish filled reefs, probing deep blue holes, and over dry desert islands with a single coconut tree, so small they sometimes looked like they came from a cartoon. It was not at all exciting.

We flew over a fishing boat, and in the distance spotted a naval patrol aircraft from somewhere (we weren't sure where) heading north-east away from us. On the horizon the ships were endless. And then Tarik said something that got us all talking.

*"Hey guys, I seriously gotta take a leak."*

He broke from the line and flew down to a small island of white sand no more than two hundred meters long. It was kind of embarrassing. We were circling around above and watched him land and emerge into the glare of the bright white sun. There were no bushes to hide behind, just a bit a dune. We all backed off while he did his business.

A few minutes later he was back in the air again.

"*It's great down there, yeah? Really warm, with great sand. It's like a resort or something.*"

We flew around for a while all thinking the same thing. How much we'd like to go for a swim.

"*Pity we didn't bring our baggies,*" Scott said.

"*Let's check first. Just because the water looks nice doesn't mean anything,*" Cam pointed out.

She swooped down to the lagoon where Tarik had landed and we saw the splash as her speeder cut into the water. Tarik peeled off and dove after her. Tahira and I circled wide keeping a look out while Sam and Ashley watched them from above.

"*Lot of seasnakes here,*" Cam pointed out.

"*We can scare 'em,*" Tarik replied.

"*There's sharks further out too,*" Scotty said.

I noticed how we had got used to the protection the suits gave us and how we'd become cautious about going into a new place without them.

"*But swimming without a suit has to be worth trying,*" I said.

"*We'll come back and try it, but I don't want to fly in Sparrowhawk all wet and salty,*" Ashley said.

Which was where we left it. We all took a turn at some point to land and feel the sand on our feet but we didn't do much more than paddle in the warm tropical water. By three in the afternoon we were getting hungry.

*"We could fly to Saigon from here and buy from some of the markets,"* Cam suggested.

*"Did you bring money?"* Scotty asked, interested.

*"Uh no, I forgot,"* she replied disappointed.

So we flew home only to learn our day's scanning had found nothing.

We went to bed early that night because the Nathans were meant to be going to school in the morning and we were hoping to walk with them.

**[+]**

Control woke us up at one thirty in the morning. Grandpop was waiting in the theatre. We were still yawning and looking tired as we ambled in.

"OK guys each team has their Nathan. One of you watch the address to see when he leaves. The other find a landing zone and plan your interception route."

Me and Tahira had Nathan Green again. He lived with his mother, father and sister. We watched his early morning routine on a corner of the holodeck. It seemed very familiar. Meanwhile Tahira had worked out his likely route. As they started to leave the house we bent. We came out from behind our dumpster, hoping the cop wasn't about, and wearing our imitation green and tan uniform with snow jacket. We ran back along the road to make sure we caught up with Nathan. We got to the front door of his block in perfect time. The only problem: no Nathan. We waited in confusion for about three minutes when the underground garage door opened and a car drove out carrying the whole Green family. They were driving the kids to school four hundred meters away! There was no way we were going to be able to get to him like this, so we bent home.

Ashley and Scotty had no luck with Nathan Montgomery either. He'd just never come out of his house and they both had a feeling he simply wasn't there. Tarik and Cam had managed to trail along after Nathan Roberts but he had two older brothers who had butted in on conversation all the time.

Dr Prosperov was fairly sure Nathan Roberts was the one because the name Raman and he had found in the future sounded more like "Roberts" than "Green" or "Montgomery". We went back to bed and awoke ready for the Nathans to go home again. It was rather cool to know we'd slept through Nathan's whole school day. We made the suits look like school uniform, then Control put us into the toilets at the Mall across the road from the school and we walked through it in time for the 3:15 p.m. home time.

**[+]**

There were hundreds of kids coming out of the school and we could easily blend in with them. A lot were black but there were also a lot of brown kids like me, Tahira and Tarik. There were enough other Vietnamese to cover Cam and, of course, Scott wasn't out of place either.

We pushed through the crowd looking around. I was wishing I'd brought Cheeky because it was hard to get a good view from the ground. In the end, though, Cam and Tarik found Nathan Roberts again, and trailed him home again. Our target, Nathan Green, was still inside. Me and Tahira decided now was the best time to try him, so we went back to the Mall toilets, and Control bent us back inside the school.

**[+]**

Finding him wasn't so easy. There was still a lot still happening at the school, but Control guided us to a particular class where

**386**

Nathan was part of a group rehearsing a play. We waited outside
in the corridor, as people pushed past, working out a plan
silently between us. There was no way we were going to be able
to join in this play, so we asked Control for the name of a teacher
Nathan knew and who had an office as far away as possible.
Then we could pretend the teacher had asked us to go and get
him. We knocked and went in. Three kids with books were
reading parts to one-another while a bunch of others followed
along. The teacher was a young man who seemed quite nice.
Normally I'm a bit shy around strangers but for some reason the
weirdness of the situation changed me. I think it was because I
was in my suit, they had no idea who I was, and I would be able
to vanish and never see them again in a few minutes.
We went up to the teacher (a Mr Brown) and waited for the kids
to stop talking. Finally they stopped reading and Mr Brown
asked us what we wanted. We said Ms Jackson wanted to talk to
Nathan about something before she left in the next few minutes
and if he could come. Mr Brown shrugged and a black boy with
glasses came forward curiously.
We led him out of the class over to Ms Jackson's classroom. It
was weird pushing through the fire doors in a school where we
only knew where to go only because Control was feeding us the
route, but it was completely new to us as well. Of course Nathan
wanted to know what Ms Jackson wanted, but we said we had
no idea. Then he wanted to know who we were, and where we
came from. We said we were exchange students from Britain.
We said the school looked amazing compared to the ones we
were used to.
He said it was money the principal Mrs Ross had got from her
friends at The Foundation. He said it was an experimental

school programme for minority students which was why they
had so many tests and the teachers came and went all the time.
They even got free medical care. He said it was just a school even
though it was better than most of the other schools he'd ever
heard of. This Nathan seemed a bit of a nerd.

Halfway there we ducked off claiming to need to go somewhere
else. We found a broom closet and bent home.

[+]

We climbed out of the jumpstation and found Dr Prosperov in
the holotheatre watching Nathan arrive at Ms Jackson's locked
office. We sat down and watched with Dr P as Nathan realised
Ms Jackson had long gone, and we had wasted his time.

"Is it him, Dr Prosperov?" I asked.

Dr P pulled a face.

"Is uncertain. Some indicators say 'yes' some 'no'. Boy may be
different from man. Tomorrow search for Montgomery boy.
Perhaps then, is clearer."

"But it's not Nathan Green is it?" I pressed.

"Green has two indicators. Roberts five. Out of possible eleven.
Can probably exclude Green."

He got up and threw a glance at the holotheatre which was now
dark, as Cam and Tarik came in, then packed his stuff and left.
We all went up to join Scotty and Ashley in the Café having a
second breakfast with Grandpop.

The next day Patricia and Ken flew to Washington. Ashley had to
be almost dragged into the sleeping bag to go join them because
she hated flying in planes so much. Even three hours annoyed
her. When he came back Scotty told us that Ken and Patricia had
stopped being polite to each other and now just laughed a lot

which seemed to please the adults – especially Zoe. We went to bed early because we had to get up at midnight to start looking for Nathan Montgomery.

By now the grind of constant missions was beginning to get to us. We had been going pretty much nonstop for two months, so when I was awoken in the middle of the night by Control bleeping my screen again, my first thought was not about helping the future of humankind, but staying in bed a little longer. Unfortunately I knew making everyone else wait for me would be a bad look, so I dragged myself up, braved the ghosts, and went downstairs.

"It looks like we have a big problem," Grandpop began the briefing.

"Nathan Montgomery is gone. His mother, June, has called him in sick, but he isn't at home, and he hasn't been home for at least a day or two. As far as we can tell she hasn't called the cops yet, but she is worried about him. He may have run away for some reason."

He sucked his teeth thoughtfully.

"So what we've gotta do is find out where he's gone, and why he went there. We have no idea how far he could have gone. We don't know how much money he had on him, nor anything about his family. The school record mentions only one parent. Dr Prosperov says that if this is the right Nathan, his mother had, or seeing as it's now we are taking about, has, a bad drinking problem, and he ended up living with his grandmother. This may be when that happens."

"So anyway, it's now six thirty in the morning D.C. time. So my plan is pretty simple, but it involves changing your teams around a bit because Ashley's not here. So Tarik, Scott and

Sam your job is to spread out and search the places a kid might hide up in Columbia Heights. Move fast. If we're lucky and he's just cooling off somewhere maybe we'll catch him sleeping. It's still dark but this is the best time to search the streets because gangsters generally aren't that great early in the morning, so you shouldn't have any interruptions."

"Tahira and Cam you guys search closer around Nathan's home. At eight though, meet at his house. Then your job is to knock on the door and ask to see Nathan. Tell his mother you're asking for Ashley who he stood up. Try to read his mum as well as you can."

So we flashed into the dark streets of Columbia Heights.

## [+]

Given it was a weekend it was pretty quiet at that time in the morning. A few cars nosed through the dark, cold streets with their lights on, but generally everyone else was doing what I wished *I* was doing: sleeping.

I mooched along in the dark. I almost wished I had pockets I could put my hands in. I picked dull colours for my clothes. A black jacket, gray pants and my bag was black too. I decided to search as quickly and thoroughly as I could.

My area was west of the school, which wasn't as bad news as the areas east or south of it. I relied on my thermal imaging to seek out pockets of warmth that might mean someone sleeping, but there just weren't any.

*"You know we'd cover more ground on our bikes,"* I told Grandpop.

There was a pause. I could tell the others agreed.

"Yeah, alright, come in when you can," Grandpop agreed.

*"Shaheen and Hooty also,"* Tahira suggested.

"Let's do the animals in the morning when they're awake and it's warmer."

I thought the animals were getting a better deal than we were – and I wasn't the only one. But rather than gripe I looked for a quiet alleyway, turned into it, and folded home. I trudged past Grandpop who was dozing in his chair (but I knew better than to imagine he was asleep) grabbed my bike, pushed it back to the jumpstation, and returned to the alleyway.

[+]

It was hard riding on the right side of the mostly empty roads (which felt wrong because I'm used to riding on the left), so I stuck to the sidewalks. There was still a little ice and slush but the bike cut through it. The main thing, though, was it was way better to ride than to walk. It was just faster. Every now and again I'd stop to check a place out. A park, a toilet, under a bridge. There was no-one much about because it was so cold. The sun was only just starting to light the sky in the east. It was like I had the whole city to myself, with only the occasional jogger or dog walker around.

I rode as far as the zoo. I was getting readings all the time, like psychic smells of ideas or feelings, but there were no signs of Nathan living rough in the sub-zero temperatures of a Washington winter. I even doubted that any twelve-year-old would not find a better way to get shelter somehow.

We didn't see each other for the hour and a half we were searching. I found absolutely nothing. Scotty found an old "Bergie" (alcoholic) who was unconscious, wrapped in two coats and an old torn quilt while the air temperature was just below freezing.

[+]

391

Finally Tahira and Cam tried the mother. We boys gave up
and bent home to watch them on the holodeck. It took ages for
Nathan Robinson's mother, June, to answer the door and when
she did she looked a wreck. It was early in the morning and
she only opened thinking that perhaps Nathan had come back.
Her eyes were glassy, and Tahira and Cam thought she stank of
alcohol. She was still drunk.

They asked her where Nathan was. It took June ages to
remember she was still pretending he was at home, but she
finally said he was asleep. Our girls asked to see him anyway
when June changed her story and said he was sick. She was
clearly angry with all the questions and said he had measles.
She started saying he was up all night with chicken pox. Then it
was flu. Tahira and Cam kept saying they were immunised and
wanted to cheer him up. Finally she got sick of them and blew
up screaming he could go live with his father for all she cared
after what he'd called her and slammed the door in their faces.
The girls bent home immediately.

So Nathan had walked out to go live with his father! Now
the question was, who was Nathan's father, and why did he
suddenly think he could find him? Had he got a letter or email to
make him think he could live with him? Where did he think he
would find his father? We had no idea.

We went back to bed and slept until lunchtime. Then we had
a day at the beach. We waited until eight in the evening when
it was two in the morning in D.C. Then Tarik, Cam and Scotty
went back to check out Nathan's room. Tarik brought Peter
the Spider to put up a web to pick up cordless and cell phones,
and Cam released a couple of flies to watch June. Tarik copied
the old PC in the living room and Scotty read that Nathan had

packed his schoolbag and worn his warmest jacket.

June Montgomery must have heard them because she called out for her son. She rushed into the small messy living room, so they had to zap her memory, knock her out, and put her back to bed. It was quite sad really. They said the reading they had was that Nathan expected to meet someone close to him from a city further north. It was a woman, not his father, and she would take him to his father. He had made plans involving a bus and was happy and excited at the prospect.

We didn't know then that the combination of a bus and someone from further north totally put us on the wrong track for about a week or two.

We went to bed knowing that Ashley, who was travelling with her mother Patricia, and Khenbish, would be waking up in Washington at 2 a.m. our time and could do the morning shifts for us. Scotty had volunteered to wake up early and bring her back to Renwick so she could hit the streets.

I missed all that, and slept until eight on a lovely, hot day on Aotea Island. We had breakfast, then Grandpop rounded us up and we went downstairs for a briefing.

"OK," Grandpop began, in the decisive way that he used when he didn't really have much for us.

"Control's been through the logs, hacked the Hotmail accounts, and followed everything he can find. Unfortunately there's nothing there. We have no idea who Nathan has gone to meet or where he might have gone. We're making contact with Dr Morozov's friends at para.no.ID who have more experience with getting into bank accounts. We think that Nathan must have some money somewhere so we want to see if he has made any withdrawals, we can track. It looks like he's planned this trip well and he's done most of it by phone. We need to do a bit of work looking for his mum's phone bills and possibly the school's as well."

"Ashley's been at the school most of the day trying to work out who Nathan's mates are and see if they know anything. So far she's got their names and pictures but she hasn't had a chance to talk to them yet. The two guys are Errol and Ricky."

Two clips of two black kids appeared on the holodeck. Errol was big, and fat. Ricky was small with glasses. You could just tell these guys just weren't into sports.

"So this is one for the girls. These guys probably don't get too much female attention so they should be pretty easy to get talking. If you guys bend to the Mall Ashley will meet you outside Starbucks and give you more information."

Tahira and Cam got up, gave me and Tarik a small wave and took off for the changers. Scott was still sleeping off his morning. Grandpop turned to me and Tarik.

"OK you guys may as well check out the intercity bus stations. There are only a few. In theory they aren't meant to take unaccompanied twelve-year-olds like Nathan who show up without a care-giver. So Ken and Patricia have got some American currency for you both. See if you can get on a bus to Chicago with it. If they call the cops go to the loo and come home."

So we got changed and bent to Ken and Patricia's Washington hotel suite which was pretty nice. As always we arrived in a flash of brilliant light.

## [+]

Ken and Patricia were sitting at their table wearing sunglasses and holding cellphones to their ears with the notebook in front of them. It looked kind of odd.

"Hi guys, welcome to grand central station," Ken said.

We opened our facescreens.

"Hi Ken, how's it going?" I asked.

"I dunno, Control was just giving us a run down."

He took off the shades.

"They sent us some of the toys Hekati gave you guys," he said.

"Anyway we're going to hire a car tomorrow which will make us a bit more useful. There's talk of flying one of your Speeders out, but we haven't worked out what we do when we leave for Europe," he said.

He slid over two envelopes.

"So here's the money. We've got you $300. You'll need $100 to $130 for a bus ticket to Chicago. How do you think you'll do it."

"Bribery," said Tarik confidently.

"Hmmm might work," said Ken doubtfully. "But they'd really have to hate their jobs."

"No, not the bus company people, just some random adult. I'll bribe him to say I'm his son. Then they can go on the unaccompanied minor form for me."

"That might work," Ken admitted. "What about you Sam?"

I hadn't even thought about it.

"I dunno, I thought I'd tell them some sob story about my father had sent me some money."

"Hmm not so likely to succeed," Ken said.

"But it's a good idea to try it and see what happens," Patricia put in. "Nathan may not have had anything better than that either and it will give us some idea what happens if you try it."

I felt a little less dumb.

"Yeah," said Ken doubtfully. "Anyway we've got two of the bigger bus stations here and here," he said pointing to the map on his notebook screen.

"So, I dunno, which ones do you want?"

We divided them up.

"OK, well good luck," Ken said.

"Do you have any onions?" I asked.

"Onions?" Ken and Patricia looked at each other.

"No. Why do you want onions?" he asked.

"I may need to cry a bit."

"Oh, good idea!" said Patricia encouragingly.

"Sorry, no onions here," Ken said." You might be able to buy some."

"It's OK." I shrugged.

So we said goodbye and folded away into nothing.

**[+]**

I arrived in a doorway in an alley some distance from the bus station. I have to admit I felt a bit nervous. I had no idea how I could convince some strange adult to let me get on a bus without my parents behind me. I also had no idea about travelling long distance on a bus at all. I'd never been on one myself. It all made me feel a little nervous and sick.

I walked out of the alleyway. It was about four in the afternoon local time. The sky was dark gray and it was getting pretty cold. It was probably going to snow.

I decided I'd have a look at the bus station before I tried to buy the ticket. For some reason the walk to the station made me feel more nervous. I started to wonder if I was picking up on something because really, I personally had no reason to be nervous at all. I wasn't planning to spend ten hours in a bus going hundreds of miles north to meet someone I didn't know in the hope of something I wasn't sure of.

The more I thought about it, the stupider it seemed to me to do. Did Nathan really know who he was going to see? How did he know they were who they said they were? How could he contact them if something delayed him? How would he get back if something went wrong?

Of course I didn't know him then, and maybe I would have asked myself different questions if I had had some idea of what he's like but those were the ones that occurred to me, in his situation. I kept walking the four or five blocks until I found the bus station.

From the outside it looked big, concrete and unfriendly. It also had cameras. I wasn't sure I liked the cameras and called in. "No, don't zap the cameras Sam. Just ignore them. It's OK," Grandpop reassured me.

So hiding under my hood I went across the road, and across the parking lot, into the bus station, feeling a bit odd in my tummy. I was really out of place.

The bus station was surprisingly empty. I had hoped there would be a crowd to hide in, but it must have been a quiet time because there was hardly anyone there. The place had a worn down look about it and the staff were chatting behind the counter, laughing about someone. They didn't even notice me at first as I looked at the timetables and stuff trying to feel better about going up to the counter. Finally I went over and stood there behind the glass, watching them talk. There was an old, thin, white woman with gray hair and wrinkled skin from too much smoking. She had a dull uniform on and was chatting to an old black man with gray hair and soft brown eyes with goo in the corners, and a fat young black woman. They all wore the same uniform.

"And what can we do for you young man?" the gray haired woman asked me sharply, looking over at me from where she sat behind the counter.

"Ah ... I wanna get a ticket to Chicago," I mumbled.

"Sorry son, can't hear you," she said tilting her head.

"I ... I wanna get a ticket to Chicago," I said loudly, already knowing it was hopeless.

"Why d'you wanna go to Chicago?"

"My dad wants me to come see him. He sent me the money for a ticket."

The gray haired woman glanced at the black man.

"I think I might ..." he said to her, nodding at me.

"Thanks Sam," she said to him.

The black man went out of sight and came through a side door over to where I was waiting.

"Come over here, son I just want a word."

He led me over to a couple of seats.

"Sit down," he said gently and took a seat next to me.

"What's your name?"

"Sam," I said.

"What's your last name?"

"Sam Brown."

"OK Sam Brown well my name is Sam too. Now tell me about this trip o' yours to Chicago. Does your Dad know you're coming?"

"Yeah, He sent me the money."

"Sure, so you've got his address and phone number with you, right?"

This was annoying because I had no idea what I could use for an address and phone number in Chicago. I didn't even know the

Zip codes. So I sat there with a stupid look on my face. Old Sam just sighed.

"Look, I'll tell you straight son, there's no way you can get on a bus without your parent or guardian. We aren't allowed to put unaccompanied minors on a bus journey that lasts more than five hours[†], and its almost double that to Chicago. Plus kids can't travel alone at night and there's two transfers and unaccompanied kids aren't allowed to do any[†]. So even, if you are tellin' the truth – and I'm not sayin' you ain't – your dad should know there ain't no way you can go to him on any bus in this whole country. But the main question I got for you is why do you want to go at all?"

"I want to go to see my dad. He's sick. He may be dying," I told Sam, making it up.

"And your mum doesn't want you to go?"

"She says he's never shown any interest in me and I should forget about him."

Sam bit his lip.

"Yeah ... Well I can sorta see where you are coming from. You want to know what he's like, right?"

"Yeah," I said getting caught up in my own story.

"Well, I can appreciate that but that doesn't change anything about transportation in the United States. Now one more thing 'Sam Brown' where you from? Because you sure don't talk like anyone I ever heard before."

"I was born in Australia."

"Is that a fact? OK, I got one bit of advice for you Sam Brown and I want you to think about this one, pretty hard. If you leave your mom what is she gonna do?"

"I dunno, probably nuthin."

"Probably somethin. Like that other kid who tried to get on one of our buses a few days ago. She'll call the cops, and they'll call youth services and then they will be on your case for the next ten years. And frankly I know those folks mean well but the way things work is if you ain't careful you can end up in some kind of institution and they just ain't good places to be. So what I'm sayin' to you, Sam Brown from Australia, is don't mess with them if you can avoid it, and if things are real bad, or even if you just need to talk things over with someone call the national runaway switchboard on 1-800-runaway⁺. They're good people. And they're better to talk to than some old guy down the bus station."

He stood up. I stood too. I liked this guy.

"So don't waste your time Sam Brown. Go home. And if you have problems make that call. 1-800-Runaway. You got that?"

"Yessir," I said.

He watched me all the way out of the station. It was dark now. There was no-one on the street and it was really cold so I did up my facescreen. Cars swished by and I could tell they were watching me curiously. I walked back to the alley and folded into the darkness.

[+]

It turned out Tarik had had less luck than I had. He'd spent $200 on a bribe and still hadn't got a ticket because of all the rules. But we did know Nathan had not left town on a bus. We went into the Holotheatre to find Scotty, now suited up, watching our girls. They were talking to Nathan's friends in the mall. They'd been at it for over an hour. It was pretty painful.

"God, I hope I *never* look that lame," Tarik commented.

The boys were so excited by these "British" girls showing

interest in them that they were showing off, and snorting at their own jokes. Tahira was particularly good at getting information out of them but Cam was cunning too. Ashley however found it hard to hide the fact that normally she would have nothing to do with such a couple of total losers.

What they found out was interesting. It turned out that Nathan had told them he'd had a call from his father's mother. The reading had been right! He didn't know his father who had split before he could remember him. June hadn't even told him his father's name.

His father had been badly hurt. Errol and Ricky didn't know how, or how bad, exactly. But apparently he wanted to see his only son in case he died. Nathan, somehow seemed to think he might inherit something from his father and wanted to make sure he got it directly, because if anything went to his mother he didn't trust her not to steal it and drink it all. I found it spooky that it was pretty close to the story I'd made up at the bus station.

Errol and Ricky said they thought the grandmother came from Detroit because Nathan had talked about catching a bus to that city but they hadn't thought he'd actually try it. They doubted he'd be allowed by himself. They said Nathan's mother was "a real bad drinker" who in the past had a number of boyfriends who had beaten up Nathan and robbed her.

Nathan had learned not to trust his mother and had lots of secrets from her: Places he hid things; a knife he often carried; and machines he nicked money from. He often stayed over with Errol and Ricky to avoid his mum's boyfriends. But even while his life was pretty tough, he always avoided joining the gang. He'd been jumped once or twice but he didn't want to be a part of it. He said he didn't want to go to jail and he didn't want to be killed.

Instead his big interest was trading stuff on eBay. Car badges and collectibles were his speciality and he was pretty good at thieving them. They said he was really good at making things sound good, even if they weren't and he did it just as well in person as online.

"*Ask his eBay username,*" Tarik prompted the girls.

The answer came back a few minutes later: Junebug77. It was his mother's. They also let slip that he'd had a secret hidey-hole in one of the local parks he'd shown them.

"Scott, go check out the hiding place, he may have gone back there," Grandpop suggested.

Scotty slipped off to the jumpstation.

The girls kept Errol and Ricky talking but it was clear they had told us everything they knew. So Tahira made an excuse and the girls went off to the toilets and came home. Scotty was back a short time later saying the hiding place might have been used once but wasn't now.

Control showed that Nathan had been selling quite a few things on his mother's eBay account up until recently but had nothing currently for sale. So the only clue we had was that Nathan had tried and failed to get on a bus to Detroit. But that still didn't tell us where he was. He could be still in Washington somewhere, on the road in between somewhere, or in one of half a dozen northern American cities. Finding a runaway teen that way would be like looking for a needle in a haystack.

Control thought the best clues would come from the phone calls to his grandmother. If we could locate her we would hopefully work back the other way. But we weren't sure who she was. If we could get her phone number we would be halfway there.

This meant going back to Nathan's mother's house, first to find out who Nathan's father was, and second whether Nathan had ever called his grandmother, leaving a number on her bill. Tahira and Cam didn't want to talk to Nathan's mother again. She was already drinking at five in the afternoon and going to be pretty hopeless pretty soon. We also agreed that June Montgomery wasn't likely to discuss Nathan's father with some nosey kids who had been hassling her the day before anyway.

That led to Dr P suggesting that as Nathan clearly was actually missing we should report it to the police. If Nathan really was in trouble, the more eyes looking for him the better. So Control networked Patricia through June Montgomery's bugged phone and she called the police claiming her son was a runaway.

It was pretty impressive what happened after that. A cop car was around within an hour, and although the drunk June Montgomery denied making the phone call, she couldn't deny Nathan was missing. The cops questioned her, took old pictures of Nathan, and copies of all his records. By eight this huge system had swung into action to find Nathan. Messages were on highways, on cell phones, on TV, everywhere.

So our new plan was simple. We were going to watch his police file and do our own check of his mother's place. But that meant waiting until our evening before we could go to Washington, so that it would be two in the morning.

Of course, Ashley couldn't last that long. She'd been up since three in the morning our time and was looking stuffed. Scotty, who was looking pretty stuffed himself, volunteered to take her back to Ken and Patricia's hotel in a sleeping bag. But Grandpop wanted them both ready to go in the morning, D.C. time, so he

**403**

organised with Zoe and Patricia for them to stay in their suits and sleep at the hotel in Washington with Ken and Patricia. It was a bit of a funny moment really. The suite had three bedrooms. Patricia wasn't quite ready to admit to Ashley she was sleeping with Ken so she thought she and Ken should be in separate bedrooms. But if they slept apart, Ashley and Scotty would have to sleep together, and she wasn't sure about that either. Patricia wasn't sure what the right thing to do was. We, of course, knew Ken thought he and Patricia should admit they were sleeping together because we could tell anyway, but Patricia felt a bit self-conscious about Ken with her daughter around. Scotty offered to stay at Renwick, but Grandpop wanted them together, Ashley wanted him to stay with her, and Scott's mum, Zoe, didn't mind either way. In the end Patricia decided it was OK if Ashley and Scotty slept in their suits on the double bed. It wasn't like they could take them off anyway. It was the first time any of us had ever done that.

They stayed in contact with us for a while making smutty jokes up about Ken and Patricia which none of the adults could hear. Cam seemed to find them especially funny which surprised Tarik. Ashley was really mean about her mum but Scotty seemed to know not to be rude about Patricia too, because we all knew mother and daughter were really very close.

Eventually they went to sleep. We had nothing to do, so Grandpop sent us upstairs to work for Mrs Jones.

It was actually a nice day outside. The sun was all golden in the early evening and I was a bit pissed off that I'd missed a nice summer day again. I found myself remembering the previous summer with Emma and that annoyed me, thinking about her with David.

"Your problem is she doesn't zink you care for 'er at all," Tahira said polishing the brass wall socket.

"Yeah I *know* that. But what can I *do* about it? We're always busy, doing missions and stuff."

"Zat is only part of your problem," she said.

"Well, what can I do when I'm all over the world and never where she is?"

"I've watched you wiz 'er Sam. You are so Mr Cool. You never flirt. You never chat wiz 'er about what she likes. You don't make 'er feel special. What is there for 'er to like? Some boy who ignores 'er all times and 'ardly says anyzing."

I was bright red. It was true. But it was because I felt so shy around her.

"Sam you are clever and brave. I know. I 'av seen it. But wiz Emma you are a big fat chicken."

"It's not as simple as that..." I started, my cheeks still red and focusing on my light switch.

"Puk ... puk ... puk."

I glared at her. She was grinning.

"I don't know what to *do*," I blurted out, frustrated with her. Tahira rolled her eyes.

"Uuuuh!" she groaned. "Why are boys zo dumb about zere 'earts?"

"We aren't dumb!" I complained. "Nobody tells us what to do."

"Hah! It is zooo simple!"

She threw down her rag and walked up to me. She closed with me her brown eyes focused on my mouth. I noticed the way she had shaped her eyebrows. Her breathing was deep.

"I can't sleep for zinking of you," she moaned. Then she casually

**405**

turned and walked back to her socket, picked up her rag and gave me a glance of pure desire and went back to her polishing.

"OK, Mr Cool, tell me you would forget *zat*!"

I thought for a moment.

"This switch is about as shiny as it's going to get," I noticed.

"Mine also."

We moved along to the next ones.

"So … you think I need to be more pushy."

"No! no! *not* pushy!" she stamped her foot. "No pushy is rude and selfish. Pushy is ze exact *opposite*. Iz passion Sam! Passion! In Persia boys and girls zey cannot touch, zey cannot even be *alone* til zey married. So 'ow do you theenk zey arrange zere love affairs? Because zey 'av love affairs Sam. Zey are 'uman. But ze Persians are *romantic*, Sam! We *invented* romance and romance means we 'av passion. We write letters, and poems. We use flowers. We send books, presents, and food. We look! A look can say very, very much. Zis is romance!" she argued with the light switch.

And you know what? I got it! I could see it in her. To her life was *all* about romance. It was an art, like Mr Trân's food or Mariko's designs. She believed in the art of romance. It was like opening a door into a new world. I stopped cleaning. I was just staring at her. She glanced at me as she reapplied cleaner to her rag.

"What?" she asked.

"You're amazing."

"Me?" she half laughed. "Why?"

"You just are," I said turning back to my polishing.

She muttered something to herself about me being easily impressed but I couldn't hear it. A bit later she was just whistling while we worked and we ended up having a rag

fight before Mrs Jones told us to go to dinner, but I felt I now
discovered a new way of seeing the world and it gave me some
hope with Emma when the holidays were over.

The missions that night were split between the usual pairs. Cam
and Tarik had to raid the Washington cops. Me and Tahira had
to do Ms Montgomery, looking for her telephone accounts. We
already knew she wasn't the most organised of people so finding
things in her flat wasn't going to be easy.

**[+]**

We flashed into her living room at two in the morning and
fluffed up our feet at once to make less noise. The whole place
was a mess and not that large, so it was difficult to move around.
We decided to split the job. Tahira would look for the phone bill
and because I seemed to have some connection with Nathan, I'd
see if I could read June Montgomery and make sure she didn't
interrupt Tahira.

I slipped down the passage and came to the room of the woman
who was snoring softly in the dark. Of course I could see her,
lit by the alarm clock saying it was 2:09 a.m. and the light
coming from under the door to the living room. I sat down in the
doorway and focused on Nathan's mother.

Her dreams were nightmares where Nathan was being driven off
in a car while policemen stood in her way and gave her a hard
time. I tried to make her think of Nathan's father. It took a bit
of leading but all I got was a dark room with flashing lights and
people dancing. She had felt happy there. But thinking about it
now made her feel guilty. She needed to find Nathan.

I sat with her for about an hour. Finally it struck me that Tahira
was taking a very long time to find an envelope so I asked her
what she was doing.

*"It's so disorganised I couldn't find anything so I'm tidying up."* she explained.

I wondered if I should ask June where the bill was. It was a risk. If she thought of it she might wake up. I decided it was worth a shot. I warned Tahira what I was going to do because we might have to dodge. She suggested we ask Control for a landing zone nearby. He had one ready in seconds. Then I softly suggested telephone bills to her.

It took a while for her to focus. She stopped snoring and started to move in her bed. She was looking for it. Looking for the bill. She wondered if she had thrown it out. Then she wondered if it had arrived yet. Was it on the fridge magnet? I passed that back to Tahira. Or was it in the shoebox by the phone? Again I passed that to Tahira.

*"I've got some bills in here,"* she announced.

June was starting to think she had got her bill and it was there somewhere. She woke up.

She would have walked along the passage and found the door to the living room closed but the light on. When she opened the door and found it all neat and tidy with her phone bills spread out on the table she must have been pretty creeped out. But Tahira had scanned all of them and we were on the other side of the world.

## [+]

It took Control a wee while to check out all the numbers on the phone bill. In the meantime Tarik and Cam came back. They had spent ages helping Control break into the Youth Services computer system. They had discovered the police were already ahead of us. They had a name for Nathan's father.

He was Richard David Robinson who had a criminal record and

originally came from Detroit. The record was mostly for minor drug offences, car conversion, common assault and petty theft. He was obviously no angel but he wasn't exactly a major league crim either. He just looked like some of my cuzzies. The kind that never learn that shortcuts are usually longcuts in the end. It had been a long and tiring day and we'd missed out on more of the summer. Frankly, I was getting a bit sick of America, nor was I alone. We got changed and went upstairs to play pool. Even that broke up early, we were just too tired.

Aunty Liz came in to see me off to bed.

"How are you Sam?"

"Pretty tired Aunty Liz. I hope we can find this damn Nathan soon," I sighed.

"I think you guys are working too hard. I've never seen a group of kids work as much as you guys do."

"Yeah ... It's also well ... we're missing out on summer. We spend all day in the cold and dark and when we come home we don't get a chance to enjoy it."

"I'll talk to dad about it. See if you can get some more treasure missions or something. Maybe you can take your sister somewhere. Maybe even me too!"

"I'd really like that mum ... Aunty Liz." I corrected myself sleepily.

The next thing I knew it was a sunny morning on Aotea again. I plodded down to the café and joined the others. There was a lot of chat going around and it was then that I learned that Nathan's father was Ashley's uncle.

Patricia had recognised him as her husband's brother when she'd been briefed in the morning. That meant Nathan's grandmother was also Ashley's grandmother and Patricia's

**409**

mother-in-law. But even Patricia couldn't get through to
Margaret on the phone.

Everyone thought this connection was pretty amazing. Some
suggested Lucky was involved but Dr P flatly said Lucky had
nothing to do with it. Tarik cleverly suggested that maybe part
of the reason Nathan could become President was that Ashley
was his cousin and helped him. It might be true, but as I say, we
didn't know what Nathan was capable of yet.

Ken and Patricia had checked out of their hotel and rented a
car. Their plan was to drive the most direct route to Detroit and
provide a base for Ashley and Scotty's searching along the way.
Meanwhile Ashley and Scotty were working hard checking out
every possible way Nathan could have found to travel north.
Then, just to make matters worse, it started snowing hard[†].
Seriously hard. It was under minus ten centigrade with wind
chill. Ken and Patricia were taking their driving very carefully. If
Nathan was outside in this his chance of getting hypothermia or
frostbite had become serious. The police were worried.

The only good news for us was it made bending around America
dead easy. In the whiteout nobody was going to be standing
around wondering what a flash of light meant. We tended to
wear our suits white so we just vanished into the snow. We
checked huge goods trains by running along the top of them,
cowboy style, as they crawled through the icy blast using our
wings and claws for stability. We flashed into stinking loos
in truck stops, service stations and diners. We bent to muggy
shelters, where old winos huddled against the polar cold. We
even went to churches that might provide some sanctuary.

For three hours we searched along the obvious places along the
120 kilometers between Washington and Hagerstown. But we

couldn't go everywhere. The area was just way too huge. It felt like three hours of nonstop running in slippery, white, semi-darkness. By six local time it was dark and we needed a break.

## [+]

We came back to Renwick where Ashley and Scotty were coming out of the sea with Mariko, Rewa and Asal all of whom were carrying some respectable fish and with huge smiles on their faces. We all got changed and had a Vietnamese style fish lunch with salads noodles, and loads of spicy soup in the sun along with Australian ginger beer. It was great to be somewhere bright and warm for a change.

Occasionally we'd think about poor old Nathan but after trying so hard for so long we felt like we deserved a rest. After lunch we went for a mooch along the bays and ended up surfing near the cave bay I'd spent so much time with Emma the year before. I felt bad knowing she was down south with that pretty-boy David. At three in the afternoon Grandpop wandered over wearing flip-flops and shorts with his hands in his pockets and said it was time for Ashley to go home to bed.

Ashley had been snoozing in the sun in her swimsuit, doing what none of the rest of us dared to do in the vicious New Zealand sun. She was tired but didn't want to go back. We kind of rallied around and said there was no special need for her to go back, she could stay with us, so Grandpop wandered back to check that out with Patricia.

It turned out Ken and Patricia were hunkered down in a small hotel in Hagerstown while outside it was turning into a regular snowstorm. They seemed quite happy not to have Ashley with them that night. But we had to drag Ashley home to her bed in Renwick at four. Zoe looked after her, and Ash and Scotty were fast asleep in their own rooms by five. Even Patience was still running around.

The next day was pretty much a repeat of the day before except Ken and Patricia ended up in Pittsburgh. We were starting to feel pretty sure that we were on completely the wrong track and that Nathan had never left D.C. The problem was no-one was answering the number in Detroit and Control couldn't see anyone there. Ashley and Scotty went ahead but the house seemed packed up, almost as if the owner was moving out. Police information was coming in too. Richard Robinson had joined the Army and they were asking them for his whereabouts. They also had had no luck getting in contact with Margaret Robinson, Richard's mother.

For a second night Ashley preferred to stay at Renwick rather than join her mother in Pittsburgh. The weather on Aotea was way better and again we spent the afternoon swimming while the snow whined and whirled around the northern United States[†] closing roads and airports and generally making sure everyone stayed indoors.

But by ten the next morning local time the case was solved. Nathan had been found with his grandmother by the Washington Metro Police at the National Rehabilitation Center hospital just a few kilometers from Columbia Heights where his father was a patient. Control picked up the police call in that they were bringing in both Nathan and his Grandmother. Ashley and Scotty got the news while checking out a goods van in driving snow storm. Ken and Patricia were just about to set out west and now had to turn around and head back to Washington again. Control spotted a Youth Services case worker had gone on leave and gave Ashley and Scotty some names from his files and sent them to sit in a waiting room, their suits adapted like a jacket over a school uniform.

The cops were just trying to sort out why Scott and Ash were waiting for a case worker who wasn't there, when Nathan came in looking a bit annoyed and a bit scared. His grandmother Margaret Robinson was with him and they took them away into an interview room but not before Ashley had released a fly which followed them in. By five our time they were back at Renwick watching the interview in the Holotheatre with sound provided by the fly.

It turned out that Nathan had been faking calls to his mother so his grandmother, Margaret, thought June had given her permission for Nathan to visit her. Nathan told his interviewer he knew his mother wouldn't have let him visit his dad, but his grandmother said his dad might die and he had always intended to find him.

It wasn't much of a first meeting with his dad, though. Richard was now a tetraplegic and very depressed. He had shown much less enthusiasm for Nathan than he'd hoped. Though the specialist had said Nathan could make a very big difference to Richard's long term mental health. He'd stayed at Margaret's hotel, sleeping on a mattress in Margaret's room.

The reunion with June was not the best. She was angry with everyone and had drunk a bit before coming. The Youth Services people warned June she was under investigation and that just made her more angry and abusive. The way she told it she worked herself into an early grave with no help from Richard or Margaret and Nathan was selfish and disrespectful. But when Margaret offered to help with Nathan, June swore at her for ten minutes until they were separated.

When I watched it with the others four hours later I couldn't help thinking Nathan was handling himself extremely well. He calmed down his mother and put up with a long police lecture on not going off by himself again which he listened to carefully and seriously. Then asked a series of 'just checking' questions which seemed to be an afterthought but which were carefully phrased so he could base excuses on them afterwards.

The cops were still dealing with June who wanted to take a protection order out against Margaret and were too distracted to realise what Nathan was really doing. Eventually he went back home with his mother who spent the next hour and a half shouting at him, then crying and then hugging him. I could see Nathan thinking his life was far too crappy. But for the moment he needed his mother and he couldn't do much without her.

We, however, were happy. We had found our third target. That evening me and Tahira took one of Hekator's injector insects and flashed into Nathan's room at two in the morning local time. We had to knock Nathan out because he woke up. But when we left it was a huge relief knowing that we finally had him tagged. Now he could take off as much as he liked but we would always know where to find him.

•••

## CHAPTER FIFTY SEVEN: A HARD PLACE

S am, we are going to need you on standby," Grandpop tells me suddenly.

I look at Sue, lying in her hot pool, trying to remember what the others are up to. Oh, yeah I was meant to be rescuing Sir Michael's daughter and testing their trap. For the life of me I can't remember why.

*"What's happening?"*

"We've reconnoitred the castle but it's closed up. We've put Shaheen and Cheeky in but the windows are curtained and they can't see anything. You'll see for yourself when you fly Ka-rea-rea around. Von Streicher's phone's coordinates are still inside the castle and we've confirmed that the para.no.ID feed is accurate. Tarik found Von Streicher's car in the private carpark in the courtyard so you'll see that too."

I still feel a bit unwell and to be honest I don't want to go anywhere.

*"What about my quarantine? I've only been here one day."*

"You won't be cleared to go on to Fae but they've cleared you for operations with us."

*"What about Sue?"* I ask, stalling.

"She'll be safe."

I thought privately, "she'll be bored stiff."

"*Sam will you be OK?*" Sue asks using her tiara.

"*I hope so,*" I say, not being at all sure. I don't feel that great. And Grandpop's news is not comforting either

"Sam, we don't think you can do all of this from Ka-rea-rea. You will be forced to get out and check inside. We've done what we can. Mariko and Cam even went inside the tourist part of the castle but the private part is locked up. We didn't dare push it in case they recognise us and realise we're all back."

I have to remember that keeping the others return secret will allow us to resettle somewhere else on Earth, hopefully without being attacked again.

"Anyway, we have a landing site where you can land Ka-rea-rea, but it looks like they want you to break in ..."

"*Great,*" I interrupt sarcastically. "*Then they'll probably shoot me.*"

"They won't if they don't know you're there."

"*Do I get one of those new suits?*" I ask, hopefully.

"Sir Michael saw you get back into Ka-rea-rea in your Aussie clothes remember?"

"*Oh yeah,*" I remember. "*Can't the new suits look like that?*" I check.

"No, we checked but they were too light for a suit to mimic."

I wondered why I hadn't simply replaced the black hoody and jeans I'd had on when I went into the caves with Emma and Sue. Probably because it was so hot on the Gold Coast when I'd bought my clothes at Pacific Fair.

"*Well, now the Fae destroyed them when I got here, so I haven't got anything to wear,*" I complain.

"Don't worry Hekator's copied them. He's beefed them up a bit."

That's still not very comforting. Because having spent a day in the comfort and safety of the quarantine station with Sue my original plan to fly off and do battle with the forces of evil all by myself now seems a bit desperate. Of course I *had* been getting desperate – especially when I heard about Lana – and then when Sir Michael had invited himself into Caz and Julia's safehouse. Realistically, if I hadn't zapped Rocelli's car and injured him I was on the brink of being captured. It was the others suddenly showing up that had saved my arse.

"Is Sir Michael's daughter really *that* important?" I wonder aloud, not wanting to get into any more danger than I need to. "I mean if I'm caught this could be serious for the whole of Fae." I'm wriggling, trying to get out of it.

"It's not just about Sian, Sam. We need to find out how they nearly caught us – remember? Otherwise they will catch us again and we might not be so lucky a second time."

I remembered thinking this was important – and it is – but after being hyped up for a week, the relief of being safe in this quarantine base was making me less keen to race back out into danger again. I don't want to even get out of my hot pool.

"I just think they will have a trap waiting for me."

"Probably Sam. But you would expect that. Look, I know it's hard but I know you. You're careful. You would never have charged into danger if we weren't here and now that we are, we don't want you to do it either. If you get hurt your Aunt will kill me, for one thing. We'll do as much of this as we can by remote control. But you may have to get out, just once in plain sight to prove that you really are in Ka-rea-rea."

That was true. Just as I'd had to show Sir Michael I would have to show Von Streicher. The difference was Von Streicher was powerfully psychic and he scared me.

"Oh, OK. Where are the clothes?"

"Waiting at the place where you came in, along with a transporter."

The 'angel' hologram appears. I notice she has Sue's attention again. The 'angel' smiles at me and signals I should follow. I sigh and get out of the water, feeling weighed down by more than gravity.

"I hope I'm not too long," I tell Sue.

"Be careful Sam. Don't do anything dangerous you don't have to do."

"Believe me, I won't," I reply, dripping everywhere.

I follow the 'angel' Fae through the maze of tunnels and waterways we'd come in through, until we come to the garden where we'd first appeared. A coffin box is waiting for me. I touch it and think "open" and it does. This one is different. It's really like a coffin. All padded and stuff. It looks quite comfy really. The clothes and a towel are inside. I dry myself and pull them on. There's also a new watch, which looks just like Qi, some shoes and a handkerchief.

The clothes are extremely silky and light, so they feel very comfortable. Grandpop fills me in on them, as I put them on.

"Hekator's done as much with the clothes as he dares without making them look different. He's made them water repellent and fire retardant. You could stand in a furnace in them. They're especially slippery making them hard to grab. They won't tear but they are not bullet proof so don't get cocky."

"The sneakers and fingerless gloves have climbing fibres built into them. They will help you climb up smooth stone surfaces."

"What's the watch for? I've got Qi, somewhere."

"Well Sir Michael saw you have a watch but *they* don't know what it does. This one will be more useful than Qi. It is a light psychic shield. It sucks up energy from other dimensions or something. Don't ask me about that stuff. All I know is it's to help you get away from Von Streicher. It also has a serious laser built into the winding knob. A light press on the face lights the targeting dot. A heavy press let's them have it."

"And the handkerchief?"

"Is a defence against gas. It changes colour from white to red if there is an abnormal air mix. It will form into a filter when pressed over your face."

"Do I have any break in tools?"

"No, but you never did so you'll have to improvise. My advice is use Ka-rea-rea and don't get out if you don't have to. But don't forget. If you need back-up we're listening in, and ready to go."

I sigh and step into the coffin and it closes around me. I just hope it won't end up being used as my real one. I ask it to take me to the place I left Ka-rea-rea and the mind bending journey begins.

## [+]

When I arrive I find Cam's waiting. I must have looked dazed, getting out of the coffin. It's night time. The sky's cloudy, the moon shines through occasionally, and it's cold.

"You OK, Sam?" she asks softly.

She looks a little different in the new suit. A little older.

"Yeah," I reply. "A bit nervous," I admit.

She looks at me for a moment, and then hugs me. She looks me in the eyes. She's really worried, which doesn't make me feel any better.

"Keep safe," she says. Then she kisses me lightly.

"For luck," she says blushing. Then she steps back, pulls up her hood, seals her face, and vanishes into darkness. I suddenly feel a bit like I'm about to go on stage with my old kapa haka group back in Northland. I look down from the high mountain to the small town of Belzer on the other side of the alpine valley. The castle is on the small hill above the town[†], in the moonlight. The sky is overcast and the moon comes and goes, as does a cool breeze.

I go over to Ka-rea-rea and open him, take out the ball receiver, and close it into the coffin transporter. It vanishes. Then I hop into Ka-rea-rea, take one last look around and pull down the lid. I take off and fly up over the big valley using adaptive camouflage. The streets beneath me are lit up in orange sodium lights except around the dark hill where the castle is. The castle has some orange lights on its walls but mostly it's dark. I circle around the valley quickly to make sure there are no nasty surprises hiding behind the mountains. I don't really need to do this because the others had been keeping watch but it's just instinctive – and as if I was still alone.

Then I zoom up directly to the castle, hovering over it out of the light.

It's a fairly typical German medieval castle. There's a big six-storey Keep in the middle which has a very steep roof with windows in it. Around the Keep is an outer wall, about ten meters high, on a very steep hill which rises up from the town below. There are two courtyards either side of the tall Keep. One courtyard is between the Keep and the outer wall. This is where Von Streicher's car is parked. An alley wide enough for vehicles to drive around the Keep connects it to a much larger courtyard between the Keep and a fortress.

The fortress is a big round block about four stories tall that was obviously built as a battle platform to prevent entry and protect the Keep. The fortress sits astride a gate which leads out to a drawbridge. The drawbridge crosses a gully to an outer tower two stories high and a gateway. Outside the castle are a couple of churches, a car park and what looks like a tourist café.

Looking at it all I can't help thinking that those medieval guys sure knew a thing or two about making a building hard to get into. The whole castle is built just to keep people out of the tall Keep. I fly lower, with adaptive camouflage making me almost transparent, and start moving slowly around the castle checking it over.

"We thought you could land under the drawbridge and climb up the wall into the first courtyard," Tarik says.

"Hmm let me look around," I reply.

I really don't like that idea at all. It might be sneaky but it exposes me to a lot of danger. Especially if I have to run away fast. I really don't like the idea of having to climb down a ten meter wall – especially if someone with a gun is chasing me. I hover about inspecting the castle. The cellphone is definitely still in the Keep and Von Streicher's car is one of the four in the back courtyard.

I start to think about the problem as if I'm by myself without the new clothes or any back-up. The more I think about it, the more I think there is no way I would get out of Ka-rea-rea. In fact I would be in no mood to be sneaky at all I would just burst in a zap everyone.

"What dya reckon Sam?" Grandpop asks.

I explain my thinking and Grandpop gets it straight away.

"You're right Sam and us nagging won't help you either. Look, we will back off and let you do this your way. We'll only come in if you're in trouble. Out."

Which gives me more time to think about it.

The first thing I wonder about is whether I should take out Von Streicher's car. If I immobilise him he's stuck there, with nowhere to go. That could be good. On the other hand it means he would hole up in a castle which is built to stop people getting into it. A car on the open road is a much easier target for me. Much easier than a castle. By leaving that door open I might encourage him to run.

I fly around getting lower and closer. There's something about the Keep. I try looking in at the windows. I use thermal vision and my beam microphones but the coloured glass blocks thermal imaging and the double glazing means the beam mike picks up nothing. I even try radar but the returns are so narrow it's hard to work out what I'm looking at.

I fly right down and check out the Keep's doors. The only thing that gives away my position is Ka-rea-rea's fuzzy shadow on the cobblestones. There's a big heavy wooden door in the front courtyard, and a smaller, but just as heavy one, at the back. It's likely the tower and the Keep are connected by tunnels but I have no way to be sure. That means that if I go in normally I would have to go through one of two heavy doors. I don't like that idea. It's too easy for them to ambush me.

And then it comes to me. I can fly *through* the windows!

I switch to inertialess and from stationary shoot off in a blur back to the mountains from where I'd come from. If there was a UFO watching they'd assume I'd seen something and chase. But nothing happens.

Five, ten minutes. I fly over the valley, watching the sky, hemmed in by the alps; watching the castle and the traffic in the streets below. Now I feel fairly confident I'm not going to be snuck up on from behind while I'm distracted. I line up on the window I'd chosen earlier, and, staying inertialess, fly at enormous speed straight back at it.

It's another one of those times I'm glad Ka-rea-rea does the real flying. We approach the window above the big front doors so fast I can't help closing my eyes. I hold my breath hoping we won't end up smeared on the stone. We shatter through the coloured glass and stop. I open my eyes, heart pounding. Ka-rea-rea is inches from a stone column as thick as a tree. I'm so shocked by the column it seems the crash of smashing through the window comes *after* we've stopped. Then I remember to breathe. I pant for a bit getting my heart under control, then look around.

We're in a big hall. Everything is stone and wood with big woollen hangings on the walls. It looks great. A real display for the tourists.

I slip sideways around the column to see a huge chandelier all lit up. A few meters below me is a balcony that runs around the hall. To the left is a grand staircase descending from a balcony on either side of a double door. It looks like a ballroom, but much bigger and grander than the one at Renwick.

There's no-one in sight. I fly down into the hall below. The silence is a bit eerie. After my violent entrance I half expect people to come running but the castle is as silent as a tomb. The lights are on but no-one seems to be home. No one who cares about one of their windows being smashed, anyway. I go looking for doors.

The obvious one is under the grand staircase. It's a big double door. I nudge it open and fly inside into a horrible scene.

The dining room is centred around a huge table made of dark

wood. The walls are deep red. There are heavy wooden shelves with plates, dried flowers in baskets and various other knick-knacks on the side. The room is lit by black candles along the centre of the table. At the end of the table to my right there is a group of three men and a woman sitting. But lying on the table is a skeleton-thin girl with long blonde hair dressed in a thin, white dress staring up at the ceiling. Plastic tubes, dark with blood, come out from beneath bandages in her wrists which lead to the guests around the table.

The foursome look around at Ka-rea-rea, smiling. I recognise bony Father Enrico Rocelli with a bandage on his face, his dark brown eyes glittering, and pretty, round Mrs Huuygens with her white skin, black curly hair and blue eyes. The big, balding, pale, white man with the blond beard in the badly fitting suit I don't know. Erich von Streicher holds a wine glass with a small amount of dark red liquid in it. He's wearing a dark, expensive dinner jacket sitting at the other end of the table.

"Sam Kahu," he laughs, "you're late. Ve vere beginnink to vorry." The others chuckle.

"Keeping Sian alive has been so very difficult, indeed vere ve to cease our ministrations ze poor girl vould die almost at once." They all smile grimly at me, in a knowing way. So if I take them out, Sian's dead. I can leave but what would that achieve? One pointless death. On the other hand she's one person. If I'm caught the safety of Fae could be at risk.

"Sam are you simply going to sit in zat box staring at us? As you can see ve are unarmed. Ve are merely concerned for zis poor girl's ... health. Vhy don't you set it down and come and talk to us like a gentleman? Ve have a proposal you may find interesting."

It's true, technically they are unarmed. But I know from bitter experience that infiltrators are never truly unarmed. They're all dangerous psychics and my watch shield isn't a proven defence yet. On the other hand I have Ka-rea-rea and an unjammable communications link. If they try anything Ka-rea-rea's beam could waste the lot of them in a second.

I hesitate.

I do have the option to zap them all now and evacuate Sian in a coffin transporter back to safety in seconds. If I was just here to rescue Sian that's what I'd do. The point was they really *were* there to talk, and so was I.

*"Grandpop my necklace still works doesn't it?"*

"Yup."

*"And it can connect through Control to Ka-rea-rea?"*

"Of course," Control said.

*"Ka-rea-rea if you lose contact with me take them all out immediately, all power necessary, then evacuate me to the hillside we started from, OK?"*

"Will do."

I settle Ka-rea-rea at the other end of the table, nose first, so he can zap them. Then I pop the hatch and get out, uncomfortably, feeling much more defenceless than I really like. I leap lightly off the table.

They sit there doing nothing as I take a chair at the far end of the long, long table opposite Von Streicher. I sit down, in the dark, peering over Ka-rea-rea, and feeling small.

"Good evening Sam, thank you for joining us. Sir Michael suggested you might be coming," Von Streicher is sitting at his end, looking very comfortable, swirling his drink. The others smile evilly.

"What do you want?" I ask, trying to sound in charge and not succeeding even to my own ears.

"Perhaps it is more what ve *all* vant. After all you need not assume our goals are mutually exclusive," Von Streicher says, comfortably.

He pauses for a moment.

"You see your ... sponsors ... and vee haf the same ultimate goals. Vee oppose the Center, zhey oppose the Center. Vee believe in freedom, zey believe in freedom."

"But they don't eat people," I object, waving at Sian.

Von Striecher freezes for a moment, thinks for a moment and then smiles.

"Do you like our castle Sam?"

"Is it yours?"

"Not exactly, but it is a castle vich some of us have lived in before and vich the current owners dare not prevent us using. It is sort of a fairytale castle."

"Sure, it's great. Are you selling it?" I ask him cheekily but to make him get on with it.

"No. But I make the point that it is a 'fairy tale' castle for a reason, Sam. Given your 'fairy' sponsors you should realise, better than most of your kind, that fairy tales are not simply idle stories for little girls. For example do you know the story of Snow White, Sam? Not the Walt Disney version, I mean the original version."

"Uh ... no," I say as if he's asking something incredibly dumb. Besides these people scare me, I don't want to get sucked into agreeing with them because that's how they hypnotise you.

"I thought not. But it is very relevant to our situation here, Sam. You see, Sian? She is like Snow White. See how very beautiful she is, all pale and golden, sleeping as if dead."

"What does that make me? The handsome Prince?" I ask, being smart.

"Perhaps? In ze original story the princesses mother pricks her finger and let's fall a drop of blood in ze snow. She makes her vishes for her daughter's good fortune. Ze mother dies and is replaced by a vicked stepmother whose vanity leads her to plot against the King's daughter. The story is quite confused with that of Sleeping Beauty. In Sleeping Beauty twelve fairies bless the Princess but the thirteenth fairy curses her so that on her sixteenth birthday she will die. The twelfth fairy commutes her death to suspended animation and, as in Snow White, they both lie as if dead until reanimated by the kiss from the eponymous Prince."

"In fact zhey are both ze same story." Von Streicher continues, lazily. "I know zis because I told it *here* first to *my* daughter," he inclines his head towards Mrs Huuygens, "some centuries ago. It voz a story for *her*."

"Congratulations, it's been a huge hit."

"Yes, but the meaning has been lost. You see my original story was about Lilit, ze first mother of vee, zer Iyrin."

And now I realise he's going to tell me something interesting, so I nod and say, "OK."

"Five tausend years ago, in an effort to bring peace all ze galactic civilisations vorked to create a new hybrid race from the genetic stock of all ze known humanoid races here, on zis planet. Our purpose vas to vatch over primitif humanoids und teach zem. Ze Earth vas our birthplace. Ze hope of ze uzzer races vas zat our existence vould be a force for unity in zer galaxy. A source of empathy and pride among all ze species zat vere our forebears. If

**427**

nuzzink else they would all be our parents. Zat is the metaphor of ze princess, Lilit."

The others nodded as if remembering.

"Hang on." I interrupted.

"He," I pointed at Rocelli, "wasn't born on Earth."

Von Streicher glanced at Rocelli.

"Vee *all* started on Earth but some vere expelled to uzzer Administration vorlds, but zat is anuzzer story. Zis story is ze genesis of our race's great mother, princess Lilit. Vat matters about vat happened to her is ze actions of ze vicked stepmother, or ze zirteenth fairy: Morganne Queen of Fae."

I have to admit I'm a bit shocked. Our entire project was all because of Morganne. She was difficult, but she was our most important ally. This was a story I hadn't heard before but I wasn't going to let him rattle me. I stared rudely at him like he was Mr Wakefield being boring.

"Queen Morganne iz, I suspect, ze root of your power, but our problems. She is a vain and vicked woman. It vas she who made ze Iyrin fall. It vas her experimental material zat made us dependent on stem cells from beings like ourselves. Ze Fae zemselves take blood and bone from *any* living creature. Only ve are forced to feed on zhose like ourselves. It vas also she who indirectly led to the rise of ze Synthetics who now rule ze Center. Do not make our mistake Sam. You cannot trust her."

This is huge news to me on two counts. First the sketchy accounts of the Iyrin that were in Hekator's knowledge beads hadn't really told me anything much about them. Second, they blamed Morganne for everything. It makes me rather start to wonder if we are, really, on the right side. But I also know I have to be careful. I already know these guys have powers – powers they can use cleverly so you hardly even notice them, to make you fall under their spell. So I brush Von Streicher's words aside in order to keep my mind clear.

"Baron, it's you I don't trust. You would sell me out to the Center in a minute."

"Wrong Sam. Quite wrong. Yes, I would have the Center destroy Morganne in a minute. Our var is with her, her followers and ze Synthetics she encouraged. Zere is no reason for your kind or the other Fae to be harmed."

I don't believe a word of it. He's drinking Sian's blood right in front of me and telling me this shit! I suspect my watch is stopping his hypnotic attack, because he would normally combine telling a cute little story with a subtle bit of mind control to get me agreeing with him, no matter what kind of vile nonsense he spouted. That is their usual technique. But it did make me wonder why he was bothering to tell me this.

"What does this have to do with me, or with her?" I ask pointing at Sian.

Von Streicher, suddenly sits forward, businesslike. Perhaps he realises his attempt to lull me into agreement has failed and has decided to try something else.

"Exactly. A fair question. Our desire is to live quietly on ze planet of our origin."

I snort with disbelief. Live quietly? Quietly killing people he meant.

"... Until," Von Striecher carries on, "ve are able to reverse the effects of Morganne's mutilation and until ve are able to release ze Center from zhe grip of zhe Synthetics."

"So another thousand years or so?" I jeer.

"Razzer less than zat," Von Streicher says icily, not liking my

**429**

lip. "Ze Synthetics do not seem to realise just what a beautiful and very *dangerous* world zis one truly is. Zey are a reflection of Morganne's vanity and that is a terrible veakness."

He smiles thinly. Then it hits me. The Synthetics are made, not born. There's no natural biochemical variation among them. They're all exactly the same. If a disease can kill one, it will wipe out them all! The infiltrators came here to find a biological weapon to eliminate the Synthetics! Something hard to detect, but incurably lethal, just like HIV. It would have to spread differently, of course, but the HIV experiment obviously had paved the way for something new. And if Von Streicher was telling the truth they believed they were close. He went on.

"No, our main delays are still due to our difficulty with regenerating our own cells without genetically similar donors," he indicated Sian. "A technique we know ze Fae solved but did not zink to share with us."

"So," I repeated, "what do you want from me?"

"Your friend Dr Prosperov," he stopped.

"Wherever he is," I said automatically. Perhaps too quickly. They glanced at one another.

"How did he manage to find, contact and convince ze Fae to assist him? He achieved vat ze Center has failed to do for zousands of years! It is something ve struggle to understand."

I shrug.

"He's a good scientist and a good talker."

A look of fury crossed Von Streicher's face and he exchanges a look with father Rocelli whose eyes looked at me like brown pools of poison.

"How did he contact ze Fae in ze first place?" Von Striecher spat, barely containing his annoyance.

"Just lucky, I guess," I smile, realising only after I have spoken, that it *was* Lucky and what I've said is the literal truth.

"Luck had nuzzink to do viz it. The Fae haf kept zemselves secret for three thousand years. Zey hav eluded ze greatest cyberminds in ze galaxy and ze greatest star fleet. So vhy reveal zhemselves to Prosperov?"

I suddenly realise what an incredible shock Prosperov must have been to the Fae. Suddenly a species regarded as primitive bypassed all their security and secrecy and swiped a Queen's daughter right from under their noses. If the Center ever discovered how Prosperov had done it, the Fae were history. This was where the pressure would come on, and I didn't want any. I get up suddenly and step onto my chair toward Ka-rea-rea.

"If you think I would just tell you *that* just because you ask, you're a bigger idiot than I thought you were," I tell him, preparing to get Ka-rea-rea to zap them all.

Suddenly, before me, Sian opens her eyes. A horrible expression is forming on her face, as she lies on the table, feet toward me. I wonder what is about to happen when she screams so loudly it's hard to believe her tiny frame is able to make so much sound. Everyone winces away from her wide open mouth. Von Streicher grins grimly.

Sian begins to shake violently, her mouth still screaming but with no noise coming out any more, like she is at the end of a breath but can't stop. It's horrible! I can't stop staring.

Then she sits up suddenly, like doll folded at the waist. Her body is caked in sweat. Her eyes are crazily wide and they swivel blindly until they find me, frozen where I stand on my chair, ready to get into Ka-rea-rea.

I notice the room is suddenly, deeply – supernaturally – cold. I can see breath mist in front of my face, and also from the mouths of everyone but Mrs Huuygens and Sian. I suddenly notice a pain on my wrist. My watch is hot, and starting to burn me! Instinctively I go to take it off, and then I realise. It's *protecting* me. It's dangerously overloading – sucking in more psychic energy than it can handle – but if I take it off I'm lost. My brain would be mush.

The pain is bad! I'm in serious trouble! I need backup! Then the awful realisation: the necklace communicator is as dead and as useless ornamental stones. Comms have gone! So why isn't Ka-rea-rea firing?

"*Ve* are losing patience," Von Streicher snarls.

I leap onto the table and press my hand to Ka-rea-rea's panel. Nothing happens! Shit! I look up to see Sian stand suddenly like a puppet, trailing tubes from her wrists. She's standing on the table, taller than me, pale, but her eyes have changed. Now they're angry and bright. She's completely possessed.

And now I see, behind her, something I'd missed before because it had been hidden behind her head where she lay. Small and shiny, it's a silver skull and I've seen it before. I feel sick.

Now I know I'm deep in the shit. No escape, no weapons, my only defence overloading and causing me so much pain I'm struggling not to scream and no way to call for backup. It's the trap I warned them about and now I'm cursing them for putting me here, and cursing myself for letting them talk me into it. Suddenly I'm picked up, as if by a gust of wind, and thrown hard against the back wall. I throw out my elbows to soften the impact but my head hits the wall with a crack. For a moment I see only white. Then I fall a meter to the floor with a splitting headache; when I hit the ground my legs buckle under me, but I stay conscious.

I feel like I'm four years old all over again. Just like when Ax threw me and went on to kill my mother. I'm almost paralysed with fear. Dizzy, I stagger to my feet.

There's a deep rumbling sound, like an earthquake coming, from Sian. I look up at her standing on the table, her eyes popped. Then she raises her arm and an invisible force closes around my throat and slams me against the wall. At the same time an idea hits me like an express train.

*"How did Prosperov find the Fae?"*

Now I'm really scared. I'm struggling to breathe. I have only a faint idea of what is asking me this, or how it has so such power over me or Ka-rea-rea. I'm going to crap myself.

"Lucky ... it was Lucky," I gurgle desperately, trying to breathe. Then the feeling like an earthquake. The whole room and my whole body seem to vibrate. The idea and the word seem the centre of my world.

*"ANSWER!"*

I feel like an ant about to be stepped on. And yet, somehow, something odd is whispering in the back of my mind. Something is waking; excited; almost turned on by my clenched gut, shaking hands and cold sweat. It is close by, but just watching me being tortured. Judging me.

*"Ka mate? (Death?) "* it whispers.

I'm shaking uncontrollably like a mouse caught by a cat. My mouth babbles as if talking will keep me from drowning.

"Lucky ... spirit ... in Prosperov ... out of world tree."

The pressure comes off my throat. I'm surprised. It wants to hear me, not crush me. I'm gasping, and I stink. I *have* crapped myself. It doesn't smell good.

"SPEAK!" it demands out of Sian's mouth but with a weird male voice.

"Fourteen years ago ... Dr Prosperov freed him by accident," I gasp. "He was doing an experiment. He didn't understand the tree. The world tree Yig-something but he didn't know what it was. Something came out. He said it was Lucky. It possesses him."

The room is already cold, but what I've told them has added another kind of chill to it. The infiltrators at the end of the room are looking at each other very concerned. I can tell I've made an impact because my watch isn't burning me anymore, although my wrist still hurts like hell. I look down. I wish I hadn't. The skin on my wrist is raw and red looking. Even so I won't take it off. It's my only protection. I'm still shaking all over. It's sooo painful but better the sharp, cold pain than losing my mind altogether.

Suddenly Sian collapses onto the table. The force which has been holding her up has gone. The skull is no longer bright. The others are whispering. I notice Sian's going to slide off the table. I'm just two meters away so I crawl over and catch her head as she slips off. It's surprising, and disturbing, how light she is. The infiltrators are having a whispered debate. I look down. Sian's eyes flicker open and she is back behind them. She's barely conscious.

"Qui ..." Sian begins in French, and then faints.

I lower her to the floor. I'm not strong enough to lift her back onto the table. The temperature in the room has warmed. Whatever the power was that overwhelmed me, seems to be gone, for the moment. I test the communications necklace silently.

"*Grandpop?*"

"Sam?"

I pretend to nurse my wrist and cry. Well, actually I *am* nursing my wrist and crying.

"*Grandpop I'm in big trouble! It's the Bruderschaft Totenkopf spirit that nearly got me and Tahira in Elan. It cut off my coms and Ka-rea-rea isn't responding.*"

Grandpop swears in surprise.

"*Don't send anyone else! It's too dangerous! They'll be caught. I need a distraction. A big distraction. Set fire to the castle or something!*"

"OK, Sam we're on it. We'll do what we can," he promises.

The whispered debate at the end of the table has ended and now they're all looking at me again. I chance a frightened glance up at them. I'm surprised to find they look more worried by me, than they had before.

"Please sit down Sam," Von Streicher instructs. He seems more grumpy and distracted than angry. I'm worn out, despite the agony of my wrist and my stink, I'm glad to obey. There's a pause and then he speaks again.

"Vell, it seems ve haf *all* had some unpleasant surprises tonight," he states, looking at the others and thinking.

I fiddle with my watch, Loosening it from my skin and blowing on it. The pain jangles up my arm, in fresh waves of steely agony.

"Still, it has provided useful food for thought. Sam, ve vant to know vere is Dr Prosperov now?"

I take the question totally literally so that I give nothing away.

"I really have no idea Baron Von Streicher. He could be anywhere," I reply clearly.

**435**

"Have you been in contact with him since he ... escaped?"

"No."

The trick to lying is to keep it short and totally believe what you are saying. I must have been convincing because Von Striecher said nothing. I keep on tending my injured wrist.

"We should check. He seems to respond to pressure," Mrs Huuygens suggests to the others. I have to interrupt. I won't survive another torture session like that.

"Baron you said you had a proposal. What is it?"

He looks uncertainly at me.

"Perhaps ze time for it has passed, Sam," he says looking at Huuygens. They all look to him. I can't tell what's passing between them but I know they're telepathic. He looks around the group, then appears to give way.

"Very vell. Ze proposal vas ... is to provide our protection against ze Administration in exchange for information about ze Fae."

I consider it.

"The alternative being?"

"Ve hand you over to ze Center as requested."

"What about Sian?"

"She is irrelevant," he waves vaguely. "She can go."

"And I would have what guarantees?" I press.

Von Streicher laughs at my cheek.

"Vat guarantees do you haf now?"

"Sir Michael offered me a private education and a lot of money," I answer cautiously.

"Hamilton-Smythe is a puppet with two masters," Von Streicher sneers. "Ze Center tells him one thing. Ve tell him another. He makes up stories to suit himself. Besides he vould still hand you over to ze Synthetics. He has no choice."

"And you do?"

"Ve haf more choices. Our ... guide assists us," he nods at the skull.

"Yet you have lost friends to the Administration."

It angers them because we all know it was because of us that the Administration arrested some of them at a gathering in Elan, France.

"Ve must be prudent Sam – for the moment."

"And they weren't?" I ask, indicating Mrs Huuygens and Father Rocelli who were also arrested by the Administration at Elan.

"Ze situation has changed since then," he says coldly.

"How?"

"You. Your sponsors' intervention has aroused the curiosity of ze Administration. You had been irritating our people for some time, but zhose operations vere secret und ve could not report zem to the Administration. Ven you reported *us*, however, zat raised concern, and so for six months ve haf been cooperating viss ze Administration to track down your operation."

"What if I refuse?" I ask, testing a new track.

"Ve have ozzer vays to find out vhat you know. None of zem pleasant," he says sourly.

We all know I can't stop them. Eventually they would get what they wanted, eventually everyone breaks. So my next question is genuine.

"What do you want to know?" I check.

"Ve vant to know vat Dr Prosperov and the Fae are doing, and vhy."

"Why do you want to know that?" I wonder, genuinely puzzled.

"Because zey vould not be doing it at all if it vasn't important. Ze Fae risk too much zey don't need to. Zey have been successfully hidden for three thousand years. To risk working with you indicates that they are after something very important. It may have a bearing on vhat ve are doing, also. So vhat is so important about Nathan Montgomery?"

"Who?"

They glance at each other. Von Streicher sighs and continues.

"Ze Administration traced Ashley Robinson to your base in New Zealand. Zere is no point denying it."

"Nathan's Ashley's cousin. She visits him because he has a pretty hard life."

"Does she visit all her couzins?"

I knew better than to answer that. What I needed to do was divert his interest.

"We all visit our friends and relatives. I've been all sorts of places to visit people. It's one of the benefits of the mission. We get to wear all this cool-as gear."

"Yes. Zis could certainly make a difference on zis primitive planet. It could even make someone President."

I smile to cover my fear. The pain helps enormously.

"Even the Americans don't vote for Presidents based on what they wear. Besides Nathan doesn't know anything about the Fae."

"Neverzeless he zinks he vill be President."

"He's probably not the only one."

"He's has an alien vorld on his side."

Now I laugh, briefly. It sounds ridiculous.

"What?...you're kidding right? You think the Fae give us all this technology so we can get our *cousins* elected President? Man, you should meet *my* cuzzies," I laugh thinking of Rebecca's family stealing things in the White House. "That's really funny."

There's an icy stare from the other end of the table. I stop laughing. People who can torture you aren't very funny.

"Vat zen of Jeanne Mazuri, Diana Popovic and Sarah Kogan. Your people are related to zese girls also?"

He knows mentioning all these names will chill me, and it does.

"No," I admit, quietly, bothered by the fact that, of course, since Elan they have also known about all these girls. The only one they don't know about is Khadiyeh.

"Zen perhaps you vill enlighten us as to your true intentions."

I think about it for a second, but it's totally no go.

"No, I can't tell you that," I say quietly, shaking my head.

"Can't or von't?" Von Streicher asks lazily.

"Won't," I shrug. I'm already in a lot of pain. Now I know it's about to get a whole lot worse.

"I zhought not. Sven? Zhe young man's vatch is troubling him. Please help him remove it."

The big bald man gets up with a grin. I've been playing with my watch the whole time. I look up, press the face and put a brilliant white dot on his chest. He doesn't see it, but Mrs Huuygens does.

"Sven he...!" calls Mrs Huuygens in alarm.

He glances back at her in confusion.

I quickly move the dot onto the side of his head and yell "Look out!" loudly at him.

He can't stop himself. He looks back at me. I press the watch face down. The white dot hits his eyes, there's a hiss and steam bursts from his face as he slaps his hands to his eyes, and keels over screaming. The others turn to him, and I run for all I'm worth toward the double doors. I know I have only seconds to get away.

**439**

I throw open the doors and a huge wall of smoke hits me. I start coughing. My eyes sting, full of tears. Suddenly the doors slam back in my face. Although smoke hangs in the air, it's gone cold again. My wrist sears with pain, my already raw skin screams in protest. I turn around. The pain is incredible. The silver skull is brilliant. I try to aim the steaming watch as it sears my wrist like a branding iron, the white dot weaves around. Then my head begins to hurt and my vision blurs. I can't keep my arms up. Sven, is staggering back, his hands over his face roaring with pain. A fire alarm is screaming now as well. Mrs Huuygens has got up and gone to help Sven. Father Rocelli is quietly disappearing through the door behind Von Streicher. But Von Streicher is showing no fear of my beam and standing, hands on the table, over the bright skull in the dark room.

"Ze problem wiz you children, is you haf no idea vhat you are involved in, or ze forces your friend Prosperov has unleashed. Maybe you vill understand as you die."

A rainbow haze is forming above the table. Smoke is starting to come from the door behind Von Streicher. Rocelli delicately covers his face and runs out. Mrs Huuygens leads Sven out. The alarm is drilling into my skull. My head pain is becoming intense and even competing with the agony of my wrist, which smells like burning meat.

Sian jumps up again like a puppet but turns away from me to Von Streicher. Von Streicher raises his arm at me and I'm picked up and slammed bodily back against the wall again. I'm winded by the impact. The rainbow haze is growing to the size of an adult human figure. I have no idea what it is but I doubt it will be good. There's a bright light in the interior to the figure. Sian gets to Von Streicher and Von Streicher takes her arm as she slumps onto it. Half carrying her, half walking her, he turns his back on me and walks out the back door leaving me alone with the silver skull and the rainbow haze, with smoke spreading along the ceiling as I lie slumped in the corner.

Despite all the pain I'm suffering in both my wrist and my head I'm noticing that it's becoming incredibly cold in this room, like all the energy is being sucked towards this bright figure. My breath is fogging to ice and my nose and mouth are starting to freeze. I'm being branded and frozen to death simultaneously! I'm shivering uncontrollably again. I scramble, desperately to my feet, trying to escape like some insect in a jar. My eyes are becoming sore. I have to get out of here fast! It has to be minus forty in here and sinking.

Then just as I manage to stand I'm lifted off my feet and smashed up against the ceiling. Again the impact almost makes me faint, but not quite. I'm freezing, burning, I can scarcely breathe and now I'm five meters up. The thick smoke makes me gasp and cough. I'm asphyxiating!

Somehow I stay conscious. And the whispering in my head, "*Ma-té (death)! Ma-té (death)*!" as my ancestors reach out to me, makes me suddenly feel much stronger. Psychically I shove back against the force holding me in the smoke, and feel its grip on me fail.

I fall four meters to the table swinging around so my feet hit first breaking my fall slightly. I still slam hard into the solid wood but at least I can breathe. My bones shock with pain and I crumple, but they are a distant third to the vicious pain in my wrist and the splitting pain in my head.

The smoke is getting lower. I'm trapped in this building, which is on fire, and I'm starting to wonder if I won't simply die in

here. I'm coughing, freezing, and choking. I try to roll off the
table and hide underneath it but the chairs slam tight against
the table to stop me. Then suddenly my head is picked up and,
unable to stop it, my face is slammed down into the chair back.
Blinding pain! My nose is flooded with the smell of blood and
my lip is torn. But unlike the agony before, this pain is different.
It pisses me off. It stokes a raging fire of anger in my soul.
Despite the extreme cold I feel hot. I can feel the spirit of my
ancestors inside me and although I'm still struggling with injury,
and coughing on the smoke, the bright figure in front of me
wavers.

Suddenly there's a huge bang behind me. I look around. The
double doors have been forced open by a shock of warm air.

To my astonishment a man with wild gray hair and a goatee,
wearing an expensive suit and carrying a silver walking stick has
burst into the room. Smoke is pouring in behind him. He's lit by
flickering red flame.

I can't believe who I'm looking at. Never, ever before, have I
seen Dr Prosperov look like this. He glances at me and I can see
the wicked dark eyes are not his. I see Lucky, and he's furious.

I glance back and then throw myself aside as a heavy chair flies
out from under the table at Dr Prosperov. It stops in mid-air and
just hangs there.

Dr Prosperov or Lucky keeps walking forward, face set. Then the
noise like an earthquake rumbles again filling the whole room
with vibration and I'm picked up off my feet and fly headfirst
toward the freezing brightness inside the rainbow figure, then,
like the chair, I stop.

I'm hanging in mid-air, my head and arms being pulled toward
the freezing light, but the rest of my body is held still. I focus my

rage on myself and the hold on me falters so that I fall onto the table.

Smoke's pouring into the room. I'm coughing, but at least now I'm not freezing at the same time. The suspended chair behind me falls with a thump and topples over. With surprising speed Dr Prosperov steps up onto the table and begins advancing along it, behind me, toward the rainbow haze. The cold bright figure seems to shrink from him. With a stab he plants the point of his stick into the light. A huge round rainbow begins to shimmer and shake where the stick has gone in.

The whole room seems to shake with terrible violence although nothing actually moves. Whatever this rainbow figure is; it is now, itself, in pain. The shaking goes on for five seconds as the bright centre shrinks, smaller and smaller. As the cold retreats so too does my feeling of connection with my ancestors. Now I'm just an injured fourteen-year-old. And the fire and smoke surges.

I can't keep my eyes open and I'm coughing all the time. Suddenly I feel one of the others grab me and lift me off the table as easily as if I was a kitten and sit me on a chair, wiping my bloody face.

I can't see but I know that mind. It's Tahira. By keeping my lids mostly closed and breathing in tiny sips, I peek over her shoulder as she wipes my face with my handkerchief. I can just make out what's going on.

The rainbow haze has contracted to a brilliant ball of light around Dr Prosperov's stick when with a final stab, it winks out. Dr P steps lightly off the table and advances on the silver skull. It's still brilliantly bright. For a second the table gives a jump as if it's going to rear up but it hasn't the power to do anything. I can't see what Dr P does next because he's between me and the skull but the light vanishes.

It's over. Smoke drifts even thicker. I start coughing constantly and shaking, my nerves are all over the place. My wrist hurts more than I had ever thought anything *could* hurt, but my face is trying hard to keep up. I fumble for the strap and the watch falls off taking a layer of white skin stuck to it revealing the dark red flesh beneath. The pain is incredible.

Another figure, like Tahira, in a faceless hoody and jeans, comes in with the bowling ball remote control interface Hekator had used to control Ka-rea-rea. It's Scott. He needs to put it inside Ka-rea-rea. Tahira picks me up and carries me over to Ka-rea-rea who opens for me. Scott slips the ball inside, and closes him up again, while Tahira gives me a handkerchief to breathe through. Dr P comes over, bends down and looks me in the eye. He's totally Lucky. I'm surprised by the look of concern on his face. He pats my shoulder, then stands and walks out into smoke filled hall.

*"Can you walk?"* Tahira's thoughts come through with surprising clarity.

I try to move but everything hurts. She just picks me up over her shoulder and carries me into the smoke. I can't keep my eyes open. Cold water's gushing down through the smoke. The water lashes me like small whips, especially on my wrist.

Suddenly I'm dumped on my back inside something. My back feels all gooey and disgusting as things writhe and wriggle beneath me. Then I feel my clothes being torn off me. It had to be inside a Fae coffin. A tentacle covers my face and a tube pushes into my mouth and starts pumping cool clean air. Another covers my eyes. Something holds my wrist and something sharp pricks me briefly.

"*Where am I going?*" I ask Tahira, silently.

"*Back to quarantine hospital,*" she tells me.

Suddenly the rain stops hitting me and drums on the outside instead. The tentacles close all around me. My eyes feel wet and better. My wrist pain has vanished and something cool squishes around it and my nose. All of my remaining clothes are being taken off me so that the warm wetness of the gooey inside covers my whole body. Then the room folds and spins, and I'm on my way.

## [+]

The mind bending trip is such a relief. I'm surprised to find my ancestors closer and approving of me and I'm almost disappointed when I arrive a minute later. I sort of expect the coffin to open and some band of Fae doctors to race up and tend me like something out of TV. Instead nothing happens. I try to open the coffin but it refuses telling me I'm too injured, and it's still working on my injuries. It tells me to rest as this will take quite a while.

"Sam, are you alright?" Grandpop asks, guiltily.

"*Yeah ... I'm ... I'm a bit tired. Bit smashed up really but I ... can't feel anything. The pain's gone. I just feel really tired.*"

"Tahira was worried. She didn't want to say anything to Liz or Rewa in case they panicked."

"*What was that thing?*"

"I don't know. Dr P has just come back and had another fit. Mrs Jones is with him. He was definitely Lucky when he left here."

"*I know. Lucky kicked its butt too. How did he get there?*"

"Sleeping bag. Look Sam, he left instructions. He said it's vital you find Von Streicher again. Lucky said that now you have been

**445**

seen the infiltrators will have no doubts you are inside Ka-rea-rea. Can you do that Sam?"

"*I guess*," I sigh wearily. "*What am I doing now?*"

"Rescuing Sian."

"*Oh yeah, I forgot.*"

My eyes are jammed closed like a tiny kitten's. I turn my mind to Ka-rea-rea who wakes at once.

It's as if he's just been switched off and not noticed. An alarm is sounding constantly, which is not doing my head any good. The room is full of smoke and fire. Ka-rea-rea lifts, silently off the table, alone in a room filled with fire, and glides smoothly out into the smoky hall where the sprinklers are pouring down through the smoke. He rises up into the gloom. Then by memory, and radar he noses back out the smashed window. Ka-rea-rea emerges from the Keep amidst the smoke pouring from the broken window. I adopt adaptive camouflage and slip out into the outer courtyard above the battle platform, still lit by orange sodium lights under the stars. There's a cloud of smoke building up over the castle in the cold air around the Keep. Down below I can hear fire engines racing through the streets. It's time to go. I switch to inertialess and Ka-rea-rea shoots up like a blur into the night.

Seeing the starry sky and enjoying the remote sense of acceleration gives me a slight lift despite feeling so tired and beaten up. But I still have a job to do: find Von Streicher and stop him escaping with Sir Michael's daughter Sian Hamilton-Smythe.

I know there are only two routes Von Streicher can take: north-east or south. I didn't even bother with the southern route. I'm certain Von Streicher will head home to Austria. He will be driving north-east following the motorway which doubles back around the big mountains behind the castle and then east to Innsbruck.

He didn't have a huge headstart. Maybe half an hour. The roads aren't especially busy so assuming he drives at a hundred and fifty he would probably be about fifty to seventy five kilometers ahead. If I go about three hundred kilometers an hour faster in theory I would catch him in ten minutes. That was if I followed the road. But Ka-rea-rea could cut over the mountains.

So we fly up over the big mountains to the deep valley in Austria on the other side, and, avoiding the power line, fly back toward Lichtenstein along the motorway to the turn off from Lichtenstein he had to take. It was pretty in the starlight. Rural and full of forests and mountains.

Seven minutes was all it took for Ka-rea-rea to find Von Streicher. He's driving around the base of a range of mountains through the forest. He's doing a relatively slow one hundred and twenty kilometers per hour. Obviously he didn't imagine I would be coming after him.

I turn around and quickly catch up, following two hundred meters above, and four hundred meters behind him. It's time to check back in with Grandpop to see what comes next.

"The idea is to panic him into calling the Administration for help," Grandpop tells me.

"*Why?*"

"To test the connections with the Administration."

"*What about Ka-rea-rea? They'll catch him.*"

"Hekator's managing that. He and Dr P have some plan. All I care about right now is that you're safely out of the way, so let's see what happens. Give Von Streicher a fright. Scare the shit out

**447**

of him if you like."

After the way he'd scared me that had a lot of appeal.

"*Oh, I like. I like a lot,*" I reply grimly.

I get Ka-rea-rea to become the local cell base station so that Von Streicher's phone links direct to me. Then I ask Ka-rea-rea to put me on his network disguised as Sir Michael's aircraft's satellite phone. Then I make the call remembering his number from the original message para.no.ID intercepted.

"*Hallo Michael?*" he answers the unexpected late night call from Sir Michael in a surprised tone.

"Kapo rere te kuri (dogs run)," I tell him and hang up. He has no idea what I've said but he knows it's me when I drop Ka-rea-rea down on his car's roof and grab on. The car swerves all over the road. For a moment I wonder if he's going to lose it but he straightens up and slows right down. Now he's worried but he can't see me and doesn't know what I might do.

I get Ka-rea-rea to pick his car up. Suddenly all he knows is that there's no sound coming from the wheels on the road and his steering wheel's stopped working. But rather than risk him jumping out I decide to speed up to about three hundred kilometers per hour.

We're screaming along the motorway now! It must be pretty scary for Von Streicher because he has no control and doesn't trust me. I find it scary enough and not only do I trust Ka-rea-rea completely, I'm not even actually there!

There isn't a lot of traffic but what there is, we pass at fantastic speed. I laugh hoping there's a speed camera so Von Streicher can get some *huge* speeding tickets. Then Ka-rea-rea's field sensors have bad news.

We are not alone.

I can see the bright light of an Administration scout UFO coming down from the stars between the tall, snowy mountains behind me. It's gaining fast. I speed up to four hundred. We zap past a truck lumbering along at one hundred so fast its almost like its standing still. Things are getting busy.

The scout slows over the valley. Then I realise I'm OK. The road goes into a tunnel[†]. It won't have time to pink light me.

They know it too! Instead of diving at me, there's a flash from the saucer and a boulder from the high cliff on the mountainside above the tunnel begins to plummet. We can make it!

We shoot into that tunnel as the rock hits the road behind us. Immediately I have to slow from four hundred to one hundred behind a truck and trailer just ahead without inertialless drive to help. The car almost hits the back trailer.

I'm stoked. The scout now has to guess where I am. Question is do I come out of the tunnel as expected or do I drop Von Streicher and double back? If I keep going the scout will easily zap me from above as I come out. But if it's high enough it can cover both ends of the tunnel.

As the tunnel exit comes up I get a new idea and turn Von Streicher's car upside-down, above me, wheels to the sky! Now he's my shield. Then as we burst into the open I zip the upside-down car over the truck in front. I'm sandwiched between Von Streicher and the truck. I can't see it, but Ka-rea-rea's sensors show the scout's field above. Its light's flooding down around us, but *they* can't get a shot. Even if they pink light me I may drop Von Streicher and kill him.

Underneath, but above my head, the truck shudders as the driver sees the strange light in the sky, and puts his foot down. The next tunnel isn't far away. With seconds to spare I fly over the truck at high speed causing it to lurch as the truck driver sees a car overtake his rig flying upside down over his head!

We enter the next tunnel and I turn the car right way up. The truck follows after. Behind me the scout has probably leapt up into the sky looking for the next tunnel exit. The time has come. I won't get away with the same trick twice!

Slowing down I drop Von Streicher's car back on the road, where he starts skidding. I stop. The following truck powers through the tunnel beneath me. Then I double back putting on my warp invisibility field.

I speed out of the tunnel, invisible, low and fast, then up the mountainside over the previous tunnel exit hoping to get away somewhere and lie low. I zip up this pine clad mountainside when I find myself almost colliding with a *second* brilliant disc coming down the slope.

A second scout!

Swearing, I dodge hard left, back down the slope into the valley, hoping like hell my warp invisibility field holds and the Scout couldn't pick up my field. Unfortunately it must have noticed something because it zips up into the sky and sits over the whole Valley, dominating everything.

Its scanners will find me in seconds like this. My only way out now is underwater in the shallow black river at the bottom of the valley. I zip over to it and sink like a stone into the water, switching off everything with an emission signature, annoyed to find the river is only two meters deep.

I've played my part as well as I could. If I'm lucky I'll escape. If not I need something to negotiate with. I need to generate antimatter fast. The more antimatter Ka-rea-rea holds in its vortex the bigger the explosion if I'm forced to detonate him.

I give the command that if he loses contact with me, he's to detonate.

Still, as far as I can tell the scouts haven't noticed me. I just have to keep still and lie low. I can't risk trying to see how their search for me is going. If I look they will see me. Ka-rea-rea lies cold and still at the bottom of the river while I lie, tapped into him from a medical coffin light years away.

Nothing happens. Slowly I start to relax. As the seconds turn to minutes I start to think back over my own lucky escape from the castle.

I wonder about the silver skull and Dr P, or Lucky or whoever he was. We had seen a skull like that before in Elan, France. I wanted to ask Dr P or Lucky what that thing had been. It had felt like an ancient ghost but I had never met an old ghost who still had so much physical power. Normally such things just possessed minds, and it had certainly tried. I was sure the watch had never been built to withstand the attack it had been under. It may have burned my wrist but the way whatever-it-was had controlled Sian had shown me what would have happened if I hadn't had its protection.

That showed that while we thought we knew what we were up against, after two years, we were still very ignorant of our enemy's powers or purpose. And what about those accusations against Morganne? What had that been about? What had she done to these people that they hated her so much? They were almost immortal but they acted as if they were entitled to it. As if it was Morganne's fault their immortality was flawed in some way. They were so arrogant that the idea of dying naturally as everyone else would – Morganne included, I supposed – was simply unthinkable. They would kill any number of people just to remain alive.

A light was heading toward me up the river. It was brilliant. They were scanning for me. It would not be long now.

"*Grandpop?*"

"Yeah, Sam?"

"*Should I make a break for it?*"

"How are you feeling?"

"*Really tired.*"

"Then leave it Sam. The plan works whether they catch you in the river or flying around."

"*Does it?*"

"You've done really well Sam. Your antimatter level's good."

"*Thanks Grandpop.*"

I feel like I'm seven years old again and tired-out after a day's swimming in races at school.

The light comes close and envelopes us. Then there are different coloured lights and Ka-rea-rea is being raised out of the water. The saucer is right above me. Ka-rea-rea goes through a round hole in the middle of the bottom of the saucer into a round room full of light. The round door closes and the light dims. Two short gray humanoid creatures with black eyes approach. I tell Ka-rea-rea to shut down his visual and radar sensors and wait.

Ka-rea-rea's world goes dark.

Sue learns the hard way just how intense the conflict between the Changels and their enemies is. But the battlefield is not just a physical one. Sam's struggle has been as much about his spiritual growth as well. Just how important that is only becomes clear when the mysterious Yemeni girl, Khadiyeh, begins to appear in Sam's dreams.

**To get your copy visit the website: www.changels.info**

# FACT OR FICTION?

As a work of fiction most characters are fictional and any resemblance to any person living or dead is coincidental. Actual persons such as Colonel Laurent Nkunda are, of course, real. There are, however, some amalgalms of fact and fiction in the work. This section is intended to clarify the fact from the fiction.

While the character of Jeanne Mazuri is fictional, Bravo Brigade of the National Congress for the Defence of the People (CNDP) did raid schools for child soldiers around Masisi in North Kivu, Democratic Republic of Congo in September 2007 (among other times and places).

The history of the Congo wars as told by the character Bernard Khumalo is historically accurate.

The massacres and horrors in North Kivu described in this story are collations of actual events. Most were considerably worse than depicted in this book. The Kivus have been described as the 'rape capital of the world'. The situation in the DRC has been neglected by Western media allowing the largest war since World War Two to pass seriously under-reported. Since this book was written the situation in the Kivus has changed but not significantly improved. The CNDP was disbanded but the rise of the M23 movement in 2012 shows that the unresolved issues caused by the borders set by the League of Nations after World War One remain.

Trafficking in women and girls from Moldova is documented very well on the www.atnet.md website. The story of Diana and Elena is considerably softer than the much more brutal reality.

Flights from Luuataken Finland to Brussels Belgium only started when Ryan Air introduced a service in 2010. As the action in chapter 49 takes place in 2008 this service would not have been available.

Laser dazzling of drivers is usually illegal and dangerous to both drivers and dazzlers. Use of the technology at military check-points has not proved particularly effective.

The most recent understanding on the origin of HIV/Aids is very well explained on the Avert.org website. While the scientific community has worked hard to determine the origins of HIV/Aids through evolutionary biochemistry, it has shown a notable reluctance to examine any connection to secret biowarfare researchers, vaccine campaigns or therapeutics manufacturers who have scarcely been inactive during the 1960s-1980s period. The suggestion that this would give credence to these conspiracy theories has completely backfired and conspiracy theories have taken a strong hold in Africa precisely because of this reticence. While it is possible HIV/Aids has been an entirely natural phenomenon it is also possible that it has been given a 'helping hand' at various times either deliberately or inadvertently. The inability of science to investigate politics is a crucial theme of the story.

Project Coast was a documented effort by the apartheid regime in South Africa during the 1980s to develop race-specific bioweapons (mostly toxins). It was investigated by the South African Truth and Reconciliation Commission. The British Medical Association did issue a warning against such weapons in 1999. The author is extremely concerned that biowarfare is recognised as one of the most serious WMD risks facing forthcoming generations. Of all current human epidemics only HIV has had a potentially racially selective effect, a point not lost on many Africans.

The Soviet agency Biopreparat is well documented in Ken Alibeck's book "Biohazard" although his focus is on development and internal politics rather than the epidemiological side.

The immunity of Nordic Europeans with the CCR5 delta-32 mutation has since been eroded by new strains of the HIV virus. There are other forms of immunity to Aids but none of the others is race specific.

The character of Klaus Hassler is inspired by Dr Klaus Schilling who was hung at Landsberg Prison in May 1946 for conducting medical experiments on inmates of Dachau concentration camp. The character of Hathaway was inspired by the trial evidence against Dr Wouter Basson, the former director of Project Coast and a former special forces soldier. There is no connection between these real historical persons, nor does inspiration constitute a portrait.

Columbia Heights in Washington DC does not have a school named Columbia Multicultural Institute. The physical attributes of this school are inspired by the real Columbia Heights Educational Campus. The characters depicted as staff, administrators and sponsors of the Columbia Multicultural Institute are entirely imaginary and any resemblance to any present or past member of the staff or administration of the CHEC is coincidental. Note also that the school uniform described is green where the CHEC uniform is burgundy or blue with khaki or white.

Nathan's move from his mother, June's home in Columbia Heights, District of Columbia to his Grandmother, Margaret's new home in Capitol Heights, Maryland is outside the scope of the story, but is alluded to.

The Baha'i Temple in Haifa was actually closed on the weekend of 8th December 2007 when Sam and Tahira fictionally visit it.

The character of Mordechai Ceder is entirely fictional. The account of the Treblinka death camp and other elements referring to the "Bruderschaft" is based on fact. Treblinka is often neglected because it was destroyed by the Nazis in 1943 but was a more efficient murder centre than Auschwitz Birkenau. Only sixty rebelling Jews of 900,000 victims sent there survived.

According to "The Devils Disciples" by Anthony Read Heinrich Himmler was the Nazi organisation's main backroom political fix-it man prior to the Nazis coming to power in 1933. Himmler certainly committed suicide by cyanide pill in 1945 but his body, after a quick burial at night, was lost somewhere in the Luneburg Heath. Its current location is unknown. The suggestion that Heinrich Himmler was an alien of any kind is obviously nonsense. This also applies to his daughter Gudrun who is (at time of writing) still alive.

Most (80%) of the senior Nazis involved in the Shoah (Holocaust) were never prosecuted. Many escaped on their own, while others were assisted by either Gudrum Himmler's Stille Hilfe organisation, the Roman Catholic Church, the Red Cross or the CIA under Operation Paperclip after the war.

Gutenburg Castle above Belzer, Liechtenstein is owned by Gutenburg – a spiritual, psychological and personal development institute. The design of the castle, its use and its occupants as depicted in this story are entirely imaginary and have nothing to do with the real place or its occupants.
Baron Von Streicher is named after the odious anti semite Julius Streicher, the Nazi propagandist executed at Nuremberg in October 1946.

The fall of the Iyrin (Aramaic for Watchers) a form of angel, is sourced from the Books Of Daniel and Enoch which have been dated to the first or second century BC. The story in Enoch is that God appointed angel Watchers to watch over humankind, but that two hundred fall; that is decide to "go native" and interbreed with human women to create the Nephilim, or giants. This leads God to start the flood in order to wipe out this unauthorised departure. Lilit or Lilitu was a Sumerian or Babylonian demon going back to the seventh century BC. Obviously this does not square with the claim of Baron Von Streicher that events took place "five thousand years ago" which would be considerably earlier. This is all invoked purely for artistic reasons.